The prosecutor stood directly in front of Callaway and spoke to him slowly and distinctly. "Captain, I want you to be very careful in your choice of words in answer to what I am going to ask you next. Will you please tell this board of court-martial, what were Captain Boone's exact words to you and the others in explanation of the capture of his party?"

Callaway nodded and spoke just as slowly and distinctly. "Captain Boone said—and I quote him as nearly as I can recall—'I led the Indians who captured me back to our camp. They sent me in and I told our men to put down their weapons and surrender to them, and this is what they did.' That," said Callaway, "is just how he said it."

"In other words, Captain Callaway, by Daniel Boone's own admission to you and others here in this fort, he voluntarily led the Indians to where his men were camped and then ordered his men to surrender without resisting?"

"Yes, sir," Captain Callaway said, "that is just what he told us."

Bantam Books by Allan W. Eckert
Ask your bookseller for the books you have missed

THE NARRATIVES OF AMERICA SERIES
    THE FRONTIERSMEN
    WILDERNESS EMPIRE
    THE CONQUERORS
    THE WILDERNESS WAR
    GATEWAY TO EMPIRE
THE COURT-MARTIAL OF DANIEL BOONE
THE SCARLET MANSION

THE COURT-MARTIAL OF DANIEL BOONE

★

A Novel by
ALLAN W. ECKERT

BANTAM BOOKS

TORONTO • NEW YORK • LONDON • SYDNEY • AUCKLAND

*This low-priced Bantam Book
has been completely reset in a type face
designed for easy reading, and was printed
from new plates. It contains the complete
text of the original hard-cover edition.*
NOT ONE WORD HAS BEEN OMITTED.

🐤

THE COURT-MARTIAL OF DANIEL BOONE

*A Bantam Book / published by arrangement with
the author*

PRINTING HISTORY

*First published in October 1973
Bantam edition / February 1987*

ISBN 0-553-26283-1

Published simultaneously in the United States and Canada

*Bantam Books are published by Bantam Books, Inc. Its trade-
mark, consisting of the words "Bantam Books" and the por-
trayal of a rooster, is Registered in U.S. Patent and Trademark
Office and in other countries. Marca Registrada. Bantam
Books, Inc., 666 Fifth Avenue, New York, New York 10103.*

PRINTED IN THE UNITED STATES OF AMERICA

O   0 9 8 7 6 5 4 3 2 1

Author's Note

Although this book is a novel, practically all of the characters depicted here were actual persons who were part of the incidents described. Considerable effort has been made to portray them as they actually were—the things they did, their manner of speech, their style of dress, and their customs, habits, character and individual intelligence.

The Court-Martial of Daniel Boone *is based on a very well-authenticated but quite obscure incident in the life of the famed frontiersman. It is known that Daniel Boone was indeed court-martialed in 1778. The charges under which he was tried are known, as are the specific counts of those charges. It has been recorded who his accusers were, who the president of the court was, and who some of the members of the court were. There are vague and tantalizing hints as to how the court-martial progressed, including Daniel Boone's own unusual posture in it. The final result of the court-martial is also a matter of record. Nevertheless, a great gap exists in regard to the specific details of the trial, since all official records pertaining to it vanished within a few years. The whereabouts of these records, if they still exist at this time, remain a mystery.*

What we do know of The Court-Martial of Daniel Boone *has been painstakingly gleaned from numerous scattered sources and brief references to it which were made at the time in letters and diaries or in personal reminiscences which still exist today. It is essentially in the matter of the actual proceedings of the court-martial—the style in which the trial was held, the actualities of examination and cross-examination of witnesses, and the interchange of trial dialogue—where fictionalization has taken place.*

The author gratefully acknowledges the assistance of the Cincinnati Historical Society in providing unique and highly

important research materials from their extensive library
during the preparation of this novel.

ALLAN W. ECKERT

Englewood, Florida
February, 1973

*For the guidance and help
he has given me over the past
decade, as well as for his
unswerving friendship and concern
at all times,
this book is dedicated
with great warmth and esteem
to my agent*
MALCOLM REISS

1

Three times in succession the young man bobbed his head as he listened to his instructions. He was acutely aware of the large group of people seated or moving quietly behind him, aware that for the moment practically every eye present was locked upon him and every ear straining to hear the words being said to him. Never before in his life had Aaron Hathaway been the center of attention at any gathering and the effect it was having upon him now was profound.

The officer speaking to him took note of the rapid movement of the youth's adam's apple, the faint beading of perspiration on his brow, the slightly glazed appearance of his eyes and misinterpreted them as a manifestation of fear. His voice gentled and became less official.

"There's no need to be afraid, Aaron," he said. "He won't harm you."

"Again the youth nodded and for the briefest moment a nervous smile touched his lips. "I know that, sir," he said. "I'm not afraid of him."

Colonel Daniel Trabue felt the tuggings of a smile at his own mouth corners and smothered the impulse. The fifteen-year-old standing before him at a ramrod-straight interpretation of the stance of attention reminded the colonel of himself at that age. How deeply the young were affected by relatively simple things. Though what was happening here was important, the boy's part in it was minute; yet there was no doubt in the colonel's mind that Aaron Hathaway would remember this moment, this time, with crystal clarity for as long as he lived. Eighty years from now, perhaps, this same individual might well be telling his great-great-grandchildren about this day and repeating with remarkable accuracy the exact words he spoke now, the sensations he felt, the words he heard, and

1

perhaps embroidering them only insofar as him own small part in the matter was concerned.

Behind the boy, Colonel Trabue could see that practically all of the people were seated now. Every available chair in the place was being put to use, as well as a large number of log sections, inverted powder kegs and small rectangular wooden boxes stood on end. Even then there were not seats enough and many of the spectators had simply seated themselves upon the ground or were standing in a variety of slouching poses at the rear and side perimeters of those who were seated. For the third time since taking his place behind the long central table, Daniel Trabue wondered if he was making a mistake by allowing these proceedings to transpire in the public eye. Hardly a person on hand was not deeply involved in one way or another and emotions were likely to rise. Yet, as he had already justified it to himself, he could see no way of excluding the public; to do so would be unreasonably thwarting them. Still, the very act of including them had caused a considerable delay in opening the first session of the court-martial, as reasonable seating arrangements had to be made. He had hoped to begin no later than nine this morning, but that time had long passed and they were only now ready. He returned his attention to the youth before him, at the same time removing a heavy, deeply engraved gold watch from the pocket of his uniform waistcoat. "It's now..." he paused and glanced at the dial as the watchlid flipped open with an automatic movement of his thumb, "...almost eleven and past time to begin." He looked at the young man directly as he replaced the timepiece in his pocket. "You understand what it is you are to say and do?"

"Yes sir, Colonel Trabue." Hathaway saluted clumsily, self-consciously, turned on his heel, and moved stiffly away along the central aisle separating the spectators. From both sides he could hear whisperings and a suffusion of pink crept up his neck and onto his cheeks. He avoided looking directly at anyone, fearing he would see his parents or some friend and would not be able to keep from breaking into an idiotic grin. His responsibility here called for grave decorum and he was determined to maintain such a posture. He had hardly emerged from the overhang of the wide flat roof when he executed a smart left turn, walked to the corner of the overhang, and then locked his gaze on the structure that was his destination, perhaps eighty feet away. He moved in a direct line toward it, stiff-legged in his attempt to remain at attention even while moving, thus walking almost as if he were on stilts. A faint tittering from the crowd now behind him made his blush grow more intense.

The building he was heading for was essentially the same as the other seventeen at intervals in the large rectangle which formed the stockaded structure called Boonesborough. Each was a cabin of rather roughly hewn logs, notched and fitted at the ends. They were each twenty feet in length and fifteen in width, with the rear wall windowless and forming part of the outer wall of the fort. Six such cabins were on each side of the 260-foot length of the walls on east and west sides. There were no side windows and on the cabin wall facing the interior of the fort each had a single narrow door and one window. The cabins on these walls were ten feet apart. Upright sharpened logs protruded from the earth and, side-by-side, formed the cabinless walls. In the center of both east and west walls was a gate ten feet wide separated from the cabins on each side of it by fifteen feet. At each of the four corners were very crudely built blockhouses forty feet square, each projecting twenty feet outward from the main walls so that defenders at the small, eye-level portholes in the upper portions would have clear vision along the outside length of the wall on both sides. The north and south walls were each 150 feet in length and had no gates. Four cabins, similar to those on east and west walls, were part of the south wall, each separated from one another and from the blockhouses at the corners by six feet. Only the north wall broke the pattern of conformity. Here there were only two cabins close to the northeast blockhouse and most of the remainder of the north wall formed the back of a large roofed-over area under which the crowd had now gathered. It was obvious that this structure had just recently been enlarged, because of the raw, unweathered wood of that portion closest to the wall. As a matter of fact, the enlargement had only been completed the day before. The roofed-over area had been a combination stock corral and central meeting place without walls or floors which had originally been built thirty feet from the north wall and twelve feet from the three cabins on the northern half of the west wall. It had formerly measured sixty feet by forty feet, but over the past ten days the length had been extended to ninety feet and connected to the north wall. It was from

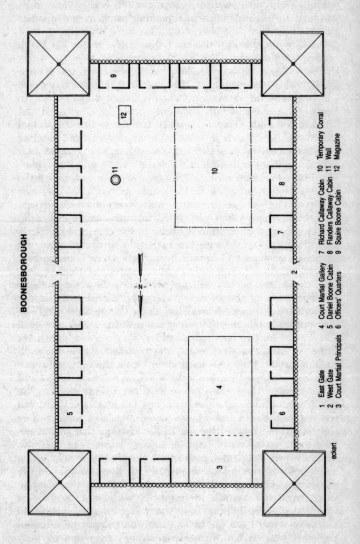

BOONESBOROUGH

1 East Gate
2 West Gate
3 Court Martial Principals
4 Court Martial Gallery
5 Daniel Boone Cabin
6 Officers' Quarters
7 Richard Callaway Cabin
8 Flanders Callaway Cabin
9 Squire Boone Cabin
10 Temporary Corral
11 Wall
12 Magazine

eckert

this open-sided structure that Aaron Hathaway now walked toward the cabin on the east wall closest to the northeast blockhouse.

A thin youth about the same age as Hathaway was leaning against the outer wall beside the door in an indolent manner, a flintlock rifle within easy reach also leaning against the wall. He straightened as Aaron approached and grinned insipidly.

"Ready?" he asked, as Hathaway was still a dozen feet away.

Aaron frowned at the nonchalance of the other and spoke curtly as he came to a halt before the door. "Yes, it's time. You're supposed to be on guard and at attention, not falling asleep."

"Hell, Aaron, I ain't asleep. No point in me standin' attention if they ain't no one lookin' at me. Anyways," he dipped his head toward the cabin, "he ain't goin' nowhere."

"You'll never make a good soldier with that kind of attitude, Fitz," Hathaway said, smiling in spite of himself. Jim Fitzgerald somehow had a knack of making anyone smile who talked to him. "Well, never mind that. Open the door."

Fitzgerald grunted something unintelligible and pulled a wooden plug out of the latch on the door which had prevented it from being opened from the inside. He stepped back as Hathaway pushed the door open and entered the cabin. For a moment the dimness inside made indistinct shadows of the table, chairs, two small beds and other furnishings, but then his eyes adjusted to the change and he saw the individual who lay on his back on one of the bunks along the rear wall, his hands clasped behind his head. The reclining man turned his head slightly toward the visitor.

Once again, as it had before when he gazed upon this man, young Hathaway's pulse quickened and a faint welling of fear rose in him. Though clad in familiar ash-grayed buckskin trousers, simple and unfringed, the man appeared to be an Indian. He wore no shirt and the skin of his chest was deeply tanned. The hair covering his scalp was very short except for a topknot of longer hair that fell to one side and covered an ear. The short hair had evidently only recently been allowed to grow out. Embarrassed because of the way the man's appearance was affecting him, young Hathaway stammered slightly as he spoke.

"C-Cap'n, sir, the colonel—Colonel Trabue—sent . . . he . . . ah . . . he sent me to fetch you, sir. It's . . . ah . . . The . . . uh . . . They're ready to begin now."

Daniel Boone swung his legs around and sat on the side of his bed. His piercing hazel eyes seemed almost black in the gloom, accentuating the Indian-like appearance he presented. He bent and quickly slipped dusky, well-worn low moccasins on his feet and stood. A soft, considerably stained leather shirt was draped over a low stool beside the head of the bed and he put it on over his head. Though fully two inches less than six feet in height and only of medium frame, he gave the illusion of being a bigger man. The shirt fit rather snugly and showed the swell of powerful chest and arm muscles as he tugged it into position. Not until he was clad did he glance at the young man and smile. It was the smile that changed his whole appearance, dispelling the thread of fear still bothering Hathaway. It was the old smile that Aaron had seen scores of times; the smile belonging to the man he had known and trusted and deeply respected for so long.

"If they're ready, I'm ready too, Aaron," Boone said.

Hathaway swallowed and his adam's apple jiggled vigorously again. He cleared his throat and spoke apologetically. "I'm supposed to make sure, Cap'n Boone, that you don't have any weapons on your person when you come. Colonel Trabue," he added hastily, "said it isn't permitted."

Boone, still smiling, raised his arms a bit and then let them drop back down along his sides. "No weapons, Aaron, but you can search me if you like."

Hathaway cleared his throat and had difficulty meeting Boone's eyes. "I believe you, sir, but the colonel said I had to check."

Hesitantly at first, but then with growing confidence when Boone evinced no sign of irritation at the indignity, he patted Boone's waist, sides, the small of his back and then stooped to swiftly run his hands down both sides of each leg. Finished, he stood and nodded. His continued stiffness and the frequent nodding of his head gave him a puppetlike demeanor of which he seemed to be unaware.

"Now, sir," he said, "I am to lead you to where you will sit. There are a lot of people that we'll have to walk past, but Colonel Trabue said I should tell you that you are not to speak to anyone and in fact not to say anything except to the colonel himself or to whom he gives you permission to speak."

Boone nodded without speaking and Hathaway continued. "The colonel also said to tell you that every courtesy possible will be extended to you throughout, sir, and except for the fact that you must at all times consider yourself in custody, you will be allowed every opportunity to defend yourself. He said he'll explain everything to you right at the beginning. Is there anything you need before we go out there?"

"Nothing," Boone said, then added, "You're doing just fine, Aaron."

Hathaway colored under the praise and bobbed his head. For a moment he was silent and then he blurted, "For what it's worth, sir, I don't believe you're guilty of treason."

Daniel Boone chuckled and squeezed his shoulder with a strong hand. "For what it's worth, Aaron," he said, "I'm glad you feel that way. Let's go."

They left the cabin and walked side by side toward the crowd gathered beneath the roofed-over meeting place. Jim Fitzgerald, his rifle now cradled in his arms, fell in silently behind them. A quick murmuring rose and fell among the gathered people and every head was suddenly turned in their direction. Probably over two hundred individuals were assembled and there was hardly a person among them whom Boone did not know personally and well. The numbers exceeded his expectations and automatically his eyes went to each of the blockhouses in turn. With so many present at the meeting place he was concerned that caution had fallen by the way, but he nodded with a certain grim satisfaction as he noted guards posted as lookouts. Without exception they were young men in their late teens and, Boone reasoned, probably none too happy to have to stand guard duty when the doings of greatest interest would be taking place below at the meeting place. At the opposite corner of the fort he could see Sergeant-at-Arms John Tibbs just emerging from the southwest blockhouse leading a squad of eight men.

As they walked, Boone's keen eyes took in the whole of the interior of Boonesborough. Considering what the place had just been through, it was really not in bad shape. Hardly a square foot of the upper portion of the walls did not bear the fresh nicks of bullet scars, but except for that and the small fenced plot near the southeast blockhouse where the mounds of three new graves could be seen, there was not much to indicate the frightful time this little fortification had just passed through.

By this time they had reached the meeting place and were moving down the central aisle, with all heads swiveling to follow their progress. Many among those seated here smiled or nodded at Boone—among them his daughter, Jemima—but many more remained expressionless. The prisoner paid no attention to them, his own glance taking in the long central table behind which at midpoint sat Colonel Daniel Trabue, resplendent in his uniform of blue coat and white waistcoat. To each side of him sat six officers, equally in uniform, all of them watching Boone's approach with varying degrees of interest. In front of each officer was a quill pen and fresh paper, with a well-filled oversized inkpot on the table between each two. To Boone's right in front of the long table was another table, much smaller and nearly square, behind which there were three chairs occupied by two men in civilian dress and one in uniform. To the left, also in front of the central table, was another small table behind which were two chairs, only one of which was presently occupied.

About fifteen feet directly in front of the central table and facing it at a slight angle was an unoccupied armless ladder-back chair. The first row of spectators was another fifteen feet beyond that. Reaching the front and turning to their left, the trio walked to the smaller table where Aaron Hathaway indicated that Boone should seat himself in the empty chair beside the individual already seated there. This man half rose as Boone took his seat and shook hands with him.

"Sort of surprised to see you here, Sam," Boone muttered.

Samuel Henderson grinned and winked. "Guess you didn't get advised I'd be sitting here, Dan," he replied in a low voice, "but the colonel asked me to come up, despite what you told him about not wanting anyone." He dipped his head to indicate the officer at midtable. The fact that Boone did not appear especially appreciative of his presence did not seem to bother him. Henderson was a rather short man, not quite corpulent and yet soft-looking. Though not more than twenty-five, he was already nearly bald. His eyes were hardly more than slits in the thick flesh of his face, disturbingly veiled and heavy-lidded and not really in keeping with his generally innocuous bearing. He shot a quick glance over his shoulder and the two young escorts, Hathaway and Fitzgerald, backed off a short distance, looked around them with some evidence of disappointment at not finding anything to seat themselves upon, and finally sat cross-legged on the ground at the base of one of the uprights.

The spectators had been largely quiet as Boone arrived and took his seat, but now a hum of conversations began rising, growing rapidly louder until suddenly chopped off by a single loud bang from the center table. Colonel Daniel Trabue, clenching a smooth, eight-inch section of wood—a neatly sawed portion of a branch about two inches in diameter—brought the end of it down onto the table a second time in the manner of a makeshift gavel and then laid it to one side. With unassumed dignity he slowly rose and in silence allowed his gaze to sweep across the assemblage before him, stopping with his attention fully upon Daniel Boone. When he spoke his voice was well modulated and resonant, carrying well to the farthest spectator, his words clearly enunciated and his manner of speech refined.

"Ladies and gentlemen of Boonesborough and others of the Kentucky settlements," he began, "we are gathered here on this twenty-eighth day of September in this year of seventeen seventy-eight to hold a trial by court-martial under military law. It is required under such law that the charges against a defendant must be instituted by two officers who are of good character and high moral standing, knowledgeable of the gravity of the charges they make and prepared to substantiate, under oath and to the best of their ability, the charges they have brought."

Colonel Trabue dipped his head to his left toward the table where the three men, only one of them uniformed, sat silently. "This requirement has been met in the charges that have been placed before this court by Captain Richard Callaway, resident of Boonesborough, and Colonel Benjamin Logan, resident of St. Asaph, also known as Logan's Station and Logan's Fort. The defendant in this action," he now turned and dipped his head to the right, "is Captain Daniel Boone, resident of Boonesborough, sometimes known as Boone's Fort."

Trabue paused for a long moment, almost as if reluctant to go on, then continued in a voice that was utterly without emotion. "The charges instituted by Captain Callaway and Colonel Logan are that in six specific instances occurring during this year, Captain Daniel Boone has committed acts of treason against the people and government of the United States of America."

II

Although it was common knowledge among everyone present what the charges were under which Daniel Boone was to be tried by court-martial, there was nevertheless a distinct stir among the spectators at the declaration of the president of the court.

No person on hand had not in some way become acquainted with Boone. Many, in fact, knew him about as well as Boone ever let anyone know him. These were his neighbors and friends whom he had led into the Kentucky wilderness several years ago; people who had trusted him and who had helped him carve a toehold of white settlement in this hostile land. More than a few owed their lives to him and had never expected to reach a point where their overwhelming trust in him might waver. Yet, in the scores of faces now turned in his direction, there was little evidence of trust or faith or even sympathy. Mostly there was an uncomfortable sense of incomprehension, coupled with an air of judgment reserved. In some there was a distinct aspect of antagonism and anger.

Boone had obviously changed. Everyone knew that. In the months past they had become painfully aware that he had done things that were inexplicable at best, and for which Boone himself had volunteered no acceptable explanation or justification. And while many on hand had in the past had their own lives or the lives of loved ones saved through Daniel Boone's efforts, by the same token a good many of those presently on hand had lost husbands, sons, brothers or friends through Boone's actions this year. Thus, more than anything else, the people congregated here seemed to be waiting for what would develop in this, the first court-martial to be held in the Kentucky country.

Colonel Trabue was still standing behind the central table, a tall, rather hawkish-featured but distinguished-appearing officer of near fifty. His military career spanned many years and this was not the first court-martial of which he had been a member, nor by any means the first time he had sat as president of such a body. He had risen in rank the hard way, beginning as an ordinary soldier of infantry in England over thirty years ago. Parentless and without connection in high places, he had entered the Royal Service at the age of seventeen. He was imbued with a keen natural intellect tempered by a pronounced degree of patience; a man accustomed to biding his time and ultimately reaping the rewards of his patience. It was how he had slowly, steadily risen through the ranks and at last, through dint of courage and presence of mind under conditions of extreme stress, had been taken under the wing of a shrewd commanding officer and promoted to lieutenant. By the time the Seven Years War had broken out in Europe and its offshoot conflict—now called the French and Indian War—on the North American continent, Trabue had become a captain in His Majesty's Royal Regiment. As such he had been placed in command of a company sent from England by the king to reinforce the army of the American colonies under General Edward Braddock. He had been with Braddock at that general's overwhelming defeat on the banks of the Monongahela in 1755; had become, in fact, a close companion of another young officer in that action, a Virginian named George Washington. Though Braddock's army had been thoroughly whipped in that battle by a mere handful of French soldiers supported by numerous Indians—Frenchmen who had quickly realized the value of fighting from cover in the Indian manner and had thus devastated the ridiculously exposed British troops—Trabue had acted gallantly and with considerable coolness. He had subsequently continued in his commanding position and by the war's end, when the French capitulated to General Amherst at Montreal, he had become a major. But like so many officers before him, Trabue had gradually become dissatisfied and disillusioned with his life as an officer of the Crown. The New World excited and fascinated him and he wanted to become a part of it. As always when he reached a decision, he was not long in acting.

Daniel Trabue had resigned his commission, married, and taken up residence in Virginia on a small plantation awarded him for his many years of loyal service. Still maintaining his friendship with George Washington, he became involved with the colonists in their growing antagonism toward the distant arm of British rule which was so thwartive of freedoms the colonists felt they deserved. Through the urgings of Washington, he reentered the service, but this time in the Virginia militia with the rank of colonel. Then came the shattering declaration by the colonists of their independence from Britannic sovereignty and the Revolutionary War was full upon them.

Now, in this year of 1778, the war was still raging in the East and there was no way of knowing which side would emerge victorious, though things were not going well for the erstwhile colonists. Three years ago George Washington had been elevated to command of the American troops and again Trabue was fighting beside him. But as if matters in the East were not enough to occupy the first General of the American Armies, matters on the western frontiers sorely needed attention. Indian attacks against settlements were increasing and settlers were demanding help from their new state governments. It was slow in coming and inadequate at best and, as a result, certain of the frontier areas were vacillating in their allegiance. The newly opened Kentucky country was a prime example. To settlers here, in what was the westernmost county of Virginia, the Revolution was a distant matter. Preservation of their own lives under the attack of Indians gave them little time or inclination to be overly concerned about how the war in the East was going. In fact they were not altogether sure, exposed as they were, that it was to their advantage to support their mother state of Virginia. The frontier settlements such as Boonesborough had thus remained essentially uncommitted in their loyalties where the Revolution was concerned—a situation of which both American and British leaders were painfully aware, and the Kentucky settlements were in essence being wooed by both factions for their allegiance.

For the British, operating out of their principal western wilderness fort at Detroit, gaining the allegiance of the Kentucky settlers could provide them a back door through which to attack the Americans from their virtually unprotected western flanks. Realizing this, the Americans stepped up their own efforts to aid the wilderness settlements, but there was in fact precious little aid they could send. It was at this juncture that General Washington wisely tapped the abilities of Colonel Daniel Trabue, placing him at the head of a company and dispatching him to the West to aid and protect the settlers wherever possible and to uproot the undermining activities of the British in that region. And it was through his position now as military commander in the western-most county of Virginia that Colonel Trabue was acting as president of a board of court-martial before which the defendant, Daniel Boone, was standing accused of treason. Now the colonel waited until the murmuring diminished and then continued.

"The specifics of the charges being levied against Captain Boone will be stated in detail presently," he said, "but first there are certain matters concerned with this court-martial which must be established and placed in their proper perspective in the minds of all persons present. For example, the right of this court to so try him must be firmly established and accepted by both prosecution and defense.

"America, as we are all aware, is not yet secured as an independent nation in her own right, though she has declared such independence. Whether or not she will win the right to maintain her own identity is still a point under dispute and a matter of which we here cannot be concerned at this moment except insofar as it affects the procedures in which we engage."

Colonel Trabue paused, noting the degree of concentration in the expressions of some as they endeavored to follow what he was saying; noting equally the evident lack of understanding among others. There were numerous intelligent, educated men here, he knew, but also there were many whose education was sorely lacking, even to the point of illiteracy, and to these people he owed a greater degree of clarification.

"What I am leading up to," he continued, "is simply this. Does this court-martial proceed under long-established British Crown regulations which set forth the limits under which it must be governed, or does it attempt to regulate itself under a new set of standards not yet really established by a developing independent Republic? In other words, is Captain Boone to be court-martialed under British or American rule?"

Again he paused as a murmur stirred the assemblage. To his left he noted that the two complainants, Colonel Logan and Captain Callaway, had their heads together in whispered conversation with the uniformed officer seated between them. Boone, to Trabue's far right, sat quietly and seemed unconcerned by the question, paying no attention to either the crowd or to Samuel Henderson who was frowning beside him and jotting some words onto a piece of paper. For the second time this morning, Colonel Trabue wondered if he had been wise in appointing Sam Henderson to act in defense of Boone, especially since Boone had made it clear that he felt no need for legal representation. In, when they came to that point of the matter, Boone still insisted that he wished to handle affairs by himself, then there would be no alternative but to instruct Henderson to step down. For Boone's sake, however, he hoped this would not be the case. The man had always been his own master in every respect and yet he was embarking into a set of conditions now with which he was wholly unfamiliar and under which he might well do himself more harm than good.

Trabue cleared his throat gently and spoke again. "Over the past several weeks, since the charges were filed with me and the need for a court-martial established, I have considered this point in depth. Although isolated here, we are nevertheless still a portion of Virginia—her westernmost county—and Virginia is no longer a Crown Colony but rather a state in the newly declared Union of the United States. As a state rather than a colony, she must be governed by the central government of the United States, however ill-formed that government may yet be.

"Yet, because—since the Declaration of Independence—the energies of Virginia and the other states have been devoted entirely to fighting a war to cement this new status, little opportunity has been given for setting up new rules of courts-martial. I feel quite certain, in fact, that even when and if time for such consideration does transpire, the process of courts-martial in the United States must be closely patterned after that which has been so long established for the Crown. Therefore, unless there is justifiable objection to our doing so here and now, I herewith declare that this court-martial shall be conducted along the lines of established British courts-martial proceedings. At the same time, there will of necessity have to be a certain amount of divergence from established regulations and because of this, our proceedings here will be to some degree less stringent. Every possible avenue of prosecution and defense may be considered and, if not too far beyond the limits of reasonability, allowed. Do either prosecution or defense have any statement germane to this issue that they might wish to make at this point? Colonel Bowman?"

At the prosecution table the judge advocate, Colonel John Bowman, pushed back his chair and stood. He was a well-built officer of around thirty who was just beginning to develop a bit of a paunch. A boyish shock of hair and large and rather protuberant blue eyes gave him a deceptively ingenuous aspect. He seemed rather young to be a colonel and undoubtedly would have appeared even younger had it not been for the carefully nurtured chestnut-colored moustache he wore. He smiled pleasantly as he faced the president of the board of court-martial.

"Colonel Trabue, the prosecution at this time has nothing specific to offer in this respect, but assumes that considerable leniency will be offered during the course of these proceedings to discuss and weigh debatable issues which may arise as matters progress. Prosecution is interested only in seeing that justice is done and due punishment is meted out to the accused . . ." he paused, and just as the frowning Colonel Trabue was about to speak, finished his comment with, ". . . . if he is found guilty by the esteemed members of this board of court-martial."

Still frowning, Trabue nodded. "Prosecution," he said drily, "has already launched himself into these proceedings with more alacrity than is yet demanded and I would recommend that he move with more verbal discretion as we continue. I would hope that this opening comment of yours—which I would judge to be more prejudicial to the accused than germane to the question—is not indicative of how you intend to pursue your case throughout this court-martial. Leniency in proceedings will, as a matter of fact, be greater than is customary, but there will still be distinct bounds and limitations beyond which I will not permit us to stray."

Bowman, not in the least chagrined by the mild rebuke, simply continued smiling as he nodded and resumed his seat between Ben Logan and Richard Callaway. Colonel Trabue turned his gaze to where Henderson and Boone were seated and said simply, "Mr. Henderson? Captain Boone?"

Samuel Henderson shot a glance at Boone, who remained silent, and then looked back at Colonel Trabue.

"The defense wishes to offer no comment at present, Mr. President, but as the judge advocate has pointed out, we also should like to feel privileged as we move along to discuss procedural points which might conceivably be inappropriate to our own peculiar situation here."

"Of course," Colonel Trabue said. "If there is no objection by either side, then, as to the legal jurisdiction of this court-martial in trying the matter presently before it, we will continue."

There was no comment and so after a moment Trabue turned his attention to Daniel Boone and addressed him directly.

"Captain Boone, I would ask you now if you are familiar with the process of courts-martial and of your rights and requirements as a defendant in court-martial action?"

Boone straightened in his chair but made no attempt to rise. "Colonel," he said, "I never sat in on one before, but I sure know a court-martial is a military trial. Not too sure what my rights are in it, but I know I'd better be able to show I ain't guilty of treason or it'll be my neck."

A smattering of laughter broke out among the spectators, silenced almost at once by the glowering of the president, who returned his attention to Boone.

"As in a civil court of law, you are here assumed innocent until proven guilty, and the burden of such proof lies with the prosecution. In a moment I will explain more fully our process here to you and if you have any questions beyond that you may feel free to ask them. However, there is one important matter to settle first. This is the nature of your defense and your right to counsel. At the time when the charges were made against you and you were confined to quarters until such time as a court-martial could be seated, you were asked whom you wished to have representing you as counsel. Your reply at that time was that you neither wished nor needed representation, that you felt capable of stating your own case. This is both irregular to the proceedings and dangerous to yourself because of unfamiliarity with either courts-martial or general trial procedures. Do you still maintain that you will act as your own defense in the matter before us here?"

Daniel Boone thought this over briefly before replying. "I still don't reckon I need someone else to talk for me, Colonel, because no one else knows just what I'll want to say."

Trabue shook his head in a little agitated movement. "I would like to remind you, sir," he told Boone, "that the charges against you are numerous and extremely grave, and that if found guilty of any one of them you could be executed as punishment. While I sympathize with your desire to defend yourself as you have heretofore been accustomed to doing in your own way of life, I must also attempt to make you realize that it will be greatly to your benefit to be represented by able counsel. I have, contingent upon your approval, appointed Mr. Samuel Henderson, attorney and son of your former employer, Judge Richard Henderson, to act as counsel for you. Bear in mind, Captain Boone, that in an action such as this you must not only be able to verbally defend yourself, but there is also the matter of cross-examination, and one not skilled in such matters may not have the ability to draw from witnesses the information or admissions he is seeking. As I say, I have appointed Mr. Henderson to act in your behalf, but if you would prefer someone else in his stead or even in addition to him, this would be permissible. I ask you again, are you still determined to act in your own defense?"

For the first time since the proceedings began, Boone got to his feet. He moved with fluid assurance and once again his similarity in appearance to an Indian caused a stir among the onlookers, but he ignored them. He moved behind his chair and placed his hands upon the high back of it, facing Colonel Trabue.

"Meaning no disrespect, Colonel," he began, "I think I'd like to take care of my own end of it myself. I don't doubt that there's a whole lot about trial procedure and cross-examination and likesuch that I ain't too knowin' about, but I've always found out that the best way to go through something you don't know anything about is to go ahead into it and learn by the doing of it. Now maybe that's being pigheaded, and I'm willing to agree that probably some good advice wouldn't do me no harm at all as we go along here, but I'd as soon have it be just that—only advice, and taken or not taken as I see fit. I've known Sam here for a number of years and know him to be a pretty good lawyer. What he didn't learn from books or schoolin' or in trials he was at, I reckon he picked up from his paw, who's pretty shrewd at legal workings himself, except for one thing I can think of."

Sam Henderson rolled his eyes in mock horror and there was a burst of laughter from the spectators at this and at Boone's subtle reference to Judge Richard Henderson's recently collapsed grandiose land scheme in which he negotiated privately with the Indians to buy the Kentucky country for his own purposes. It had been Judge Henderson's great dream, his greatest scheme, and equally his greatest failure. Boone grinned along with the crowd, gave Samuel Henderson's shoulder a brief squeeze and then continued as the laughter abated.

"Anyway, Colonel, I do believe Sam could be of some help and if it's allowed, I'd sort of like to have him stay here so I can play buzzard and pick his brains as we go along." Ignoring the new laughter, he continued. "But as for me having others to do the questioning and such for me, I guess I'll handle that end of it. There's just one other feller I'd like to have giving me some support and if he could sort of sit up here along with Sam and me, I'd appreciate it."

"Who is it, Captain Boone?" Trabue asked.

"Well, he ain't no lawyer," Boone said, "but he's got enough book-learnin' to be one. It's Jim Harrod."

Colonel Trabue gave one curt nod and looked out over the gallery. "Is Captain James Harrod present?" he asked.

Close to the center aisle at about midpoint of the onlookers to the court's left a medium-sized man with thinning brown hair and an air of assurance rose and held up one hand. He was not in uniform. Immediately the judge advocate was on his feet.

"Mr. President," he said, "it was a consideration of prosecution to possibly call Captain Harrod as witness."

"There is no reason," Trabue said, "that you still cannot do so. His acting as counsel or advisor to the defendant does not preclude him from also being called as witness, just as any member of this board of court-martial could be called to testify. There is, in fact," Trabue continued, now directing his remarks more to Boone than to Colonel Bowman, "no person present here today who cannot be called as witness by prosecution or defense. This includes the judge advocate, any member of the board of court-martial, or the president of the court-martial. Such individuals may be called, sworn in, give their testimony and then return to their duty when excused. The only possible exceptions are these: Captain Boone may, if he chooses, be a witness, but he also has the right to refuse to testify, since no man can be forced to incriminate himself. By the same token, if the wife of Captain Boone is present, she may not testify either for or against her husband. But in this present situation, where Captain Harrod would be acting as advisory counsel to the defendant, this would not, as the judge advocate well knows, preclude him from being sworn in to testify as a witness."

"Yes, sir," Bowman argued, "that's true, but if he is acting in behalf of Captain Boone then he will necessarily be prejudiced against the prosecution."

"That is a possibility," Trabue admitted, "but if such should develop, then this court would permit leave for prosecution to question him as a hostile witness." He looked again toward the gallery where Harrod still stood by his seat. "Captain Harrod, have you any objection to acting as advisor or counsel to Captain Boone in the issue under consideration here?"

"None, Mr. President," Harrod said. "In fact I would consider it an honor to do so."

"All right then," the colonel said, "please bring your chair to the front with you and take a place at the table with Captain Boone and Mr. Henderson."

James Harrod, founder of Harrodsburg which lay some forty miles almost due west of Boonesborough and less than twenty miles northwest of Benjamin Logan's station of St. Asaph, raised his empty chair high to clear the ducking heads of people between himself and the center aisle and then came to the front with it, taking a place at the defense table. In a moment the general rustling of the crowd had died away and again the president of the court was directing his remarks to Daniel Boone.

"Captain Boone, matters are well enough established at this point that I think we can more pertinently approach the matter at hand. It is the standard procedure in courts-martial such as this to first read to the accused the charge or charges that have been lodged against him. After each such charge has been read, you are required to respond to the question; that is, to state whether you are guilty or not guilty of the specific charge. Since it is the responsibility of the judge advocate to advise and assist the defendant as well as to prosecute him, and since he is very familiar with the military responses and their meaning, I will ask Colonel Bowman now to repair to your table and make such explanation to you.

"At the same time," he added sharply, as another new murmuring started in the gallery, "I must state to the onlookers here that in most cases courts-martial are not public affairs and that I have made exception to that in this present instance because of the closeness with which virtually everyone here is connected with the case. However, I have no intention of having this court-martial disrupted by outside disturbance. I will order the sergeant-at-arms to remove any person guilty of such disturbance and should the gallery in general become disruptive, then I will order that the remainder of the court-martial be conducted behind closed doors as is customary."

With that he picked up some papers on the table before him and then leaned toward the officer to his right and began conversing with him in an undertone inaudible to anyone else. At the prosecution table, Colonel Bowman came to his feet and walked to the table behind which sat Boone, Henderson and Harrod. He smiled in a genial manner but did not offer his hand to any of them.

"Just want to say at the start," he said to Boone, but only

loudly enough for just the three at the table to hear, "that I think you are a son of a bitch and I intend to see you hang."

The smile had never left his lips as he spoke, but it also had never reached the protuberant blue eyes. As cold and hard as blue marble, they held not the faintest trace of amity. James Harrod slammed the palms of his hands against the table to shove himself erect, but Bowman's own hand flashed out and gripped the nearest wrist, staying him.

"Sit still!" Bowman hissed. "Make a fuss to Trabue and I'll deny it and it'll only make you look bad." He released his grip and Harrod remained where he was, his face pinched and angry. Continuing to smile, Bowman looked at Boone again. "Just wanted you to know at the onset where I stand," he murmured.

Daniel Boone's expression had changed only in that his eyes had narrowed and his right jaw muscle was alternately swelling and relaxing. Though his hands on the table still seemed perfectly relaxed, he suddenly seemed to be a very dangerous man.

"To the matter at hand," Bowman said cheerfully. "Colonel Trabue will call you to the bar and read off the charges. After each you'll respond with the words 'guilty'—which you are," he added smoothly, but continued without pause, "—or 'not guilty.' If you plead guilty, there will be no further need for trial and you will be sentenced—in your case, to death by hanging. If you plead not guilty, the trial will continue with the presentation of such evidence as is available, primarily the evidence of testimony of witnesses interrogated through direct examination and cross-examination by both prosecution and defense. Through what is determined in such testimony thereby given, the members of the court-martial will ascertain in their own judgment the matter of your guilt or innocence."

"And if he refuses to make any plea at all to the charges?"

Bowman shot a glance at Henderson, who had asked the question. The officer sighed. "I thought we could avoid all that," he said. To Boone he added, "Making no reply at all to the charges means 'standing mute.' There are several forms of standing mute. Not answering at all is just one of them. It is possible that in some cases the defendant stands mute because he has no choice; for one reason or another—through being struck mute with fear, through being a mute to begin with—he is not physically able to respond. In such instance this is called standing mute *ex visitatione Dei*—in other words, as an act of God. In your case, Boone, it wouldn't apply, as you've already exhibited speech. If you then refused to respond it would be standing mute as an act of malice. For this the result is the same as if you were to respond to the question with impertinence or in a manner foreign to the purpose. As such it will be interpreted as an admission of guilt and you will be instantly convicted and suffer *peine forte et dure*—that is, strong and hard punishment. I could only wish," he added darkly, "that you stand mute."

"What's meant by 'strong and hard punishment'?" Harrod asked. "The same as conviction after trial would have given? Hanging?"

Bowman shook his head slowly and smiled more broadly, relishing his own response. "Not at all. Under *peine forte et dure,* the accused is returned to the prison or place where he's been awaiting trial. There he is laid naked on the ground or floor on his back and spread-eagled with tight cords from his wrists and ankles to the four corners of the room. Then an iron weight is placed on top of him—as great as he can bear—and remains there. On the second day he is given three small pieces of dried bread to eat but nothing to drink. On the third day he can have three swallows of stagnant water. That's how it alternates from then on."

Harrod's eyes had widened in disbelief. "My God," he whispered, "for how long?"

"Until he dies."

Before any of the three could say anything, Colonel Trabue's makeshift gavel had smacked the table sharply again. They all looked toward the bar.

"Has the judge advocate nearly finished instructing the defendant?"

Bowman's reply was prompt and courteous. "Very nearly, Colonel Trabue. May I ask for just a moment or two longer?"

At Trabue's nod he turned back and was met by an incredulous whisper from Harrod.

"That's insane! With such a punishment for standing mute, no one in his right mind would ever elect to do so."

"Wrong," Bowman replied. "Some have—not here, but in England. There, if convicted of a felony, the guilty individual is not only punished, he also forfeits his entire estate of landed property, thus leaving his family destitute. But in standing mute and thereby undergoing the judgment of *peine*

forte et dure, even though it result in his death, there is no
such forfeiture of his estate, which thereupon passes into the
hands of his heirs. You'd be surprised at how many have
preferred it that way. Care to have a go at it, Captain?"

Boone made no reply and Bowman obviously expected
none, for he continued without pause. "The only other pleas
are not applicable in your case. One is *autre fois acquit,*
which is simply to say you've already been tried and acquit-
ted of the crime and cannot legally be placed in second
jeopardy. Another is *autre fois attaint ou convaincu,* meaning
you've already been tried and convicted of the crime in
question and cannot legally be punished a second time for it.
You could also plead a change of venue on the grounds of
questioning the jurisdiction of the court, but since you have
already indicated to this court-martial your acceptance of its
jurisdiction in the matter, that plea is negated." Bowman
straightened. "Thus," he concluded, the irritating smile spread-
ing his lips again, "you have no choice but to plead guilty or
not guilty. Do yourself and the court a favor—plead guilty.
It'll save time. One way or another, Boone, I'm going to
watch you get hanged!"

With that he turned and strode back to the prosecution
table, nodding pleasantly at Colonel Trabue as he passed to
signify that he had indeed instructed Daniel Boone in his
rights of plea.

III

Although he had earlier hurried the judge advocate along,
for fully two minutes after Bowman had returned to his seat
at the prosecution table, Colonel Daniel Trabue busied himself with checking certain points in the small sheaf of papers
on the table before him. Twice he conferred in whispered
tones to the officer seated on his left and once with the officer
on his right. At one point he arose and walked to the second
officer to his left, stood behind him and briefly whispered in
his ear, then returned to his own chair. At last he looked up
and spoke to the assemblage in general.

"It is not customary," he began, "to explain in detail the
mechanics of courts-martial to the accused or to any who may
be in attendance. In most cases it is entirely unnecessary,

since they are military people and have an obligation to be familiar with at least the basic rules of procedure in a military trial. To some extent, however, I am going to stray from this custom at the present time. I have two reasons in particular for doing so. One is that we have on hand here quite a large number of individuals who have never before in any way participated in a court-martial, either as principal or as spectator. To them it would be unfair to plunge instantly into proceedings that are apt to be rather confusing if not clarified to some degree.

"Secondly," he continued, "this body is acting under an unusual—in fact, a unique—set of circumstances, in that it is basing its procedures on rules established by a country with which this country is currently at war. There is altogether the likelihood that in certain respects, this board of court-martial will have to stray from rulings established in—and predicated upon—a Monarchy, and therefore adapt as well as possible to new precepts more in keeping with the structure of a Republic. In this light it will become necessary to point out to defense and prosecution alike, as well as to the officers acting as members of this court-martial, where we are altering rules of procedure."

Colonel Trabue paused for a moment, glancing down at the piece of paper upon which he had jotted some notes to himself during the interval when Colonel Bowman had been in whispered conference with the three men at the defense table. In a moment he looked up, cleared his throat lightly and resumed speaking.

"Already I have noted a few minor points about established British courts-martial proceedings which are no longer quite applicable to our situation here. That we are within our bounds to hold court-martial at all in the matter of charges of treason against Captain Daniel Boone is beyond dispute. It is not only our duty to do so, but it is also the right of Captain Boone to be afforded such court-martial. This stems from the twenty-ninth chapter of the Magna Charta which declares that no freeman shall be taken, imprisoned or otherwise deprived of his freehold or liberties or free customs—or be outlawed or exiled or otherwise destroyed—and that no sentence shall pass upon him nor shall he be condemned except through lawful judgment of his peers or by the *lex terrae*, which is the law of the land. In our particular case, in a state of war and with civil jurisdiction nonexistent, martial law is quite certainly a part of the *lex terrae*.

"It will be noticed that seated with me here are twelve other officers who, with the president of the court acting as the thirteenth, constitute the customary number of members of a board of court-martial. Some of these officers are higher in rank than the accused, at least one is lower, and some are the same, but the very fact of their being officers establishes their peership with the accused. No officer of this board is compelled to judge in any way other than that dictated by his own conscience, irrespective of rank. Thus, it is customary, when judgment is called for, that the least in rank among these members cast their opinion first and in this way be in no manner swayed by the opinion of a superior officer on the same board.

"Such opinions," he added, "are in most circumstances given verbally, but I have long been personally convinced that the method used by the French Service is less subject to one member being influenced in his own opinion by the opinion of another member, and therefore more just. It is that method which I purport to have this present board of court-martial follow when the time comes. When all evidence has been presented and it becomes time for judgment, I will ask the lowest-ranked member of this board to write his opinion at the top of a sheet of paper, then fold it over so none can see what he has written and pass it to the next higher in rank so he may do the same. This will continue until my own opinion is called for as last. The paper will then be unfolded and the opinions counted. As has always been customary under the rules of courts-martial, the opinion of the president of the court shall be counted as two voices if in favor of the defendant, but only as one if against him. Since treason is an offense punishable by death, the opinion of two thirds of the members of this board must concur in the guilt of the accused before the death penalty can be passed. Does Captain Boone understand this fully before we progress to other matters?"

Daniel Boone was sitting silently, hardly appearing to be listening to what Colonel Trabue was saying. Sam Henderson leaned over and whispered to him and in a moment James Harrod joined in their conference. Boone nodded and looked at the president of the court.

"I understand," he said simply, "but it doesn't strike me as being fair that you get two votes and everyone else up there gets only one."

Colonel Trabue looked shocked. "But that is entirely to your benefit, Captain Boone. My opinion is worth two voices only if it is in your favor. Otherwise it is worth just one."

Boone shrugged. "A vote's a vote, and that's how I always figured it."

Colonel Trabue wore a pained expression now and shook his head. "In most cases where a vote is concerned you are, of course, correct. However, in the case of courts-martial a favorable opinion for the defendant by the president of the court has been established over many years as being two voices, and I see no reason at this juncture for altering that procedure."

Boone shrugged again, but when he said nothing more, Colonel Trabue went on. "In times past, the judge advocate has been the true mainspring of a court-martial, since it is largely upon him that the court-material depends for information concerning the legality as well as the regularity of the proceedings. He is well-versed in military law and if he errs, then it is quite possible that all may go wrong. He prevents members of the board of court-martial from engaging in illegal proceedings, since most often the officers sitting as members of a court-martial have not had specific training in such matters and may be ill-informed in respect to finer points of military law. Fortunately in this case, I have myself on numerous occasions acted as both member of boards of court-martial and also judge advocate, so our combined knowledge here will undoubtedly see us through very well.

"The role of judge advocate has always been a most difficult one," he went on. "That is part of what I hope we can simplify here. In the past the judge advocate has had to be something of a Proteus—changing sides to aid both the prosecution and the defense. Though he acts as prosecutor—formerly for the Crown but now for the government of the United States—he has also been expected to assist the accused in his defense in order to see that he has law and justice. He does this by pointing out to him the proper mode of supporting his cause and making his defense, as Colonel Bowman has just done in part by instructing Captain Boone in his rights of plea. However, to me it has always been inconsistent with justice and common sense—no matter how well imbued he may be with impartiality—to expect the judge advocate to be thus active in both prosecution and defense. Therefore, in this transitional period of military law, it is my ruling that he shall on this occasion act principally as prosecutor, with the continued privilege and responsibility of instructing the court and its members in any matter regarding legality or procedure."

For just a moment it appeared that Colonel Bowman would rise and take issue with this, but then he seemed to change his mind and settled back in his seat complacently.

"It has equally been the province of the judge advocate," Trabue was saying, "to perform the office of clerk or register of the court. Again, I find this to be divertive to his basic role as prosecutor and have therefore asked that Captain George Michael Bedinger assume the duties of clerk and take down the record of what occurs here."

The president dipped his head to his left where, a few feet from the central table, a small table was situated at which sat a youthful officer already swiftly penning what was being said, in many cases using his own forms of abbreviation to facilitate his speed in writing.

"Does the judge advocate," Colonel Trabue inquired, "have any objection to these relegations of authority which are normally in his province?"

Bowman waved a hand airily without rising and said, "I have no objection to them, Colonel."

Trabue smiled. He had never been in a court-martial before in which Bowman had taken part and was not sure as yet how to read the man. He was pleased to find him so cooperative and took it as an indication that the proceedings would undoubtedly move along smoothly.

"There is, then," he went on, still speaking generally but directing his monologue mostly toward Bowman, "only one other point to cover here insofar as the duties of the judge advocate are concerned. It is incumbent upon him to administer the necessary oath to the members of the court. However, prior to them being sworn, the judge advocate is to see that the accused is informed of the rank and name of each man acting as his judge upon this board of court-martial. The accused or his counsel, as well as the prosecution, may thereupon challenge any whom either side feels might be prejudiced against his cause."

Colonel Trabue turned his attention to the defendant. "Captain Boone, since you may be unfamiliar with the meth-

od of challenge, I will briefly explain that you are permitted—
as is the judge advocate acting for the prosecution—an unlimited number of challenges with cause. In other words, if you
can show good cause why any juror here might be biased
against you, that juror will be removed and replaced with
another. Normally under the rules of courts-martial the accused is further permitted to have a maximum of twenty
peremptory challenges—that is, challenges without any cause
shown. It may be that without substantial justification, the
accused simply feels he does not wish a certain member of a
board of court-martial to sit in judgment of him. On peremptory challenge, such a juror is excused and replaced. The
prosecution has the same right. Such, however, is not the
case here. When the charge is high treason, as it is in the
matter before us, peremptory challenges are not permitted,
although challenges *with* cause remain unlimited."

Trabue looked from the defense to the prosecution and
then back to defense again. "I caution both sides, however,"
he added, "against acting with abandon in the matter of such
challenges, since by their very nature they tend to impugn
the character of the challenged—saying, in effect, that this
officer is incapable of arriving at an impartial opinion on the
evidence presented. Further, and admittedly this is of much
less consequence and not a determining factor legally,
Boonesborough is a frontier post with a very limited number
of replacements available, and it would not be difficult to use
them all up. In such case the court-martial would have to be
postponed until new jurors could be brought in, or else the
trial itself be moved elsewhere."

Colonel Trabue put down the piece of paper he had been
holding. "I believe, with that," he said, "we are now ready to
begin. Colonel Bowman may now establish the rank and
identity of officers seated here as possible members of this
board of court-martial, following which the period of challenges, if any, shall be opened. I would also instruct the
defendant that with no challenges, or once challenging has
been completed, the judge advocate will swear in the members and after that point challenges are no longer acceptable.
Colonel Bowman, you may proceed."

As if magnetically drawn, virtually every eye of those in the
gallery locked on the judge advocate. Bowman, with an air of
practiced confidence, placed a smooth round stone half the
size of his fist on the middle of the small stack of papers

before him and came quickly to his feet. He walked across
the space before the court-martial table without looking at
any individual seated there until he stopped at the end
closest to the defense table. The outermost officer, six seats to
the right of Colonel Trabue, was about twenty-two years of
age and impeccably clad.

"Lieutenant," Colonel Bowman said, "would you please
identify yourself?"

The young officer dipped his head and, looking in the
direction of the defense table, said, "Lieutenant David Gass
of the Virginia Militia, sir."

The judge advocate took a full pace backward to stop
before the officer to the left of Gass. "Sir?" he asked.

The officer, burly and somewhat unkempt despite a fresh
blue uniform, had heavy features and dense black hair. His
hands, folded on the table before him, were meaty and
broad, though short-fingered. Curling black hairs grew heavily on the backs of his hands and fingers. He smiled, exposing
stained teeth.

"William Bailey Smith, Major, Virginia Militia."

The next officer, a captain, was the largest man of the
thirteen members of the court. Seated, he was half a head
taller than any other and powerfully built, though his facial
skin was somewhat puffy and his cheeks were red-stained
from subdermal capillary ruptures. His voice, despite his
size, was remarkably high-pitched. "Cap'n McGary," he said.
"Hugh McGary. Acting Colonel, Virginia Militia."

To his left, as if in contrast to McGary's bulk, sat the
slightest of the court members, who identified himself as
Captain John Holder, resident of Boonesborough and acting
major of the Boonesborough Militia. Thin and hatchet-faced,
he sported a narrow black moustache with a substantial gap in
the center.

Another captain was next—a tall but well-proportioned and
quite handsome officer of about twenty-eight who identified
himself as James Wilkinson, formerly of Massachusetts but
now a regular of the Virginia Regiment who had accompanied
Colonel Trabue to Kentucky.

Colonel Isaac Shelby sat between Wilkinson and Colonel
Trabue, a stern-faced man with full, close-cropped salt-and-
pepper beard, bushy brows and a long, rather sharply pointed nose. A Boonesborough settler, he was also an officer of the
First Virginia Regiment.

The judge advocate then asked Colonel Trabue to identify himself, which the court president did in clipped words, as if anxious to get this detail out of the way and the actual trial proceedings begun. Two majors sat to his left and in turn identified themselves as Bowman stopped before them. The first was Major Robert Anderson, about forty, a well-known settler of the area who was presently residing at Harrodsburg. He had been a member of the Queen's Rangers some years before but, like Colonel Trabue, had retired his commission to become a resident of the New World and wound up reentering military service, but this time in the militia of Pennsylvania. He was an outspoken critic of the past policies of William Pitt and King George.

After Anderson came Major Arthur Campbell, an entirely bald, rotund officer with quick bright eyes and a jovial appearance. Despite his hairless pate, his eyebrows were dense and nearly white. A member of the Pennsylvania Second Regiment of regulars, he perpetually supported his head with his left hand under his chin and elbow anchored to the table. A resident of Philadelphia, he had come to the Kentucky frontier as adjutant to Colonel Trabue's command.

Four captains followed, all but one members of the Virginia Militia. They were James Galloway, John Todd, James Wood and John Floyd. Galloway, one of George Rogers Clark's officers, had been prevented by illness from accompanying Clark in his present campaign against Kaskaskia and Cahokia in the Illinois country. Todd, his left arm in a black sling, had similarly been prevented from being with Clark due to a bullet wound in the upper arm. He had been fired at from ambush and though the assailant had escaped, it was presumed to have been a roving Shawnee who had taken one snap shot at the officer and then fled. Todd was the only regular officer of these four, having received his captain's commission from Clark a year and a half ago, on March 5, on direct order from the governor of Virginia, Patrick Henry. Wood, who was deemed by certain of his fellow officers to have Tory inclinations, though an unjustified accusation, had been a member of the General Assembly of Frederick County, Virginia, until his move last year to Logan's Fort. He was presently of the Virginia Militia as a detached service. Floyd, who had the acting rank of colonel, was originally a Boonesborough settler, but who spent more of his time in recent months at Harrodsburg—lured there, it was whispered, by the charms of a certain lady not yet positively identified but probably one of a pair of not unattractive widows.

With the identifications completed, Colonel Bowman returned to his seat as the president of the court spoke to the defendant.

"Captain Boone, do you wish to challenge the seating of any of these officers in the court-martial about to commence against you?"

Boone stood up deliberately and for a few moments said nothing as he allowed his gaze to move from left to right across the seated officers. At length he looked at the middle officer and gave a little grunt, then a shrug.

"No, sir."

"You may be seated. Does the judge advocate have any challenges to make in the members being seated for this board of court-martial?"

"None, sir," Bowman replied.

"Then will you please swear in this board?"

"Yes, sir." Bowman busied himself with his papers, selected one from the pile and approached the principal table. He spoke first to the president of the court.

"I have, Colonel Trabue, pursuant to your instructions prior to this time, adapted the British oath of court-martial to our present situation as representing the government of the United States. Little modification was required and the oath is primarily the same as when established in Great Britain under the Mutiny Act, Section One, Articles of War, Section Fifteen, Article Six. Mr. President and members of the court, kindly rise and raise your right hands, listen to the oath as I read it and then signify your acceptance of the responsibilites of this office by responding to the question."

All thirteen officers at the table stood and raised their right hands as Bowman read slowly and clearly from the paper he was holding.

"As officer in the service of the Government of the United States, being called upon as a duty and privilege to act as member of this board of court-martial now being seated, I solemnly swear by Almighty God that I will faithfully and truly turn my efforts to just consideration of the issue before this board; that I will be guided by my conscience; that I will not be swayed in my opinion by the opinions of others, even though they may be of higher rank; that I will administer justice without partiality, favor or affection, and without bias, predetermination or prejudice; and that I shall well and truly try and determine, according to the evidence in the matter now before me." Bowman lifted his eyes. "Please signify your acceptance of this responsibility by your utterance of the words: This I do solemnly swear, so help me God."

In precise chorus of voices, the thirteen officers swore their oath, lowered their hands and resumed their seated positions. From the gallery came a shuffling of feet, scattered coughing and then a pervading silence. A quickening of interest was visible on every face. With a sudden crack almost like that of a rifle, the crude gavel in Colonel Trabue's grasp smote the table resoundingly.

The court-martial of Daniel Boone had begun.

IV

"Captain Daniel Boone, rise and approach the bar."

The words of the president of the court-martial punctured the quiet overhanging the spectators at Boonesborough and, like a whisper of escaping air, a soft collective sighing sound came from the gallery. It was a sound not quite of anticipation, not quite of regret, yet somehow a combination of the two, as if those gathered here had abruptly come to the realization that an irrevocable line had been crossed, a step taken from which there could never be a turning back.

Daniel Boone moved to a point about ten feet in front of the long central table, facing Colonel Trabue. At the age of forty-four, the frontiersman showed no sign whatever of aging. Through years of habit he moved with a peculiar animal grace and bearing that suggested enormous reserves of strength and endurance. His hair—the long dark topknot from his crown which swept back and down behind his left ear and almost to his shoulder, as well as the short new growth over the remainder of his scalp—was a deep brown, almost black, without any vestige of gray. His skin was deeply tanned, imparting an additional flavor of the Indian aspect, and his features were even and unreadable, giving no indication of what might be passing through his mind at this critical moment of his life. When he stopped and waited before the bar, he exhibited not the slightest trace of self-consciousness or concern. He stood comfortably erect, quietly dignified, his arms straight down, his well-formed hands half-curled, his stature that of a man in full though relaxed possession of every faculty.

Colonel Daniel Trabue looked up from the paper before him on which were row after row of neat cursive lines in the delicately flamboyant hand of a skilled penman. His gray eyes carefully studied the man who stood before him. As a relative newcomer to the Kentucky country, he hardly knew Boone at all on a personal level, yet he had heard a great deal about the man from a wide variety of people. On one level of his intellect he was glad he did not know Boone better, therefore allowing him a greater deal of impartiality in his judgment of the man now; yet on another level was an indefinable sense of regret at not being more familiar with him. Beyond any doubt, Daniel Boone possessed that rare aura of a man who was something apart from other men, a quality of intense individuality that Trabue had seldom encountered in his many years of dealing closely with men from all walks of life.

"Captain Boone," he began, "you appear before this body charged with the crime of treason on six specific counts. These charges have been imputed, as prescribed by the military code of justice, by two of your fellow officers, Captain Richard Callaway and Colonel Benjamin Logan. The judge advocate has explained your rights of plea to you. In addition, previous to this court-martial you were presented with a full written copy of the charges, but it is still required by regulation that I read the individual charges aloud to you, asking of you your plea to each specific charge before passing on to the next."

He lowered his eyes to the paper before him. "It is charged," he read, "that Captain Daniel Boone, on the seventh day of February in this year of our Lord, 1778, did voluntarily absent himself from a party of twenty-seven Boonesborough men under his command; that these men, encamped at a place known as the Blue Licks, were engaged in the manufacture of salt from springs in that area; that Captain Boone, having been absent from his party for a period of approximately thirty-one hours, did return on the next day, February 8, approaching the encampment at first as if he were alone; that soon eight Indians became visible a short distance behind him and were led by him into said encampment; that in addition to those eight Indians, over one hundred other Indians had secretly surrounded the said encampment, which fact Colonel Boone knew before reentering the encampment; that Captain Boone did voluntarily call his men together and order them to lay down their arms and surrender themselves into the hands of these Indians; that these men were thereupon made captive without the opportunity of defending themselves; that the capture of these men left the settlement of Boonesborough in an extremely vulnerable situation for further attack by the Indians, the fort at that time being left with only ten men, twenty boys and fifty women and girls to defend it."

Trabue lifted his eyes to Boone, whose expression had not altered. "Captain Boone," he said, "how do you plead?"

"Colonel, I reckon I plead guilty, since everything you read there happened just about the way you read it."

There was a gasp from the gallery and above it the voice of Boone's young married daughter, Jemima, cried out clearly, "Oh, Father, *no!*"

Colonel Trabue was surprised. "You are pleading guilty, sir, to this first charge of treason?"

Daniel Boone frowned and shook his head. "No, sir," he said, "I ain't. I'm pleading guilty to doing all those things you read off that I did, but I sure ain't guilty of treason."

"Captain, the *prima-facie* evidence inherent in the statement of actions is what has led to the charge of treason. If you plead guilty to the actions described, then you are pleading guilty to the treason charge. Do you wish to retract your plea of guilty and enter a plea of not guilty?"

"Don't rightly see any way I can do that, Colonel; because like I said, I *did* do those things it says, but I ain't guilty of treason."

The president of the board of court-martial sighed and turned to the officer rapidly writing at the same table to the left of the court. "Captain Bedinger," he directed, "let the record show that Captain Boone has pleaded guilty to the action, but not to the first charge of treason itself."

At the prosecution table Colonel Bowman half rose to his feet, then settled back and swiftly paged through the papers before him, finally stopping on one and studying it carefully, his brow faintly furrowed. Colonel Trabue saw this but made no comment. He read from his own charge sheets again.

"In the second count it is charged that on or about the thirteenth day of March in this year of our Lord, 1778, Captain Daniel Boone, having been transported to the British fort at Detroit, did voluntarily meet and hold conference with the British commander there, Governor-General Henry Hamilton; that this occurred at a time when the United States was engaged in active warfare with Great Britain; that he did collude with said Governor-General Hamilton and accept numerous favors and goods from him; that Captain Boone did agree to subsequently turn his allegiance to Great Britain; that Captain Boone did conspire with Governor-General Hamilton in that he promised to encourage his followers in Boonesborough when he returned to them to similarly turn their allegiance to Great Britain; and that the said Captain Boone did conspire with Governor-General Hamilton in that he further promised to surrender the settlement of Boonesborough to the British without opposition at a given time. Captain Daniel Boone, how do you plead?"

Boone scratched the side of his jaw and squinted. "Colonel, it sure don't sound so good the way you read it there, but I got to admit that I did what it says."

"You are, then, on this charge, pleading guilty to treason?"

"No, sir, I ain't! Only to what it said there," he pointed to the paper before Trabue, "that I did. There was no treason involved."

"I have never," Colonel Trabue said, a slight edge in his voice, "encountered a situation quite like this. Does the judge advocate wish to make any comment at this point?"

John Bowman did not look happy. "Mr. President," he said, "with all due respect to the court, I fail to see how, under the rules of courts-martial as clearly delineated in the Articles of War, a defendant can plead guilty to the act but not to the crime. Even less," he added tightly, "do I understand how the president of this court can direct that such a plea be accepted and recorded. The Articles, sir, do not allow for this. The matter is quite clear; the defendant is either guilty or not guilty and his plea must be one way or the other. It cannot, under British military law, be both."

"That is quiet true, Colonel Bowman, but again I would remind you that we are in a strange situation here, trying an officer of the United States under the British rules of courts-martial, on charges of acts of treason against the United States in favor of the British. As specifically stated in the beginning, numerous adjustments will undoubtedly have to be made as this trial progresses to alter the established rules of courts-martial to fit the situation prevailing. In this respect, though it may not coincide with previous standards of procedure, it is the discretion of this court to allow the seemingly contradictory plea of guilty of the act but not of the charge to stand. Let it so be written, Captain Bedinger."

Bowman was getting angrier by the minute and showed it. "I must strongly disagree, sir," he said heatedly. "As judge advocate it is my prescribed duty to clarify areas of legality or illegality in procedure, should any points of law arise, as they have now. If the president of this court persists in the judicial discretion he has claimed in this matter, then I must insist that my utmost objection to it be written into the record for later review by higher authority."

Bowman's demand did not altogether surprise Colonel Trabue, although the judge advocate's anger did. He nodded and remarked that it was only as he expected Colonel Bowman to react, then directed Captain Bedinger to record the objection as stated. Bowman, however, was not in the least intimidated by the court and his next remark did indeed catch Trabue off balance.

"As judge advocate, I must also demand at this point, sir, that the members of this board of court-martial be polled in an aye or nay vote in regard to accepting the contradictory plea as you have suggested—their votes also to be written into the record—and this court thereupon to abide by the ruling of a simple majority upon this issue."

Trabue's lips thinned. Bowman had adroitly sidestepped him, taking the decision out of his hands alone and placing it in the hands of the court as a body. There was nothing he could do but comply with the demand, with the galling realization that a degree of his own power as president of the court had been stripped away and that his own decision might now be reversed. If such became the case, it could well become an ugly blight on his own record, possibly even leading to reprimand and demotion. Even worse, as Trabue viewed it, the polling of the members over this issue would almost certainly split the court into factions, thus tending to reduce its effectiveness and impartiality as a cohesive body.

"The judge advocate's demand," he said coldly, "is within the purview of his office. It will be met. This board of court-martial will now be polled on the question. An aye vote will signify acceptance of the dual plea of guilty to the act but not guilty of the charge. A nay vote will be a vote to accept only a simple plea of guilty or not guilty. Captain Bedinger, you may poll the panel and record the vote."

George Michael Bedinger, a pale-complexioned individual with tight dark red hair, closely cropped, and ice-blue eyes, bobbed his head once and said, "Yes, sir," as he continued swiftly writing without looking up. In a moment he lifted his quill pen, dipped it neatly into the immaculate hexagonal crystal inkpot and sat with it poised just above the paper. Without having to be told to do so, he polled the members of the court in the order in which they were subsequently to be polled for their opinion in the judgment of Daniel Boone— from the lowest ranked officer to the highest—calling out the officers' names and jotting down the vote of each as it was given.

"Lieutenant David Gass."

A momentary pause from the junior officer and then the response: "Nay." Gass shot a nervous glance at Colonel Trabue, but the president of the court was looking straight ahead, seemingly lost in his own thoughts.

"Captain John Holder."

Quickly and decisively, Holder said, "Nay."

"Captain James Wood."

"Nay." Now the onlookers murmured faintly among themselves and the court president's calm gaze dropped to the table in front of him. He seemed unperturbed.

"Captain Hugh McGary."

"Nay." It was not an unexpected vote.

"Captain John Floyd."

The officer seated closest to where Bedinger sat recording the vote nodded and said quietly, "Aye." Someone in the gallery clapped twice and then abruptly ceased.

"Captain James Galloway."

An aye vote had been anticipated by many of the onlookers and when the sandy-haired Scotsman said "Nay" the atmosphere became suddenly charged.

"Captain John Todd."

"Aye."

"Captain James Wilkinson."

"Nay."

Breaths were being held. With eight members polled the vote stood at six nays, two ayes. It now appeared that Bowman would surely win his point and the faintest suggestion of a smug little smile touched the judge advocate's lips. With five votes yet to be polled, only one more nay would signify a significant psychological victory for Bowman.

"Major William Smith."

"Aye," Smith called out loudly and not unexpectedly. He and Daniel Boone had often roamed together.

"Major Arthur Campbell."

"Aye." The tension intensified.

"Major Robert Anderson."

The officer to the immediate left of Colonel Trabue hesitated only an instant and then replied softly, "Aye."

For the first time, Colonel Trabue reacted visibly. Although his expression did not alter, he folded his hands together on the table before him and the knuckles became suddenly white with the pressure of his grasp. Colonel Shelby, seated to his right, was known as a "by-the-book" officer, and the frown that had been creasing Shelby's brow over the past few minutes had grown deeper. An almost palpable hush overhung the assemblage now and the judge advocate, the vague smile still tilting the corners of his mouth, flicked the tip of his tongue swiftly across his lips.

Captain George Michael Bedinger's voice breaking the silence came as something of a jolt. "Colonel Isaac Shelby."

No response prior to his had been so long in coming. Half a minute plodded by as every ear strained to hear his reply, but finally it was Bedinger who spoke again.

"Colonel Shelby, sir?"

Shelby turned his head to look at the clerk and then he nodded. "Aye," he said.

Reaction was mixed. Among the spectators there were perhaps more groans than sighs of relief, although a brief scattering of applause broke out. The judge advocate's eyes had become veiled, his expression unreadable. At the prosecution table with him, Richard Callaway was obviously angry and Benjamin Logan was frowning. Across from them Sam Henderson and James Harrod were openly grinning. Colonel Trabue looked oddly disturbed and only Daniel Boone, still standing before him, seemed completely unconcerned about what had taken place and merely waited with his characteristic patience for the proceedings to continue. Captain Bedinger's call for the final vote was anticlimactic.

"Colonel Daniel Trabue."

"Aye," said the president of the court. He had won a narrow victory but, though he preferred it to defeat, he was not pleased. Against his will and realizing the pointlessness of reacting in such a manner, he was nevertheless irked at

Boone, regarding him as responsible for causing this early crisis in the proceedings. Bowman, even though having lost, had been successful in hammering a wedge into the panel, dividing them evenly into two factions and quite possibly undermining to a greater or lesser degree their ability to be wholly impartial. The element of competition, greatly out of place in any jury, had been introduced to them through Bowman's strategy. In a way, though the judge advocate had lost, he had also won. Colonel Trabue had never doubted the intelligence of this fish-eyed colonel, but with a grudging admiration the president of the court now reevaluated and elevated his measure of John Bowman's shrewdness. He also experienced a twinge of pity for Boone, whom he suspected had encountered very few, if any, adversaries of the caliber of Colonel Bowman—and these two men were now in the preliminaries to engaging in battle in the arena most favorable to Bowman's talents and least familiar to Boone.

"We will go on," Trabue said, once more consulting the charge sheet before him. "In the third specific it is charged that Captain Daniel Boone, during the late winter and throughout all of spring of this year of our Lord, 1778, did voluntarily consort with the Indian enemies of the white settlers of Kentucky, namely the Shawnee Indians in the Ohio portion of the Northwest Territory; that the said Captain Boone, at a time when all white settlements in Kentucky were and are in grave jeopardy of Shawnee attack and many of his companions had already been killed and their property stolen or destroyed by said Indians, consorted with this heathen foe to the extent of emulating their manner of dress, personal grooming and action; that the said Captain Boone did also during this time actively hunt for and with them, using his skill with firearms to provide them with meat for their continued sustenance; and that the said Captain Boone did also, in addition to performing many other favors for these Indians, use his considerable skills in weaponry to repair faulty rifles and other weapons being prepared for use against the Kentucky settlements. Captain Daniel Boone, what is your plea?"

The reference to Boone's emulation of the Indians had had telling effect upon the spectators. No settler present had not in some manner been harassed or damaged through attacks of raiding Shawnee Indian war parties. Many had had their cabins burnt, their crops ravaged, their horses stolen and their cattle killed. And hardly a person here had not suffered the loss of a close relative or friend to the Indians, either through being killed or taken captive. Now the resentment over this, heightened by Boone's present blatantly worn Indian haircut and apparel, seethed and boiled over.

For the majority here, it was the first time that they had heard the specifics of the charges against Boone. This frontiersman had long been their friend and protector, or at least had effectively led them to believe he was. Now he was suddenly and quite specifically accused of having consorted and collaborated with the enemy they most detested and feared. No voice was now raised in his behest. Instead, an ugly, inchoate anger fired them and fragments of epithets mingled, in which the phrase *"hang him!"* was most recognizable.

It took several minutes for Colonel Trabue, flushed with suppressed anger, to gavel them into silence. Yet, surprisingly— evidently expecting and understanding the outburst, though not condoning it—he neither threatened them again with resumption of the proceedings in private nor even verbally castigated them. He simply waited until silence had been restored and then repeated his question to Boone.

For the first time, Daniel Boone's composure seemed to be somewhat shaken. His eyes had widened at the outburst and he had turned to partially face them, his muscular body tensed while Trabue pounded for silence. He had recognized the unsettling sound of pure and unbridled hatred directed at him and for a brief moment had felt the edge of one of the most terrible blades of fear that man can know—the unreasoning animalistic fury of the mob. The moment passed as quickly as it had come and now, a certain wariness still gripping him, he faced the bar again.

"Same answer," he said shortly. "I did what's said, but I committed no treason."

"A plea of guilty to the action, not guilty to the charge on the third count," Trabue said to the clerk.

For a considerable while Colonel Trabue studied the sheet in front of him, preoccupied with his own thoughts. The charges against Boone were growing progressively more damning and, having read the next one through twice to himself, Trabue was sure the reaction to it among the onlookers would be even stronger. Again he mentally questioned his own wisdom in opening these proceedings to the public. Abruptly he beckoned the non-commissioned officer standing at the rear of the assemblage, who immediately strode to the front past Boone and stopped at the table.

Colonel Trabue leaned forward and whispered in his ear and twice the man nodded and murmured, "Yes, sir." Soon he spun around in a neat about-face and returned to the rear. The president of the court continued watching him as he moved purposefully to eight men scattered at the back of the spectators; men who had been casually holding or leaning upon their grounded rifles. Now each in turn, after a few words from the noncommissioned officer, became more alert and moved his weapon to a ready position of ported arms.

"Ladies and gentlemen," Trabue said abruptly, "due to the gravity of the continuing charges against Captain Boone and as a result of the outburst that transpired on the reading of the third charge, I have directed Sergeant-at-Arms John Tibbs to keep his squad in readiness to maintain order—by force," he added, "should that become necessary. I am aware of the terrible losses suffered by many of you who are in attendance here and both understand and deeply sympathize with what you feel. I do not wish to deprive you of what I am convinced is your right to witness these court-martial proceedings; yet neither can I tolerate outbursts which could possibly become so heated as to grow out of control. I say, therefore, as an assurance as well as a warning, that any display of violence on the part of the gallery here will be immediately quashed in whatever manner is required—even," he added darkly, "to the point of gunfire should that become necessary."

A distinct aura of stunned surprise encompassed the spectators. Most of them were well enough acquainted with Daniel Trabue to know that he was a reasonably mild-mannered officer, slow to anger, easy to get along with, and just strict enough to maintain both good discipline and a high degree of respect among his subordinates. What they were witnessing now was a new and disturbing side to the commander and it caused a vein of fear to throb through the crowd. There may have been some who doubted that Trabue would follow through with his threat but, if so, they were in the minority. Most of them knew Colonel Daniel Trabue to be a man of his word in every respect.

"We will now continue with the fourth charge," the president of the court said. The attention of the six officers on either side of him was undivided as again he read:

"That on or about the twenty-seventh day of April in this year of our Lord, 1778, Captain Daniel Boone did become, through actual tribal adoption, the son and ward of Black Fish, principal chief of the Shawnee nation; that he thereupon took up residence in the domicile of this chief; that he frequently sat in tribal council with said chief; that further, while some of his companions were still being held prisoner in the same village by these Indians, the said Captain Boone was shown highly favored treatment at all times; that he was permitted entire freedom to move about as he wished without restraint, but that he refused for many weeks to act on this and return to his own people at Boonesborough, but instead remained in evident contentment with these enemies of his own people; further, that in war councils which were held in said village by Chief Black Fish, where attack was being planned against the settlement of Boonesborough, the said Captain Boone, of his own volition did forward a plan to the chief in council whereby Boonesborough could easily be taken without the Shawnee Indians themselves being exposed to danger. Captain Boone, how do you plead?"

"I reckon," Boone replied, nodding slowly, "that while it ain't quite complete what it's said there that I did, what is said is true as far as it goes. But at no time was treason involved. I ain't guilty of that."

The reaction of the crowd was different this time. Trabue's threat had tempered them and they were practically silent, but the ill-concealed contempt and hatred in the looks cast at Boone were so pronounced that they became a blanket which enveloped him in a suffocating manner. He listened morosely as Colonel Trabue directed Captain Bedinger to record the same split plea as on the other counts. Without more than a momentary pause, Trabue went on to the next charge.

"In the fifth count of treason against you, Captain Boone, it is stated . . ." he glanced down at the paper and read:". . . that on Captain Daniel Boone's return to Boonesborough on the twentieth day of June in this year of our Lord, 1778, after having allegedly escaped from the Shawnee Indians, said Captain Boone, though expecting imminent attack on Boonesborough by the Indians, and despite the arguments of many of his fellows to the contrary, did in fact lead a large party of men away from Boonesborough; that in doing so he once more exposed Boonesborough and its settlers to grave danger in an unduly weakened state; and that he did needlessly and deliberately expose the men who were with him to extreme peril by leading them into the midst of the Shawnee country north of the Ohio River; that he did these acts by nature of his commanding position at Boonesborough and in direct and continued opposition to the advice of his friends and subordinates; and that two of the men who accompanied Captain Daniel Boone on this abortive mission have been lost. Captain Boone, how do you plead?"

Boone was suddenly upset, and this was unexpected for he was a man well noted for his imperturbability even under the most trying of conditions. He spun around, pointed at the judge advocate and rasped, "This is your doing! There's distortion there! The things it's said I did, yes I did do them, but I did more than that. Those two men were among my closest friends. What happened to them was no doing of mine. This whole—"

Trabue's gavel slamming to the tabletop cut him off and Trabue stood swiftly, glowering angrily at Boone who had whirled around to face him again. "Sir!" Trabue snapped. "Silence! You are standing here to make your plea and not at this time to argue your case. I ask you again, what is your plea?"

Boone spoke, but in such a muttered voice that not even Colonel Trabue, who was closest to him, could make out what he said.

"Repeat, Captain," Trabue demanded, "and speak up! What is your plea?"

The emotion was gone from Boone as swiftly as it had come and he hunched his shoulders in a careless shrugging gesture, saying loudly, "The same."

Captain Bedinger nodded at his table and was already recording the split plea. Still angry, Trabue regarded Boone silently for a time and then slowly sat down again. He consulted his papers and without raising his eyes went into the sixth and final charge.

"It is further charged that on the seventh day of August in this year of our Lord, 1778, Captain Daniel Boone did return to Boonesborough with his party of men, excepting two of that party who did not return; that said party arrived in the fort with a force of well over four hundred Shawnee Indians less than one day behind them; that when this force did in fact arrive and take attack position around Boonesborough, the said Captain Boone did voluntarily leave the fort and converse with Chief Black Fish, his Indian father, who was leading the Indian attackers; that he did also engage in negotiation with Chief Black Fish and with British officers who were with the Indians in regard to surrendering the fort of Boonesborough to them and surrendering the people of Boonesborough into captivity; that in the process of said negotiations, Captain Boone did in fact, through negligence, carelessness and design, expose his fellows to mortal danger; that through the actions of the said Captain Boone on this occasion, eight of Boonesborough's finest defenders were brought into the hands of the enemy; that only through the Grace of God were those men able to escape back into the fort with their lives, though at the cost of one of them being wounded by a tomahawk blow and another, the brother of Daniel Boone, being grievously shot; that because of the actions of Captain Boone on this occasion, Boonesborough was placed under siege by the attackers and survived only through the Grace of God and the refusal of the relatively few defenders of the fort, gravely outnumbered, to capitulate to the enemy. Captain Boone, how do you plead?"

"The same way, Colonel," Boone said, calm now despite the steadily increasing current of anger and loathing from the gallery.

"Let the record then show," the president of the court directed his clerk, "that on all six counts of treason against him, the defendant has pleaded guilty to the action but not guilty to the charge of treason. The defendant may now return to his seat and the judge advocate may address the members of the court in opening statement, or else call his first witness for the prosecution."

V

Colonel John Bowman took his time. He exuded an air of supreme confidence and smiled frequently as he conversed quietly for several minutes with both Colonel Benjamin Logan and Captain Richard Callaway at his table. Logan appeared nervous and could not seem to keep from looking over toward Boone, but Callaway paid no attention whatever to the defendant. He listened to what Bowman was saying and then nodded and settled himself comfortably in his chair.

The judge advocate swiftly jotted down a few words on a small piece of paper before him and then with easy deliberance he stood and walked to the bar. For a long moment he looked up and down the line of thirteen officers seated there and finally allowed his gaze to settle on Colonel Trabue.

"Mr. President," he began, then shifted his attention and continued, "esteemed members of this board of court-martial, it is the intention of prosecution to present its case as briefly but as completely as possible. With witnesses and the presentation of supportive items of evidence, it will not take prosecution long to show—indeed, to *prove*—that the defendant in this case, Captain Daniel Boone, is guilty of treason."

He had begun by speaking smoothly and calmly, but already his words seemed to crackle with intensity in the stillness. He turned and glanced toward where Boone was seated and then looked back at the bar.

"Gentlemen," he continued, "we will show that in full knowledge of what he was doing and of the consequences of his acts should they ever be brought to light, this man," again he looked at Boone and this time took several steps in his direction, "Captain Daniel Boone, acted in a manner highly detrimental to his country, to his state, to his community and to the individual people here who placed their full trust and faith in him. We will prove," his accusatory gaze locked on Boone, who met it directly, "that Captain Boone knowingly and willingly deceived, deserted, betrayed, and in some instances helped to destroy those whom it was his responsibility to protect to the best of his ability."

The spectators were listening closely, their expressions a variety of coldness, hatred and contempt. Few individuals exhibited attitudes that might have been interpreted as concern or sympathy for the defendant or disbelief of the prosecutor. The only sound other than the whiplash cracking of Bowman's words in his accusation of Boone was the brief and muted barking of a dog from one of the closed cabins along the east wall of the stockade and a vague rumble of thunder far in the distance, although the early autumn sky directly above Boonesborough was free of any clouds. Bowman paid no attention to either as he glared at Boone contemptuously and then turned, speaking again as he returned toward the bar.

"We will show, gentlemen, that Captain Daniel Boone voluntarily and with deliberate malice toward his fellows, associated and consorted not only with the British, with whom America is currently at war, but equally with the Shawnee Indians whose avowed intention it is to destroy all Kentucky settlements and settlers. We will prove that this man, acting with a fiendishness difficult even to describe, conspired with these enemies against Boonesborough and even helped provide weapons to those Indians so that they might use them in their attacks against the weakly defended settlements of Kentucky. We will show how this officer, entrusted with the life, liberty and safety of his fellows, knowingly and willingly and with full intention of his acts, maliciously betrayed such trust in numerous instances; that he knowingly and willingly and with malice became derelict in the duties of his office, and that he voluntarily and to his own benefit dealt with the enemy to the extent of forcing his own men to surrender to them. Gentlemen, beyond any shadow of doubt the prosecution will prove Captain Daniel Boone to be a liar, a coward, a renegade, a pawn of enemy interests, a thorough disgrace to his uniform and his command and, in numerous respects, a traitor to his country!"

At the defense table Samuel Henderson pursed his lips in a silent whistle and then leaned across the table, touched Boone's arm to get his attention and whispered, "That no-good bastard is trying to get you hung even before calling any witnesses!" Boone hardly appeared to have heard and only turned his head back toward Bowman who, after a dramatic pause, had resumed speaking.

"Mr. President and members of the court, the prosecution will prove to your fullest satisfaction that Captain Daniel Boone has engaged in active negotiation with the enemy not merely with the intent of the overthrow of the settlements of Kentucky. The intent, gentlemen, as we will show, has been the destruction of the western frontier defense of the United States, upon which the heart of our nation could be attacked from unexpected and unprotected quarters, and the continued existence of the United States placed in extreme jeopardy!"

John Bowman had succeeded in working himself into a distinctly agitated state and now he paused, breathing a bit heavily, to let the effect of his words sink in. The officers of the board of court-martial had been listening attentively, though with surprisingly little overt reaction to Colonel Bowman's damning accusations. At the defense table Daniel Boone still successfully masked whatever he was feeling and continued watching John Bowman. James Harrod and Samuel Henderson, on the other hand, were obviously infuriated with Bowman's inflammatory declarations and they divided their attention between brief whisperings to one another and glances swinging back and forth between Bowman and Boone.

Bowman's final remarks were presented more calmly and addressed most pointedly to the president of the court. "We will show," he said, "that Captain Daniel Boone did all of this and more in full possession of his faculties and in full knowledge of the gravity of his acts, and that he is, in the fullest meaning of the words, of distinctly traitorous character and entirely guilty on all six counts of treason against the government and people of the United States of America. And in proving his guilt," he added coldly, "the prosecution shall demand the harshest punishment allowable under military law—that this man," he stabbed a pointing finger unwaveringly at the defendant, "—Captain Daniel Boone, be found guilty on all counts by this board of court-martial and that for his heinous crime of treason he be afforded no mercy whatever but instead be forthwith sentenced to death by hanging!"

As Bowman finished and strode back to the prosecution table, an excited hum of conversation rose from the gallery and for the moment Colonel Trabue allowed it to run unchecked. At the bar, some of the members of the board of court-martial talked softly to one another. Bowman beckoned a youngster of about fourteen to him from the front row of the gallery, spoke to him briefly and then turned to talk with the complainants at his table as the boy raced off. Bowman glanced at the bar, nodded in response to the questioning glance in return from Colonel Trabue and half rose. "I'll call the first witness for the prosecution in just a moment, Colonel."

By the time the judge advocate had finished conversing with Logan and Callaway, the boy had returned with a heavy white pitcher and three well-battered pewter mugs, which he set on the table. Bowman smiled and thanked him, poured water into each of the mugs and took a hasty swallow from one as he began rising to his feet. The bang of Colonel Trabue's gavel restored silence to the gallery and immediately Colonel Bowman spoke loudly.

"The prosecution calls as its first witness, Captain Richard Callaway."

Callaway stood and, as he had evidently been instructed to

do by Bowman, walked to the empty chair fifteen feet in front of the bar, midway between prosecution and defense tables. A corpulent man with angular features, he was about fifty years old and seemed well possessed of himself. His black frock coat and trousers were well cut and except for the heavy gold watch chain spanning his broad middle he bore a markedly clerical aspect. His stride was purposeful and when he stopped in front of the witness chair he automatically raised his right hand shoulder high and palm forward as Bowman took a position before him.

"Do you solemnly swear," the judge advocate intoned, "that in the testimony you are about to give in the matter presently before this court, you will speak the truth, the whole truth, and nothing but the truth, so help you God?"

"I do."

"Please be seated."

Callaway sat down, his spine rigid and not touching the high backrest of the chair. His eyes remained on Bowman, who had moved lightly away toward the left side of the bar. The prosecutor faced him and spoke clearly.

"Would you please state your name in full and your place of residence."

"Richard Callaway. I am a resident of Boonesborough."

"You are a captain?"

"Yes, sir, in the Virginia Militia."

"And how long have you resided in Boonesborough?"

There was a smattering of laughter from the gallery and Callaway himself smiled. "Sir, I am one of the original founders of Boonesborough."

"When and under what circumstances, Captain Callaway, did you help to found Boonesborough?"

"Just about three and a half years ago. Judge Henderson—Richard Henderson—of North Carolina, along with a group of other men of financial means, formed a land syndicate which they called The Transylvania Company. Their purpose was to deal directly with the Cherokee Indians in the purchase from them of a large section of land. It was a tract which Judge Henderson initially proposed to make into an entirely new country, but which he later decided to mold into a new colony—the fourteenth for the Crown on this continent—and name it Transylvania. He—"

"Excuse me, Captain," Bowman interrupted, "but can you

tell this court where the land to be purchased was located and how large a parcel it involved?"

"Yes, sir, I can. It included this area where we are right now. As a matter of fact, it included just about everything to the south of the Kentucky River and north of the Clinch—a total of approximately twenty million acres."

"I see," Bowman said. "Please go on."

"Well, he—that is, Judge Henderson—consummated his deal with the Indians in March of 1775 at Sycamore Shoals in the Watauga country just west of North Carolina. It was not a cash purchase, but rather one of goods. It amounted to a wagon-train load of goods brought to the site by Henderson's agents from Cross Creek, North Carolina, and worth ten thousand pounds sterling."

"Did Judge Henderson and his colleagues have plans for this land above and beyond merely the establishment of a fourteenth Crown colony?"

At the defense table Samuel Henderson stood. "Mr. President," he said to Colonel Trabue, "it seems to me that Colonel Bowman is straying from our purpose here."

Trabue transferred his attention to Bowman. "It does seem," he agreed quietly, "that prosecution is moving rather far afield."

Bowman shook his head. "Sir, I think not. Mr. Henderson may prefer not to have the details of his father's land scheme discussed here, but I feel they are necessary in order to establish a foundation from which the examination may proceed. The witness, in this present testimony, is establishing not only his knowledge of this country but, as will be seen, his close association with and knowledge of the defendant himself."

"Very well," Trabue said, "but the witness should make every effort to be brief in his explanations and move as quickly as possible toward the issue being considered."

"Yes, sir," the judge advocate said. "There are only a few minor points of establishment remaining which should be clarified before we move on. Captain Callaway, sir," he said, turning back to his witness, "allow me to rephrase the question. What plans, if any, did this Transylvania Company have for the land in question other than the establishment of a new colony?"

"Well, the proprietors, including Judge Henderson, wished to retain large tracts of it for their own personal estates.

Beyond that, they planned to advertise and sell the rest to settlers, although 'sell' is not quite the correct word to use here. It was actually to be a rent, since title to the land would remain in the name of the proprietors of the Colony of Transylvania in America, and they would charge settlers a perpetual quit-rent for every acre sold. They also wished to retain special power among themselves in governing the new colony."

"Was that not rather romantically feudalistic, sir?"

"Yes it was, Colonel Bowman, and also illegal. The purchase, though consummated, was subsequently declared illegal by Governor Martin of North Carolina and the company dissolved, but that wasn't until much later. For the time being Judge Henderson was moving ahead with his project and right at the time the land purchase treaty was being signed with the Indians at Watauga, he commissioned Daniel Boone to lay out a trail into the Kentucky country and establish a station here, which would eventually become the capital of Transylvania."

"When did your involvement in it begin?"

"About the same time. I had been a neighbor of Boone's before this and when he needed a party of able-bodied men to go along with him on his mission to erect this station, I was one of those he asked."

"You were well acquainted, then, with the defendant even before any settlement had begun in this country. What was your impression of Boone at that time?"

"Like everyone else's, I suppose. Everyone knew he was a good woodsman and liked to explore, though mostly he was pretty much a loner. He didn't like to have to depend on anyone else, especially not out in the woods. But we all considered him capable and trustworthy then."

"You say 'then,' Captain. Evidently your opinion has changed?"

"Yes, sir," Callaway said, turning a cold stare on Boone. "I now consider him to be wholly untrustworthy and a traitor."

There was a pause, Bowman waiting for the expected objection. When it didn't come, Colonel Trabue spoke up. "In the absence of any comment in regard to this from the defense, I would like to remind prosecution that insufficient groundwork has been laid to permit such a conclusion on the part of the witness. Prosecution is ordered to keep his witness within the acceptable procedural framework, and the witness is cautioned against expressing opinion instead of fact. The defendant is cautioned to maintain a better eye and ear to his own defense. Examination may continue."

"Yes, sir," Bowman said. He moved a few paces toward the defense table, stopped and placed a hand under his chin and maintained this pose as he turned to face his witness again. "Captain Callaway, you said you were one of a number of men who accompanied Captain Boone here. Who were the others?"

"Daniel Boone's brother, Squire, was along, plus their good friends Michael Stoner and Benjamin Cutbirth. Then there was also Captain Abraham Twitty, along with a number of his Negro servants, who joined us just before we left. Captain Twitty also brought along seven men that he knew from North Carolina."

"That was all of the men involved?"

"Oh, no, sir. There was a Mr. Walker—Felix, I think his first name was—and a few friends of his. Also Sam Tate, Tom McDowell and Jeremiah McPeters and their men. Beside all these, there were also a number of men whom the Boone brothers hired to do labors on construction of the station when we got here."

"It was quite a sizable party then. When did you leave?"

"On the tenth of March."

"And that was three years ago, in 1775?"

"Yes, sir. Three and a half year, actually."

"And how long did it take you to reach this site—the site of present Boonesborough?"

"Twenty-one days. We reached here late in the afternoon on March thirty-first and started building the station the next morning."

"And that station was the beginning of this present station of Boonesborough?"

"Yes, sir."

"What was to be your remuneration for helping to establish this station, Captain?"

"I was promised a grant of five hundred acres. The same grant had been promised to the other principals of our party—Captain Twitty, Mr. Walker, Mr. Tate, Mr. Cutbirth, Mr. Stoner, and Squire Boone."

"What about Daniel Boone?"

"He was to be given a grant of two thousand acres."

"Did not you and the others consider that unfair in view of the allotment you were to be given, and similarly in view of the effort that all of you were equally making, and the risk that all of you were equally taking?"

"Some of us talked about it, yes, and I guess there was some degree of resentment about it, but that's the way it had been set up and there didn't seem to be anything we could do about it."

"Knowing Daniel Boone as you do, would you consider him to be a man who is land-hungry?"

"Object!" It was Harrod. "Conclusion being called for."

"Opinion more than conclusion," Trabue said, nodding. "Inadmissible in either respect. Would prosecution care to rephrase?"

Bowman thought for a moment, then asked, "Captain, of your own knowledge, to how many acres of land in this Kentucky country does Captain Boone now hold claim?"

"Sir, the last time he and I discussed such matters, Captain Boone told me that he had already claimed ten thousand acres but that he was planning to claim much more."

Major Arthur Campbell, second to Colonel Trabue's left, suddenly spoke up. "Mr. President, I fail to see where any of this line of questioning by the judge advocate is taking us. As yet, he has touched upon nothing except in the most tangential manner that is even remotely associated with the specific charges against Captain Boone."

Bowman had reacted angrily even while the court member was speaking, taking a widespread stance and leaning forward in a pugnacious manner. Before Colonel Trabue had a chance to remark, the prosecutor answered Major Campbell directly. "Sir," he said, "it is and has been my intention through the early phase of this questioning to establish points in regard to the character of the defendant. May I point out to you, sir, that already in this early testimony we have seen that there is certainly reason to suspect that Captain Boone is definitely not deserving of the glowing reputation which precedes him; that of being the amazingly resourceful woodsman and selfless leader. Even so early in his peregrinations in this Kentucky country a picture is evolving of a man who is greedy, domineering, and ineffective at best and, at worst, quite possibly dangerously defective as a leader. I request that the court permit me to continue my questioning along these lines of character establishment so that when we reach the points of issue it can more clearly be seen how this man could so effectively exist in an aura of adulation from those around him while at the same time, in secret, be the greatest enemy of their lives! He is—"

"Mr. President!" Two voices had burst out as one and both Harrod and Henderson were already rising. They looked at one another and it was Harrod who indicated to Henderson to go ahead and sat down.

"Mr. President," Henderson said, "the defense must take great issue with what is occurring here. The prosecutor is leading his witness and drawing him into opinions and conclusions which, even if stricken from the record, cannot help but remain in the minds of the officers of this court, though they be instructed to ignore them. Not satisfied with that, the prosecutor now presumes to stand before this board of court-martial and, virtually in a presummation, expounds on his own conclusions as to the character and supposed guilt of the defendant. Military law is most certainly not my forte, but I do know enough of it to realize that already this court-martial has teetered dangerously close to grounds for a mistrial. May I remind the court that under the Articles of War governing the process of courts-martial it is stated that even though the judge advocate may be acting as prosecutor, he must also be imbued with impartiality and that he should be particularly careful not to let one part of his business prejudice him in the conduct of another, nor lead him to endeavor to bias the court. Certainly what we have just heard here is a most blatant attempt on the part of the judge advocate to indeed bias the court against the defendant."

"The astute observation of Mr. Henderson is well taken," Colonel Trabue said, impressed, "as the judge advocate has in this instance rather seriously overstepped his bounds and has comported himself in a manner quite opposed to the rights of the defendant and the regulations governing courts-martial proceedings. There are harsh penalities which can be—and which will be—enforced against him if any further suggestion of this type of behavior is engaged in by him. Does the judge advocate clearly understand this?"

Colonel Bowman had paled under Trabue's sharp rebuke. For a long moment he appeared at a loss for words, but at last he faced Trabue squarely and spoke.

"Mr. President, I understand, and I most sincerely apologize to this court and to the defendant and his counsel."

Trabue nodded curtly, scarcely mollified in his irritation

with the prosecutor, and then faced toward Major Campbell. "In response to the comment by Major Campbell, I agree entirely that prosecution has veered much too far from the purpose of this court-martial. It is not a matter of our consideration here what amount of land holdings Captain Boone may have; no more than it would be to know how much money he has or how often he bathes. Such matters are irrelevant and immaterial to our issue, and while this court will allow the greatest possible latitude in the examination of witnesses and the development of foundation, it will not permit casual and, for all intents and purposes, pointless wanderings. The issue before us is the charge of treason on six counts against Captain Daniel Boone, and that must remain our only concern. Prosecution is hereby directed to move at once to matters of relevance in its attempt to establish proof of the guilt of the defendant under the specified charge. We will now continue."

Only once before in his career had John Bowman been so harshly rebuked by the president of a court, though he had many times overstepped his role in the vigor of his prosecutions. He had expected Trabue to be less than really knowledgeable in courts-martial procedures and as dependent upon the judge advocate for points of legality as most court presidents turned out to be. It had been a serious mistake, an almost disastrous underestimation, and now he was forced to reassess his whole structure of planned operation in this case. He took his watch from his waistcoat pocket, flipped open the lid to check the time and then addressed the president of the court as he returned the watch to its pocket.

"Mr. President, having begun later than customary this morning, it is now just after two o'clock. Procedure requires that courts-martial may not continue to sit after three o'clock. Although I have not yet finished in the examination of this witness, I should like to request that we adjourn for the day and resume tomorrow, at which time I will be prepared to move along swiftly."

"Request granted," Trabue said. "The sergeant-at-arms will escort the defendant back to his quarters where he will remain under confinement, though permitted to confer at will with Mr. Henderson and Captain Harrod. This court-martial is hereby adjourned until eight o'clock tomorrow morning."

VI

With more horses and more people in Boonesborough than ever before in its brief history, the little station was extremely crowded. Despite the fact that this meant every cabin of the place and even the blockhouses were a confusion of movement and conversation, the residents of the station did not mind. With so much manpower on hand, it was the first time in more than half a year that the residents felt reasonably safe. Having just recently emerged from a desperate siege at the hands of an enemy that had outnumbered their fighting force by close to eight to one, they were in no way inclined to grouse over the inconvenience of crowded conditions. But with anywhere from eight to twelve people in each of the tiny one-room cabins and all four blockhouses filled, there was indeed the sense of people falling over one another.

Every available scrap of bedding had been used and makeshift beds had been prepared on floors, on tables, on platforms and under ladderwells in the blockhouses, beneath the large roofed-over area where the first session of the court-martial had been held, and elsewhere. The normal guard-posting of four lookouts had been increased threefold and was to be changed four times during the night rather than the usual twice.

Horses and cattle had been indiscriminately herded together in a crude and hastily formed temporary corral of sorts in the southwest quadrant within the fort and they added to the confusion with a bedlam of snorts and stampings, whinnies and lowings and bawls. Around thirty youngsters—boys and girls alike—were doing their best to tend the stock, providing them with freshly cut bundles of grass and lugging interminable buckets of water from the adjacent Kentucky River to fill the big tubs scattered at intervals among the animals. The children thought it terribly unfair that the Boonesborough well, so much closer to the cattle and horses than the river, was not finished yet.

Smoke billowed in blue-white plumes from every chimney and from scores of cooking fires that had been built on the ground within the fort. Men were returning to the station in the twilight from hunting, having gone out in numerous parties of from three to eight men each shortly after the adjournment of the court-martial. Some came back empty-handed, but others arrived with an unusual variety of game—a few deer, one elk, dozens of rabbits and squirrels, numerous raccoons, a few opossums, several muskrats, a few turkeys, scores of passenger pigeons. Feathers, fur, feet, hooves, claws and viscera of the game being cleaned were tossed on one central pile to be carried out later and buried, but in the meanwhile a dozen or more nondescript dogs and several bold cats were howling and yapping, snarling and yowling and clawing as they vied for the remains.

Weary women worked at great pots overhanging the fires, stirring, tasting, adding ingredients, and then ladling huge servings of their bubbling concoctions into bowls and dishes of wood or pewter or crockery. Cooking and eating utensils clattered and banged. And adding to the general cacophony came the overriding laughter, shouts, curses, cries, singing, shrieks, calls, whistlings and conversations of nearly three hundred men, women and children.

It was bedlam; a combination of state fair, party, reunion, banquet, picnic, slaughterhouse, stable, barn, stockyard, kennel and circus. Never before in its brief forty months of existence had Boonesborough been so filled with people and animals, sounds and smells and good-natured confusion. Not even during those times when battle had raged here and the little fort had trembled under days of siege at the hands of a savage host had there been such a continuous peak of surging activity. Boonesborough's star had risen.

At first following this opening day's adjournment of court-martial proceedings, necessary chores to be done had kept everyone busy and there was little time for talk; but as day progressed into evening and then into night, knots of talking people developed everywhere—leaning against the walls or structures, squatting or sitting in circles on the ground, perched in groups on the chairs and logs still in their uneven rows under the roofed-over area, gathered in the cramped interiors of the cabins where they sprawled before the fireplaces or leaned with their backs against rough-hewn walls. The clouds of cookfire smoke and the aroma of stewing meats and vegetables became gradually replaced by smaller clouds of smoke from a multitude of pipes and a smaller number of cigars, and with the aroma of tobacco.

Practically without exception there was but one topic of discussion—Daniel Boone—and arguments rose and fell over the conjecturings on his guilt or innocence. Probably no other individual in the Kentucky country was so well known by everyone as Daniel Boone, with the possible exception of Simon Kenton, who was last known to be in Indian captivity and who might now quite possibly be dead.

Boone and Kenton—great, powerful frontiersmen who had for years strode with incredible confidence through the wilderness where other men slunk furtively and were haunted as much by the enemies in their imagination as by the foe lurking in the undergrowth. Boone and Kenton—strong, self-assured, dependable guardian spirits of the frontier; men who had saved the lives of dozens, scores, perhaps hundreds of others and who had avenged those they had been unable to save; men who moved unseen and unheard through the midst of the Indians in their own domain; men who thrived and blossomed with the very peril of their daily existence. This was how the settlers had come to know them—this pair named Boone and Kenton. These were the men who were the epitome of frontier existence, without whose influence and assistance the settlers would never have come ... or stayed. They were the strength, the hope, the salvation of the pioneer settlers. They were the men who bested the Indians at their own game.

Suddenly the world of these settlers now gathered at Boonesborough was being violently rocked. Kenton was gone; the man who moved with impunity through danger-filled woods, the man who laughed at peril, this young striding giant of a man who, in the minds of all who knew him, could be bested by no foe and who was immune to all harm—this incredible guardian spirit and avenging angel of the frontier— was at last gone, captured by the Indians and probably dead, at the age of only twenty-three.

And Boone! Daniel Boone, the forty-four-year-old pillar of strength and assurance for all of them, wise in woodland knowledge beyond all others, guardian and mentor and so greatly loved by so many for so long; now he too was gone, but in a different and more tragic and unbelievable manner. All that he had been to them was suddenly eroding away. How could it be that this man—this kind, quiet, good-natured, powerful and incredibly able man who had so closely held their trust and their faith and their love—had betrayed them?

Deep into the night the arguments rose and fell over the issue of his guilt or innocence. There were some who, no matter the strength of the argument against him, absolutely refused to believe that Boone could have betrayed them. There were equally those who were convinced that they had been thoroughly duped by Boone, made fools of and secretly laughed at by him, and they could not believe other than that he was at least as guilty as charged, if not even more. But on this first night after the beginning of the court-martial, by far the greater majority were hurled and tossed, battered and bruised by the conflicts within their own minds and hearts over the question. They did not know what to believe and they vacillated from one extreme to another, rarely staying in one frame of mind for long. These were the people who wandered from one cabin to another, drifted from one camp-fire to the next, from one circle of talkers to another, their trust or mistrust of Boone ebbing or swelling with the tide of conversation in the group where they happened to be. They were confused and hurt and largely lost within themselves, believing yet unbelieving, in a mental turmoil of warring thrusts of faith and distrust, love and hate, trust and fear. A hundred times at least Daniel Boone was declared guilty, and a hundred times at least proven to be innocent.

Only the members of the court did not speak of Boone. Crowded together in the single-roomed cabin along the west wall and closest to the northwest blockhouse, the thirteen officers ate their unsatisfying meal in an aura of moody silence, hearing but not hearing the banging, braying, shouting welter of confusion outside their walls. They did not speak of Boone, yet he was dominant among them, pervading their thoughts—at times crushed by the charges against him and at other times thrusting his way above them. He was with them as they silently ate, with them as they made their pallets for the night, with them as they lay down in the early darkness to sleep, with them and filling their minds so that sleep for all was long in coming. But of Daniel Boone they did not speak.

Across the interior of the fort, directly opposite the quarters of these officers, in the cabin on the east wall and closest to the northeast blockhouse, the object of all this activity and discussion and soul-searching stood quietly. Daniel Boone, bare feet planted solidly in an open stance on the hard-packed earthen floor and clad only in his soft ash-grayed buckskin trousers, stood with his back to the fireplace. His chest and features were only dimly visible, but his form was outlined with a soft glow of highlight from the fire behind him. The only other light source was a single stubby tallow candle glowing on the table between the shuttered window and closed door. In the single chair at that table sat James Harrod, staring somberly past Boone at the dwindling cookfire. On the bunklike bed along the outer wall sat Samuel Henderson, a dim shadow amid darker shadows.

For five hours—since seven in the evening—Harrod and Henderson had been conversing with Boone, attempting to formulate their defense, trying to minutely cover every aspect of each of the counts of treason lodged against Boone. The aura of gloom pervading the quarters, as much from the two men themselves as from the lack of illumination, attested to the trend of their talk and the mood which filled both Henderson and Harrod. Boone, as always, had done far more listening than speaking, to the exasperation of his two companions. What they needed from him was help in the defense, ammunition they could use to counter the damning evidence that would be building to a mountain against him; evidence that promised to crush him in an avalanche.

One of the chief points of discussion was the desperate plea from both men to Boone to let them have control of his defense; to let them, when the time came for it, proceed with cross-examination of the witnesses who testified against him. But Boone refused to be budged, simply shaking his head and saying gently but firmly that he would handle it. They argued the matter with him until they were nearly hoarse, trying to make him comprehend that there were techniques of courtroom procedure with which he was totally unfamiliar, avenues of defense of which he was unaware, methods of cross-examination that could be of immense benefit to him but that would be lost through his ignorance of them if he were to handle the questioning. And finally, wearied of his taciturn stubbornness, they gave in, having exacted from him only the promise that he would continue to listen to their advice, but not be bound by any promise to use it.

They had experienced considerable difficulty keeping Boone's mind on the subject at hand. He had constantly disrupted the flow of trial discussion and planning with other matters. He wanted to know about his brother: was Squire doing all right? Was he in much pain? Had the rampaging infection abated yet? How was his daughter bearing up: was Jemima holding her own? Was her faith in him unshaken? Was her husband becoming a problem over this matter? But most of all he kept coming back to the subject of Rebecca: when, exactly, had his wife left Boonesborough? Was she able to bear up well under her conviction that he was dead? What had been Becky's reaction last February when he had failed to return from Blue Licks with the saltmakers? When had she finally given up her last cherished hope that he was still alive? Had there been any news from her at all? Had she made it safely back to North Carolina and found her parents still well?

Henderson and Harrod had answered him as best they could, which was not well at all since they really did not know, and it left him even more distant and less communicative. At last they realized that there was nothing further to be gained by staying with him and they prepared to leave, doing their best to appear optimistic, but neither convincing themselves nor Boone. Things looked bleak, with the promise of becoming much worse. There were few witnesses that seemed likely to be of any help at all to Boone, and of what weight could Boone's own denials be against an intricately woven phalanx of evidence against him, as presented by the skilled, methodical and dangerous prosecutor, John Bowman?

At the doorway, as the portal was opened for them by the outside guard, Jim Harrod paused and looked back at Boone, still standing where he had been most of the evening. Henderson had already stepped outside and for a time Harrod said nothing. At length he sighed, smiled wryly and shook his head.

"With everything else stacked against you the way it is, Dan, I sure as hell wish you didn't look so much like a damned Indian!"

In a moment the door had closed behind him and he joined Henderson. The turbulent activity that had been rocking Boonesborough for so many hours had finally died away, hastened to rest perhaps by the gentle drizzle that had begun falling in the midnight darkness. They paid little attention to the misty rain as they headed for the southwest blockhouse where they had earlier left their bedrolls and effects. At first they were silent, lost in their own thoughts, but then Harrod, not looking at Henderson, muttered softly, "It really doesn't look very good for him, does it, Sam?"

Henderson shook his head but continued walking in silence for another dozen paces. "What bothers me most, Jim," he said at last, "is that four times tonight, in four different ways,

I asked Dan a question, and each time he skirted it without giving me an answer."

Harrod stopped and frowned, trying to remember. He looked questioningly at his companion. Henderson had stopped when Harrod did and now stood with his head bent as he kicked mechanically at a small root protruding from the ground. The angle at which he held his head hid his expression but his voice, when he finally spoke again, was heavy with sadness.

"I asked him," he said softly, "if he was guilty."

2

The court-martial resumed promptly at eight o'clock in the morning, September 29, under conditions of weather far less pleasant than those of the day before. By dawn the light drizzle that had fallen most of the night had turned into a drumming downpour of rain, turning the interior of Boonesborough into little short of a quagmire. The cattle and horses, nervous and uncomfortable, made considerable commotion, bellowing or snorting, constantly stamping about in their confined quarters until they were wallowing in a sea of mud which reached nearly to their knees. With a score of men and boys herding, they had been driven out the west gate and into the more spacious but hardly less muddy permanent outside corral about thirty yards from the wall.

Fortunately, an hour after daybreak the rain began easing off and by the time Colonel Trabue's gavel had brought the proceedings to order, it had slackened to a steady light rain—more than a mere drizzle but certainly not the downpour it had been. There was no wind accompanying it to blow it underneath the roofed-over area and even further dampen the huddled spectators, but the gloominess of the morning seemed to be an augury that affected the people and most faces were grim.

After the minor formalities of opening the session, the president of the court turned the floor over to Colonel Bowman, who recalled Captain Richard Callaway to the witness chair, reminded him that he was still under oath, and resumed his examination.

"Captain Callaway," he began, "I would like to begin today's questioning by calling your attention to matters which have transpired here at Boonesborough during the past three months, since June 20. Will you kindly tell this court what event of significance occurred on that date?"

"Yes, sir," Callaway said. "June twentieth was the day that Daniel Boone returned to Boonesborough."

"Returned to Boonesborough from where, Captain?"

"From his supposed captivity among the Indians."

"Supposed?" Bowman said and then, having glanced at the president of the court, continued, "Well, never mind that for now. Captain Boone returned here on June 20. How long had he been absent from Boonesborough?"

"Almost exactly six months, sir."

"Under what circumstances?"

"On the first day of January this year, Captain Boone set off from Boonesborough with a party of thirty men. They were heading for the Blue Licks, which is approximately fifty miles due north of us, along the Licking River. The three settlements—Boonesborough, Harrodsburg and Logan's Station—were all very much in need of salt. There are no finer salt springs anywhere in this country than the Blue Licks. Therefore, Captain Boone led his men there to make enough salt to see the settlements through for a considerable while."

"I see. Now, was Captain Boone in charge of this party?"

"Yes, sir, he was."

"These were all Boonesborough men?"

"Yes, sir, they were."

"Did not the departure of so many men leave this place in a rather weakened state?"

"Yes, sir, it definitely did. When they left there were only ten able-bodied men remaining to defend Boonesborough, along with twenty boys and fifty women and girls."

"Was no objection made to Captain Boone about leaving Boonesborough in such a relatively defenseless state?"

"There were quite a few objections, sir, including my own. I very strongly argued against it, even to the point of positively refusing to accompany them myself, but Captain Boone put up a pretty good argument and convinced them that everything would be all right."

"How did he do this?"

"Well, from past experience we were aware that the majority of Indian raids against the settlements have occurred during seasons when the weather is not so severe. Attacks in December are rare and attacks in January, February and March are practically unheard of. Captain Boone convinced the men that such would be the case this time, and the need for salt, especially for the preservation of meat, was so great that it was agreed to chance it. Anyway, a train of horses was made up and packed with big iron kettles and other saltmaking gear. Those kettles, incidentally, were a gift from the Virginia government the preceding year. With them and other necessary equipment packed, the party set off for the Blue Licks on the morning of January first."

"Were these thirty men that Boone was leading armed?" Bowman asked.

"Of course. Each man had his rifle and sufficient powder and lead, as well as tomahawk and knife. Boone had insisted on this, in the event they ran into any difficulty."

"Continue."

"Well, they reached Blue Licks without problem and set up camp there and started boiling the water to make salt. They—"

"Mr. President," interjected Sam Henderson, rising, "the witness has now entered into an area of testimony in which his knowledge is only hearsay and thus unacceptable as evidence. Since he stayed behind at Boonesborough, he cannot legally testify to what occurred at the Blue Licks."

"Mr. Henderson is correct, Colonel Bowman," Trabue told the judge advocate. "The witness will confine himself to firsthand testimony."

Bowman seemed not in the least disconcerted by the ruling. He bowed slightly and continued. "Captain Callaway," he said, "what was your next personal contact with any of these men?"

"Three of our men returned from the Blue Licks on February second," he said. "They told us they had been sent back by Boone with some of the salt already rendered, so we could use it here for our immediate needs. They brought a quantity amounting to about six bushels, but told us that the party at Blue Licks was doing just fine and had already rendered an additional three hundred bushels, which would be brought in by the whole party when they returned. The three men remained at Boonesborough for four days—through February sixth—and then started back to Blue Licks around noon on February seventh to help finish making the salt and bring it in. We thought they'd be gone for at least another two or three weeks, but on the fifth day after they left they came back with the dreadful news."

"Which was?"

"That the camp was abandoned, the salt discarded, and that Boone and his twenty-seven remaining men were gone. They said that Captain Boone had forced his men to surrender to a party of Indians which Boone himself had led to the camp."

"Objection!" James Harrod was standing. "That is hearsay and not admissible, Mr. President. On the very face of it, it cannot possibly be true. If the three men, as Captain Callaway says they claim, found the camp deserted when they returned, they might possibly have been able to deduce from footprints and the like that the party had been captured by Indians. However, there would have been no way whatsoever for them to have reached the conclusion that those Indians had been led to the camp by Captain Boone who thereupon forced his own men to surrender."

Trabue nodded. "Captain Callaway?" he said.

Callaway faced the president of the court, flushing slightly. "I guess that's right, sir. I'm afraid I've gotten a little ahead of myself. It was only later on that we learned from one of the saltmakers, Andrew Johnson, who was one of those taken by the Indians and later escaped from them, what the details were."

"Then that is information you are not permitted to give testimony to, sir," Trabue said, "since it is evidence not of your own knowledge but secondhand. Members of the court are instructed to ignore the final remark of the witness, which will be stricken from the record."

"Colonel Trabue," said the judge advocate, "this matter will be more fully developed later, with another witness, in a more proper framework. For now we will move on to another matter. Captain Callaway," he said, once again facing his witness, "getting back to June twentieth, you said this was the day that Captain Boone returned to Boonesborough. What were the circumstances?"

"He reached here on foot in ragged condition, sir, and looking so much like an Indian that our sentry very nearly shot him before he had a chance to identify himself. However, he did call out who he was and, recognizing his voice, we opened the east gate and admitted him."

"What did he have to say by way of explanation concerning his absence and return?"

"He told us that while he had been out hunting for meat

for the saltmakers he had been surprised and captured by the Indians."

Bowman held up a hand and stopped him from going on. He had been standing about a dozen feet from the witness but now he came back and stood directly in front of Callaway and spoke to him slowly and distinctly. "Captain, I want you to be very careful in your choice of words in answer to what I am going to ask you next. Will you please tell this board of court-martial, what were Captain Boone's exact words to you and the others in explanation of the capture of his party?"

Callaway nodded and spoke just as slowly and distinctly. "Captain Boone said—and I quote him as nearly as I can recall—'I led the Indians who captured me back to our camp. They sent me in and I told our men to put down their weapons and surrender to them, and this is what they did.' That," said Callaway, "is just how he said it."

"In other words, Captain Callaway," Bowman put in quickly, "by Daniel Boone's own admission to you and others here in the fort, he voluntarily led the Indians to where his men were camped and then ordered his own men to surrender to the Indians without resisting?"

"Yes, sir," Captain Callaway said, "that is just what he told us."

There was a deep murmur from the gallery and for the first time the officers of the board of court-martial were exhibiting some reaction to the testimony. Several had looked at one another with significant glances and at least four were jotting something on paper in front of them. Henderson shook his head in a barely perceptible movement and Harrod looked disturbed. And incredibly, Daniel Boone sat quietly in his chair with the faintest of smiles upon his lips.

Bowman let the silence run just to the point where it seemed to be getting interminable and then he resumed his examination of the witness, once again tossing a question casually behind as he moved slowly away from him.

"Captain Callaway, did Captain Boone ever tell you why he gave his men orders to surrender without any attempt at their own defense?"

"Yes, sir, he did. He told me that he thought it was for the best."

"The best? Now that's odd. The best for whom, sir? Well," he added hastily before Callaway could answer, "never mind that. What else did Captain Boone tell you on that twentieth of June by way of explanation of his extended absence?"

"He told us that he had been held captive by the Shawnees in their principal village of Chalahgawtha for a short time and then, along with some of his men, taken to Detroit."

"And what did he say happened there?"

"He told us that the eleven men who were taken there with him were sold by the Indians to the British there."

"But Captain Boone was not?"

"No, sir, he was not. He said the Indians had suddenly taken a great liking to him and didn't want to sell him, and that they turned down a great deal of money's worth of goods from the British for him."

"Did not that part of Captain Boone's story strike you as peculiar, Captain?"

"It did, Colonel, and it still does."

At the defense table Harrod and Henderson were staring incredulously at Boone. When he glanced their way, Henderson whispered urgently, "For God's sake, Daniel, is that true?"

Boone was laconic. "Yep," he said, turning his attention back to the prosecutor and witness. Harold and Henderson looked at one another and Henderson rolled his eyes up as if in Divine appeal.

"Did Captain Boone have anything to say about the treatment he received in Detroit?" Bowman asked.

Callaway nodded. "He said that he had been treated with the utmost courtesy and that he had enjoyed many long talks with the commandant there, Governor-General Henry Hamilton."

Bowman had grown suddenly tense. He spun about and lowered his head toward Callaway as if he were going to charge the man. "Captain," he said, his voice so low that the gallery automatically leaned forward and cocked their heads to make sure they wouldn't miss what he was about to say, "what did Daniel Boone tell you that he and Governor-General Hamilton discussed during those long talks that he enjoyed so much?"

"Sir, he told me that Hamilton had asked him if he would consider switching his allegiance to the British."

"And did he say what his reaction was to that preposterous suggestion?" Bowman continued in that hushed voice.

"He did. He said that he agreed to switch his allegiance to the Crown."

There was a universal gasp from the gallery but Bowman thrust his next question at Callaway instantly, cutting short the outside sound. "At any time did Captain Boone make any statement to you in regard to turning over Boonesborough to the British?"

"Yes, sir. Daniel Boone told me that he had agreed to surrender Boonesborough to the British as soon as they would appear at the fort and that he would surrender all his people here to be conducted to Detroit."

A bubbling turmoil of exclamations erupted from among the spectators and even the officers of the board of court-martial were obviously shocked. Harrod, taking advantage of the momentary disruption of testimony because of the disturbance, stood up suddenly, placing himself between Boone and the bar. He leaned down so that none in the place other than Boone and Henderson could hear him."

"God help us, Dan," he said. "Tell me you didn't make any such admission as that. For heaven's sake, please tell me you didn't."

Boone looked up at him and shook his head faintly. "Wish I could tell you that, Jim, but I can't. Dick Callaway's telling the truth so far. He just ain't telling all of it, yet. Matter of fact, I reckon he don't know much more than he's telling."

"That's enough for him to know, Dan," Henderson growled. "It's more than enough. How could you possibly have admitted things such as that to him? Were you just joshing him and he took it seriously?"

"Oh, I reckon in a way I was sort of joshing him. It tickled me to see him look like he was going to have heart failure when I told him about it. But though I was having fun with him, what I told him was true."

Both Harrod and Henderson looked at him as if he had taken complete leave of his senses. For a moment neither man could even say anything. Then Harrod, his shoulders slumped and his tone of voice despondent, muttered, "Oh hell, Dan...oh, *hell*!" The words were all he could say but they were pained and more expressive than a diatribe. Harrod straightened, returned to his side of the table, and sat down.

For the first time since the opening of this day's session,

Colonel Daniel Trabue was forced to use his branchwood
gavel to restore silence. He shot a questioning glance toward
the table where Boone and his companions sat. "Does defense
wish to make any objection over this present testimony?" he
asked.

"No, sir," Henderson replied. "We have no comment to
offer at this time."

Trabue looked at them for a moment perplexedly and then
turned away and nodded to the judge advocate. "Continue
with your examination, Colonel Bowman."

The prosecutor smiled, pleased at the way matters were
moving now. He stepped behind the high-backed witness
chair and placed his hand on one of the ball-topped uprights.
"Captain Callaway," he said, in a mildly conversational tone
now, "would you please continue with what you know about
Captain Boone's return to this place?"

"His return here, sir, or his return with the Indians from
Detroit to their village?"

"Pick it up," Bowman said casually, "with what he told you
occurred on his departure from Detroit."

"Captain Boone said that shortly after his talks with Governor-
General Hamilton he left with the Indians to return to
Chalahgawtha. The other eleven men, he said, stayed in
Detroit. He said they were to remain there as prisoners of
war."

"So they returned to the village on the Little Miami River.
What happened then?

"He told us—"

"By 'he,'" Bowman interjected swiftly, "you are referring
to Captain Boone?"

"Yes, sir. Captain Boone told us that he was brought back
to the village and then adopted by the principal chief of the
Shawnees, Chief Black Fish."

"*Adopted!*" Bowman seemed amazed. "Do you mean
actually adopted in our understanding of what that word
means?"

"I do. Captain Boone told us that he became the son and
ward of Chief Black Fish and that, as such, he acquired a
special place of honor in the tribe and was afforded the
freedom to move about as he wished, without restraint and
often without anyone even watching him."

"Most interesting," Bowman said. "When did this occur?"

"Boone said the adoption ceremony took place around the end of April."

"But, Captain Callaway," Bowman was feigning puzzlement, "you have testified that Captain Boone did not return to Boonesborough until the twentieth of June. Do I understand you correctly in your statement that although Daniel Boone was no longer treated as a prisoner by the Indians after the end of April and free to come and go as he wished, that he actually elected—that he actually *chose* of his own volition—to remain with them and not depart from them until almost another six weeks had gone by... even though he had not been home since January the first?"

"That is what he told me, sir."

"How extraordinary! Well, then, he must have given you some sort of reason for his staying with them so long when he didn't actually have to."

"He said, sir, that he found it to be an immensely enjoyable experience to live with them and hunt with them, and that there were numerous things that he wanted to learn about them."

"What sort of things, Captain?"

"He did not explain that to us, Colonel. He just said that since he had the opportunity, he intended to stay with them and learn some things about them. I do not know what things he was referring to."

"Did he make any reference to what he actually did during this interval of voluntarily living as an adopted son amongst them?"

"Only in a very general way. He did mention that he often hunted with them and that he joined in shooting competitions with them, and foot races and that sort of thing. He also said that they depended very much on him for the repair of rifles they had which had become inoperable. And he—"

"Hold it!" Bowman barked, swinging himself around the witness chair so that he was once again in front of Callaway. "Are you implying that Captain Boone *fixed* their defective rifles?"

"Not implying it, sir," Callaway said archly. "I am telling you what Captain Boone himself told us that he did."

"This is fantastic!" Bowman exclaimed, placing a hand to his cheek and allowing the protuberant blue eyes to grow even wider. "He must have known that such weapons could and very probably would be used against Boonesborough and other settlements, didn't he?"

"He admitted to us that he considered this to be a possibility, Colonel."

"And yet he still went ahead and did it?"

"That's what he told us he did."

"Did he ever mention any concern for the people of Boonesborough?"

"Well, yes, he said he often thought about them and hoped they were all right."

"That was very kind of him," Bowman said sarcastically. "Did he ever mention any attempt on his part to communicate with his wife, Rebecca Boone, who was here at Boonesborough at the time—or with his daughter, Jemima, who was also here, or with his brother, Squire, who was here, too?"

Daniel Boone had suddenly straightened in his seat at the mention of his wife and his left hand, resting on the defense table, had abruptly knotted into a fist. John Bowman noticed the reaction and pressed in.

"Especially, Captain Callaway," he added, "did he indicate any concern whatever for Rebecca Boone?"

"He did not say so."

"Did he mention whether or not he knew that Becky actually thought he was dead?"

"No, sir, he didn't."

"Did he mention any concern whatsoever over the fact that although he could have walked away from the Indians at any time after the end of April and put the fears of his wife to rest, he did not do so? That instead, he was completely content to have her suffer the agony of a broken heart at the belief that her beloved husband was dead, and that—"

"Bowman, you son of a bitch!"

Daniel Boone had leaped to his feet and it was taking the combined effort of Henderson and Harrod to prevent him from charging at the prosecutor. The sergeant-at-arms raced down the central aisle, followed by two of his men, and in a moment had pulled Boone back and all three soldiers were forcibly holding him down in his seat. The gallery was in an uproar. A scream had come from one of the women—possibly Jemima—and men were shouting. Practically all the spectators were on their feet and for a long while the vigorous and continued pounding of Colonel Trabue's gavel went unheeded.

Only gradually did the first burst of excitement die away. Trabue continued pounding and little by little the spectators took their seats once more. Boone was no longer struggling to rise, but he was still being held firmly by the three guards. Harrod and Henderson stood in front of the table, both of them shaken and excited. Callaway had paled somewhat but Colonel John Bowman, standing beside him, had put a hand reassuringly upon his shoulder. Bowman himself wore a faintly amused expression.

Henderson was first to speak and his words tumbled out in a veritable torrent. "Mr. President! *Mr. President!* Objection, sir, objection! Sir," he walked several steps toward the bar as he spoke, "this has been a blatant attempt on the part of prosecution to bait the defendant into just such an act. It has been a calculated effort on the part of prosecution to undermine and, if possible, destroy the character of Daniel Boone and to completely prejudice the members of the court against—"

"Silence!" roared Trabue suddenly. He slammed the gavel so hard to the tabletop that a large sliver broke from one side of it and spun through the air to the ground several feet in front of the bar. "Silence!" he repeated. "There will be order here!" He pointed accusingly at Boone and his cheeks shook with the fury that was raging in him.

"Captain Boone," he rasped, "you have used foul and unseemly language before this court and moved in a manner threatening to an official of this court." He was calming even as he spoke, but his voice still was strained. "Such behavior cannot and will not be tolerated. If you do not, here and now, swear that you will not again act in such manner during the remainder of this court-martial, I will order that you be shackled hand and foot to a stake driven into the ground beside your chair."

Boone's eyes were still flashing dangerously but he was otherwise in complete control of himself again. He dipped his head toward the president of the court and spoke levelly. "Colonel Trabue, I apologize for both my words and my actions. It will not happen again."

Only partially mollified, Colonel Trabue motioned to the guards. Sergeant-at-Arms John Tibbs reluctantly, rather gingerly, released his hold on Boone. At his muttered command the two guards also let go and stepped back. Boone remained seated. After a moment Tibbs nodded to his men and the three moved to the extreme right of the roofed-over area, perhaps a dozen paces from the defense table, and stood there, still taut and ready to spring into action again if need be. Henderson slowly resumed his seat, but Harrod did not move from where he stood. The onlookers had all seated themselves again by this time and were no longer whispering. At the bar, Colonel Trabue spoke again with well-controlled remonstrance.

"What has just happened here has been a disgrace," he said. "The defendant, however, is not solely at fault. The inflammatory statements of prosecution have acted as a goad. The judge advocate's questioning was proper enough to the point of his final remark, but there it ceased being examination and instead became comment intended to enrage the defendant, and that, too, will not be permitted. The judge advocate," he added, his gaze now narrowed onto Bowman, who stood quietly facing him without expression, "has been testing this board of court-martial to the utmost limits and dangerously approaching the point of an official reprimand. The court understands and applauds the vigor which the judge advocate has exhibited in his prosecution of this case, but feels that prosecution has tended to be carried away in his own fervor so that he loses perspective. The charges in this issue are clear and the prosecutor must, of course, use his whole effort to prove those charges are true, but he must do so only within the framework of proper courts-martial procedure. If again he varies from such procedure in so deliberate and calculated a manner, attempting to provoke disruption in this court, he will be removed from the office of prosecutor."

"The prosecution understands, Colonel," Bowman responded quietly, "and regrets that he did indeed express himself in a manner the court deems as having been inflammatory. However, may I point out to the court that part of what we are determining here is, and must of necessity be, the character of the defendant. Captain Daniel Boone has long enjoyed the reputation of being the self-denying, solicitous guardian of the settlers, remaining calm, cool and collected in all situations. That, sirs, is a characterization wholly inconsistent with the perpetration of acts of treason, and equally inconsistent in respect to what we have just seen here—the action of the defendant to an incident of relatively mild stress. Further, sirs, in mentioning the wife of the defendant, who was indeed greatly distraught, and Captain Boone's apparent lack of concern about this, prosecution has merely been attempting, perhaps somewhat too strongly, to prove that in reality the defendant is possessed of a callousness of nature that would allow him to commit without hesitation or remorse the acts with which he is charged here."

"The court does understand that, Colonel Bowman," Trabue answered him stiffly, "but it behooves prosecution to do so under the guidelines of direct examination rather than through statements calculated to goad retaliatory reaction on the part of the defendant. The fact that Captain Boone did not express to Captain Callaway some degree of concern is certainly not proof that concern did not exist." He paused and seemed about to say more to Bowman, but instead abruptly turned his attention to James Harrod who was still patiently standing, and said, "Captain Harrod?"

"Mr. President and members of the court," Harrod said, "there is one point I should like to make clear concerning the defendant, in the nature of an apology. Captain Boone expressed himself in language unbecoming to these proceedings, and while the court may have been shocked, those persons gathered here who have enjoyed years of close association with Captain Boone are far more shocked. I personally have known Daniel Boone for over three years and have been his companion in many types of conditions, including some of considerable danger or stress. Yet, in all this time I have heard him utter the mild profanity of 'hell' or 'damn' not over two or three times. I have never heard him mutter a curse stronger than that. He is not a man who loses his temper easily and I know he regrets his outburst, but I also understand how deeply incensed he had to feel at the words of prosecution in order to so veer from his normal character. I hope the court will understand this."

"The court does understand, Captain Harrod," Trabue commented, though without much warmth. He looked again at Bowman. "May we now proceed with examination?"

As James Harrod returned to his seat, Bowman moved to stand again before his witness and smiled pleasantly at him. "Leaving for the moment Captain Boone's sojourn with the Indians, Captain Callaway, will you now please tell this court what the defendant did when he returned to Boonesborough?"

"Yes, sir. He told us that the Shawnees were mounting a major force to come against Boonesborough, and he ordered that we set about improving our defenses at once, since they were in a bad state. The stockade at that time had an extremely weak west wall and both the southwest and northwest blockhouses had not been completed. The other two needed repair, and at other places the palisade uprights had separated. There was also no water supply in the fort and Captain Boone ordered that a well be dug. We first made sure all water vessels were filled from our usual source which is Lick Spring, located outside the fort, and then set about digging the well and making the repairs as directed."

"With this threat of attack that Captain Boone warned of hanging over Boonesborough, Captain, how many men did the fort have at this time for its defense?"

"A few families had come in during the late spring from North Carolina and several individuals had rafted down the Ohio River. There were also two men who came here in April from Harrodsburg and one from St. Asaph—Logan's Fort. At the time Captain Boone returned we had, including Boone himself, twenty-five men."

"Why so small a number? Weren't there usually about sixty or seventy men here?"

"Yes, sir, but in addition to the saltmakers who were captured, a large number of our men from all the settlements, Boonesborough included, had been conscripted and were gone—and still are," he added, "with George Rogers Clark on his campaign to the Illinois country."

"Did Daniel Boone take any steps to remedy the shortage of manpower here?"

Callaway nodded. "The day after his return he dispatched two of our young men to the settlements south of the mountains on the Holston River for reinforcements. They subsequently returned with a party of sixteen men. By then we had also gotten some more substantial help from both St. Asaph and Harrodsburg. Colonel Logan only had a total of thirty-nine men at his place, but since his was least likely to be attacked, he sent us fifteen good men. Harrodsburg was more subject to attack than St. Asaph but not as much as Boonesborough, so Captain Harrod also sent some men to us—eight of them. So we then had sixty-four men. When Simon Kenton came in with news of Clark's capture of the British post at Kaskaskia, that made our manpower total sixty-five."

"And did the attacking force of Indians come as Captain Boone had warned?"

"No, sir, they did not. Captain Boone had told us they would be attacking us in a matter of days, but by the middle of July there was still no sign of the enemy."

"How was Captain Boone able to account for this in view of his dire warnings?"

"He wasn't. None of us could understand it, but then on July seventeen another one of the captured saltmakers came in, having escaped."

"Who was that?"

"Me!" shouted a voice from the gallery, and a large, heavily bearded settler stood. "Willie Hancock. I got away from 'em, by God!" He was terribly proud of himself.

Trabue's gavel cracked, cutting off the sprinkling of applause and laughter that had begun, and Hancock, looking a little sheepish, sat down. Bowman continued.

"Captain?"

"It was William Hancock, sir. He was in pretty bad shape when he got in, but he made it."

"What was his report?"

"He told us that the Shawnees were extremely upset by Captain Boone having left them and that because of it they had postponed their attack against Boonesborough. It was then reset for three weeks from the day Mr. Hancock escaped. Mr. Hancock had taken nine days to reach us, though, so that meant that we could expect their attack in another twelve days."

"What was Captain Boone's reaction to this news?"

"To some of us, sir—and we remarked about this among ourselves at the time—he seemed to be oddly disappointed that they were going to take so long to get here."

"Objection," Henderson said, holding up his hand. "Conclusion on part of the witness."

Bowman opened his mouth to reply, but Trabue spoke first. "I think in this instance I'll let the response stand. While it is a conclusion to some degree, it has firm grounds for establishment and relates to an actual and observable physical reaction on the part of the defendant at the time, as well as relating a matter of factual discussion entered into then, and therefore not merely an opinion formed just now by the witness. Prosecution may continue."

"Knowing this attack was in the offing in twelve days," Bowman went on, "what did Captain Boone do after that?"

"With each day that passed," Callaway said, "Captain Boone

appeared to grow more impatient. Finally," he shot a look of disgust toward the defendant, "on the eleventh day he mounted a party of men to leave Boonesborough."

Bowman's eyes widened and there was a sudden hush in the gallery. "To *leave* Boonesborough? For what conceivable purpose would he have done that at such a time?"

"Captain Boone proposed to lead an expedition across the Ohio River and into the Shawnee territory—specifically into the valley of the Scioto River in the Ohio country."

"Wait there a moment, Captain," Bowman said quickly. "I want to be perfectly sure the court understands the implications of what you are saying here. Are you absolutely positive that on the very day before a major attack against Boonesborough was expected to commence, Captain Boone intended to lead a party of his men *away* from Boonesborough?"

"It was more than merely his intention, sir," Callaway said pointedly. "He actually did so!"

"Let's back up just a moment, Captain," Bowman said. "What was the reaction in Boonesborough when Captain Boone first broached this incredible plan?"

"Most of us were pretty upset about it, Colonel Bowman. We argued considerably with Captain Boone about it, trying to impress him with the danger of weakening Boonesborough in any manner at that stage, but he was quite adamant about going."

"What was his argument in return, Captain?"

"Sir, he told us that he was now convinced that something had occurred to make the Indians change their minds and delay the attack still more, and that the expedition he was proposing was to attempt to spy on the enemy and discover what the intentions of the Indians were."

"How many men did he plan to take along with him?"

"Thirty in all, including himself."

Bowman expelled a great gust of wind and shook his head unbelievingly. "Thus, with attack expected on the morrow, Captain Daniel Boone proposed cutting the manpower of the fort virtually in half by setting out on a mission that at best had an extremely nebulous goal?"

"Yes, sir, he did."

There was a stir among the officers of the court and a look of disbelief matching Bowman's own on some of their faces. Captain Hugh McGary issued a muted groan but cut it off instantly at a sharp look from the president of the court.

"Was there any other basis forwarded by Captain Boone that could better justify his planned mission, Captain Callaway?"

"Well, sir, Captain Boone had returned from a brief reconnaissance just before this and he reminded everyone that he had seen nothing to indicate that an Indian force was moving against Boonesborough yet. When it appeared that we who were arguing against the mission were making headway, Captain Boone then added that he would lead the men who went with him to a Shawnee village near Paint Creek—that's a major tributary of the Scioto River—where he knew the Indians had a large number of horses that had been stolen from the Kentucky settlements. He hinted that some of them might be recovered. Almost all of us had lost horses to the Indians, sir, and we were very much in need of them. The idea of possibly getting a number of them back definitely appealed to a good many of our men and they began to fall in with Captain Boone's plan."

"Was there anything else he used as an argument to encourage them to leave Boonesborough with him?"

"Yes, sir. He also said the Indians had laid up a considerable number of beaver skins in the Paint Creek village and that there was every chance we could get those as well as some horses. As he put it to us, we could make a great 'speck' in taking beaver skins, recovering horses and still get back here in time to oppose a big army of Indians."

"And so, despite your own continued objections and those of others who were there, twenty-nine other men did fall in with Captain Boone's plan and embarked on this mission?"

"Yes, sir, they did."

"You didn't accompany them?"

"No, sir, I most certainly did *not* accompany them. I felt that it was my responsibility, since Captain Boone was taking it upon himself to leave with half our force, to see as best I could with what we had left to the defense of Boonesborough." A decided note of smugness and self-approval was evident in Callaway's voice.

"I know, Captain Callaway, that you are aware of what occurred on Captain Boone's mission," Bowman said carefully, "but since you did not accompany it and only learned the details from others, you may not testify to these matters. However, please tell us what happened at Boonesborough after the party left."

"We saw to the defenses, Colonel, and tried to calm the

women and children, some of whom had become hysterical at the departure of the party. They felt they were being abandoned by Boone to a terrible fate at the hands of the Indians."

"Objection!" Henderson put in quickly. "Witness cannot testify to his interpretation of the feelings of others."

Bowman nodded and rephrased without waiting for a ruling by Colonel Trabue. "What did the women and children here at Boonesborough actually do and say, Captain?"

"Some of them cried. Others stood at the gate as the party filed out and begged them not to go. Some who were there shook their fists at Captain Boone, called him a traitor and asked him if he was now going to turn this party of men over to the Indians, too, as he had turned over his party of saltmakers to them."

Harrod seemed on the point of making objection, but Henderson touched his arm and shook his head. Harrod sighed and settled back in his seat, looking at Boone with an expression of misery as Bowman continued questioning.

"And after the party left, what then?"

"On the fifth day after they left, sir, just over a third of them—eleven men, to be exact—returned. They told us they had gone with Boone as far as the Blue Licks and at that point, at their camp there, which was right on the site where the saltmaking party had been taken last February, some of the men gave way to second thoughts about leaving Boonesborough so weak, so they broke away from Boone and returned here."

Bowman considered this. "Captain Callaway," he said, "since eleven men returned to the fort then there were obviously eighteen others who stayed with Captain Boone. Can you tell us when these men returned to Boonesborough?"

"Not until the afternoon of August seventh."

"And all this time during Boonesborough's being so weakened, you were expecting attack?"

"Yes, sir. It is very difficult," he added in a voice suddenly charged with emotion, "to adequately express to you the terror that prevailed in the fort here. All of us expected to hear the shrieks of attacking Indians at any instant. I must admit that I myself have never before experienced such presentiment of danger, and," he added defensively, "I am not ashamed to admit that I, along with everyone else here, was much afraid."

Bowman smiled and touched his witness on the shoulder.

"A most understandable reaction under the circumstances, Captain Callaway. Even the bravest men experience fear. Courage lies in performing your duty in the face of fear, which is evidently what you did and what Captain Boone failed to do."

"I think," Colonel Trabue interposed mildly, even as Henderson prepared to rise, "that the judge advocate can avoid comments of such philosophical nature in the future. This board of court-martial is quite capable of forming its own opinions as to whether or not Captains Boone or Callaway acted with courage. Continue."

"You say, Captain Callaway," Bowman went on, "that you expected attack by the Indians momentarily, but evidently such attack did not materialize before Captain Boone and his men returned."

"Captain Boone returned," Callaway rejoined with heat, "at about five o'clock in the afternoon of the seventh, minus two of the men who had accompanied him—Simon Kenton and Alexander Montgomery—and by the following dawn, only about twelve hours later, Boonesborough was invested by a force of about four hundred and fifty Indians, along with some British support."

"And," Bowman said, "did these returned men—less the two missing men—bring back with them the object of their mission, the beaver skins and the recovered horses?"

Callaway snorted derisively. "They most certainly did not! They were as empty-handed when they returned as when they left, but with two of their party left behind in the Indian territory."

It was at this point that Colonel Trabue tapped his gavel gently and spoke. "Questioning has continued unbroken for quite some time now, and if prosecution is at a point where he can hold off further examination for a while, I would propose a recess of ninety minutes."

Bowman hesitated, evidently loathe to stop now, yet as aware as Colonel Trabue had been of a growing restlessness on the part of the gallery and even to some extent among the officers at the bar. The pangs of hunger and a desire to smoke was sitting heavily on some, and the continuing rainfall was conducive to a need for many here, including Bowman, to relieve themselves. He wanted the members of the court fresh, comfortable and alert for the testimony about to come, so he nodded in agreement.

Again Colonel Trabue tapped his gavel and recessed the proceedings until noon.

II

In the hour and fifteen minutes since the recess had been declared, James Harrod and Samuel Henderson had had precious little time to confer with Daniel Boone. He had been too busy and kept putting them off until now only a short quarter hour remained until the court-martial would again be called to order.

First, as had the others, Boone—with a guard on either side of him—had joined the stream of men leaving the west gate of the fort toward the wooded ravine a couple of hundred yards away where the outside latrine of the fort had hastily been enlarged before the court-martial began. It was used only by men, with the women relieving themselves within their own quarters and a regular procession of them carrying heavy chamber pots to a pit which had been dug not far from the riverbank on the downstream side some forty yards below the fort.

When Boone and his guards had reentered the fort he was met by his daughter, Jemima, an unusually attractive girl of sixteen, who almost exactly one year ago had married Flanders Callaway. And Flanders Callaway was none other than the nephew of Boone's principal accuser, Captain Richard Callaway— which placed the young man in a difficult position. Jemima, unaccompanied by Flanders at the moment, kissed her father warmly on the cheek and smiled brightly, but she appeared wan and drawn. Her long dark chestnut hair was tightly braided and laced in a circle to the back of her head. She handed Boone a wooden bowl and spoon. A curl of steam arose from a soup so thick with meat and vegetables that it was more like stew.

Despite the gentle objections of Henderson and Harrod who had come back into the fort a few yards behind him, Boone had followed Jemima to a bench and, with the guards standing a respectful distance away to either side, sat with her and chatted while he ate. Others, elsewhere inside the fort, were similarly eating. Jemima refused her father's offer to share what she had given him, saying she had had a bite or two just before he had returned to the fort. Though he didn't really believe it, Boone made no issue of it.

Daniel Boone's expression had softened greatly, as it always did when he looked at her. She looked so much like her mother had looked when Daniel had married her in 1756, though Becky had then been a year older than Jemima was now. In many of her actions, too, Jemima was a great deal like her mother and Boone never tired of being near her. By the time he was finished eating and they ended their little discussion about Rebecca, about how she was getting along with Flanders, and how Squire Boone was doing—she had been tending him with great care since he was wounded—it was time to get back to the roofed-over area.

Now Boone was again seated at the defense table with only these few minutes left to confer with his two friends, who leaned their heads close to his and spoke in whispers.

"Dan," Henderson began, "you've got to know that it's going very badly for you so far. Bowman's building a strong case against you, and he's far from finished yet. Are we going to be able to break Callaway down in cross-examination?"

"Hard saying, Sam. He's pretty much told the truth, except for a few things that he got a little mixed up. I expect there's a few things he said that I'll be able to change around a little."

"A little!" Harrod exploded. "Damn it, Dan, you don't seem to realize the spot you're in. With this one witness alone Bowman's already all but got your neck in a noose, and God only knows what he's still going to do up there or who else he's going to call. I'll ask you once again—plead with you, if it'll do any good, Dan—please, *please* give Sam or me a go at cross-examination when it comes time."

Boone looked at him levelly and then smiled and put his hand on Harrod's arm. "Jim," he said, "and you, too, Sam, I know you're both considering my best interests as you see them, but there are things you don't know and which there's no way for me to explain to you now. No, you can both give me suggestions if you want, but like I said before, I'll be the one to do the talking."

Henderson got angry. "Never considered you to be a fool before, Daniel, but damn my soul if you aren't just about the biggest fool I ever encountered. I've half a mind to walk away right now. I don't much like the idea of sitting here and

watching you crucify yourself, knowing we can help but not
being allowed to because you won't let us."

"I'd be sorry to see you walk off, Sam," Boone said softly,
"because I know you want to help and I think I'll need it. But
I ain't keeping you from helping me like you're saying. It's
just that I've thought on it for a good while and know what I
want to say and don't want anyone else to try to say it for me."
He paused and then added, looking from one to the other, "I
appreciate all you've done so far, but if you don't want to
continue, I'll understand and you don't need to feel bad about
going. You suit yourself whichever way."

The officers of the court had filed in and taken their seats
and now the president rapped his gavel and reopened the
session. Sam Henderson, at a glance from Harrod, whispered
quickly, "We'll stick with you, Dan, but damed if I know
why."

As the shuffling, whispering, rustling and coughing from
the spectators died away, John Bowman resumed his questioning of Richard Callaway.

"Captain Callaway, we've come a long way in your testimony and I promise that I won't be questioning you too much
longer. However, there remains one extremely important
matter which needs to be discussed. At this time, as briefly
yet as thoroughly as you can—and I will endeavor to keep my
own interruptions to a minimum—I would like you to explain
to the court exactly what took place after the hostile force of
Indians had surrounded Boonesborough. Again, that was on
the morning of August eight of this year?"

"Yes, sir, that is correct." Callaway cleared his throat and
then began. "During the night of the seventh the Indians had
evidently camped in the woods behind the hill across the
river from us and then, just before dawn, they crossed the
river at a place we now call Black Fish Ford, just upriver
from us a short way. They took cover behind the ridge in back
of the fort, to the west"—he pointed—"and in that way
spread out all the way around us and crept up pretty close
under cover of trees, brush and stumps. At first we didn't
know they were there. Captain Boone and a couple of his
nephews, Isaiah and Moses—sons of Squire Boone—were
outside the east gate watering some horses when the two
boys saw some men moving and pointed them out to Captain
Boone. He looked, saw they were Indians and immediately
sent the boys running into the fort with the warning, and he

entered close behind. They were the only people of ours who were out at the time, fortunately, so we closed and secured both gates at once. Lookouts in the blockhouses kept calling out that they were seeing more and more Indians at various places, but still too distant to be fired at effectively. Then a man approached from across the east clearing, waving a white flag on a stick and hailing the fort. He was asking if Captain Boone was here."

"This was an Indian who approached and called out for Captain Boone?"

"No, sir, it wasn't. It was quite a large Negro man. Captain Boone took one look at him from over the top of the palisades and told us that he was an escaped slave from Virginia who had gone West and joined the Shawnees and was now living at Chalahgawtha, which was where Boone said he knew him from. The Negro's name was Pompey."

"Go on."

"We didn't answer at first but when Pompey kept right on shouting—he had a powerful voice—Boone himself looked over the wall again and answered with the word 'yes.'"

"Just that one word, 'yes,' Captain Callaway?"

"Yes, sir. Evidently the Negro recognized his voice immediately because we heard him laugh. Then he said that he was there speaking for both the Shawnees and the British and that General Hamilton now expected him to live up to his promises and surrender Boonesborough to them peacefully."

Bowman was suddenly as alert and tense as a stalking cat. "Captain Callaway," he said quickly, "you yourself actually heard this Negro tell Boone to live up to the promises he had made to Hamilton to surrender Boonesborough to them?"

Callaway nodded vigorously. "I did. His exact words, as I recall them—and I don't think I'll ever forget them—were these: 'Cap'n Boone, sir, I got a message for you straight from the gen'rel himself. Gen'rel Hamilton says to tell you that he now expects you to live up to the promise you made to him last spring and surrender your fort and everyone in it without no fuss.' I guess," Callaway went on, "most of us inside the fort at that time were looking at Captain Boone, and he was just standing up there grinning and looking very pleased."

"What was Captain Boone's response?"

"He yelled out 'Hello there, Pompey. How are you feeling these days?' And then he laughed, too."

Bowman was aghast. "He asked to this man's *health*? A

man who had come to demand surrender of this fort—and a *black* man at that?"

"Yes, sir, he did. We all heard him. Then this Pompey reached inside his coat and pulled out some folded white papers and yelled back that he was feeling just fine and thank you and that he had some letters for Captain Boone from the 'Gen'rel' and that he wanted Boone to come out alone and get them."

"Did Boone do so?" It was the first time Bowman had referred to the defendant by his last name alone, but no one seemed to notice.

"Not right away. I think he might have if we hadn't stopped him, sir, but we held a hurried counsel of officers and then yelled back to the man outside that Captain Boone would not come out, but that if the man would bring the letters to the gate they would be accepted."

"Did the black do this?"

"No, sir. He seemed nervous then and undecided about what to do. Just about that time, an Indian decorated with lots of war paint and other regalia and with a bright red blanket over one arm stepped into view from quite a ways in back of the Negro Pompey. Right away Captain Boone told us that this was Black Fish."

"*Chief* Black Fish, the principal chief of the entire Shawnee tribe?"

"Yes, sir. The same. He called out loudly to Captain Boone, but calling him by the name Sheltowee rather than Boone."

"What does Sheltowee mean?"

"It means Big Turtle. Later on we found out that this was the name that the Indians gave Captain Boone when Black Fish adopted him."

"What did Black Fish say? Did he speak in English?"

"He spoke in English, sir, but not really too well. His words, as I remember him using them, were: 'Black Fish come, speak Sheltowee. My son come. Speak to father.'"

There were some decidedly ugly murmurings from the gallery, but Bowman gave them no chance to swell. "What then?"

"Captain Boone didn't wait for us to discuss it any further, saying there was no time or need for that. He just called back that he would come out to meet his father Black Fish at a very broad white oak stump that was just to the left of where Pompey was still standing, about fifty yards from the fort.

Maybe sixty. He opened the gate and walked out, and we immediately locked the gate behind him, as he had told us to."

"Did Captain Boone take a gun with him?"

"No, sir, he left that inside, along with his tomahawk and belt knife. Pompey had come closer to the gate and met Boone and at the same time two other Indians who were war-painted but not so decorated with ornaments joined Black Fish and were walking with him toward the stump. They got there first and spread out a blanket. We could see them indicate that Boone was to sit down on it. He did so and then the chief, the other two Indians and the Negro all sat down also. We could clearly see Boone and Black Fish shake hands. We also saw Black Fish take the letters from Pompey and hand them to Boone, who opened them and read them. Then they immediately began to talk."

"You could not hear what was said?"

"No, sir, they were too far away."

"Continue."

Callaway glanced at the officers seated to the right of Colonel Trabue and smiled briefly at one of them, but none of the officers changed expression. Callaway coughed once into his hand. "Excuse me," he said. "After a little while Boone got up, shook hands all around and came back to the gate alone. The others remained seated where he had left them. We admitted Boone and he told us that he had pretended to them that because he had stayed in their village so long, that he was no longer in charge of Boonesborough and that a bigger chief of the whites was in the fort. Boone said he told them that for this reason he was no longer in a position to order the surrender of the fort to them, but that he would come back to the fort and bring back out with him the officer who was now in charge and they could try to convince him to do so."

"Who was the officer he planned to pawn off on the Indians as the higher commander at Boonesborough?"

Callaway pointed at the member of the board of court-martial seated fifth to the right of Colonel Trabue. "Major Smith, sir," he said.

"Let the record show," Bowman said to Captain Bedinger at the clerk's table, "that Captain Callaway has indicated Major William Bailey Smith, member of this board of court-martial. Now, then, Captain," he said, returning his attention to the witness, "did Captain Boone have some sort of plan which he explained at this time?"

"Yes, sir. He asked Major Smith if he would mind getting dressed up in a uniform as gaudily as he could and coming back to the conference with him. Major Smith agreed and very quickly put on an old scarlet officer's coat with brass buttons, which was in a trunk here, along with one of the elaborate formal uniform hats fitted with a bit ostrich plume. The major cut quite a figure in that outfit, sir."

There was a burst of laughter from the gallery as well as among the members of the court and Smith dipped his head in amused acknowledgment of the attention he was getting.

"Major Smith and Captain Boone thereupon went out of the fort?"

"Yes, sir, they went directly back to the conference where they sat and talked for the better part of an hour, at which time they came back to the fort by themselves, and told us what had been discussed. They said that they were scheduled to meet and talk with Chief Black Fish and his Indians again the following morning, but at that time there would be some British officers in attendance as well. It was at about this time, sir, that I am afraid I became extremely upset with Captain Boone."

"Why, Captain Callaway?"

"Well, first of all because Captain Boone said he had told the enemy to help themselves to whatever they needed of the fort's cattle and crops and to make themselves comfortable. He then, along with Major Smith, called a council of all our officers and put the question to us. Boone asked us if we were willing to surrender peaceably."

"Was he in favor of such a surrender, Captain?"

"From what we could determine through his actions and words, sir," Callaway nodded, 'he was in favor of such a surrender. He explained to us in a very persuasive way that the Indians had promised to take all of us safely to Detroit without harming us if we surrendered, and he was sure they would live up to their word. He also told us that if we resisted and lost, there would certainly be a dreadful massacre which was sure to include the women and children. There was no doubt whatever in my mind, sir," Callaway added bitingly, "that Captain Boone was doing all in his power to sway us to the advantages of surrender to the enemy without resistance."

"Captain," Bowman said softly, looking at Boone as he

spoke, "will you please tell the members of this court what your own personal remarks were to Boone at this time?"

"Yes, sir. I became very angry. That was the first time I openly accused him of being a traitor, although for some time I had harbored the feeling. I also told him that *my* family, at least, was not going to grow up among the Indians or even among the British."

"Was anyone else of the same mind?"

"Indeed yes! Everyone was. Even his own brother. Usually Squire Boone went along with everything Daniel suggested, but this time he objected strongly. He vowed that he would never give up, that he would fight until he died if that was the way it had to be. Everyone else agreed with Squire and me."

"And what was Daniel Boone's reaction to this?"

Callaway shook his head disgustedly. "He just threw his head back and laughed at first, but then he gave us an odd look and said that he reckoned he'd die along with the rest of us."

"That was nice of him," Bowman said with syrupy sarcasm, then added quickly, "Captain Callaway, with everyone inside the fort opposed to surrender but the defenses of the fort still not terribly good and the defenders outnumbered about eight to one, what was the plan of action then followed?"

"Well, Captain Boone led the discussions and he insisted that we had to delay the inevitable fight for as long as possible."

"Why?"

"He said it would be to the enemy's disadvantage to do so, because he said the Indians tended to lose heart for a fight if they didn't engage in it right away. He maintained that the longer we could continue negotiations with them and make them think we were going to surrender, that the shorter an eventual siege laid against Boonesborough would be. He also contended that it would give us that much more time to see to our defenses, to try to complete the well, which was only half dug, and that it might even afford us an opportunity to preserve as many of our cattle as possible."

"The same cattle that he had already so magnanimously offered to the enemy for their sustenance?" Bowman put in.

"Yes, sir."

"Go on."

"Captain Boone and Major Smith both told us that the

Indians had agreed to camp for the night and that they had demanded that first thing in the morning there should be another meeting, attended by Boone and Major Smith and a third officer, to discuss the surrender which Boone had made them believe was still going to be the result."

"And your reaction to this was what?"

"Since a third officer was to be included, I demanded to be a part of the next meeting. Captain Boone made it clear that he didn't want me along, but Major Smith agreed with me, so I was the one included."

"The fort experienced no attack that night?"

"No, sir. All was quiet. We continued our defense preparations and the digging of the well. Along about dark some of the cattle that the Indians hadn't yet killed came to the fort to be milked, which was usual, and we managed to get them safely inside the walls. After dark several of our young men slipped out and brought in whatever vegetables they could find in the fort garden that were ripe."

"Did you not, during this night, Captain Callaway, devise a plan to further delude the Indians?"

"Yes, sir, I did." A note of pride crept into Callaway's voice. "From what Major Smith told us, it seemed that the Indians were under the impression that we had a great many more people inside the fort than was true. In order to perpetuate this belief, I ordered that every extra hat and jacket in the fort be dug out of storage and dummies be made up. I told them that when daylight came and the Indians would be watching us closely, I wanted them to think there were even more men here than they already believed. Most of the women dressed themselves as men, in whatever uniforms we had, and children were sent up to the lookout walkways just below the tops of the walls to walk along there, themselves hidden, but each one carrying two upright sticks, and on the top of each a hat that could be seen over the top of the wall. It was also my plan that when Major Smith, Daniel Boone and I went out to meet them again in the morning, that the gate be left open behind us—ready to be slammed and locked at once if danger threatened—and a constant movement of people with weapons to be occurring inside."

"Very commendable, Captain. This plan worked?"

"Yes, sir, it worked quite well. I'm sure the enemy thought we were a much larger force than they had even anticipated."

"Tell the court, Captain, what happened at the meeting

next morning. You three did go out and meet with the enemy?"

"Yes, sir, we did. There were more Indians attending this time—about twenty of them, including not only Chief Black Fish, but also a very old chief named Moluntha. Boone later told us that he was chief of the Maykujay Shawnees, which is one of the five septs or clans which make up the tribe. Then there was also the British commander, only it turned out that he was a French-Canadian who had turned his allegiance to the British after the last war."

"What was his name?"

"Well, he wore the insignia of a lieutenant, but he was addressed as Captain Antoine Dagneaux De Quindre of the Detroit Militia."

"Any other British there?"

"Yes, sir, two; that is one true Englishman, who was Lieutenant Peter Drouilliard, and then another French-Canadian who was in the British service. His name was Lieutenant Isadore Chene—pronounced 'chain' but spelled 'c-h-e-n-e' —and he was acting as interpreter for De Quindre and Drouilliard."

"What was discussed at this meeting, Captain Callaway?"

"Well, first of all, though there was much of it I could not understand—" he paused and added accusingly, "—I don't speak or understand the Shawnee tongue as Captain Boone does—but we all sat on panther skins which were spread on the ground while some warriors held leafy branches over our heads to shield us from the sun. Chief Black Fish talked at length, though I don't know what he said and Boone said it was just formal preliminaries, and then he held up a large belt of wampum in three colors—white, red and black."

"What did this wampum belt signify?"

"Well, according to Boone, the white, which predominated, stood for peace. Red meant war and black meant death. As it was explained to me, Black Fish was offering us peace, primarily—meaning that if we surrendered to them voluntarily we would be well-treated, but that if we resisted a fight would begin and then there could be no alternative but death to all in the fort. The chief talked for quite a while and then he finally ended by saying to Major Smith in pretty good English, 'I come, take you away easy.'"

"Did Major Smith reply?"

Callaway frowned. "Yes, although I thought he would tell

them flatly that we had no intention of surrendering. He didn't." The witness glanced at Major Smith at the bar and then looked hastily back to Bowman. "All he said was that it would be difficult to transport so many people, especially the Boonesborough women and children who would not be able to walk all the way to Detroit."

"And Black Fish's response was?"

"He spoke in Shawnee, but Lieutenant Chene interpreted and said that the chief was saying that he was well prepared for this and had brought along a great many extra horses, because he knew the old people, women and children of Boonesborough would need to ride."

Bowman leaped on this. "You are saying then that Black Fish was so assured of Boone turning over this fort to him that he had actually brought along extra transportation for those who would be surrendering?"

"Yes, sir, that is correct."

"What was the response to this?"

"There was none, sir, either by Captain Boone or Major Smith, because just about then we had something happen which made us interrupt the discussion."

"What happened, Captain?"

"Well, sir, Pompey, the big Negro, had moved a little bit away from us in the direction of the fort and was closely observing all the movement that was taking place inside—the moving hats and people. Captain Boone at this time jumped to his feet and called him to come back, that he was going past the neutral line and that if he did not come back he would surely be shot."

"He came back?"

"Yes, sir, he did."

"Had he seen through the deception?"

"I didn't think so, sir, nor did Major Smith, but Captain Boone was very suspicious of him and suddenly quite eager to get back to the fort. He asked Chief Black Fish for all the rest of that day and the next to consider the request to surrender. Black Fish did not at first seem too willing to do this, and he was somewhat reproachful of Boone, whom he had alternately been calling Sheltowee or 'My son.'"

"But he finally agreed?"

"Yes, sir, he did."

"Was there anything else he agreed to? What about Boone

himself? Did Daniel Boone at this time indicate that there would indeed be a surrender?"

"Oh, yes. Everything he said, sir, gave the enemy the undeniable impression that we would certainly surrender just as soon as we had talked it over among ourselves, but that if we were too hard-pressed then we might balk. For the moment the Indians agreed to approach no nearer than thirty yards of the fort, and Boone agreed that the whites would do no shooting and would carry no weapons outside the fort. At that point Chief Black Fish presented Captain Boone with seven smoked buffalo tongues, which he said were a gift for the women of the fort. He also said that he and some of his warriors would like to come to the fort and see Boone's squaws, as he put it. Captain Boone thanked him for the gift but told the chief that his women were very much afraid of Indians and that the Indians would see them soon enough when the fort was surrendered."

"He said *when*, Captain, not *if*?"

"He said *when*!"

"Did the chief seem to harbor any doubt that there would be a surrender?"

"Sir, he seemed positively convinced that there would be a surrender and for this reason did not seem to mind agreeing to the delay."

"Thank you, Captain." Bowman seemed very pleased with Callaway's concise explanation of what had occurred, and that there had been no interruption by objections from defense. He clasped his hands behind his back and strode a few steps away, then continued speaking with his back to the witness. "Let's move on, Captain Callaway. Will you please tell the court as briefly as possible what transpired during the two days of grace period?"

"Yes, sir. We held numerous meetings and every person in the fort was given his own task to continue in the strengthening of the fort's defenses."

"Did Captain Boone make any further overtures to the Boonesborough people about surrendering?"

"No, sir. He seemed to realize that we would never give in and that no matter how much *he* may have wanted us to surrender, we wouldn't."

"Objection! Mr. President," said Sam Henderson, rising and shaking his head, "defense has allowed the judge advocate to question at his own pace and in his own direction without making objection, although several times there were certainly grounds for such objection. However, defense has refrained in the belief that it was helping to speed along these proceedings. But we cannot sit idly by and permit the judge advocate to lead the witness and the witness himself, for that matter, to state his own conclusions as established fact detrimental to the defendant."

Colonel Trabue thought this over for a moment or so as Henderson sat down and then looked at the judge advocate. "Colonel Bowman," he said, "the court feels that the objection by defense is justified. We are gratified that examination has moved along well, but there have been several occasions when you have teetered on the boundary of improper examination procedure. Prosecution will please refrain from doing so and continue his examination by adhering only to those matters to which the witness may answer in fact and not in opinion or conjecture. The witness, too, is enjoined to refrain from expressing his personal opinion."

"Prosecution," Bowman said with elaborate contriteness, "apologizes and will continue as directed." He was just about to ask Callaway another question when Colonel Trabue interposed.

"Colonel Bowman, it is now nearing two o'clock. Much ground has been covered and if prosecution would care to entertain a motion for adjournment for this day, the court would so grant."

Bowman thought a moment and then shook his head. His examination had been rolling along well and he didn't want to lose the impetus built up already. "Mr. President," he said, "we still have an hour remaining before this court-martial is required to adjourn and I would prefer going on if it does not inconvenience the court. I feel sure I will be finished with my examination of this witness by that time."

Trabue looked as if he would have preferred adjournment, but he merely nodded and said, "Proceed."

Bowman faced Callaway again, his expression becoming a little more grim. "Captain Callaway, will you please explain a little more specifically what sort of defenses were being repaired or made ready during the two-day interval that was granted?"

"Mostly standard battle preparations, sir. During the day powder was served out to everyone, bullets were being molded as rapidly as possible, flints were picked and chipped and set in their locks on the rifles, and the rifles themselves were cleaned and checked for any possible defects. We had numerous sentries on the walls standing guard all night against possible treachery by the Indians, but all remained quiet. In fact, everything remained peaceful until early the next evening when Lieutenant—or Captain, whichever the case—De Quindre and about nine or ten Indians walked to the meeting place carrying a truce flag. They stopped there and De Quindre called and asked if we were now prepared to surrender."

"Do you recall his exact words?"

"Yes, sir. He directed his remarks to Captain Boone and—"

"Not to Major Smith, who was now allegedly in command of Boonesborough?" Bowman put in quickly.

"No, sir! Quite distinctly to Captain Boone. He said, 'Captain Boone, your time for deliberation has now ended and I call upon you in the name of His Britannic Majesty to surrender at once.'"

"Did Boone thereupon go out and confer with him?"

"He did not. He climbed to the top of the wall on the southeast and cupped his mouth with his hands and called back to De Quindre."

"Saying what? His exact words, if you please."

"He said: 'Captain De Quindre'—he called him captain instead of lieutenant—he said: 'Captain De Quindre, we sure have appreciated all the time you've given us to prepare our defenses. Bring on your fight if you mean to, but we won't surrender, not if we have to defend this place until everyone's dead.'"

"What was De Quindre's reaction?"

"He seemed absolutely flabbergasted. He just could not seem to believe what Boone was saying and he repeated the question, to which Boone gave him the same answer, adding that we were now very strong and if they decided to attack, there were going to be a whole lot of people dead—mostly Indians and a few British."

"Then?"

"De Quindre argued with Boone, asking him—no, demanding would be more correct—demanding that Boone reconsider, and couldn't he see the horrible folly of trying to resist? It would, De Quindre called to him, be suicide, because once the station fell by force then there would simply be no way to restrain the Indians in their desire for

vengeance. He shouted that Boone had given his word to
Governor-General Hamilton and he was expected to live up
to his promises. He also said that Black Fish would be
extremely disappointed in his son. To these remarks Boone
made no reply. As we watched him, then, the officer turned
to the Indians who were with him and spoke with them at
length. Then he turned back and called out to Boone again.
He insisted that they had come prepared to take Boonesborough
peacefully, not through warfare, that Hamilton had ordered
them to avoid bloodshed if at all possible. He said they were
offering their hearts and hands in friendship, not in hatred.
He also said that the very fact that they had allowed the
cattle to come back to the fort to be taken inside should have
proved to us that their intentions were peaceable. It was at
this stage that he suddenly surprised us all by saying that if
we Kentuckians were changing our minds because we didn't
want to leave our homes here and go to Detroit, then he
could certainly understand that, and perhaps we could negotiate a treaty which would not make it necessary for us to give
up what we had here or to leave the place."

"Did he elaborate on this?"

"No, sir, at least not at that time. But he did say that if
Captain Boone and eight other top-ranking officers here in
Boonesborough would agree to meet in conference with them
in the morning, he was sure that a suitable negotiation would
ensue in which the Boonesborough people could remain here
in their fort unharmed."

"What was Boone's reply to this?"

"Well, before he could answer I spoke up and said that I
was sure it was nothing more than a trick to get some of our
men outside the fort in order to take them unawares and thus
weaken the fort for their subsequent attack, which I was sure
was coming, no matter what."

"Did Captain Boone disagree with this view?"

"Well, no, not really. He agreed that what I said was
possibly the case, but he strongly argued that we chance it
anyway. He said we could negotiate with them and promise
them anything they asked, as long as they left Boonesborough
alone. He argued that any promises that we would make
under threat of death could not be considered as binding in
any respect and that we would not be dishonoring ourselves
by not abiding by whatever promises were made. He was
very convincing and gradually the others fell in with his way

of thinking about it and agreed that, for the sake of our women and children, it was worth a try. Captain Boone thereupon called back over the wall to De Quindre that he and eight others would meet with them an hour after daylight the next morning in the hollow at Lick Spring, where we get our water."

"Why there?"

"Because there weren't as many stumps around there behind which the Indians could take cover if trouble broke out. In addition, it is only about eighty yards from the fort, which is within good rifle range of the walls. It was the plan to have every rifle available in position to cover the party and be prepared to shoot instantly at the first sign of trouble."

"Whose plan was this, Major Smith's or yours?"

Callaway looked uncomfortable, as if he hated to make his next admission, "No, sir, it was Captain Boone's plan."

Bowman looked as if he wished he hadn't asked the question, but went on. "Captain Boone expected treachery, then?"

"No, he didn't say he expected it. In fact, he said he fully hoped and expected that something could actually be worked out whereby Boonesborough would not be destroyed or its people hurt. He said he did not believe it was possible that we could hold against them if attack was launched. Even though he was hopeful that some kind of treaty could be arranged with them yet, he still insisted that the negotiation party be well covered from our walls just in case."

"This meeting was held as planned?"

"Yes, sir, but with one change that we made. We showed up for the negotiation with only eight men instead of nine. We simply felt that nine men going out would just weaken us too much. I argued strongly for only five of us going out, but the rest agreed with Boone that we should keep the number reasonably near what the enemy had requested or they would be suspicious of our not acting in good faith. When we showed up with one less than they had asked for, we told them that one of our principal negotiators had fallen sick during the night but had told us to go ahead with the discussion without him."

"They accepted this?"

"They seemed to, sir."

Bowman turned and looked at the board of court-martial. "Tell us, Captain," he said quietly, "about the negotiations, beginning with the identity of the eight who left the fort."

"Yes, sir. First of all there were the Boone brothers, Dan and Squire. I came, along with my nephew, Flanders. Major Smith was one of us, too. Then there were the Hancock brothers, Stephen and William, along with William Buchanan. We walked in a group, unarmed as promised, toward Lick Spring, and found that a table had been set up there, covered with a clean linen cloth and with two flags on sticks set up behind it."

"*Two* flags?" queried Bowman. "Why wouldn't just one Union Jack have sufficed?"

"It *was* just one British flag, sir," Callaway explained. "The other was the flag of France."

"France!" Bowman seemed genuinely surprised. "Why would this be the case, when France is an ally of the Americans?"

"I don't know, sir, and no one brought the matter up. I wondered about it and thought that perhaps it had been set up to represent us, since France is supposed to be our ally. Either that or else De Quindre and Chene and Mr. Beaubien had set it up simply as a token of continued devotion to the mother country, and the Indians seemed to think nothing of it."

"Wait a minute, Captain. Who was this Mr. Beaubien?"

"Another French-Canadian we hadn't seen before this. He was acting as clerk to record the decisions we made and to draw up the treaty for our signatures. The whole setup was really quite formal."

"How many Indians were on hand?"

"There were only a small number, Colonel Bowman. In addition to Chiefs Black Fish and Moluntha, there was Black Fish's second-in-command, Catahecassa—Black Hoof, as Boone called him—and a Chippewa chief named Blackbird. Then there were also twelve other older chiefs, none of whom Boone recognized."

"Go on."

"Behind us in Boonesborough the people were still moving back and forth, just visible over the walls, in a show of force, and the riflemen under Captain Holder were in the block-houses with their weapons aimed and ready. At the confer-ence we sat on animal skins and began with some good food and wine which had been provided, we were told, by the British commissariat at Detroit for this purpose."

"Was an agreement reached, as Boone had expected?"

Callaway shrugged. "Of sorts," he said. "We talked until

almost evening and by that time had come to agreement that Boonesborough was to declare its allegiance to the Crown in the present war. A document was to be prepared by Mr. Beaubien during the night to this effect, to be signed the next morning by all the officers who had attended this meeting. The British representatives would then also sign it and, after them, the Indians would make their marks. As soon as that was done, they promised us, they would withdraw and leave us in peace."

"You returned to the fort then?"

"Soon, but not just yet. Chief Black Fish said he would return the next morning with eighteen Indians attending him. We objected to this and—"

"Boone, too?" Bowman interrupted.

"Yes, sir, Boone more than any of the rest of us. By that time all of us but Captain Boone were quite sure that we had actually managed to pull it off and that in signing the treaty, we would be left in peace. But Boone was more suspicious than we'd seen him get before. He was most pessimistic."

"Why?"

"Well, later on, when we were back in the fort, he said it was because the Indians had smoked their pipe but had not passed it to us to smoke, too, which he said was the custom. We pointed out that they hadn't passed it to the Crown representatives who were there, either, but this didn't seem to matter to Boone. But anyway, when Black Fish said he'd have eighteen men, we objected. Black Fish insisted that the eighteen were village chiefs, each representing one of the villages of the tribe and that each would have to make his mark on the articles or the Indians would not regard the treaty as binding. We had no way to counter this, so had to agree. We then returned to the fort."

"Did you really plan to return in the morning to sign the articles of treaty, knowing you would be outnumbered more than two to one at the scene of the negotiation and that you would be unarmed?"

Callaway grew a little uncomfortable. "Well, again Captain Boone and I had a few words on this. He was suddenly against going back out in the morning. However, I—and I must say that all the others agreed with me—I contended that we had gone this far and if there was the least chance that we could prevent attack from occurring against Boonesborough by signing the treaty, then we should do so. We voted Boone down on this, so he finally agreed to go along with it."

"What happened then?"

"In the morning he led us out. Because he and Squire brought guns out, I think it was his fault that everything fell—"

"Objection!" called out Henderson. "Witness is again stating an opinion."

"Sustained. The witness will confine himself to relation of what actually took place."

Callaway grunted, thought a moment and then began again. "When we left the fort in the morning, Squire and Daniel were armed, but they leaned their rifles against the wall of the fort outside. The Indians could not help but see this. Once again we had every available man in the blockhouses and on the walls with rifles, ready to fire. Major Smith at first gave them orders to fire if he waved his hat, but Boone countermanded that. He told Captain Holder, who was in charge of the riflemen, that if there was trouble there might not be any time for hat-waving and that if anything occurred which indicated trouble, they'd know it right away and they were to fire at once."

"All right," Bowman said in a clipped manner, as if anxious to get away from anything which might show Boone in a favorable light, "what happened when you reached the council area?"

"They were all there as before, but this time Chief Black Fish had eighteen young men with him, including none of those that had accompanied him the day before. When we objected that they were not the same chiefs, Black Fish had the gall to insist they included the twelve who had been there the day before. It was pointless to try to argue with him about it but from that point on the rest of us were as suspicious as Boone had been. We talked a long while and went over the articles of peace one by one."

"Just what were the terms that you were agreeing to, Captain Callaway?" Bowman asked.

"What it amounted to was that in signing the documents we were signifying our oath of British allegiance as well as establishing peace with the Indians. The treaty stated that thenceforth the Ohio River would become the boundary between Indians and whites; that no white settlement was to be undertaken north of the river; that hostilities would cease between Indians and whites; that no Indian raiding parties would any longer come south of the river; that no white raiding parties would go north of the river; that we would live in peace together as neighbors for as long as the sun would shine and the rivers flow. We all signed and then Black Fish and his men in turn made their marks—usually scribbly little lines or crude drawings of animals—and then Black Fish said he would have to announce the peace agreements to his men. He stepped to one side and called out a very loud and long collection of words that none of us understood."

"Not even Captain Boone?" Bowman asked quickly. "You said he understood the Shawnee tongue."

"He does, but he said he could not understand the words Black Fish used then. He thought it might be the Huron language. As soon as Black Fish finished he came back to us and announced that with this conclusion of a treaty of peace, it was customary for the Indian negotiators to shake hands with the whites. Since there were twice as many Indians as whites, then to save time two of the Indians would shake hands with each white man simultaneously."

"Did you not consider that a rather extraordinary suggestion?"

Callaway nodded and grimaced. "Of course we did, but," he added defensively, "after all, all the proceedings had been rather extraordinary and this was only one more. We were anxious to get back into the fort and have the enemy gone and so, with all the Indians laughing and in what seemed to be a very good humor, we agreed. We held out our hands and each of us was gripped by two of the Indians. But suddenly these grips became tighter than they should have been and I yelled out that it was a trap."

"What happened then?"

"We all heard Black Fish yell out the word "Go!" About a hundred yards away from us an Indian stood up, pulled a rifle from under his blanket and fired it into the air. At this, each of the Indians holding us tried to drag us over a little incline nearby which would have carried us out of sight of the fort, so we began struggling. I was first to break away and run, and the others followed as soon as they could break loose themselves, although for some it was very difficult."

Callaway's words had become charged with emotion as he verbally relived the exciting moments and the gallery was listening intently so as not to miss a syllable of what was being said. The witness paused for only a moment and then went on.

"Right away the lookouts realized there was trouble and they began to shoot. It allowed us the distraction to the Indians that we needed in order to get safely into the fort, although by this time many hidden Indians were shooting at us as we ran."

"Who among our men were hurt, Captain Callaway?" Bowman asked.

"Squire Boone was quite seriously wounded in the shoulder as he ran, sir. Major Smith took an ugly gash in his hip from a tomahawk that was swung at Daniel Boone. Boone saw it coming and leaped away and it struck Major Smith glancingly. There was a lot of confusion and yells and shooting. A number of the Indians were shot down by the fire coming from the fort, but other than Squire's wound and that suffered by Major Smith, the rest of us escaped with only minor cuts or bruises. We were all very lucky. Bill Buchanan was luckiest of all, I guess. He fell on the way back and twisted his ankle so badly that he couldn't run, so he took refuge behind a stump. Evidently the Indians thought he had been shot dead, since they didn't shoot at him anymore, and after darkness fell we managed to get him in. That, sir," he concluded, looking at Bowman, "was the start of the siege which lasted for nine days and ten nights."

"Captain Callaway," Bowman said softly in the silence which had followed his final remark, "on the basis of all the facts you know in this case, do you at this time consider Daniel Boone to be guilty of treason?"

Even as Callaway began to nod in response, both Harrod and Henderson were on their feet shouting objections, and simultaneously the gavel in Colonel Trabue's grip slammed the table repeatedly, cutting off the reply that Callaway might have made. Trabue waved Henderson and Harrod back to their seats and, with the spectators silenced, shot a frosty glance at Bowman.

"The judge advocate," he said, "seems to take delight in ignoring both courts-martial procedures and the warnings of this court. An official statement of his behavior will be prepared and appended to the minutes at the conclusion of this matter before us, with the recommendation that disciplinary action be taken. This court, Colonel Bowman, will not be treated lightly!"

John Bowman, standing at attention, bowed gravely to the bar and nodded. Such a reprimand, he knew, could be most damaging to his career, but only if Boone were cleared of the charges against him. If he were found guilty, the reprimand would be essentially meaningless and probably not even lodged. Colonel Bowman was not in the least concerned. There was not the slightest vestige of doubt in his mind that Daniel Boone would be found guilty as charged on each of the six counts of treason against him.

"The prosecution," he said smoothly, "has no further questions of this witness on direct examination, Mr. President."

Colonel Daniel Trabue rapped his gavel on the table at once. "This court is hereby adjourned until tomorrow morning at eight o'clock," he said, "at which time defense may begin its cross-examination."

3

As the spectators took their places in the roofed-over area of Boonesborough just before eight o'clock the next morning, their prevailing mood was as bleak as the weather. All through the court-martial proceedings yesterday the rain had fallen— not hard, but steadily, depressingly. Throughout the night it had continued falling and this morning, instead of slackening as everyone hoped, it was whipping up into more of a storm. Occasional gusts of wind sent a dreary misting of rain deep into the shelter and many of the spectators were wearing oilskin ponchos to protect them, especially those sitting closer to the outer edges. Now and again thunder rumbled menacingly, causing the ground to vibrate and glasses on the tables to rattle and clink against their neighbors. A dog in one of the closed cabins howled miserably and continuously in its fright and it was an unsettling sound. Twice lightning had struck reasonably close, lighting the morning gloom with a brilliant blue-white flash and causing momentary consternation with the almost instantaneous ear-splitting crack and the frightening smell of ozone.

Daniel Boone, flanked and followed by his guards, had been taken to the defense table about fifteen minutes before the session was due to begin, and he had settled into his seat beside Henderson and Harrod who were already there. Neither of these men appeared happy and though both nodded to Boone as he arrived, only Henderson managed a half-smile which faded as swiftly as it had come. They did not engage in conversation. For Harrod and Henderson, there seemed nothing left to say. Both had talked with Boone until their throats were raw, beginning their conference immediately after adjournment yesterday and continuing until well after midnight. Boone's vaguely expressed ideas of how he intended handling his own defense had both shocked and confused them at first, and then angered them the more they discussed it. Not only was it an improper method of conducting a defense, it was certainly not in accordance with regulations governing military courts-martial. They had tried to make him see the error of attempting it, make him understand the gravity of tinkering with established procedure, but he would not listen. They had tried as well to pry from him an explanation of how, if he was so determined to handle it his way, he was going to present his own defense, but even in this he had been uncooperative, giving them replies that continued to be vague or misleading or evasive and in all respects unsatisfying.

Their dinner had been brought to them in Boone's cabin confinement, but only Daniel had eaten heartily, listening attentively to their arguments and advice as he ate, occasionally nodding or shaking his head, but saying very little himself. And finally, after over nine hours of conferring with him, the pair had left dejectedly, no closer to having established a workable outline of their defense than when they had arrived. It was Samuel Henderson who had paused in the doorway and peered back through the firelit dimness at Boone.

"Daniel," he had said, shaking his head morosely, "you are beyond any doubt the stubbornest individual I've ever encountered. My pa told me you were that way, but I never really understood what he meant until now. I hope you'll be able to handle it all right, but I doubt it. I truly don't believe you have much of a chance, even if you had a well-planned defense; and doing it your way . . ." he paused and sighed and slapped his arms to his sides, ". . . I think you're committing suicide just as surely as if you put a gun to your head and pulled the trigger."

Boone hadn't answered but merely looked at him with an oddly sympathetic expression. In a moment Henderson had gone, leaving his confused and disappointed words echoing in Boone's mind. Now, with the members of the court filing in to take their places and this day's session about to begin, Henderson's visage was little different than it had been at the time of his departure last night.

Both Henderson and Harrod were painfully aware of the surliness of mood enveloping the gallery—partially induced by the weather, but more so as a result of the testimony given yesterday by Richard Callaway. With almost every statement he had made, Callaway had gravely damaged Boone, undermining his character, underlining his seemingly treasonable actions, filling the minds of all who listened with an ever-mounting revulsion for Boone and increased distrust of him, solidifying their conviction of his guilt. Their anger and bitterness overhung the assemblage in an almost palpable way and the prevailing desire among them at this moment seemed to be nothing less than to see this traitor hanging limp and lifeless at the end of a gallows rope.

Across from Boone's table, John Bowman, judge advocate and prosecutor, was deep in whispered conversation with his principal witness, Captain Richard Callaway. The portly Callaway listened carefully, nodded frequently, but seldom spoke. He seemed very nervous and frequently glanced toward the defense table, although he avoided meeting Boone's eyes directly. Colonel Benjamin Logan, sitting with them, also said little but was attentive to what was being discussed. His face was expressionless and he seemed unaffected by what Bowman was saying to Callaway.

With the members of the court having all settled themselves in their chairs behind the long central table, Colonel Daniel Trabue looked at his watch, snapped it shut and suddenly sat straighter in his seat. As always, he was clean-shaven and impeccably clad, his wavy, graying hair neatly combed and imbuing him with the distinguishment of appearance that seemed so appropriate for a president of this body of men. He tapped his gavel lightly, bringing order to the assemblage and announced that the court-martial was again in session.

"Captain Boone," he began, "at the beginning of this court-martial you announced that you intended to act as your own defense. Since then, two days of intensive direct examination of a witness have elapsed. I must advise you at this point that while members of this court have as yet formed no opinion, the testimony already given has been considerably damaging to you. It is my understanding that you spent a great deal of time yesterday after court in conference with Captain Harrod and Mr. Henderson. I feel sure that both of these men are strongly aware of the manner in which the charges against you are being developed and of your pressing need for experienced assistance in the matter of cross-examination of Captain Callaway, to which you are now entitled. May I assume that you have now rescinded your previous declaration of intention to handle your own defense and will at this time permit one of these gentlemen to conduct cross-examination?"

Daniel Boone rose, shaking his head as he did so. "No, sir, Colonel Trabue, that's still not how I aim it to be. I'm grateful for the advice Jim and Sam have been giving me, but like I've told them, I still aim to take care of my own defense."

Trabue looked down at the papers before him on the table to mask the expression of mingled contempt and sympathy which flooded his features. He was surprised that Harrod and Henderson had been unable to convince Boone of the foolishness of attempting to match wits with so able an opponent as the judge advocate. When he looked up again he spoke in a level tone.

"The court cannot help but feel that the defendant is compounding his own jeopardy, but has no authority to force him to act otherwise, although you may retain the right, at any time you care to during these proceedings, to step aside and let experienced counsel continue for you. Cross-examination by the defense may now begin."

"Don't want to cross-examine, Colonel," Boone said.

Despite himself, Trabue's mouth opened in surprise. Members of the court, equally taken aback, glanced at each other and some murmured to one another or shook their heads. An excited whispering rose and fell among the spectators and at the prosecution table Richard Callaway was smiling at the unexpected reprieve from what promised to be an unpleasant session. But seated beside him, John Bowman was frowning. The judge advocate studied Boone closely and his frown only deepened. He didn't appreciate surprises like this in court, not even when they seemed to be to his advantage. If surprises were to come, he liked them to be of his own making.

"Captain Boone," Trabue was saying, "am I to understand that you do not want to cross-examine Captain Callaway at all?"

Boone shrugged. "Well, leastways not right now, Colonel. Later on I suppose it's possible I might want to talk to him a little on a few points, but not now. Do I have to cross-examine now or not at all?"

The president of the court pursed his lips as he pondered the point. "Normally," he said, "cross-examination immediately follows direct examination of each witness called by the prosecution. This, I might add, is to the benefit of the defendant, so that his counsel or," he added hastily, "you, in this case, may attempt to disprove the allegations of the witness while they are still fresh in your mind and in the minds of the members of this court. However, I must say that I personally know of no regulation stipulating that cross-examination *must* be undertaken immediately after direct examination or not at all. Does the judge advocate know of any?"

John Bowman shook his head and spoke without rising. "No, sir, although it is highly irregular, straying far from normal procedure. Prosecution would like to know, assuming that the defendant does intend to question the witness at some time, when such questioning might take place?"

"Captain Boone?" questioned Trabue, turning to look at the defendant.

Again Boone shrugged, ignoring the barely audible groan that involuntarily escaped Sam Henderson's lips. "Sir," he said, "I can't rightly answer that yet. Seems to me, though, that a man can't properly defend himself against charges until every one of the witnesses against him have had their say. I ain't too much of a talker. Never have been. I figure I could do a lot better if I hold my own talking to a minimum and not bother with a lot of arguing until I've heard what everyone has to say against me. Maybe then I'd like to toss a few questions at Dick Callaway, maybe not. But I don't know for sure, yet."

"It is," Trabue said, "as the judge advocate has pointed out, irregular to say the least. However, since there is no well-grounded objection from prosecution, then under the mantle of judicial discretion I see no reason for not letting Captain Boone wait, if he chooses, until prosecution has finished with all its direct examination before engaging in cross-examination. However, Captain Boone," he added, "this being your choice, then I must emphasize that you will not be permitted to call a witness for cross-examination out of context. That is, if prosecution has called several witnesses and still has others to question, you may not suddenly ask to cross-examine Captain Callaway or one of the previous witnesses other than the witness the prosecution has just finished questioning. Is that clear to you?"

Boone nodded but did not speak and Trabue continued. "In addition, sir, I believe the court will at this time rule that you must conduct whatever cross-examination you intend of the prosecution witnesses *before* you call any witnesses for the defense. Is this also clear to you?"

"Yes, sir," Boone said, nodding again, "but one thing I want to make sure of: I'll still be able to question any of these witnesses I want to after John Bowman's all finished with them, won't I?"

Trabue sighed, wondering if the defendant had really understood anything he had said. "You will," he said.

"Then I don't have anything more to say right now," Boone told him, taking his seat.

The president of the court seemed no more pleased by this turn of events than the judge advocate, but he merely faced toward Colonel Bowman and dipped his head. "Prosecution may call its next witness."

Bowman called Colonel Benjamin Logan to the witness chair and swore him in. Logan was a craggy individual with penetrating gaze from under dense graying eyebrows which were so long at their outer ends that they curled in a half circle.

The questioning of Logan was largely routine and unspectacular. Logan testified that he and a small party of his men had established his fort of St. Asaph, some eighteen miles southeast of Harrodsburg, in the middle of May, 1775. It, along with Harrodsburg and Boonesborough, had been one of the first three Kentucky settlements of whites and, like the other two, had suffered numerous attacks by the Indians. He testified that he was one of those responsible for the ruination of Judge Richard Henderson's grandiose plan.

"It was an intriguing idea," he explained to the court, "to think of establishing an entire new country or a new Crown colony named Transylvania, but it was entirely unrealistic. For one thing, St. Asaph and Harrodsburg were established as settlements of Virginia's Fincastle County, which extended all the way from the mountains to the Mississippi. As far as we were concerned, it was not Cherokee land that could be bought from these Indians to begin with, nor was it land belonging to North Carolina. The idea of an entirely new government was completely impractical. How, for instance, could it defend itself against the Indians that were already attacking? We had neither men nor arms. We held a meeting of the three settlements at Harrodsburg, presided over by George Rogers Clark. I and others agreed with Clark that we needed to petition Virginia to divide the Fincastle County lands and establish Kentucky as a county in its own right. Practically everyone on hand, including myself and even Captain Boone and his brother, Squire, signed the petition and elected Clark and John Gabriel Jones to represent us to the governor and at the Virginia General Assembly. As a result, the Transylvania plan collapsed and Kentucky County was formed. This was exactly what we needed in order to ask for governmental aid, but it was slow in coming."

"Your own settlement of St. Asaph continued to be attacked by the Shawnees?" Bowman asked.

"Yes, and not only ours. Every settlement that had sprung up by early 1777 was under attack—ours, Boonesborough, Harrodsburg, Leestown, McClelland's Station, Crow's Station, Hinkson's Fort. We were much too divided to protect ourselves adequately, so we began to abandon them and consolidate. By early February last year only St. Asaph, Harrodsburg and Boonesborough remained. Then, even ours was gone. On my orders we abandoned St. Asaph and joined forces with Jim Harrod at his station late that month. We remained until early April when it seemed safe to move back. Clark warned me that it was a premature move, but I thought not. As it turned out, Clark was right."

"You were attacked again?"

"Yes, sir. We were the weakest of the surviving stations, having only eleven men including myself. On May thirtieth the Indians launched a very concerted two-day attack against us, early in which four of our men and three of our women were killed. It seemed almost certain we would fall. Under cover of darkness I slipped out of the fort, managed to get through the Indians and rode for help from the Virginia government."

"Which you received?"

"Yes, sir," Logan said, smiling, "which we received. That was when you, in charge of a company of men, came here from Williamsburg to aid us."

"Was Daniel Boone of any help to St. Asaph or Harrodsburg during these attacks?"

Benjamin Logan was genuinely surprised by the question and he frowned. "No, but we didn't expect him to be. Boonesborough was being even more frequently attacked than we, and with few men for defense. We could hardly have expected him to come to our aid when he could only barely withstand the attacks he was receiving."

Bowman nodded. "Of course," he said, "but Boonesborough was not under attack at the same time that St. Asaph was, was it?"

"No, it wasn't, but—"

"And even though not himself under attack and realizing the·awful weakness of your station and the fact that it *was* under concerted attack and needed help desperately, he did not come to your aid?"

"No, he didn't, but—"

"Just confine yourself to the answer for now, please, Colonel Logan," Bowman interrupted, ignoring the angry flush that spread across Logan's face. "Let me move along, and I ask that you refrain from interjecting any extraneous material. Simply answer my questions with a yes or no unless I specifically ask you for a more detailed explanation."

"Mr. President," said James Harrod, "It seems to me that the prosecutor is treating his own witness as hostile and preparing to ask leading questions to which a direct yes or no answer will unjustifiably cast the defendant in a bad light."

"May I say, sir," Bowman spoke up quickly, "that it behooves a prosecutor to move his examination along swiftly if he can and, where possible, to elicit testimony with simple replies of yes or no. If such replies do not favor the defendant, this cannot act as a deterrent to prosecution. After all, it is prosecution's responsibility to show the culpability of the defendant in any way legally allowable. That is what this court-martial is all about."

Trabue spoke to Harrod with what seemed to be a trace of regret. "The court will have to rule in favor of the prosecution in this matter," he said. "The prosecutor has every right to question his witness in the manner that he is now undertaking. If the defense feels that material which is relevant has been omitted through such brevity, then defense has every right to enlarge the avenues opened by prosecution when and if cross-examination of the witness takes place."

Reluctantly, James Harrod sat down and Bowman smiled pleasantly at him before turning back to his witness. "Colonel Logan, have you spoken to Captain Boone privately at any time since the Boonesborough siege?"

"No, sir, I have not."

Bowman nibbled at a corner of his moustache for a moment, considering his next point. Abruptly he said to his witness, "You are familiar, are you not, with Simon Kenton and Alexander Montgomery?"

"Yes, I am."

"You know for a fact that these two men were part of the force that accompanied Daniel Boone on his mission into the Scioto River valley of the Ohio country during a time when Boonesborough was under direct threat of attack?"

"Yes, sir."

"Did you feel that Captain Boone's planned expedition at such a time was both unwarranted and dangerous in the extreme to the settlement of Boonesborough?"

"I did." Logan hesitated, then added, "And I made my feelings quite clear about it at the time."

"You advised against it?"

"I did."

"In the strongest possible terms?"

"Yes."

"Did Captain Boone ignore your advice?"

"He did."

"Colonel Logan, you know at this time, do you not, that Alexander Montgomery was killed by the Indians and that Simon Kenton was captured by them and presumed now to be dead?"

A dawning of understanding swept through Benjamin Logan and suddenly he was angry. His reply to Bowman was heated. "What you're leading up to, sir, is—"

"Colonel!" barked Bowman, cutting him off, "kindly answer the question yes or no."

Logan clamped his jaws shut and remained silent. Bowman looked appealingly at the president of the court and Colonel Trabue nodded. "The witness," he said, "will answer the question posed by prosecution."

Still Logan hesitated and Bowman prompted, "Colonel?"

"Yes!" he answered sharply.

"You are answering yes, that you do know that Alex Montgomery is dead and Kenton captured and presumed dead?"

"Yes!"

Bowman chose his next words with care and spoke distinctly. "Do you not also know for a fact, Colonel, that these two men, leaving Boonesborough as a part of Captain Boone's mission into the Indian territory, did not return to Boonesborough with the others?"

"Yes."

"And that in fact these two men never saw Boonesborough again?"

"They did not, but—"

"No elaboration please, Colonel. Is it not true that you, along with Captain Callaway, instigated the charges of treason against Daniel Boone, under which the defendant is now being tried?"

"Yes, sir, I did. I agreed with Dick Callaway to be one of the officers instituting such charges against Dan, but not for the same motivations which prompted Captain Callaway. I agreed to be a party to the charges against Boone, but simply in order that he might have an opportunity to publicly wipe away the whisperings and suspicions which were surrounding him since the siege. Captain Boone is now and always has been a good friend of mine."

Bowman sighed with dramatic exasperation. "My dear Colonel," he said, "I shall have to ask you again to refrain from adding superfluous information to your answers. The facts remain, Colonel, that even though you allege yourself to be a friend of the defendant, you argued with him over the wisdom of the mission he was planning, you endeavored to stay him from leaving Boonesborough in jeopardy and, when ignored in your entreaties, you were so convinced of Captain Boone's guilt of treason that you brought charges against him for that crime. Is that not true, Colonel?"

"Ony so he could clear himself and—"

"Colonel! Did you or did you not lodge charges of treason against Captain Daniel Boone?"

Logan's shoulders slumped and he looked imploringly at the president of the court, but Colonel Trabue merely looked back at him impassively. He nodded, "I did."

"Thank you, Colonel Logan. I have no more questions of this witness, Mr. President."

Colonel Trabue glanced toward Daniel Boone who was now standing, a faint smile tilting one side of his mouth. "Thanks, Ben," Boone said, and then added to the witness, "I don't have any questions for you now. Maybe later."

"Defendant will direct such remarks to the court hereafter," Trabue said, "and on a less personal level. The witness is excused. Prosecution may call its next witness."

"Prosecution calls Mr. Andrew H. Johnson," Bowman said loudly.

"Here!" The high-pitched voice shrilled out from the rear of the right side of the gallery and an unusually small and slight individual stood up. He looked down the length of the crowded row he was in, shook his head, stepped up onto the seat he had vacated and then nimbly jumped over the back of it to the ground behind. Ducking his head against the pelting rain, he ran to the center aisle and trotted down its length to the front. Without being bidden to do so, he moved quickly to the witness chair and stood there expectantly.

Andrew Johnson, though twenty-eight years old, married and the father of four children, nevertheless looked to be hardly more than a boy himself. Barely over five feet tall and certainly not much more than 110 pounds, his dun-colored hair was long and straggly, his actions quick and birdlike. His eyes were a disturbingly light grayish-blue and seemed incapable of resting long in one place. He habitually wore an engaging smile, exposing small, even, unusually white teeth.

Bowman came to him and swore him in and then, after he was perched on the very edge of the witness chair, began his questioning.

"State to the court, please, your full name and place of residence."

"Yes, sir. My name is Andrew Hezekiah Johnson, though everyone just calls me Andrew or Andy, 'cept Martha—she's my wife—an' she calls me Honeypot."

A gale of laughter swept the gallery and even the members of the court were grinning broadly. Struggling to keep his face straight, the judge advocate nodded and said, "Andrew Johnson will suffice. Where do you live?"

"Hell, Colonel, you know blamed well I live right here in Boonesborough."

Again there was laughter and despite himself Bowman grinned widely. After a moment, as the spectators quieted, he continued. "You were residing in Boonesborough at the beginning of this year?"

"Yep, sure was."

"At the time that the saltmaking party was organized by Captain Boone, were you one of those who accompanied the group to the Blue Licks?"

"Uh-huh. We all left here for the Licks on the first day of the year."

"What was your task among the saltmakers?"

"Me? I was a stoker. Ain't big enough ner strong enough

t'cut ner carry the wood, but I k'n hustle from fire t'fire an' keep 'em goin' hot, long as there's wood t'feed 'em with."

Bowman thought for a moment and then said, "For the benefit of the members of this court, many of whom are not familiar with the process, will you please explain how you make salt and why it is so necessary?"

"Ain't nothin' so important for preservin' our meats an' fish an' sech as salt, t'say nothin' 'bout our needin' it fer preservin' hides an' fer flavorin' cookin'. Well, to git the salt, we got these big ol' iron kettles we use. We build up a batch of close-together fire sites, put the kettles on top of 'em, fill 'em with water from the Blue Licks, which is real salt-heavy water, an' then light the fires an' boil 'em dry. The water boils away an' the salt stays on the sides an' bottom of the kettles. Then this is scraped into sacks fer totin' back to the settlement."

"How much salt is rendered from one kettleful of water?"

Johnson squinted, as if figuring, and then hunched his shoulders. "Depends," he said. "Some springs ain't too good, others are brinier than hell. Now at the Blue Licks, which are the best springs around, one kettleful don't render a whole lot. We figger it takes pert' near eight hunnerd an' fifty gallons t'yield one bushel of good quality salt."

"And how much is a bushel of salt worth?"

"Oh, 'bout a cow an' a half."

A light tittering ran through the spectators but Bowman paid no attention to it. "You say you were a stoker. What were the other men doing?"

"Well, 'bout a third of 'em was choppin' down trees, 'nother third was haulin' 'em with teams to the fires sites an' the rest was cuttin' 'em into burnables. Ain't but one stoker needed if he's a good'un, an' I'm him."

"Did you have any guards posted to watch for possible attack by Indians?"

"Nope. Ol' Dan'l, he said wa'nt no need of it, not at that time of year. Reckon he figgered the Shawnees had 'nuff t'do keepin' their own selves warm 'thout botherin' us. Reckon, too," he added darkly, sending a bleak look toward Boone, "he was dead wrong."

"So Daniel Boone, who was in charge of the party, made no effort to see to its defense?"

"Nope." He said it cheerfully, but there was a tightness in his voice that was quite apparent.

"What was Captain Boone's job during this time?" Bowman asked.

"Well, he kep' us dang well supplied with meat, what we had t'have. Pert' near ever' day he lit out 'long 'bout daylight an' we didn't see hide ner hair of 'im agin till 'long 'bout late afternoon. Usually then he was totin' somethin'—deer er turkey er somethin' like that there. Lots of times he'd send one er two er three parties out with horses t'pick up carcasses he couldn't carry—a elk, mebbe, er a buff'ler. Got t'say this, we allus had fresh meat a plenty."

"Did Captain Boone ever stay out more than just from dawn until dusk?"

"Oh, I reckon they was a time er two he didn't git back till long after dark, but that wa'nt usual."

"He never stayed away overnight, though, and returned the next day?"

"Well, I 'spect mebbe once er twice he done so, but 'twasn't usual."

"Will you tell the court, Mr. Johnson, what events transpired beginning the morning of February seven?"

"You mean what happened? Hell yes, I'll tell 'em!" He shot a pointing finger out at Boone as if to impale him. "That there bastard done turned us over t'the Injins!"

The gavel cracked and Colonel Trabue half rose in his chair, frowning deeply. "The witness," he said sharply, "will control his use of profanity in this court!"

At the defense table, Boone was staring coldly at the witness, his lips drawn in a thin white line. Johnson stared back at him, paying little attention to the president of the court. He shook his head, started to speak, stopped, then began again. "Us'ta be 'feared of 'im," he said, "but I ain't no more. I tell you true, Dan'l Boone ain't nothin' but a damn'—" he caught himself and amended hastily, "—a daggone traitor!"

Again the gavel struck and now Colonel Trabue was standing. "Mr. Johnson!" he said loudly. When the little man looked in his direction, the president of the court went on. "Sir, not only will you refrain from profanity in your testimony, you will confine yourself to answering only what you have been asked and keep all comments of a personal nature to yourself!"

Johnson had calmed down some and now he made a little show of contrition. "Sorry," he mumbled. "Reckon I jest sort'a forgot myself."

Bowman squeezed the man's bony shoulder and then stepped in front of him. "I can understand your feelings, Mr. Johnson, but I'm afraid you've gotten ahead of yourself. Let me put the matter to you in questions. Daniel Boone left the saltmaking camp early in the morning of February seventh, did he not?"

"Yep, he done like always. Left jest after daylight."

"Riding a horse?"

"He was ridin', but later on if huntin' was good, which it usually was fer him—ain't never seed a man so lucky in huntin'—he'd use the horse fer packin' his kill an' lead 'im in."

"And you saw no more of him that day?"

"Nope, ner that night neither."

"When did you next see him?"

"Not till 'long 'bout noon the next day."

"February eight?"

"Febber-rary eight," said Johnson drily, "usually follers Febber-rary seven, don't it?"

"All right," Bowman said, faintly irritated, "you next saw him about noon on February eight. Under what circumstances?"

"He come a-walkin' down the hill toward us bolder'n anything, with 'bout eight Injins follerin' in the snow 'round a hunnerd feet ahind 'im. I'll tell you true," he added, shaking his head, "they give us some start, them red niggers."

"What did you do?"

"Well, some of us jumped up an' ran fer our guns, but Cap'n Boone, he stopped us."

"Stopped you how?"

"He yelled out that we shouldn't fire, that we was all surrounded by Injins an' that iffen we fired, we was all of us sure t'be massacreed."

"And then?"

"Fer a minute it looked like as if some was gonn'a fire anyhow, 'spite of what Boone said, but then we seen a whole string of Injins in a circle 'round us, ready to fire the second we did. Boone, now, he's still a-comin' down an' he calls an' says he's done gone an' surrendered all of us to the Injins an' we're t'stack up our rifles, drop our knives an' 'hawks an' stan' in a group. Didn't 'pear like as how we had no other choice, so we done what he said. Then the whole damn' tribe of Shawnees poured in on us."

"How many were there?"

Johnson thought and then shrugged. "'Twas like they was a

thousan' of 'em at first, but we was pert' near skeered t'death then. Figgered out later on they was over a hunnerd of 'em. 'Bout a hunnerd an' twenny. They made us sit in the snow where we was at an' then they starts a-jabberin' in Shawnee."

"Was Captain Boone made to sit with his men?"

"Yep, but they sure as hell wa'nt none of us bein' overfriendly with 'im at that pertic'ler time."

"What were the Indians saying?"

"Hell, I dunno. I don't talk no Shawnee. But Boone there, he was a-list'nin' an' gettin' kind'a mad at 'em fer what they was talkin' 'bout."

"Were you near Boone? Did he interpret any of it for you?"

"He was near, but didn't tell me much. Jest said they'd promised him not t'hurt no one an' here they was a-talkin' 'bout killin' all of us 'cept Boone hisself."

"They were discussing killing everyone *except* Captain Boone? Why was that?"

"He didn't say, but it sure as hell don't take a whole lot of 'magination t'figger it out. They was gonna spare him as a reward fer gettin' us t'surrender 'thout fightin', like we should'a done!"

"Conclusion on the part of the witness!" Henderson called out, and Colonel Trabue nodded.

"Strike that remark," he directed Captain Bedinger, whose pen had momentarily paused in its racing. "Witness will answer to known facts and avoid speculation."

"Does Captain Boone speak the Shawnee tongue well, Mr. Johnson?"

"He didn't then, though I understan' he does now. At that time he was jest figgerin' out some words here an' there, but they was enough! Then that big black nigger what lives with the Shawnees—the one Boone calls Pompey—he leaves the Injins an' comes over an' sits close t'Boone an' starts interpretin' for 'im."

"Were you close enough to hear what was being said?"

Johnson nodded vigorously. "Right next to 'em, by grab, an' heered 'bout ever' word, even though they was whisperin'."

"What was the gist of their conversation, Mr. Johnson?"

"Well, the Injins, they talked for nigh on two hours an' the nigger tol' Boone they was talkin' on whether t'kill us all er not. The others of our party didn't know what was goin' on, as none of 'em spoke Shawnee an' they couldn't hear Boone an' the nigger like I could. But what I heered jest plumb skeered hell out of me!"

"From what Pompey was saying to Captain Boone, could you determine how the opinion was going?"

"Yep." Johnson nodded again. "They was damn' near split. Some was fer livin' up to a promise they'd made t'Boone."

"A promise made to Daniel Boone?" Bowman had jumped on the comment. "What was the nature of this promise?"

"That if Boone surrendered both us an' Boonesborough to 'em, they'd jest take us pris'ner an' not massacree us."

"You're sure of what you're saying?" Bowman asked intently. "You're certain that a promise was made by Boone that no one would be killed if he surrendered you twenty-seven men *and* the settlement of Boonesborough?"

"Yep. Ain't no doubt of it. An' besides, when Boone hisself got up t'talk in council, he said it right out hisownself."

"Mr. Johnson, are you saying that in this discussion over whether or not the saltmakers were to be killed, Captain Boone was permitted to speak up?"

Johnson looked at Bowman with some agitation. "Daggone it, Colonel, you ain't got no need t'make me repeat ever'thin'. Iffen I said it onct, then by grab, that's what I meant. Yes, Boone spoke to 'em."

Bowman ignored the slight man's comment and bored in. "Are you able to remember what he said? Did he speak in English or in the Shawnee tongue?"

"Boone, he talked English an' the nigger repeated ever' sentence Boone said into Shawnee. An' as fer rememberin' what he said, Colonel, they ain't a one of us still livin' that'll ever fergit it. Damn' right I 'member it."

"Then Mr. Johnson, I ask you now to repeat Captain Boone's speech for this panel as nearly word for word as you can."

Andrew Johnson bobbed his head, cleared his throat and spoke very clearly. "He started out by callin' 'em his brothers. Here's what he said. He said: 'My brothers, what I have promised you I k'n give you a whole lot better come spring than now. Then the weather'll be warm an' nice an' all our women an' chillun k'n travel from Boonesborough to yore towns an' live with you as one people.' Then, after the nigger got it all said in Shawnee, Boone talked again. He said, 'I want you should spare these here men, as they are ever' one good, strong young men an' they will make good workers an' warriors fer you an 'hunters fer meat fer yore squaws an' chillun. Iffen you kill 'em, yore surefire gonn'a make the Great Speerit unhappy an' he ain't gonn'a let you do much good in yore huntin' ner in war neither. Now these here men ain't did you no harm. They was only a-makin' salt an' jest like I promised you, they didn't make no fight whilst I 'splained you didn't mean t'do 'em no harm. You promised me they'd be pris'ners, not kilt, an' you ain't gonn'a make the Great Speerit happy a-tall iffen you don't live up to it.' That was all he said then an' fer most of us it was the first any knew what was goin' on. I tell you true, suddenlike ever'one was shakin'.'"

Bowman's eyes were glittering and his voice was nearly a whisper. "What happened then? Was there some kind of a vote taken?"

"Uh-huh. Them Injins passed a war club from one to the other an' the feller what had it either passed it on er hit the groun' with it."

"Striking the ground with it was a vote for death?"

"Yep."

"And how did the voting go?"

"They was fifty-nine what hit the groun' with it."

"How many merely passed it on?"

"Sixty-one," Johnson replied, but then amended at once, "Sixty-three iffen you count Boone an' the nigger."

Bowman remained silent for a long while and the tension became almost unbearable. At last he said, looking at Boone as he spoke, "How nice that Captain Boone voted to spare your life. I'm sure you must be very grateful to him."

Johnson looked startled, not catching the irony of Bowman's comment and for a moment not knowing what to say in reply. Bowman moved quickly on before he could add anything.

"What happened then, Mr. Johnson?"

"They was still some talk 'bout goin' after Boonesborough right away, 'fore headin' back fer Ohio country. Boone, him an' that Pompey nigger, they got up an' went over to where ol' Chief Black Fish was a-talkin' with a couple English fellers. Couldn't hear too well then, but seems as how the Britishers was fer movin' on an' takin' Boonesborough, but the Injins didn't like th' idee. They was glad 'nuff t'have tooken us, gettin' all our horses an' guns an' other sech things. Anyways, Boone an' Pompey talks with 'em fer a while an' then Black Fish yells at his men an' they start packin' up ever'thin' t'head home."

"Do you know who the two white men were who were with the Shawnees, Mr. Johnson?"

"Not right then I didn't, but later on I found out one of 'em was named Charles Beaubien, which t'me is a Frenchy soundin' name, but he was sure 'nuff in British uniform. The other one, I never did know who he was."

"What was the reaction of the saltmakers when Captain Boone entered into conference with Chief Black Fish and the British officers?"

"If ever I seen murder in men's eyes, Colonel, it was in them right then. Some of 'em was thinkin' up till then that Boone was tryin' t'help 'em, a little mebbe, but when he an' them three an' the nigger all got their heads together a-talkin' an' a-laughin' an' carryin' on, they wasn't no doubt nohow whose side he was on. Reckon," he added wryly, "iffen they was a gun 'mongst us right then, Boone'd be dead now. An' I 'spect," his birdlike gaze flitted toward Boone again and perched on him. "that it ain't all too late yet, by grab!"

Bowman, Henderson, Harrod and Trabue, along with a fair percentage of the spectators, all began talking at once at this, but with the slam of his gavel, the president of the court overrode the others. He leaned forward and stared coldly at the little frontiersman in the witness chair.

"Mr. Johnson," he said harshly, "under no circumstances whatever will any threats be made in this court—either directly or through inference. This court will not tolerate any further suggestion of such a comment, and the witness is warned not to let this occur again. The court fully understands your emotions and the hardships you and your fellows have borne, but in this court those are not mitigating circumstances at any time for such remarks." He paused, looked around and then continued in a more even tone of voice. "In order to allow passions time to subside somewhat, I hereby call a recess for two hours. This court will reconvene at one o'clock. Court dismissed."

The final bang of his gavel ending this session carried a peculiarly ominous sound.

II

The rain had ceased but there was still a gloomy overcast and the wind had a chill bite to it. People milled on the mucky ground of the interior of Boonesborough as if not knowing what to do with themselves during this recess in the trial, the passionate testimony of diminutive Andrew H. Johnson still echoing in their minds, his accusations and threats affecting them deeply. Although Daniel Boone had always throughout his life been an essentially untalkative man, more willing to listen than to speak and little concerned with what others may have thought about him personally, he was suddenly acutely aware of the intensity of feeling rising against him. Where prior to now in the trial his fellow settlers had become reserved in their actions toward him and tended to avoid contact with him, abruptly their reserve had become poorly masked revulsion and, in some cases, overt hatred. Where those people were concerned with whom he had had little previous contact, it didn't much matter to him. What hurt was that suddenly people whom he had long considered as being friends had turned against him. In just the brief two hours before the court reconvened, bitter accusations and deep insults had been hurled at him by people whom he had known and liked for years; people whom he had helped become established in this country, often at the risk of his own life. This was especially true in respect to the families of men he had led away from Boonesborough—the men who had never returned.

Only minutes after the recess began, as Boone was moving up the center isle, little Emily Montgomery, widow of Alexander Montgomery, scurried up to a stop in front of him, blocking his passage. Her face was contorted with emotion, her voice breaking as she shrieked at him. Her violent words had been almost unintelligible, but heavy with loathing as she blamed him for her husband's death. A ring of people had formed around them, listening soberly, filled with compassion for the distraught woman, augmenting her hatred of Boone with their own.

Emily Montgomery's heated words were abruptly drowned in the flow of tears from her eyes, degenerating into a nightmarish repetition of a sound like "Muh...muh... muhmuhmuh" and then, no longer able to contain herself, she flung herself at him, butting him unexpectedly in the stomach with her head, beating at his face and chest, her stubby fingers clawing for his eyes. Unprepared for the assault, Boone attempted to cover himself and ward off the blows and gougings without harming the small woman. The crowd did nothing to stop it, remaining poised as if to join her in the attack should he make any aggressive act against her. The guards behind Boone, unable or unwilling to act, merely stood and watched, and even while undergoing the attack, a small part of Boone's mind recreated a mental image for him of a scene he had witnessed years ago. For some reason a dozen or more of the fort's dogs had suddenly encircled two others—a large male and a medium-sized bitch. The onlooking dogs had snarled and slavered threateningly, baring yellowed teeth, but the bitch had attacked, ripping the male badly in her fury. Bleeding and bewildered under her onslaught, the male had quickly rolled over onto his back in the universal action of canine submission, which should have ended the fight. It hadn't. The bitch had locked her teeth in his throat and before anyone had been able to stop it, the others had joined her, ripping and tearing at the exposed belly and flanks. In mere seconds the large male, disemboweled, hamstrung, and the ripped throat spurting his lifeblood in a scarlet flood, lay dying on the ground. No one had ever been able to determine why the fight had begun and could only register mute shock as the pack had suddenly scattered and left the mutilated remains of what had just moments before been one of their number. Now, for a horrible moment, it seemed to Daniel Boone that this was what was happening to him. Some atavistic sense within him made him know that if he raised a hand against Emily Montgomery in his own defense, or if he grappled with her merely to pin the flailing arms, or if he refused to defend himself and stumbled to the ground, this human pack would similarly tear the life from him.

As swiftly as it had begun, it ended. A flash of movement through the onlookers resolved itself into Jemima Boone Callaway, furiously thrusting herself into the circle, gripping the attacking woman's disheveled hair with both hands and yanking her away from her father, spinning her off into the crowd. Hands reached and caught the older woman before she could fall, and the spell was broken. Comforting arms encircled her and led her away, while the word she had been trying to speak finally burst from her in a convulsive, reiterated gasping.

"Muh...murderer!...*murderer!*...*MURDERER!*" On and on the word came, filling the courtyard of the fort, not ending

until she had been led into one of the cabins and the door
had closed behind the little group.

Stunned by what had happened, Boone let himself be led
by his daughter to an empty half-log bench inside the enclo-
sure, hardly hearing the ugly, vituperative remarks from
those through whom they threaded their way. There were
muted threats, vile name-callings, clearly voiced desires to
see him hanged, to smite his dead body, to spit upon his
grave. The three guards had followed them, uncomfortably
attentive, frightened at the thought of what might now happen to them for their own failure to protect their prisoner.

Within mere minutes everyone in the fort knew what had
occurred and the crowd milling about beyond the expansive
roofed-over area swelled rather than diminished. Sergeant-at-
Arms John Tibbs, leading a squad of eight soldiers, shouldered
his way through the people. At his direction the eight replacements took up a rectangular position around Boone and
his daughter, bayoneted rifles horizontally at hip height, held
loosely but menacingly, and the crowd kept its distance.
Tibbs muttered curt words at the three original guards and
then led them away toward the northwest blockhouse.

Jemima was crying now, her slight frame wracked by an
uncontrollable trembling despite the reassurance of her father's encircling arm holding her close to his side, despite the
comforting whispers which he murmured into her hair. After
a little while the words he was speaking ended and they
merely sat quietly together, each mentally reliving the unspeakable horror just past.

Flanders Callaway came to the guard soldier in charge and,
at the soldier's nod, moved into the protective rectangle and
sat down on the bench so that Jemima was now between her
father and her husband. A gawky, intense young man of
nineteen, Flanders' deep brown eyes mirrored the love he
felt for his young wife, the sorrow he felt for her father. He
took her hands in his, kissed her gently on the temple,
smiled hesitantly at Boone. A longtime admirer of Boone, he
was one of the few here at Boonesborough whose devotion to
the frontiersman had not wavered, who utterly refused to
believe the charges lodged against him, who yearned to help
but didn't know how and therefore felt inadequate.

Flanders Callaway had lived in a state of mental turmoil for
well over a year, torn in his loyalties between his uncle and
guardian, Captain Richard Callaway, and his father-in-law,

Daniel Boone. Helplessly he had watched the enmity for Boone grow in his uncle until it had become a stultifying passion in the older man. Entreaties and arguments had been to no avail and each day the wedge between the guardian and his ward had been driven more deeply until at last the split had become irreparable and at the same time all but unbearable, for as much as they might differ in opinion, Flanders Callaway had always loved and respected his uncle. He also understood him better than any other person at Boonesborough, including even Richard Callaway's almost constantly whining wife; and, in understanding him, recognized only too clearly what motivated him in his remorseless animosity toward Boone. Equally, Flanders was agonizingly aware that his marriage to Daniel Boone's daughter had driven a stake deeply into the breast of his uncle, and that his uncle was convinced that he had been betrayed by the boy he had raised as his own son. Richard Callaway had two daughters, but no sons. Flanders, the son of his dead brother, had become to Callaway the son he had always wanted. And now, in Callaway's mind, Flanders had betrayed him just as certainly as Daniel Boone had betrayed his people.

The three of them sitting on the bench formed a lonely island in an alien sea, each lost momentarily in his own little sphere of depression. They did not speak. They watched unseeingly the milling of the muttering crowd, heard these murmurings gradually being lost in a growing drumming of the recurring rain, felt the vibrations of renewed distant thundering. A world they had loved was becoming sour and bleak around them. But they had each other, and that was important. Passions and hatreds might continue to rise against them, hearts and minds might be filled with intensifying bitterness toward them, but despite all this, they had each other and that was what mattered most.

James Harrod and Samuel Henderson arrived about ten minutes after Flanders, both of them having left the fort quickly at the calling of the recess. The two new arrivals stood there expressing their sympathy and concern and anger over the incident and then, with a word from Harrod to the guard in charge, they moved to the defense table, bringing two more chairs to it from the gallery so that all could sit. It was Harrod who spoke first, addressing himself to Boone.

"Dan," he said softly. "I'd like you to listen very carefully to what I have to say. You are sitting here now with possibly the only four people in this entire place who believe without reservation in your innocence. You are and always have been a strong and determined man, filled with a marvelous self-confidence far beyond what any of us have ever experienced. It is what has allowed you to survive and even thrive in a hostile wilderness that has defeated and destroyed so many others. You have lived by your wit and your strength and your skill, bending the wilderness to your own will, depending on no one but yourself. But, Dan, this," he swung his arm out in a broad, meaningful gesture which took in the entire area where they sat, "—this court—is a different form of wilderness. Believe me when I say that it can be every bit as deadly as the one out there. At the moment it is stalking you, Dan, boxing you in, cutting off every avenue of escape. And when it has you completely tied and helpless, that's when it will kill you."

Harrod paused for a considerable while and no one spoke, although Henderson vaguely nodded his head. "Dan," Harrod continued then, still speaking softly, "don't keep trying to go it alone. This is not your wilderness now, it's ours—Sam's and mine. We understand it, know its perils, know how to use it for our own purposes, just as you know how to use the forest wilderness out there for yours. In your wilderness you have always helped others to survive by giving them the benefit of your abilities. Now it's our turn. Give us the chance to help you survive. Open up to us, Dan. Talk to us. Tell us what we need to know in order to help. You're a proud man, but even proud men can't always stand alone, not if they mean to survive. Right now, this moment, you are just a whisper away from a sentence of death. For God's sake, Dan, help us to help you."

Moved by Harrod's plea, Boone looked at those around the table. The worry and love in Jemima was evident, reflected almost as strongly in Flanders. The depth of concern in all four of them touched him so deeply that for a moment he felt almost overwhelmed by it. He reached out and placed his hand on Harrod's, which were folded on the table in front of him.

"All right, Jim," he said, nodding, "let's talk."

Ninety minutes later, as members of the court filed back into place and the spectators gradually stilled their own rustling and murmuring, the five were still deep in discussion. Reluctantly they broke off, planning to resume their conference after the adjournment of this session. Jemima and Flanders Callaway returned to their own seats in the gallery. There was hardly the need for the bang of Colonel Trabue's makeshift gavel on the table as a call to order. Everyone was waiting.

The president of the court looked out over the assemblage soberly. "I think all of us," he began, "are aware that a very disturbing incident occurred during the recess. There can be no repetition of such an action or anything even remotely similar. I would take this moment to remind all who are gathered here that the defendant, Daniel Boone, though charged with treason, must be presumed innocent until proven guilty. It is not—and cannot be—the province of anyone here except the members of this court to judge the defendant, and then only when all evidence has been entered. Passions blind men, warping judgment and thus encouraging injustice. Henceforth, Captain Daniel Boone will be under the guard of four armed men who have been ordered to protect him in whatever way becomes necessary, even should it amount to violence against any who should try to harm him. I regret that such a strong step has become necessary. I had hoped that we were a more civilized people, despite an existence on the frontier. It appears that I may have been mistaken and so now protective enforcement is required. Should the defendant be physically harmed during the remainder of this court-martial, the perpetrator of such harm shall himself be brought to trial for assault. Should the defendant be slain, then all who are even remotely involved in his death shall be tried for murder—and I promise you they will be found guilty and themselves be hanged. This," he added with cold menace, "is the one and only warning this court will give to any who might contemplate taking the law into his own hands."

Trabue let an uncomfortable silence grow and then turned his eyes to Colonel John Bowman and dipped his head. "The judge advocate may now continue with examination of the witness."

Bowman reminded the little man in the witness chair that he was still under oath and then spoke steadily for several minutes, reminding court and witness of where the testimony had broken off at the time the recess was called, though scrupulously avoiding any mention of the implied threat against Boone by the witness.

"Now, Mr. Johnson," Bowman continued, "will you please tell the court exactly what happened following Chief Black Fish's orders to his men to prepare to return to their own territory?"

"Uh-huh. First of all," Andrew Johnson said in his high, thin voice, "everything was gathered up that could be carried. All our weapons an' blankets an' cookware an' likesuch, 'long with what food we still had, which 'mounted to 'bout half a bear, half a elk, some buff'ler, an' two-three deer. All this was loaded into bundles an' we was made t'carry it."

"Including the large iron kettles and the salt that had been rendered by this time?"

"Nope. They was jest too heavy t'fool with an' all of a sudden the Injins was in a hurry t'git goin'. Food-cookin' kettles an' utensils an' sech was kept, but salt kettles was left where they was, an' three hunnerd bushels of salt was dumped out in the snow."

"You say the prisoners were forced to carry all the confiscated gear?"

"Yep. Most of the stuff the Injins had of their own was loaded on our packhorses, an' so the rest had t'be hand-toted, an' we was the ones what was made t'carry it."

"What was your load?"

"'Bout a hunnerd pounds of bear meat wrapped in the skin. Ever' man had t'carry 'bout a hunnerd pounds."

"Did this include Captain Boone? Did he have to carry a load like the others?"

Once more a flickering of malevolence came alive in Johnson's eyes as he shook his head. "Nope. The chief hisownself disallowed Boone havin' t'carry anything. Ever'where we went Boone got special favors from ol' Black Fish."

Bowman nodded sadly at this, as if to say just how terrible it was that Daniel Boone should receive favorable treatment at a time when all his men were suffering indignities, but he didn't linger on the point. Instead, he directed Johnson to tell the court about the forced march into the Ohio country.

"It wa'nt no good weather t'be walkin' in," Johnson sniffed. "Colder'n a witch's tit an' deep snow. Ohio River was froze clear over. First time I ever seen it that way. Horses an' men, we all crossed over the ice in single file an' never even heard nary a crack, so thick it was. We was all tied up each night an' suffered fierce 'cause of frostbite. Hell, even some of the Injins got their ears froze. 'Cause us white men was tied an' couldn't move much, we was worser off. Five er six of us lost toes er fingers later on, 'cause of it."

"Explain how you were tied and forced to spend the nights."

"Well, first of all our arms was tied ahind us with buff'ler tugs."

"What are buffalo tugs?"

Johnson gave Bowman a pitying look for exhibiting such ignorance. "A buff'ler tug," he said, "is rawhide strips cut from cured buff'ler hides an' strung t'gether t'make a long cord."

"Go on."

"After that, 'nother tug was tied 'bout our bellies with loose ends a-stickin' out on each side. An Injin slep' one on each side of ever' pris'ner, with the loose tug end on his side wrapped 'round his wrist so's iffen we made ary move t'excape, they'd feel it. Fin'ly, 'nother tug was tied from the one 'round our arms so it went 'round our neck in a loop an' then was tied to a tree ahind us. That's how we slep' in the snow ever' night till we reached the village."

"That was the village of Chalahgawtha on the Little Miami River?"

"Yep, biggest damn' Injin village ever I seen. Mebbe two-three thousan' people. Mebbe more, countin' ol' folks, squaws an' chillun."

"How long did it take to get there?"

"Ten days an' nine nights."

"And what happened when you got there?"

"Them red niggers was damn' near 'side themselves with joy. Reckon they never afore had no war party come back with so many pris'ners, 'specially pris'ners that was all able-bodied men. We got there 'bout noon but it was so damn' cold that spit friz up afore it c'd hit the groun'. 'Spect this was lucky fer us, though."

"How so?" Bowman asked.

"We all of us had t'run a gauntlet," Johnson said, then added with a glare at Boone, "even though the Cap'n had promised us that we wouldn't none of us have t'do so. Anyway, 'twas so gol-danged cold that them Injins wa'nt any more anxious to stay outside longer'n necessary than we was. So we rung through the lines right quicklike an' took a few hard licks an' then was all tooken inside a big ol' council house."

"Just a moment, Mr. Johnson, before you go on. You say

that all of you had to run the gauntlet there at Chalahgawtha.
Did this include Daniel Boone?"

"Nope."

"He did *not*?"

"Nope."

"You're positive of that?"

"Hellfire, Colonel, that's what I'm a-sayin', ain't it? Ever'
blesset one of us ran the gauntlet at Chalahgawtha 'ceptin'
Boone hisownself. Him they took inside out've the cold
right away."

"What happened then?"

"Well, they was days an' days of palaverin' an' we wasn't
treated too bad, though Boone hisself was treated best. He
stayed in ol' Chief Black Fish's wegiwa all the time, whilst the
rest of us was parceled out into other wegiwas where we was
kep' tied an' watched 'most always."

"Was Captain Boone tied also, even though he was staying
in the chief's residence?"

"Not so's I ever knowed 'bout it. Didn't see 'im much, but
ever' time I seen 'im, he was loose as a hick'ry nut come first
frost."

"In your own particular case, Mr. Johnson, how were you
treated and how did you manage to escape?"

A mischievous twinkle came alive in the little frontiersman's eyes. "I done fooled 'em proper, that's how. Oh, they
treated me perty good—better'n most, I 'spect, 'cause I was
so small. Reckon they sorter thought I was still a boy. Even
give me a Injin name," he added with some measure of
pride. "They called me Pequolly."

"What does that mean?"

Johnson chuckled. "Means 'Little-Shut-His-Eyes.'"

"How would they come to name you that?"

"Like I said, I fooled 'em proper. First off, I pretended to
ack like as iffen I was simpleminded. Pretended to be a-skeered
of bein' out in the woods an' even when they'd want me t'go
out with 'em I'd wail an' balk an' carry on till perty soon they
didn't try t'force me t'go out of camp with 'em no more.
An' ever' time they'd shoot, why I'd jump like as iffen I was a
gun-shy pup. Sometimes they'd make me shoot at a mark on
a tree an' I'd ack so skeered of the gun that when I fin'ly got
'round t'pullin' the trigger I'd have my eyes squoze shut an'
never even come nowhere near the tree, much less the mark.
That's when it come 'bout that they called me Pequolly—

'Little-Shut-His-Eyes.' Yessir, I fooled 'em. That's how I come t'excape while Boone was up at Dee-troit. I jest—"

"One moment, Mr. Johnson," Bowman interposed quickly. "Let's back up a moment. You say Daniel Boone was in Detroit? How and when did that take place?"

"Well, let's see. We was in Chalahgawtha 'bout three weeks when the Injins decided t'sell some of us t'the British fer the bounties they was offerin'."

"Some of you?" the prosecutor inquired. "Not all of you?"

"Nope, jest some of us. Sixteen, 'cludin' me, was chose t'stay in the village fer 'doption into the tribe later on. Boone an' 'leven others, they was t'be sold t'the British in Dee-troit. Them twelve—Boone included—was marched away toward Dee-troit on March tenth. They was guarded by forty warriors, plus ol' Black Fish hisownself a-leadin' 'em."

"Did you see Captain Boone any time after that?"

Johnson shook his scraggly head. "Nope. Leastways not 'til back here in Boonesborough, when he come a-draggin' in 'bout six-seven weeks after me."

"When did you escape from Chalahgawtha and how?"

"'Bout toward the middle of April. Them Injins that'd took Boone an' the other 'leven north hadn't come back yet an' I figgered I'd better make my try afore they did. By this time I had the freedom of the village. All the Injins there figgered I couldn't git away iffen I wanted to—first of all 'cause they was sure I was skeered t'death of the woods, an' secondly 'cause they thought I was too small t'take care of myself, an' thirdly 'cause they figgered I was simpleminded, but fourthly an' mostly 'cause of another reason. Ever' time they'd say t'me, 'Huy, Pequolly, which way Kentuck?', I'd allus point in any direction 'cept the right one." He chuckled. "Damn' red niggers us'ta laugh an' slap their bellies when I'd point t'the east er north er west an' they wa'nt hardly no day went by 'thout at least one of 'em sayin' 'Huy, Pequolly, which way Kentuck?' Yessiree, I fooled 'em proper!" He laughed even louder at the remembrance of his own cleverness, then went on. "Well, anyways, 'long 'bout mid-April they was some kind of cel'bration dance held in Chalahgawtha an' whilst ever'one was occupied, I jest snuck into one of the wegiwas, picked me up a rifle, powder an' lead, 'long with a knife an' a 'hawk an' a blanket, an' slipped away. Headed almos' straight west fer a couple-three days, then turned south 'til I come t'the Ohio. Come out on it jest about right 'cross from the mouth of the Kentucky River, so's I rigged up a raft, crossed over an' then took my time an' follered the Kentuck' right back t'here."

"And you arrived back here on the sixth day of May?"

"That's right. Fact is, I got back here less'n a week after Miz' Boone tooken herself an' fam'ly—cept fer Jemima there—" he indicated Boone's daughter in the gallery with an offhand gesture of his thumb "—after she tooken herself an' fam'ly," he repeated, "back down t'Caroliny, she thinkin' all the time, of course, that Dan'l done went an' got hisself kilt."

"And it was on your return here, Mr. Johnson, that Boonesborough first knew any real details of the capture and captivity of Captain Boone's party of saltmakers?"

"Yep."

"Or even of the existence and exact location of the principal Shawnee village of Chalahgawtha?"

"Yep."

"One final question that I'd like to put to you, Mr. Johnson," Bowman said, selecting his words with great care. "Based on things that you yourself actually saw and heard during your capture and captivity, did Captain Boone act in collusion with the Indians and therefore become guilty of treason?"

"Objection!" Sam Henderson had leaped to his feet so swiftly that he turned his chair over backwards with a heavy thump, but he paid no attention to it. Henderson addressed himself to the president of the court. "Colonel, once again the prosecutor is calling for a conclusion by his witness."

Trabue was shaking his head even before Henderson was finished. "I am going to rule for prosecution in this instance, Mr. Henderson," he said. "While to a certain extent the prosecution has both led his witness and called for a conclusion, yet the court feels strongly that because of Mr. Johnson's closeness to the events which took place, he is qualified to respond based on what he actually saw and heard. But though allowing the response, the court instructs the members of this board of court-martial to accept the response with reservation."

"Mr. Johnson?" inquired Bowman, smiling faintly.

"Do I think he was workin' with the Injins agin' us?" the little frontiersman said. "No, sir, I don't think it—I *damn well know it!* If ever they was a man guilty of treason, Boone's the one!"

"Thank you, Mr. Johnson, I have no further questions," Bowman said, but his comment was lost in the uproar that was sweeping the gallery.

4

It was not until the sun had cleared the eastern horizon on the morning of October 1—fourth day of the court-martial of Daniel Boone—that the three men in the well-guarded cabin near Boonesborough's northeast blockhouse concluded their conference. A grinding weariness rode the shoulders of each of them and their eyes were red-rimmed and grainy. For fifteen hours—ever since shortly after yesterday's adjournment—Daniel Boone, Samuel Henderson and James Harrod had been sequestered in this cabin, doggedly and relentlessly retracing the events that had led up to the court-martial, then planning strategy for what was yet to come.

The invective that had been hurled at Boone from the gallery yesterday afternoon at the close of Andrew Johnson's testimony had spawned a turmoil which had taken Colonel Trabue a considerable while to silence, and at the expense of his crude branchwood gavel, which had split directly down the center for its full length as he had so vigorously pounded with it. It was, in fact, the breaking of the gavel that had enabled order finally to be restored.

Bitter denunciations of Boone had been filling the air and arguments almost to the point of blows had broken out in several places among the spectators. Hoarse voices of men and the shrill, piercing voices of women had until then intermingled in a confused and angry mélange. But the breaking of the gavel and the expression that appeared on Colonel Trabue's face when it occurred had reversed the mood of the gallery. Suddenly the anger was supplanted with laughter, deep and hearty and full of genuine mirth. Even the fierce countenance of the president of the court, which had become startled at the breaking of the gavel, half of which he still gripped in one hand, gradually turned into a smile.

This unexpected breaking of the gavel might not of itself

have been enough to counteract the mood of the crowd, but the other half of the cylinder of wood had bounded high into the air in a spinning arc and had come down with one end plunging precisely into the oversized inkpot located on the table between Colonel Isaac Shelby and Captain James Wilkinson. A geyser of ink had spurted from the inkpot in a spray that thoroughly splattered the immaculate uniforms of both officers and even reached as far as the left sleeve of Captain John Holder's coat. The slapstick effect, coupled with the absolutely thunderstruck expressions on the faces of both Colonel Shelby and Captain Wilkinson, simply sent the gallery into gales of virtually uncontrollable laughter.

The disturbance, which had begun as an evil-tempered one which Colonel Trabue had tried desperately to bring under control, had become one which he then gladly allowed to run its course. For a while after the initial cause for laughter had occurred, everything that happened seemed to provoke new outbreaks of chuckles and cackles, giggles and belly laughs. They occurred when Captain Wilkinson unthinkingly and automatically attempted to brush the ink off his waistcoat and only succeeded in badly smearing it. They occurred again when Colonel Shelby, himself grinning, gingerly reached out and removed the section of gavel from the inkpot and then they redoubled upon themselves when he turned and gravely offered the dripping wood back to the president of the court.

Even while laughter racketed back and forth, Colonel Trabue had stood, faced to his right and, keeping his face as straight as he could, bowed in a courtly manner to the stained officers and offered his apologies—and this, too, brought more laughter.

A release valve had been opened and tensions that had built during the Johnson testimony and which had increased dangerously in the uproar immediately following the last statement the witness had made, were suddenly relieved and spent because of a simple incident of a totally unexpected comedy of errors. At last, in its own time, a semblance of order was restored. Daniel Trabue had recognized fully the pointlessness and even possible danger of rebuking the spectators for their initial ugly outburst and thereby possibly rekindling it. The mood had suddenly become very light and he hoped to keep it that way as long as possible. He nodded to the judge advocate, who repeated the comment that had been lost—that he had no further questions of the witness.

Defense was queried as to whether or not they wished to cross-examine and once again it was Daniel Boone, still grinning, who declined. In this decision his two counselors seemed to be in accord with him. By that time it had been nearing the regulation adjournment hour of three o'clock and so Colonel Trabue had adjourned the proceedings until the next morning.

Less than twenty minutes later, Harrod, Henderson and Boone had begun their marathon conference which only now, in the bright morning sunlight, was ending. Meals for all three had been brought by the guards and these were eaten mechanically, with hardly any cognizance of what was being chewed and swallowed. At about seven in the evening Jemima Boone Callaway had been summoned and joined them. Half an hour later Flanders Callaway was also sent for. The young married couple had remained until nearly nine o'clock before returning to their own quarters. Just before ten o'clock, Sam Henderson left the guarded cabin and was gone for nearly two hours. His first brief stop had been at the fort's northwest cabin, where the members of the court were quartered. Here, at the door, he spoke quietly with Colonel Trabue for about five minutes in regard to a matter of procedure. Next he went to the cabin where Squire Boone lay, still being treated for the serious bullet wound he had suffered during the incident which had initiated the siege of Boonesborough. They spoke in whispers until just about midnight and then Henderson left him and moved in slow thoughtlessness back toward the confinement cabin of Daniel Boone.

On the way to the cabin, Henderson detected something of a slight commotion at the west gate. He paused and peered in that direction but could only make out that the gate had been briefly opened and then closed, and that a small number of men—guards, he presumed—were leading another man toward the officers' quarters. Henderson was curious, but even more anxious to get back to Boone and Harrod and so he moved on. A moment later he had been readmitted to the cabin.

Though weariness dogged all three men, the hours nevertheless sped by with unbelievable rapidity. The depressing rainfall had finally ended near three in the morning and within an hour the moonless sky was like a deep, midnight-blue velvet cloth in which a million brilliant little diamond chips sparkled with inner fire. By the first suggestion of dawn's light they had covered the necessary points and from then until now they had tried to tie up loose ends in their planning. Despite lack of sleep, and a little less encouragement from Boone than they had hoped for in regard to his letting them assist in greater measure with his defense, Harrod and Henderson were in a more buoyant mood than they had been since the trial began. The bright dawn promised to be an augury for them, Harrod had remarked. Only two hours remained now until the court-martial was to be reconvened, and so Harrod suggested that they end their own meeting and try to get what sleep they could, in order to have their wits about them as fully as possible. Henderson and Boone needed no further encouragement. Within five minutes all three were asleep—Boone and Harrod on the two bunks, Henderson on a pallet close by. Not one of them stirred again until an authoritative rapping on the door awakened them and the voice of the guard informed them that only about half an hour remained until court was due to begin.

Actually, it was closer to forty-five minutes before Colonel Trabue, equipped with a new gavel, rapped the court to order. By the time the president of the court had awakened this morning, a total of five new gavels had been placed on the ground before the door of the officers' quarters. All had been rapidly and more or less crudely fashioned. One had been much too small—hardly larger than a pipe. Another was so huge that Trabue would have been required to use both hands to wield it. Three were usable, two of which were simply rounded dowel handles that had been set in rectangular blocks of wood. The third showed that its maker had used a bit of ingenuity and craftsmanship. The handle of the gavel was evidently a portion of the sturdy rung of a chair, while its head was a roughly but attractively carved figure of a sitting bear. The handle protruded from the bear's back and the striking surface was that portion of the bear's anatomy where it sat. It was with this gavel that Colonel Trabue opened the fourth day of prosecution testimony.

The first witness of this day called by the judge advocate was a burly, heavily bearded man with an oddly vacant stare which took only a slight degree of liveliness while he was speaking. He was a well-featured man with nicely chiseled chin, nose and brow, but was prevented from being handsome by the presence of a growth virtually the size and texture of an English walnut which clung to his right temple.

"State your name and residence, please," Bowman directed, after swearing the witness in.

"William Hancock. I live here in Boonesborough."

"Mr. Hancock," Bowman said, standing seven or eight feet away from the witness but facing him, "were you one of the saltmakers in the party under the leadership of Daniel Boone early this year—the party captured by Shawnee Indians on February eight?"

"I was." His voice was very deep and slightly muffled, as if the dense beard was impeding the flow of his words.

"You were among those taken to the village of Chalahgawtha by the Indians?"

"I was."

"Mr. Hancock, you have heard the testimony of the previous witness, Andrew Hezekiah Johnson, in regard to details of the capture of the saltmaking party, their forced march to Chalahgawtha and early details of what occurred there. Is there anything of significance to these proceedings, overlooked by Mr. Johnson, which you might at this time add in evidence?"

Hancock thought for a moment, then shook his head. "No," he said slowly, and added with a grin, "I reckon it was pretty well all covered by Honeypot."

In the midst of the laughter sweeping the gallery, Andrew Johnson stood up near the rear and waved his cap, calling out good-naturedly, "That name's reserved for Martha, Willie."

Bowman, smiling, continued as soon as the laughter abated. "Were you among the sixteen captives who were retained in Chalahgawtha while the remainder were led to Detroit?"

"No, sir," he replied. "I was one of the twelve taken north."

"To Detroit?"

"Yes, sir, to Detroit."

"You left Chalahgawtha on March tenth?"

"That's right."

"And how long did it take you to reach Detroit?"

"Exactly twenty days. We arrived on the thirtieth."

"Did anything of an unusual nature occur during the march to Detroit?"

Hancock frowned as he thought about that, then shook his head. "Not that I can recollect," he said. "We just marched and camped pretty regular."

"Was Captain Boone, who accompanied you, shown any particular kindness or special treatment during the march?"

"Well, I guess in some ways he was. The Injins seemed to

have taken quite a shine to him and every day they was
getting to like him more. 'Course they knowed about him for
years and considered him a great white warrior. The way they
figured it, catching him was one of the greatest feats they
ever pulled off, and they were right proud of it. They liked to
show him off to everybody in all the villages we stopped off at
on the way up to Detroit. And like I say, every day they
seemed to like him even more than before. They talked a
whole lot to him and because of that he was picking up their
language pretty fast. Black Fish always wanted Boone sitting
next to him whenever we stopped for night camp and had our
meal. The rest of us always sat together in a circle with from
five to ten warriors standing guard. We wasn't allowed to talk
much, but Cap'n Boone and Black Fish, they seemed like
they never had time enough to talk all they wanted together."

"Were you or any of the other saltmakers mistreated on
this march north to Detroit?"

"Not really, 'cept for being tied up at night."

"What happened on your arrival at Detroit?"

"Governor-General Hamilton himself came out to meet us.
He was very courteous to all the Indians, but especially to
Black Fish. He gave Black Fish and his men ten pounds
sterling worth of goods—mostly ammunition, knives, tomahawks and vermilion—for each one of the eleven of us."

"Eleven? I thought there were twelve of you."

"Well, yes, countin' Cap'n Boone, but he wasn't sold."

"He wasn't? Why not?"

"Black Fish said no. Seems he took such a fancy for Boone
on the way up that he decided to take him back again and
adopt him as a son."

"Interesting," Bowman commented. "Did Hamilton make
any sort of offer to buy Captain Boone from Chief Black
Fish?"

"He sure did! Fact is, he was so anxious to get him that he
kept raising his offer every time Black Fish turned him
down."

"How high did his bid go before he gave up?"

"One hundred pounds sterling."

There was a gasp from the onlookers. Such an amount was
a small fortune to the settlers, and that amount in sorely
needed goods had to have been a great temptation to Chief
Black Fish.

"Yet Black Fish refused to sell Captain Boone? What was Daniel Boone's reaction to this?"

Hancock shrugged. "Seemed to me he was sort of glad about it."

Harrod, on the point of rising, hesitated, waiting for Bowman's next remark. Beside him Henderson muttered, "Nip him if he tries it, Jim."

John Bowman raised his eyebrows. "Really. You mean he actually wanted to live with the Indians and be adopted as the son of Black Fish?"

"Objection, Mr. President," Harrod called out now as he stood up. "Witness cannot properly answer to the feelings and desires of the defendant unless such feelings were expressed and such desires directly stated."

"Rephrase, Colonel Bowman?" Trabue asked.

Bowman nodded. "Mr. Hancock, did Captain Boone tell you that he wanted to live with the Indians and be adopted by Black Fish?"

"No, sir, I don't recollect he ever come right out and said it."

"All right, let's skip that for the moment. To your knowledge, at any time during your stay in Detroit did Captain Boone have private meetings with Governor-General Henry Hamilton?"

"Yes, sir, he sure did. Just about every day we was there."

"Which was how long?"

"They left to go back to the village on the tenth of April, so that'd be twelve days, countin' the day we got there and the day they left."

"Do you know what Captain Boone and the Detroit commandant discussed?"

"I didn't hear their discussions, but Boone himself told me a lot about what was said."

Bowman obviously was pleased. He turned away with his hands clasped behind his back and looked toward the defense table. Without turning back to Hancock, he said, "Will you now, Mr. Hancock, please tell the court what Captain Boone told you about those meetings?"

The witness turned his head to face Colonel Trabue. "He told me and some of the others that he was negotiating with Hamilton about surrendering Boonesborough to him later in the summer."

The collective gasp from the spectators was like a brief,

harsh wind, and John Bowman spun around. "You are positive, beyond any possible doubt, that this is what Captain Boone himself told you?"

"Yes, sir, there ain't any doubt at all. That's just what he said."

"What else did he tell you?"

"He told us that he had been given a horse, saddle, bridle and blankets, as well as clothing from the British Army supply store on direct orders from Hamilton, plus some trinkets made out of silver that he could use for trading while among the Indians. He was given lots of fancy foods, too, and some of the other British officers there were offering him things."

"Let's go back a step or two," Bowman said grimly. "Did he tell you anything else about his offer to surrender Boonesborough to Hamilton in late summer?"

"Yes. He said that he dropped a lot of hints that Boonesborough was by no means very strong in allegiance to the United States and that the people here at the fort would very likely welcome its conversion to a British post."

"Did not you and the other captives who heard this consider these to be treasonous statements?"

Henderson started to rise, but Boone quickly put a hand on his arm and stopped him. "Let him answer," Boone said. "Might be it could help us later on."

Both the prosecutor and president of the court had glanced toward the defense, expecting the objection. When none was forthcoming, Bowman repeated his question.

"Well," Hancock said, "like I told you before the trial, sir, at first we never thought he was doing much but funning us."

"You no longer think that?"

"No, sir! Not no more, Colonel. Reckon what he told us he said to Hamilton was sure enough what he said . . . and meant."

"Mr. Hancock, did you remain a prisoner of war in Detroit, along with the other ten saltmakers when Captain Boone returned with the Indians to Chalahgawtha?"

"I did."

"But you escaped from Detroit later on?"

"Yes."

"How did you get away, and when?"

"Oh, 'bout the first of June I was being walked by a guard to do some work in one of the gardens on the edge of Detroit. We were just about there when I sort of decided that I'd had enough of this prisoner business, so I pointed toward a tree to one side and told him to look at that great big red bird sitting there. He looked and I clouted him 'longside the head. He wasn't looking at anything after that. I took his rifle and just walked off without no one seeing me. Headed west for a while, got lost in a great big marsh and spent three-four days there, losing the gun when I stepped into a sinkhole. Finally got clear of the marsh and headed south. Didn't make good headway, though, 'cause I had to spend a lot of time trying to find food. 'Bout the third week of June I got to within 'bout ten miles of Chalahgawtha, planning to go wide around it, when all of a sudden I was standing in the middle of about twenty Shawnees."

"You were captured again by the Shawnees of Chalahgawtha?"

Hancock looked disgusted with himself and nodded. "Yep, sure was. Probably would've made it all right, but it turned out that Cap'n Boone had gotten away from them two-three days before and parties was out in all directions trying to locate him. That's how come they found me."

"You were taken back to Chalahgawtha?"

"Uh-huh. Sure was."

"Did you find any preparations going on there for an assault against Boonesborough?"

Hancock nodded and grunted an affirmation. "They was more Injins there—warriors all painted up—than I ever seen in any one place before. From one of the other prisoners still there I found out that they'd had a war party all ready to come against Boonesborough when Cap'n Boone up and walked off. They was so bothered by Boone's leaving like that, they just postponed the plan for a spell. I was captive with 'em there that second time for fifteen days and then managed to escape again on the eighth of July around noon. It was on the morning of that day that I learned the Injins planned to make their attack on Boonesborough exactly three weeks from then, so I figured I'd best try to get back here with a warning."

"Yet, Mr. Hancock, though you escaped on July eight, you did not arrive at Boonesborough until July seventeen. Why had it taken you nine days to get back here?"

Hancock grinned a bit sheepishly. "I sneaked out and stole one of their horses to get away on and rode him like hell bareback for about six or eight miles, and then while I was takin' a look behind me, that damn' boneheaded cuss run me under a low branch and knocked me off and kept right on going. I lit the wrong way and about busted my knee. It swole up like a big gourd in about five minutes. I wiped out my marks on the ground and found me a place to hide in some rocks and watched my backtrack. Sure enough, about three hours later here come a party of braves tracking the horse. They didn't even pause where I was knocked off, just kept on following the horse, so as soon as they was out of sight I fixed me up a crotchety-branch crutch and hobbled off the other way. A man can't travel none too fast with a bad swole-up knee, so that's why it was nine days, my getting here."

"Mr. Hancock, during your brief second captivity in Chalahgawtha, you mentioned that you had learned the Indians were preparing an attack against Boonesborough through information you got from one of the saltmakers still being held prisoner there. Who was this person?"

"His name's Walter Bruther. I don't know him too good because he only come to live at Boonesborough maybe a month or two 'fore we went out to make salt, but I got no cause to think he was lying to me."

Bowman shook his head, smiling. "No, that isn't what I was implying at all, Mr. Hancock. I'm quite sure that Mr. Bruther was telling you the truth." He turned to face the president of the court. "Prosecution has no further questions of this witness on direct, Colonel Trabue." He turned back and added to the bearded frontiersman, "Thank you very much, Mr. Hancock."

II

"The prosecution calls Mr. Walter Bruther."

At these words from Colonel John Bowman, Daniel Boone gave a start, frowned deeply and then looked at Henderson. Counsel for the defense was immediately concerned. He craned his neck to get a better look at the nearly bald man who had risen from his seat in the gallery and was now moving down the aisle toward the front.

"Trouble, Dan?" Henderson muttered quickly, looking back at his companion.

Boone made no reply but Henderson saw that his usual

expression of noncommittal interest had vanished and Boone was now watching the approaching witness with feral intentness.

"Dan?" Henderson asked again, but still there was no reply. Sam Henderson sighed and glanced at Jim Harrod who was seated on the other side of him. Harrod responded with a helpless shrug, as if to say, "That's Boone for you," but he, too, said nothing. Henderson made a small exasperated sound, wishing he knew what was going on in Boone's mind. Despite the rapport they had achieved at last, Boone was still nowhere near as cooperative or open as Henderson could have wished. He'd never before had any client so uncommunicative nor so hard to fathom. Although, like Harrod, Sam had reluctantly gone along with Boone's decision not to do any cross-examining of witnesses until prosecution had finished all its direct examination, he certainly didn't like it. With the last witness, William Hancock, for example, there had been several points of the man's testimony that he'd love to have torn apart in cross-examination, but Boone had stayed him. There seemed to be no way of adequately putting it across to Daniel that brick by brick, John Bowman was building a structure of guilt around Boone which, if not soon broken down, would encase him. Hourly the conviction had been growing in Henderson's mind that all the talking he and Harrod had done with Boone during the all-night session had been futile.

Samuel Henderson had always been an attorney in whom strong optimism was a key characteristic; an attitude that had worked to his advantage innumerable times in past trials, including those times when the going had become rocky. But in such cases he had always enjoyed the full cooperation and confidence of the defendant. Even though Boone had finally opened up considerably to him and Harrod the night before, it hadn't been enough, Henderson realized now, and this was one time when he just couldn't seem to generate his usual optimistic outlook. The chances for acquittal were rapidly failing. Henderson made it a habit to assiduously avoid predicting, even to himself, what the outcome of any trial-in-progress would be, and he was trying very hard to do the same here, but for once he couldn't quite shake the dismal sense of foreboding. In retrospect now, he knew very well why not; the long night of conversation and planning had made them all giddy with fatigue, and the lift they had felt in their spirits was simply an illusion. In the bright light of day his worst fears were solidifying. There was virtually nothing that had yet been given in testimony that Boone had been able to say was not true, or that had even varied much from the way the witness had expressed it. That being the case, Sam Henderson realized at this point only too well that he had no idea what kind of a defense they could present, and he was very nearly sick with the worry of it. Now he glanced morosely at the gentle-appearing, middle-aged man who had taken his place in the witness chair after having been sworn in by Bowman, and wondered what new little tidbits of damning evidence this individual would have to add to the mountain of guilt already heaped on Daniel Boone.

Colonel John Bowman exuded an air of supreme confidence, both in bearing and in speech. Rarely, if ever, in his years of courts-martial experience had he encountered a case where testimony had interlocked so tightly, where each witness had not only been able to corroborate portions of what others had testified to, but had also added strongly guilt-substantive evidence of his own knowledge. The early concern he had experienced over Boone's extraordinary decision not to engage in cross-examination immediately following direct had faded. At first Bowman had feared that Boone had some sort of trick up his sleeve, but he no longer felt that way. Because of the neatly dovetailing testimony and the lack of objective interruption by defense, he was absolutely convinced that his own witnesses had told the truth. Such being the case, he could no longer imagine any sort of trick Boone might pull which could extricate him from the more and more tightly woven skein of evidence that direct examination had brought forth. Though the defendant's heart was still beating, John Bowman had no doubt whatever that Daniel Boone was a dead man.

Now the prosecutor fixed his bulbous eyes on the amiable-featured man of about forty whom he had just sworn in and smiled at him.

"Will you please," he said, "state your name in full and your place of residence?"

"My name," said the witness in a well-polished and cultured voice, "is Walter B. Bruther and I live here in Boonesborough. I have been a resident of this settlement since the fourteenth day of November last year. Prior to that I resided in Baltimore, where I was a schoolteacher."

"Thank you, Mr. Bruther," Bowman said. Immediately he

plunged into a rapid-fire examination, bringing out the information that Walter Bruther had emigrated to Kentucky because his wife had died and he no longer had any desire to remain in Baltimore where they had lived. He stated that he had no children and that he had always had a yearning to see the western frontier of America. He had been teaching the children at Boonesborough since arriving, but because he wanted the experience and felt he was needed in other respects beside helping the community educationally, he had volunteered to assist in making salt. He had been one of the captured saltmakers taken to Chalahgawtha, but not from there to Detroit. Bruther had then corroborated much of what the witness Andrew Johnson had testified to, but up to the point where Johnson had escaped, had added little that was new. But then the questioning became more pointed.

"Mr. Bruther, what was the reaction of the Shawnees to the escape of Mr. Johnson, whom they had named Pequolly?"

"They were considerably upset."

"By that, do you mean they were angry about it?"

"No, sir, not at all," Bruther said. "It was more concern than anger. They had all treated Pequolly as if he were some sort of pet. They felt he couldn't watch out for himself at all, so they were always taking special care of him. When he disappeared as he did, they at first thought he'd just wandered off and gotten lost, as a little child might. Then, when they discovered that a rifle and other things were missing, they still weren't so much furious at him as they were disgusted. They called Little-Shut-His-Eyes a fool and they were convinced that he would die in the forest if they weren't able to find him. That's when they received the biggest surprise of all."

"Which was what?" Bowman inquired.

"They couldn't find a trail left by Johnson anywhere at all and this just completely baffled them. To them, Pequolly was such a bumbling little man, so inept and so frightened at everything that they couldn't imagine that he would be able to go *anywhere* without leaving a trail. For three days they searched for it and then gave up. By that time they were convincing themselves that the Great Spirit had himself taken such a shine to Pequolly that he had just lifted him up and taken him away. It was the only reasonable justification they could accept for there not being any trail to follow. As you must know, sir, it takes an extremely skilled woodsman to travel without leaving some sort of sign behind him here and there for an Indian to detect."

"Of course," said Bowman. "You were still a captive at Chalahgawtha when Captain Boone returned there from Detroit with the Shawnees?"

"Yes, sir."

"How long after Johnson's escape was this?"

"I believe it was about nine or ten days. As nearly as I can place it, they returned to Chalahgawtha about the twenty-fifth of April."

"What was their reaction to the escape of Andrew Johnson?"

"Well, most of the warriors seemed willing to accept what the others had already decided—that the Great Spirit had claimed him. Chief Black Fish, however, was not so sure. He is a surprisingly astute individual in many respects. He talked at length with Captain Boone about it, and I heard the captain say that all he could guess was that maybe the Great Spirit *did* take Pequolly, realizing all the while, of course, that Johnson had simply escaped. Black Fish finally gave up on the mystery of it and concentrated more on preparing for Captain Boone's adoption into the tribe."

"You actually witnessed the adoption of Daniel Boone as a Shawnee Indian?"

"I did."

"When did this occur?"

"The second day after they returned from Detroit."

"Was Captain Boone's adoption a general sort of thing, merely making him a Shawnee Indian, or was he more specifically adopted by an individual?"

"Oh, he was adopted by Chief Black Fish himself. A white man doesn't get adopted into the tribe unless a particular member of the tribe desires it, and then he becomes an actual part of that Indian's family. I never got adopted because it turned out that none of the Indians there liked me well enough to take me in as a member of his family. It's a very serious matter with them and they really have to think highly of the man before accepting him. Usually he's adopted because he has shown strength and skill and courage. You see, once he's adopted, then he's not only a member of that Indian's family, but the Indian himself becomes responsible for him, and invariably he wants someone he can be proud of. It's an important thing with them."

"You say you were not adopted. Why was this?"

Bruther grinned. "First of all, I didn't choose to be. Secondly, I had every intention of escaping as soon as I could conceivably do so, but there's a big difference between escaping when you're a captive and escaping when you're an adopted member of the tribe. If you're a captive and escape and they track you down, they just bring you back and treat you pretty roughly for a while, but that's all. However, if you escape after you've been adopted, they consider it a wholly unforgivable betrayal of their trust. If they run you down then, it means automatic death at the stake. I'm afraid," he added ruefully, "that I am neither a very brave man nor a skilled frontiersman. I was fearful that when I did make my bid to escape I would subsequently be caught. The bad treatment I could accept, but I didn't care to be tortured to death at the stake."

"But," said Bowman, persisting in his point, "how could you prevent your adoption?"

"Simply by being as utterly unappealing to them as I could. To begin with, I had a pretty bad cold when we were first captured. It only lasted a few days, but I continued to act very sick and weak and afraid. I complained a lot about everything. I also acted stupid, dull and clumsy. I didn't act simpleminded in an appealing manner as Mr. Johnson did, but more loutish and uncommunicative. I did everything wrong that I could get away with doing wrong, but at the same time I was closely observing and studying the Shawnees and their ways. I do not," he added quickly, "mean to appear self-laudatory, but I've always been very good with languages—I speak French, Spanish, Portuguese, Italian and German as well as English—and I was now learning the Shawnee language as well."

"Did someone specifically teach you?"

"Not really. By the time I'd been with them a couple of months I could understand nearly everything they said, although at no time did I let on that I could."

Only Jim Harrod and Sam Henderson, who were both so close by, noted the change in Daniel Boone. His jaw muscle was working, as it often did when he became agitated, and he had stiffened as if there was a great spring within him that had been wound to full tension. Boone noticed them looking at him and he jerked his head slightly toward the witness chair, silently ordering them to return their attention to the testimony. They did so, but both men were suddenly very upset.

"I pretended I couldn't understand a word of it," Bruther was saying, "even when a couple of them spent a number of days trying to teach me. They never did realize how much I actually learned from them. So far as they could see, I was incapable of being taught anything and, as a result, no one wanted me in his family."

"But in Captain Boone's case it was different?"

Bruther nodded. "All the difference in the world," he said. "Captain Boone could have been adopted by any Shawnee family there, but since the chief himself wanted him, that was the way it had to be."

"How did Captain Boone make himself so appealing to the Shawnees?"

"Just by pretty much being himself. He had established something of an incredible reputation over the years where they were concerned, before his capture, but in addition to that he could run, jump, shoot, and track and do just about anything else like that every bit as well as the Shawnees themselves, or even better. That's the sort of man they admire."

"He made no attempt to hide these skills from them?"

"It's a peculiar thing," Bruther said, reflecting, "and I may have imagined it, but while he made no attempt to hide his skills from them, it seemed to me that he never let them know how really good he was. It was as if he always held himself back just a little, although for what purpose I cannot imagine."

"You say he was adopted by Chief Black Fish. Did this chief have any other adopted children?"

"Not white men. Captain Boone was the only one, although it is still difficult to think of him as the chief's adopted son, since the captain is probably no more than a few years younger than Chief Black Fish."

"You say no white men. Did Black Fish have adopted Indian children or blacks?"

"Both. The Negro named Pompey was in his family, but as an adopted nephew rather than as a son, which is a prestige matter, because an adopted nephew is nowhere near as important as an adopted son. Black Fish also had an adopted daughter and five adopted sons, all of whom were Shawnee. All five were the children of the tribe's former war chief,

Pucksinwah, who was killed four years ago at Point Pleasant during Lord Dunmore's War. The two eldest were a young warrior about twenty-two years old named Chiksika and his sister, a beautiful girl of about twenty, named Tecumapese. Then there was a younger brother of about ten or eleven who was named Tecumseh. Finally, there were three still younger brothers—triplets, six years old—but I can't at this moment recall their names."

"Mr. President," spoke up James Harrod from the defense table, "it seems to the defense that prosecution is moving rather far afield. The fact that Chief Black Fish had other adopted children is really quite irrelevant. Defense cannot see how this present testimony can have any real bearing on the issue in question here."

Trabue raised his eyebrows. "Colonel Bowman?"

"Mr. President," Bowman replied, "part of the charge against Captain Boone deals with the fact that he was adopted by the Indians and in this role supported them in various ways. Granted that the information in regard to the other adopted children of Chief Black Fish may be seemingly immaterial, it nevertheless provides us with a look into the kind of family Captain Boone became a member of. Prosecution is attempting to establish with the present line of questioning the fact that Captain Boone's adoption was willingly accepted by him, that he did in fact want very much to become a member of this family complex, when he could well have taken steps to prevent it, just as Mr. Bruther has testified that he did. We wish to prove here that not only did Captain Boone voluntarily become an Indian, but that he specifically became the adopted son of the principal chief of the entire Shawnee nation—the single most dangerous enemy of the Kentucky settlers—that he aided them in numerous ways to the detriment of the Kentucky settlers and that he conspired with them, in a plan proposed by himself, to cause the downfall of Boonesborough."

"The members of the court," Trabue said slowly, "are aware of the points that prosecution is attempting to prove and have no desire to hamper him from doing so. However, Captain Harrod's point of objection seems well taken, since the present testimony seems to bear no direct relationship to those points."

"Sir," Bowman said, "if the court can be patient just a short while longer, it will be shown that the information presently being elicited from the witness will have considerable bearing in proving the guilt of the defendant."

Colonel Trabue considered this. "With the understanding," he said at length, "that this is the aim of prosecution, the court will allow the present line of testimony to continue, but if relationship is not soon shown, preceding testimony will be stricken,"

"Yes, sir," Bowman said with a slight bow. "Thank you. Now then," he continued, turning back to the witness as Harrod resumed his seat, "let us be a little more explicit in the matter of Captain Boone. Is it not true that if Captain Boone had so desired it, he could have avoided being adopted by Chief Black Fish?"

"It was possible. Yes, sir."

"But he did not?"

"No, sir."

"He chose to be adopted? Actually welcomed it?"

"Yes, sir. He said he welcomed it and acted as if he meant exactly what he said."

"And it is because of that adoption and Captain Boone's subsequent relationship to the tribe that his present appearance," he pointed accusingly at the defendant, "is more that of an Indian than that of a white man?"

"Yes, sir, but once adoption took place, he had no further choice concerning whether or not he was going to look like an Indian."

Bowman didn't care for that response. "Please," he told the witness with a trace of stiffness, "do not answer questions with additionally volunteered information unless it is specifically requested. As the court has just indicated, it is only too easy to stray off into areas tangential to our purposes."

"Especially," Sam Henderson interjected loudly, "if those tangents seem in any way to be of benefit to the defendant. Sir," he said, addressing Trabue, "it seems that there is a point of information here of possible importance to the court that prosecution is attempting to avoid."

"It seems to the court," Trabue said, "that we are discussing a point of procedure which we touched upon briefly previously, but perhaps it would be well to clarify the situation. Colonel Bowman, as prosecutor, has the duty to do all in his power to prove the defendant guilty of the charge against him. As defense must know," and here a note of chiding crept into the president's voice, "he cannot therefore be expected to have a prosecution witness provide material which is of benefit to the defendant and therefore detrimental to the aims of prosecution. If defense notes areas in which issues of benefit to the defendant seem to be skirted, then it is the right—in fact, the responsibility—of defense to pursue such matters during the course of cross-examination. I hardly need point out that thus far defense has made no use whatever of the rights of cross-examination." He paused briefly and seemed to have reached a decision, as he nodded to himself. "Yet, there is more to consider in regard to Colonel Bowman's posture in this court. His present course of questioning as prosecutor is not objectionable. Yet, while prosecution is his primary function here, he is still judge advocate as well and in this role he is, by the dictates of the Articles of War, called upon to act with impartiality and not let the one part of his business prejudice him in the conduct of another. The Mutiny Act states that his being prosecutor for the Crown—or, in our present case, the United States Government—must not induce him to omit anything in the records of the court that may be of service to the prisoner. It is rather a contradictory and untenable position, but I feel personally that it behooves the prosecutor to be motivated not as much with a desire to convict the defendant as with a desire to see justice done. The court, therefore, now rules neither for defense nor prosecution, but rather addresses itself directly to the witness, requesting him at this time to explain for the benefit of the court something about the process of Indian adoption and what he meant when he stated that once adoption occurred, Captain Boone had no choice as to his appearance. Mr. Bruther?"

Walter Bruther glanced at the prosecutor, who nodded reluctantly. "Sir," he said, returning his attention to the president of the court, "the adoption process is none too pleasant. The person who is to be adopted—Captain Boone in this case—is made to sit on the ground while several squaws little by little pull out the hair of his head by the roots. It takes quite a while and becomes progressively more painful. They pull out every hair except for that one tuft on top, which they leave alone until later when they decorate it with feathers or ribbons or bones or other things of that nature. Then the squaws take off all his clothes and march him to the river, which they enter with him. Here they scoop up handfuls of mud, sand and gravel and scrub his entire body, from the top of his head to the soles of his feet. They're not too gentle about it and this, too, becomes very painful, especially—" he glanced self-consciously at the gallery and lowered his voice, "—in the area of the private parts. This scrubbing is a symbolic sort of thing which is supposed to wash all the white blood out of him, and by the time they're done he's been rubbed nearly raw and he's quite as red as a beet. Then he is taken and dressed up Indian style, his face and chest are painted in a variety of garishly colored designs and then he's led to where all the other Indians are gathered waiting for him in the *msi-ka-mi-qui*—which is an enormous council house. The chief of the tribe thereupon makes a long speech about what a great honor is being bestowed upon him and what he has to do to live up to this honor, part of which being that he has to maintain his appearance the way it has been altered. Then he is given his new Indian name and never again referred to by any of them with his former name among the white people. After this they all smoke pipes and have an impressive feast and dance. All that is what happened to Captain Boone."

"What name," Colonel Trabue asked, "was given to Captain Boone at his adoption in ceremony?"

"Chief Black Fish named him Sheltowee, which in English means Big Turtle. It was an important name and evidently a singular honor for him to be given it, sir, since the turtle is considered to be a very powerful sign among the Shawnees."

Trabue thought this over and seemed about to ask another question, but instead he merely smiled and said, "Thank you, Mr. Bruther, for your very clear explanation. Prosecution may now continue."

"Yes, sir. Mr. Bruther," Bowman said, obviously still displeased that the explanation was given, "did you at any time after that see Captain Boone make any effort whatever to resume his identity as a white man?"

"No, sir, I did not."

"Up until the time of adoption, was Captain Boone given freedom to move about the village as he chose?"

"Not entirely, sir. He could move about much more than any of the rest of us, but never without a couple of Indians with him. And he was still tied up at night like the rest of us."

"This changed after the adoption?"

"Yes, sir. Definitely!"

"In what way?"

"Well, after that he was able to go just about anywhere he wanted to go, and without any guards, either."

"You mean, of course, just within the limits of the village, don't you?"

"No, sir, I do not mean that. He could go fishing, or walking in the woods, or go off hunting on his own if he liked."

"Hunting!" Bowman expressed shock. "Did he learn to use a bow?"

"No, they gave him back his gun—that big rifle he calls 'Tick-Licker'—and he hunted with that. He would go out almost every day with it and come back with deer and raccoon and other meat for them."

John Bowman pursed his lips in a silent whistle. "Let me be sure I have this quite clear, Mr. Bruther. You are telling this court that Captain Daniel Boone, while thought by the Kentucky settlers to be a captive of the Indians, was actually a free man among them?"

"Yes, sir."

"That he became the adopted son of Black Fish, chief of the Shawnees?"

"Yes, sir."

"And became known to all the Shawnees as their brother, Sheltowee?"

"Yes, sir."

"That he could come and go as he wished without being guarded?"

"Yes, sir, so far as I could determine."

"That he was actually armed with his own rifle and provided with ammunition?"

"Yes, sir."

"That he in fact became a hunter for the Indians, providing them with the meat they required for sustenance?"

"Yes, sir."

"That he deliberately chose to stay and live as an Indian and provide for his Indian brothers, though he could have simply walked off at any time he chose to, after his adoption?"

"Yes, sir, I believe so."

Every point being made was striking home deeply with each person present at the court-martial. The faces of the officers of the court, some looking at the witness and others staring at Daniel Boone, were stony, grim. The expressions of the onlookers registered a wide gamut of feelings, ranging from shock and incredulity and stunned disbelief to open contempt, disgust, horror and cold, implacable anger. John Bowman let the silence hang over the court for fully half a minute before speaking again.

"I'm sure the court greatly appreciates the clarity and succinctness with which you express yourself, Mr. Bruther," he continued finally, "and therefore I would like at this time to permit you a greater leeway in your response. You are aware that Captain Daniel Boone is being tried here for treason. Will you now, in your own words, kindly tell the esteemed members of this court what you actually saw and heard at the village of Chalahgawtha, from the time of Captain Boone's adoption until the day of his alleged escape from captivity, that would support the charge of treason against him?"

Walter Bruther seemed to have been primed beforehand for just this moment. He took a deep breath and then spoke in a quietly learned manner, though to some degree as if he had rehearsed his statement.

"There are a great many things that I *suspect* in regard to Captain Boone's guilt," he said, "but what I actually saw and heard leaves virtually no doubt in my mind. First of all, in addition to voluntarily being adopted and taking on the appearance and actions of the Shawnees, I witnessed Captain Boone hunting for them and with them. Sometimes he would go out in hunting parties with them for several days at a time, but more often he would go out on his own in the morning with 'Tick-Licker,' just as he was accustomed to doing for us at the Blue Licks, and come back later in the afternoon with whatever meat he'd killed, which he always gave to the Indians.

"I must add," he explained, "that he never at any time offered any of this meat or any real kind of help or comfort to us of his saltmaking party who were still there as prisoners. While we were fed the viscera of the game he slew, or sometimes some rather distasteful dogmeat, Captain Boone was living in quite regal style in the chief's own house, dining on the very best cuts of the deer, elk, buffalo or whatever else was prepared.

"Those of us," he continued, "who were still prisoners there were made to do much menial work; work that was usually done by the squaws. This included bringing food and drink to the chiefs and warriors gathered for councils. Be-

cause I did this work well and it seemed to them to be the
only thing I could do well, I was ordered to do it often.
And because they were sure I couldn't understand them,
they were not in the least reticent about speaking openly
while I was among them. I always pretended absolute incomprehension of what was being said and geared myself to
exhibit no reaction to anything they said unless they literally
yelled 'Bruther!' They had given me the Shawnee name of
Petahkenethi, which is about the biggest insult for a man. It
means 'Rabbit,' but even that I pretended not to understand
when they tried to get my attention by saying it. Only when
they cried 'Bruther!' would I look up at them as stupidly as I
could."

The witness suddenly coughed raggedly into his hand, with
a deep, rumbling sound coming from within his chest. It was
nearly a minute before he could bring the coughing under
control, apologize to the court and continue his narration.

"Anyway," he went on, "in this manner I was able to hear
portions of many of their councils. Black Fish was extremely
proud of Captain Boone, and he invariably referred to him as
'*Ni quihfu Sheltowee*,' meaning 'My son, Big Turtle.' He
always insisted that Sheltowee sit in on the councils. Captain
Boone participated in them with considerable relish and it
was at one of these that Captain Boone said he could guaran-
tee the surrender of Boonesborough to them without a shot
being fired."

"Hold it right there! Mr. Bruther," Bowman said with
dramatic emphasis, "you yourself actually heard this with
your own ears?"

"Colonel Bowman, yes, I actually heard it with my own
ears. The Indians, of course, were extremely interested in
this and Captain Boone went on to explain that all they would
have to do to accomplish this was to let him return to the fort
a little ahead of the time of the planned appearance of the
Indians themselves. They were to call to him when they got
there, at which time he promised to come outside and speak
to them, but that it would take him about two days of talking
with those inside the fort to convince them that they must
surrender or be destroyed."

"Mr. Bruther," John Bowman said in a guardedly solicitous
manner, "let me impress upon you the gravity of what you
are saying. If those are actually the words that Captain Boone
spoke to them, then he is beyond any doubt whatever, guilty

of treason. Are you positive—*positive beyond doubt!*—that that is what Captain Boone said to them during their council?"

"It is," Bruther said quietly.

No faintest whisper of sound touched the gallery. It was as if every individual in this crowd had turned to marble. They did not whisper or shuffle, they did not cough or sneeze or gasp. They hardly even breathed. The members of the board of court-martial, too, sat absolutely still, most of them looking at Boone now, their faces impassive but their eyes hard and cold.

"What happened in the council next, Mr. Bruther," Bowman said at last, his words splitting the silence almost startlingly.

"I don't know, sir," Bruther said, shaking his head. "Their council was continued but the eating was over and at that point I was sent out and not able to hear what else transpired."

"A question, Mr. Bruther, please," said Colonel Isaac Shelby at the bar.

"Yes, sir?"

"Do you know whether or not Captain Boone knew you could understand the Shawnee tongue?"

"Sir, so far as I know, until this very day Captain Boone never had any idea whatever that I could understand or speak the Shawnee language."

Bowman waited a moment to see if there was anything more that Shelby wished to ask, but when the colonel said nothing else, the prosecutor returned the floor to Bruther with a tight, satisfied little nod.

"To go on," Bruther began again, hesitantly, "there was one day when Captain Boone was out on a hunting trip with three Shawnees, that the rifle of one of the Indians broke. When they got back to Chalahgawtha, I was watching while Captain Boone took that weapon and repaired it and then returned it to the Indian in much better condition than it was in the first place. Captain Boone is a distinctly skilled gunsmith. When he did that, other Indians began bringing worn out or malfunctioning guns to him and he fixed them, also. These were mostly guns that were used for hunting, but when Chief Black Fish saw how well he was doing with them, he asked Captain Boone if he would make sure that all the guns that had been set aside for the next big war party were in good shape, and to repair any that were not. The captain set about working on those guns at once, working much harder than I ever saw any gunsmith work before, sometimes continuing long into the night by firelight. He took every one of them apart, cleaned them all and lubricated them very well with the best bear oil. I watched him do it."

"Exactly what sort of repairs was he doing?" Bowman asked.

"In addition to cleaning them? Well, where stocks or triggers or sights were broken, he fixed them perfectly. He made sure that every gun had fresh flints of the best quality obtainable, and that the pans were clean and the ports unobstructed for the flash. When he was finished, the Shawnees had a stockpile of three hundred or more rifles in the best operating condition possible, although before he went to work on them I would hazard a guess that more than half of them would not even have fired."

Bruther's forehead furrowed as he paused and thought before going on. "I guess there is only one other thing of consequence that I can recall right now. On June the first Captain Boone went away with a party of eight Shawnees and was gone for ten days. He told me that he was going with them to the Scioto River country east of us to make salt there, but when he came back on June the eleventh, he brought back no salt that I saw. However, there was a big change. He had gone away, as I said, with eight others, but when he came back he was riding with a party of around four hundred Shawnees decked out in war paint. The captain told me that the war party had joined him and his eight companions on the trail one day out of Chalahgawtha, saying they were returning from successful raids against Donnelly's Fort way up on the Greenbrier River and Fort Randolph at Point Pleasant. I saw no plunder that would have indicated this was true. The war party looked more to me as if it was gathering at Chalahgawtha to go out against the whites, rather than just having returned from attacking them. By the next day I learned that this war party was definitely preparing to go against Boonesborough within ten days, and the guns that Daniel Boone had repaired were being parceled out to them." He paused and then shook his head, adding, "That is all I can attest to of my own witness that would support the charge of treason against Captain Boone, although as I have said, there is much more that I suspect and could speculate upon."

Bowman hastily held up a hand to stop him. He wanted nothing to spoil this extremely damaging testimony in the least. "No," he told Bruther quickly, "with what you have already told us, sir, there is certainly no need—even if it were permissible for you to do so—for you to express suspicions and speculations. I have only a few other questions to ask of you. First, how long was it after Boone returned from his alleged saltmaking at the Scioto with this war party before he left Chalahgawtha to return to Boonesborough?"

"They returned, as I've said," Bruther repeated patiently, "on June the eleventh. Captain Boone spent the rest of that day and all of the next four days cleaning and repairing the rifles of the party that had just arrived with him. He finished late in the afternoon of June the fifteenth. Before sunrise the next morning, June sixteenth, he rode out on a horse to supposedly round up and bring in the horses of the Indians that had been turned loose on wide hobbles. This is what was usually done. Tight hobbles, such as we often use, keep a horse in one place without tethering, but the Shawnees have the habit of using wide hobbles so their animals can move about rather freely in order to graze over considerable distances, but restrictive enough that they still are not able to run or jump. Then the Indians just go out and round them up when they need them. That's what Captain Boone was supposed to do on the morning of June the sixteenth, but he simply rode out with his rifle and never came back."

"What was the effect of this on the Indians, Mr. Bruther?"

"Well, at first they weren't too concerned, but the later it got, the more worried they became. They sent some men out to search, because Black Fish said maybe his son had somehow gotten hurt and needed help. The men who searched found the wide-hobbled horses, but no sign of Captain Boone. Black Fish sent them out again for a closer look and then they came back in saying they had found the tracks of his horse, and that these tracks were heading south toward the *Spay-lay-wi-theepi*, which is what they call the Ohio River."

"Did they then go in pursuit of Captain Boone?"

"Yes, sir. About thirty mounted and started following his trail, but half of them came back late that night and said Captain Boone had been running his horse hard until the point where the trail had entered a stream called Caesar Creek—named after a Negro named Caesar who was also living with them, like Pompey—and here they had lost the trail. Those that had not come back were still searching for the place where the trail emerged from the creek and when they found it they were going to continue their pursuit of him."

"Obviously, since Captain Boone made it back here, they did not overtake him?"

"No, sir, but they did come back with the horse. Captain Boone had run it into the ground before turning it loose and the animal could hardly walk. It will never be a useful horse again. They looked for Captain Boone's footprints but were unable to find them. Captain Boone evidently very wisely persisted in walking in the streams wherever possible so he couldn't be traced."

"When it finally dawned on them that Captain Boone was actually gone from them, what was the reaction?"

"They were more furious than I'd ever seen them. They held a great council and voted that now Captain Boone was *cut-ta-ho-tha*, which means sentenced to death by torturing and burning at the stake. If he was seen again he was not to be killed but rather captured by any means possible to be brought back to Chalahgawtha so that the whole Shawnee nation could be summoned to congregate at Chalahgawtha in order to witness the ritual of his death. Black Fish was especially provoked at first, but also very sad. As time progressed it became his firm belief that Captain Boone had taken leave of his senses and was therefore unaccountable for his actions. He kept saying that he knew his son Sheltowee had been very happy there and that, as he put it, a bad spirit must have entered his ear and twisted his brain."

"Did this," Bowman asked, "seem to you to be a subterfuge on the part of the chief? Recalling the plan you have testified to that Captain Boone proposed to them in council, where he was to return to Boonesborough by himself shortly before the Indian force arrived, was there any indication at the time of Captain Boone's alleged escape that Chief Black Fish fully expected Boone to leave and go back to Boonesborough to await his coming with the war party?"

"No, sir, I cannot in honesty even surmise that. I am convinced that both the anger and sadness evinced by Chief Black Fish were genuine and that he had no previous knowledge of it. However, I did overhear Black Fish in conversation with his second-in-command, Chief Catahecassa—Black Hoof—in which the chief said that they would only delay their departure a little while and then go ahead as planned and trust in *Moneto*—their God—to bring Sheltowee to his senses when they should appear and make him carry out the plan that had been agreed to. It was quite apparent that Black Fish desperately wanted to believe that Captain Boone would still remain faithful to the plan. However, if at that time Sheltowee did not agree, then they would attack as if there had been no such plan."

Bowman walked in silence completely around the witness chair, considering, and came to a stop a few feet in front of the witness. "Mr. Bruther," he said, "the Indians did not appear at Boonesborough as soon as Captain Boone had warned that they would. Mr. Hancock has testified that this was because Boone's leaving Chalahgawtha caused them to postpone their plans. However, another attack was planned which should have occurred on July twenty-nine, twelve days after Mr. Hancock arrived back here. This attack also did not materialize when expected. The Indians, in fact, did not appear here at Boonesborough for another ten days beyond that. Why was this?"

"The escape of William Hancock also caused them some distress," Bruther stated. "With three of our men already gone from them—Andrew Johnson, Daniel Boone and William Hancock—some of the older chiefs were beginning to consider it as a bad omen, saying that they should not attack Boonesborough at all. This resulted in almost two weeks of counciling to decide again whether they would or would not attack. They finally came to agreement among themselves again to go ahead with it, but this agreement was not reached until the last day of July. Preparations then had to be made and a war dance held and so it was not until the third day of August that the war party actually left Chalahgawtha."

"Mr. Bruther," Colonel Trabue spoke up. "I'd like to ask a question."

"Yes, sir?" said the witness, turning to face the president of the court.

"It has been testified that when the Indians arrived here on August eight they were accompanied by some French-Canadians acting as the British representatives of Governor-General Henry Hamilton at Detroit. Did these men leave Chalahgawtha with the Shawnee war party? If so, when did they arrive at that village?"

"Yes, sir," Bruther said, nodding, "they did leave with the war party. They had arrived in Chalahgawtha the day after William Hancock escaped. About eighty Indians had come with them from the Michigan country—mainly Chippewas and Wyandots, but also a few Ottawas, Miamis and Potawatomies were with them. They came in a horse train, sir, and they had two small pieces of artillery with them—brass cannons, three-pounders—each of which was being transported on a sort of wooden platform suspended between two side-by-side packhorses."

"No such weapons were put to use by the enemy during the siege of Boonesborough, Mr. Bruther," Trabue reminded, a slight frown furrowing his brow.

"That's true, sir. This was because Chief Black Fish insisted there would be no need to have them—that to take them along would considerably slow their march, especially when they reached the Ohio River and had to raft them across."

"How were you able to learn this?"

"Two of the English-dressed Frenchmen, sir, the one named Beaubien and the one named De Quindre, were complaining about it one night inside the *wegiwa* where they were staying. I was passing by on my way to the spring for some water and heard them, so I stopped and listened."

"They were speaking in English?"

"No, sir, in French. As I mentioned earlier, it's one of the languages I speak."

"What were they saying?" Trabue asked.

"I only heard them saying that they thought Black Fish was making a big mistake by not letting them take the cannon along as a 'convincer,' as they put it, if Boone failed to live up to his promises made to General Hamilton and Chief Black Fish. Then someone came my way so I had to move off. That was all I heard."

"But they left the two swivels behind in the village?"

"Yes, sir, they did."

"I see. Thank you, Mr. Bruther. You may proceed, Colonel Bowman."

John Bowman shook his head. "I really have nothing more to ask of this witness, Mr. President, although I think it may interest the members of this court to know that Mr. Bruther himself escaped from captivity at Chalahgawtha only seven days ago and arrived here at Boonesborough at midnight last night."

At the defense table, Sam Henderson closed his eyes and groaned softly, mentally kicking himself for not paying closer attention to the mild disturbance he had noted at the west gate last night.

"Thank you, Colonel Bowman," Trabue said. "No further questions then?"

"No, sir."

"Does the defense wish to cross-examine at this time?"

Daniel Boone, still with a grim air about him, shook his head and it was a concerned Samuel Henderson who said soberly, "Not at this time, sir."

III

"Damn it, Dan, *talk* to us!" Sam Henderson slammed the pewter water pitcher down onto the rough table with such force that the remaining fluid inside spouted upward in a veritable geyser, puddling the tabletop and spattering the front of Henderson's shirt. The candle sitting nearby swayed precariously, sputtering a few times, and then settled back into its steady yellow glow.

Henderson glared at the frontiersman, who stood leaning against the wall beside the fireplace with his customary impassiveness. "Give us some ammunition," he demanded. "Stop tying our hands so there's nothing we can do but sit back with vacant looks and watch you get sentenced to death!"

He strode to Boone and stood in front of him rigidly, leaning toward him and continuing in a deeply agitated tone of voice. "Do you think Jim and I are some kind of miracle workers? Do you think *you* are? For God's sake, man, think! Just what in hell do you expect us to say?"

Boone said nothing and after a moment Henderson turned and paced away several strides, then spun on his heel and faced him. "I'll ask you again," he continued, still angry but somewhat more in control of himself, "will you let us cross-examine? Will you give us at least *that* much of a chance to counteract this case Bowman's built up against you?"

Boone shook his head regretfully. "I told you right at the beginning," he said, "and you, too, Jim," he shot a glance at Harrod who was sprawled on one of the bunks, facing them, "that I'd handle that when I was ready."

"When you're *ready*?" Henderson snorted, then repeated

himself, changing the emphasis, "When *you're* ready? Goddammit, can't you get it through your thick head that you don't have any more *time* to get ready? If you're not ready now, you've had it. You're done! Believe me, John Bowman may be a miserable son of a bitch, but he's no dummy. He's built up such a damnably ironclad case against you already— especially with little surprises like Bruther showing up from out of nowhere—that right now there's more chance of hell sprouting icicles than there is of us getting you out of all this."

"Never figured at all that you and Jim *could* get me out of it, Sam," Boone said mildly. "Never meant to depend on you to do that. You've known that from the start. You've helped me a lot already, you and Jim, and I don't want you to think I don't appreciate it. There's probably plenty coming yet that you'll be able to help me with, but it's going to have to be my way. If that don't sit well with you, then it's like I told you before; I guess you'll just have to pull out."

He paused for a long while, and when he continued his words were strained and tight, and for once he was more than just a little angry. "Do you think I've been asleep all this time? Do you think I haven't heard John Bowman's shovel digging out my grave with every question he's asked? I *know* what kind of case he's built. I *know* it looks bad for me— damned bad! I know I'm going to have to use my head like I ain't never used it before. But you listen to me, I also know some things that no one else knows. Most important among 'em, I know what *I'm* going to do tomorrow. I aim to do a little cross-examining. I aim to call a few witnesses myself, and I aim to wipe that smart-ass little bug-eyed smile off Bowman's face. I ain't hung yet, no matter what he might think, and I don't, by God, intend to be! There's one important—"

Boone broke off as there came a sharp rapping on the door and it was opened from the outside. The guard was there— the usual door guard—and beside him were Jemima and Flanders Callaway. The couple had brought food for them. Two small steaming kettles, their bottoms caked with greasy charcoal, hung from their handles in Flanders' grip. Jemima carried a large round bread loaf under one arm while holding a cloth-wrapped bundle in her hands before her. Jemima nodded and smiled prettily at the guard, murmured her thanks, and entered with Flanders close behind. She pretended not to notice the tension in the room between her father and the other two, and even as the guard closed and bolted the door behind them from the outside, she was brushing off comments by the men that they weren't hungry and was busying herself setting the table. Flanders hung the pots from the iron rod over Boone's embered cookfire and nodded in agreement as his young wife told the men they had to take time to eat.

"And we'll join you, if you'll invite us," she added, "although I guess we're not giving you much choice, are we?" She laughed brightly and without waiting for reply made things ready. She unwrapped the bundle she had brought in with her and it turned out to be a couple of bottles of wine.

"I don't think I was supposed to bring these in here," she said, "but Uncle Squire said they were the best he had and he wanted you to have them tonight. They were also the only ones he had, so I guess they *had* to be the best he had." She laughed again and her lightness was infectious, bringing out smiles on the faces of the men who moments before had been in heated discussion, dispelling the mood that had prevailed before her arrival. Again Boone reflected that she was like Becky in this respect, too.

Continuing her chatter as she worked, Jemima quickly wiped up the spilled water, set the table and got everything ready. Flanders poured wine in five glasses and distributed them as Jemima cut the loaf into neat, oval-shaped slices and filled the plates with steaming beans from one kettle and generous chunks of pot-roasted meat from the other. Three chairs, a stool and a keg drawn up to the little table gave them seats. In another moment Jemima raised her glass and suddenly there were tears in her eyes, reflecting highlights form the candle's glow, and her lower lip trembled.

"To my father," she said softly, "whom I dearly love, and to his good friends," she dipped her head at Henderson and Harrod, "who are helping him. God bless you all."

They drank the toast and Boone reached across the table to squeeze Jemima's hand. There was no need for words. His grip and the love in his eyes for his daughter expressed it all.

Talking as they ate, the reminisced about happy times of the past, discussing family and friends, commenting on the latest news of the Revolution and then finally, almost reluctantly, touching on the matter most important to them all here and now—the trial. Jim and Sam concurred in their belief that the examination of his final six witnesses by John Bowman that afternoon, following the testimony of Mr. Walter Bruther, had been relatively inconsequential. They were mostly residents of Boonesborough who had been on hand during the siege, corroborating points previous witnesses had made but adding little that was new or of a still more damaging nature to Boone. In no case had defense cross-examined any of them and none had remained in the witness chair for long. Bowman had finally finished with his last witness and rested his case just fifteen minutes before the court's regular adjournment time. Henderson opined, however, that for all intents and purposes, Bowman's case had ended with the extremely damaging testimony given by the erudite Walter Bruther. As prosecution rested, Colonel Trabue had immediately adjourned the court, instructing defense to be ready to begin its presentation when the court reconvened in the morning. For the next two hours or more after that, both Henderson and Harrod had been busy moving about from cabin to cabin in Boonesborough, talking quietly with various people, and it was not until almost six o'clock that they had joined Daniel Boone in his confinement quarters, finally engaging in the heated conversation that the young Callaways had interrupted.

By this time it was going on eight and their meal was finished. Invited to remain if they wished, Jemima and Flanders seated themselves quietly on one bunk and listened attentively as the three men began picking up the threads of the discussion that had been interrupted. The mood was better now—improved as much by the easy flow of the dinner conversation and the presence of Boone's daughter and son-in-law as by the food they had eaten and the wine they had drunk.

"You were telling us, Dan," reminded Henderson, "that you still intended to question the witnesses yourself, but that there was something else of importance you were mentioning when we broke off. What was it?"

Boone nodded. "I'm going to backtrack a little and try to tell you everything the way *I* know it happened," he said, "which ain't always quite the way it was told in court. When I'm finished, I'm going to listen to whatever you can tell me that'll help me when I do my examining. But," he said flatly, "I don't want to hear anything more about either of you having a go at the witnesses. Everyone who's going to be questioned, I aim to question myself."

Henderson blew out a gust of breath and shook his head. "I

guess we can't make you change you mind, Dan, but we still feel you're making the biggest mistake of your life. So go on, tell us what you can, and then Jim and I will give you the best advice we can, and we won't insist anymore on cross-examining any of the witnesses."

Daniel Boone grunted in a small, satisfied way and began to talk. For nearly three hours this normally taciturn frontiersman talked, and everyone present was more than merely impressed with his memory for detail. Here and there Harrod or Henderson would interject a question or comment, but mostly they just let Boone speak until he had completed his say. Then they began a discussion of what was to come and how they should proceed, beginning tomorrow morning. The three had had little more than an hour's sleep the night before and their eyes were bloodshot and sandy, their nerves more than a little frayed, their whole physical beings numbed with fatigue. Yet it was more than an hour after midnight when they finally finished. A great deal had been accomplished, although when the four finally said good-night and left the cabin for their own quarters, Harrod and Henderson were hardly optimistic. Still, they were congratulating themselves over having won at least one major battle with Boone himself.

Despite his adamant statement earlier in the evening, they had managed to convince the frontiersman to let them call and examine one key witness for the defense.

5

There had been no dull moments to speak of in the court-martial of Daniel Boone and at no time had the numerous spectators gathered under the roofed-over area of Boonesborough's northwest quadrant become restless. To the contrary, they had been keenly alert, devouring with eyes and ears the proceedings from one moment to the next.

Yet, on this fifth day of the court-martial there was an atmosphere of even increased attention among them, a marked hesitancy to cough or clear their throats or otherwise make any sound which might result in a single word being lost to their hearing. Nor was this sharpening of attitude limited merely to the gallery as Colonel Trabue's bear-shaped gavel cracked on the table before him to reconvene the court. The officers to his right and left, though never having slouched in their seats, seemed somehow to be sitting straighter and their attention to what was now being said was more pronounced. The same thought, in one form or another, seemed to be in the minds of virtually everyone present: now it was Daniel Boone's turn, and what would he do?

Among the spectators, the general feeling toward the defendant had settled into one of ominous anticipation. Few among them were not now thoroughly convinced of Daniel Boone's guilt. Fewer still felt that anything Boone would have to say by way of cross-examination or other defense could in any manner mitigate the evidence already given. There was virtually no belief that anything at this point could reverse the defendant's impending fate and oddly, because of this, their own anger and yearning for vengeance against him had tempered; it was not gone, but it was better contained. Obviously there was no longer a need for them to even consider taking the law into their own hands—a possibility that had provided no little degree of worry for Colonel Trabue

166

during the first few days of testimony—since Boone would soon, legally and with absolute finality, pay the ultimate penalty for his crimes.

"This court-martial," Colonel Daniel Trabue said clearly, "is again in session, but the court itself wishes to make a statement before matters continue."

There was neither friendliness nor hostility in his eyes as he turned his head slightly to face the defendant. "Prosecution having finished presenting its evidence yesterday, it now becomes incumbent upon Captain Daniel Boone to attempt to refute, or have his counselors refute, the testimony heretofore given in evidence against him. It is not customary in courts-martial proceedings for defense to be given an opportunity to make any sort of opening statement to the court, as prosecution is permitted to do. Yet, in many respects, as we have already seen, what we have here is a situation unique to the process of courts-martial. As has previously been pointed out, the defendant is being tried basically under the rules of courts-martial established by a country with whom we are now at war, thus demanding a marked flexibility in procedures and perhaps even departure from certain regulations. Much of what we do here may ultimately become precedent-setting standards, but in that respect we find ourselves with little choice. Therefore, if the defense—either defendant or counsel—wishes to address this court in an opening statement, it is my ruling that it shall in this case be permitted. Captain Boone?"

"I thank the court, Mr. President," replied Daniel Boone, rising, "for the offer, but I have nothing in particular to say that I reckon can't be brought out a whole lot better in questioning."

"All right, then," Trabue said, evidently not especially surprised by the response, "I have a further remark which I will at this time address to the judge advocate. Colonel Bowman," he said, turning toward the prosecution table as Boone sat down again, "considerable leeway was permitted, as you know, during direct examination and at least as much leeway will be permitted by this court to defense. Captain Boone has been given the right to counsel and has thus far refused to use it except in an advisory and procedural capacity. That is his choice and no special favor may be granted to him on that count alone. However, the court is prepared to grant him considerable latitude in the manner in which he intends to progress in establishing his own defense. Prosecution is requested to hold its objections to the barest minimum, reserving them for issues of great variance to accepted procedure. The judge advocate should bear in mind that defense may not always comport himself in formally prescribed fashion as he conducts his case, but within certain limitations this will be taken into consideration and allowed. Special favor will not be granted to defense any more than it was to prosecution, but every effort will be made to see that defense is permitted to establish its case in the most expedient and effective manner, even at the risk of possibly crossing lines of procedure."

John Bowman shifted his cold blue gaze from the president of the court to Boone and then back again to Colonel Trabue, but other than acknowledging the president's remarks with the suggestion of a nod, he said nothing.

"And now," Trabue continued after a moment, "defense having rejected an opportunity for opening statement, we will continue. Does Captain Boone still insist on defending himself?"

Once again Boone came to his feet. He inclined his head respectfully. "Yes, sir," he said, "although if there ain't any objection to it, Jim or Sam here have got some questions to ask later on."

Trabue cocked an eye at them. "You have explained to the defendant the perils of attempting his own defense?"

"We have, Mr. President," Harrod confirmed, "but he remains in his original position. We have also instructed him, as you desired us to, that he must conclude any cross-examination he may have before he may begin presentation of his own witnesses."

"Very well. Captain Boone, you may proceed."

The majority of those present evidently expected Boone first to call for cross-examination the witness most responsible for the charges against him and who had testified so damagingly and at such length against him—Captain Richard Callaway. Boone, however, did not.

"First off," he said, moving toward the bar, "I'd sort of like to talk to Andy Johnson."

John Bowman stood, called Andrew Hezekiah Johnson to the witness chair, reminded him that he was still under oath from his former testimony and turned him over to Boone with a malicious little smile. "Have fun, counselor," he muttered only loudly enough for Boone to hear him, and then added meaningfully, "while you can."

Boone seemed not to hear. He was looking at the diminutive man in the witness chair with a speculative eye. Like virtually all the frontiersmen, Johnson was an adept liar if he felt the need to be, and Boone was fairly sure that the fact that he'd sworn an oath to tell the truth wouldn't keep him from fabricating if he felt he could get away with it.

"Well, Pequolly," he began with a broad smile, "which way Kentuck'?"

There was a genuine swell of laughter from the gallery which grew even louder when, after a moment's confusion at the unexpectedness of Boone's question, Johnson altered his expression to appear vapid, almost idiotic, and then deliberately pointed north while at the same time effecting a loose-lipped grin. Though none here but Boone, Hancock and Bruther had seen the gesture before, there was no doubt in anyone's mind that this was precisely the way Andrew Johnson had acted when the same question had been posed to him by the Indians during his captivity. Boone's own smile became wider and, as the gallery settled down, he complimented Johnson.

"You do that pretty good, Andy. No wonder you were able to fool them. Let's see you do it again. Huy, Pequolly, which way Kentuck'?"

Suddenly Andrew Johnson was suspicious. The smile still on Boone's face somehow didn't quite reach to his eyes. Johnson's own expression took on a weasel-like cunning as he shot a quick glance over at Colonel Bowman. Immediately the prosecutor was on his feet.

"Sir," he said, addressing himself to the president of the court, "prosecution fails to see how this is a matter of cross-examination. The defendant is obviously attempting to humiliate the witness before the court. For one thing, his name is Andrew Johnson, not Pequolly. Allowing latitude is one matter, but this is quite another."

Colonel Trabue allowed himself a faint grimace. "Prosecution," he commented, "will, I'm sure, make every effort to see that precious little latitude is enjoyed by the defendant. I would point out as a reminder here that prosecution itself brought out the name Pequolly in direct examination. The objection strikes me as being premature and once again, for the sake of moving matters along quickly, I would caution the prosecution to temper his comments in that respect. The court, however, will rule for you in this instance, because of the possibility of ridicule of the witness, and direct the defendant to limit himself to straightforward cross-examination directed to the witness by his proper name."

Boone gave a low affirmative grunt and, while the grudgingly satisfied Bowman resumed his seat, turned his attention to Johnson again. The ferret wariness was still evident in the manner in which the witness stared back.

"Like I was saying, Andy," Boone continued, "you do that pretty good. Easy to see why you had all the Indians up there at Chalahgawtha fooled. Ever use that sort of 'dumb' act before to fool people?"

"I dunno," Johnson muttered, shrugging.

"Sure you do," Boone put in cheerfully. "Remember at Blue Licks? Don't you recollect how you pretended to be sick, so others would have to do your work for you up there? Remember how well you fooled us until that time when you let it slip to Joe Jackson that you were just faking it?"

Johnson squirmed uncomfortably, but said nothing.

"You don't much like me, do you, Andy?"

Boone's sudden change of subject caught Johnson off balance. He stared at his buckskin-clad questioner for a moment and then shook his head. "Damn' little," he admitted.

"Why?"

Johnson looked swiftly at the bar. "He's askin' it, yer Honor," he said, then replied to Boone, "'Cause you're a damn' traitor, that's why!"

Colonel Trabue made as if to speak as a stirring began in the gallery, but Boone moved along quickly. "Now that's funny," he said, briefly scratching the back of his neck, "you didn't think I was a traitor at Blue Licks before the Indians came, did you?"

"Nope. But I sure, by God, have ever since!"

"Think back a minute, Andy. There are at least two other witnesses here who'll remember as I do that long before the Indians came you told the other saltmakers there that you hated my guts, didn't you? And that was right after I hauled you out of your blankets and made you go to work, wasn't it?"

"I was jest mad."

"Now that's the truth, sure enough. Didn't you say you were going to nail my hide to the wall if it was the last thing you ever did?"

Johnson said nothing, compressing his lips and glaring at Boone. After an instant Colonel Bowman stood and addressed the court. "Sir, the defendant is obviously browbeating this witness."

Colonel Trabue was irked by the objection and snapped at Bowman. "Prosecution will be seated. The defendant is well within his rights to show if he can that the witness bears malice toward him. And if this witness did in fact threaten the defendant, then the point is quite relative to the issue. Prosecution is out of order. Witness will answer the question."

Still Johnson hesitated and Daniel Boone nudged him. "Careful, Andy," he said. "Remember, nearly everyone there heard it. Didn't you say you were going to nail my hide to the wall if it was the last thing you ever did?"

Johnson licked his lips and nodded. "Yep," he said, "but like I say, I was mad. People say things when they're mad that they don't rightly mean."

"But you meant it, didn't you? You kept on saying it, right up to the time the Shawnees took us, and then all the way to Chalahgawtha, didn't you?"

"Yes." The answer was barely audible and the president of the court admonished him to speak up. "Yes!" Johnson said again, loudly and heatedly.

"And didn't you," Boone pressed, "say exactly the same thing on a number of occasions after your return to Boonesborough? Didn't you, in fact, say it the day before this court-martial began?"

"Yes!"

Boone smiled. "Well, I'm glad we got that settled. Let's move along. You got mad at me, Andy, because you were caught shirking your work and I wouldn't let you get away with it. And even then you fooled us some more, didn't you, and still managed to get yourself the easiest job of all— feeding the fires and staying nice and warm while the others were out in the snow swinging axes or using saws or hauling wood, right?"

"I ain't very big," Johnson protested. "It's all I c'd do!"

"That's what you had us all believing, sure enough," Boone admitted, "but seems as how you were pretending again. There were men bigger than you by far who nearly died on the way to Chalahgawtha, and some of them were carrying less than you, ain't that so?"

"I carried my share!" Johnson spat out the words. "That was more'n you done, Boone!"

Daniel Boone was unruffled. He tugged at his earlobe and shook his head. "You surprised us, Andy, I got to admit that. You toted that hundred pounds of bear meat like it just wasn't much at all. I sure got to admire the way you can fool folks. Now, as I recollect from what you told Colonel Bowman before, when he was first talking to you, you said I told Black Fish it'd be easy for him to take Boonesborough?"

Johnson was visibly relieved to be getting away from the subject of his fooling people and he answered quickly, bobbing his head rapidly. "Yep, that's what you said."

"When?"

"Huh?"

"*When* did I tell Black Fish it'd be easier to take Boonesborough?"

Johnson was clever in trying to skirt the answer Boone was seeking. "Right then, you tol' 'im, Boone. We was all a-standin' there an' heard you sayin' it."

Boone sighed. "Andy, let me put it to you in another way. How many Indians were in that party that took us?"

"'Bout a hunnerd an' twenny, I reckon."

"And how many of our people had we left behind us to defend Boonesborough?"

"Eighty."

Boone shook his head with a little show of irritation. "C'mon now, Andy—I said to *defend* Boonesborough. I ain't talking about women and children. How many?"

"Thutty," Johnson grunted. "They was fifty women an' girls there."

"Thirty," Boone repeated. "Sounds like a pretty respectable force . . . but maybe not. You know, it's like pulling teeth to get clear answers out of you. Of them thirty, Andy, how many were men—able-bodied, experienced *men* who could fight Indians?"

Johnson was hemmed in and so he simply shrugged and said, "Ten men, I reckon. The other twenny was boys."

"So at the time when we were taken at our camp by about a hundred and twenty Indians, who were then all set to come against Boonesborough, this fort only had ten able men and some inexperienced boys to defend fifty women and girls and this whole fort?"

"Yep."

"And at that time Boonesborough only had three walls and two blockhouses and wasn't in any shape to protect itself even if it had a hundred fighting men?"

"I reckon."

"All right, when the Indians took us, where were they heading for? We both know that they didn't come to catch us saltmakers at the Blue Licks, 'cause that surprised them as much as it surprised us. They were right then on the march against Boonesborough, weren't they?"

"That's what they said."

"And what did I tell them about their chances of taking Boonesborough after they'd taken us?"

"That it'd be easy for 'em to take."

"*When*, Andy? *When* did I say it would be easy for them to take it?"

"Right then, when they caught us, was when you said it!" Johnson was very adroit at sidestepping Boone and the defendant for the first time appealed to the court.

"Mr. President, is it all right for me to state certain things to Andy Johnson here and then ask him to answer yes or no?"

"What you're asking, Captain Boone," Colonel Trabue replied, "is if it is allowable for you to lead the witness. In this particular case, since you have already shown through testimony that the witness is hostile to you, it is permitted."

"Thank you, sir," Boone said. "All right, Andy, just answer me yes or no. Did I tell Black Fish that we had four companies of soldiers here at the fort?"

"Yep," said Johnson reluctantly.

"Didn't I tell him that he couldn't possibly take the fort right then?"

"Yep."

"Didn't I also tell him that later on, in late spring or toward summer, after the soldiers were gone again, Boonesborough would be weaker and could be taken then without much trouble?"

"Yep."

"And didn't I say that if they came after Boonesborough when it was warmer weather they wouldn't' have the trouble getting all the women and children to Chalahgawtha that they'd have in freezing weather like we were having—even assuming they could take the fort from all the soldiers I claimed were guarding it?"

"That's what you tol' 'em."

"And ain't it true that if they *had* marched on Boonesborough right away, they'd have taken it; but that when Boonesborough realized we'd been captured and had time to make repairs to the fort and get in extra men, they'd probably be able to hold, as they eventually did?"

"Yep." Very grudgingly.

"If I hadn't been able to convince them otherwise, they would've come against Boonesborough right away, ain't that right?"

Johnson sighed. "That's right."

"Could the women and children here have survived the march we were forced to make to Chalahgawtha?"

"Not many of 'em," Johnson said, shaking his head.

"Then there was a good reason for me convincing Black Fish and his party as I did that they could take Boonesborough easy later on, but not right then?"

"I reckon you might say that," Johnson muttered.

At the prosecution table Colonel Bowman was sitting straighter and frowning, seemingly lost in a mental reassessment of the defendant, at whom he was staring intently. The previous untalkative Boone was suddenly being disturbingly vocal.

Behind Daniel Boone, at the defense table, Jim Harrod nudged Sam Henderson with an elbow and when Henderson looked at him, raised his brows in an expression of approving surprise. Henderson's own expression didn't change but one eyelid flicked in a rapid wink. His lips hardly moved as he murmured, "Uh-huh . . . but where does he go from here?"

The defendant stood a few feet away from Johnson now, appraising him. "Andy," he said, "a little ways back you said you carried your share on the way north with the Indians, which was more than I had done, right?"

"Damn right!"

"You're saying that when the Indians divvied out the parcels for carrying, I wasn't given any?"

Johnson hesitated. "Well," he said at length, "when we started north you wasn't carryin' none, like the rest of us was."

"Didn't one of the warriors—a buck named Red Fox—try to make me carry a big brass cooking kettle plumb full of bear lard?"

The little frontiersman nodded, muttering an affirmative.

"And when I refused and threw it down and he began to get mean about it, what happened?"

"You got Black Fish t'come 'twixt you an' say you didn't have t'carry no load."

"How did I do that? What happened between me and Red Fox?"

"You shoved 'im away."

"Shoved him? Wasn't it a mite more'n that?"

"I reckon."

"Didn't I hit him?"

"Yep, you hit 'im."

"Hard?"

"I reckon."

"How hard, Andy?"

Boone waited and when Johnson didn't reply other than with a vague shrug, he repeated himself more demandingly. "How hard, Andy?"

"Dammit, Boone, you knocked 'im ass over teakettle, that's how hard!"

Anticipating some sort of comment from the court as raucous guffaws broke out in the gallery, Boone continued quickly. "Where was Black Fish when this happened?"

"'Bout ten feet away, watchin'."

"And what did he do?"

Johnson shook his head as if still not able to believe what had happened. "I reckoned he'd kill you right then, but instead the damn' red nigger clapped his han's an' laughed fit t'bust, an' all the others was a-laughin', too, 'cept Red Fox."

"But Black Fish sent him away?"

"Yep, an' said as how you didn't haft'a carry nothin'."

"Now be careful how you answer this one, Andy. Did I carry nothing?"

Andrew Johnson paused and licked his lips, thinking. "Fer a spell."

"How long?"

Johnson shrugged. He seemed to know what was coming and didn't like it, but knew of no way to avoid it. Boone crossed his arms and looked down at him. "At the end of the first mile I took someone's load and carried it for about half an hour, didn't I? Whose load was it, Andy?"

Johnson's reply was so soft that not even the president of the court could hear and Trabue instantly snapped at him. "The witness will speak out clearly in answer to all questions."

Johnson nodded dolefully and responded loudly. "Mine."

"Yours," Boone agreed. "That's right. And after yours for half an hour, didn't I take Ansel Goodman's load for half an hour also?"

"Yep."

"And after Goodman's, Joe Jackson's, and then George Hendrick's?"

"I reckon."

"Isn't it true, Mr. Johnson," Boone went on quietly, addressing the witness by his surname for the first time, "that throughout the march which lasted for ten days, I was not again without someone's load except for the brief moments it took to return one man's load to him and go to another to relieve him?"

"I s'pose that's right."

"Didn't quite a few of our men openly admit by the time we neared Chalahgawtha that had it not been for the relief thus afforded, they just couldn't have made it?"

"I reckon I heered some of 'em sayin' that."

Boone nodded. "I guess you did, since I recollect that you were one of those who said it. Now, there were two men whose loads were carried for them more than the others. Who were they?"

"Anse Goodman for one. He had a swole ankle from a log what rolled on 'im an' couldn't walk so purty good."

"And the other?"

Johnson glared at Boone and didn't reply. The defendant formed the answer for him. "Isn't it true, Mr. Johnson, that it was yourself—because you were so small and all of us at that time still believed you to be weak?"

"All right!" Johnson practically shouted. "So it was mine! So what?"

"Nothing, Mr. Johnson," Boone said lightly. "Nothing at all. Just wanted to establish that little point clearly." He turned and took a step or two toward the defense table, as if he were finished, but then abruptly stopped and turned. He stood with his moccasined feet in a fairly widespread stance and his arms akimbo, his head cocked slightly to one side.

"Before I let you go, Andy, reckon I might as well clear up one other little bit of misleading you did while Colonel Bowman was questioning you. You said everyone had to run the gauntlet at Chalahgawtha when we got there except me, didn't you?"

Johnson rolled his eyes toward the prosecutor in a tight-faced, silent appeal, but Bowman merely continued fingering his heavy moustache as he had been doing for the past several minutes. In a moment the witness looked back at Boone and dipped his head in affirmation.

"Shaking or nodding the head cannot be accepted as responses, Mr. Johnson," Trabue spoke up. "You will please answer by voice the questions which are put to you."

"All of us run the gauntlet at the village," Johnson said slowly. "You didn't. That's what I tol' him." He jerked his head toward Bowman.

Boone gave a little laugh and reached up to scratch the short hair on the right side of his head just below the long tuft of crown hair. "Doggone," he said pleasantly, "you know something? If I didn't know better and was sitting up there with all the officers of this court, why I'd probably figure like they're probably figuring right now—that it sure is mighty queer that everybody had to run a gauntlet but ol' Boone. Sure would sort of tend to make 'em not feel too kindly toward me, now wouldn't it? But you and me, Andy, we know a little different, don't we? And I reckon," he added meaningfully, sweeping a hand out toward the spectators, "Willie Hancock and W. B. Bruther, sitting out there, do too, don't they? So then, just not to leave any wrong ideas behind us, reckon I'd better ask a few more questions."

He took a step or two closer to Johnson. "You seem to remember my talks with Chief Black Fish pretty well. Do you recollect how mad I got with him when we got to Chalahgawtha and I saw all the villagers come out and start setting up the gauntlet lines?"

"Yep, you was peeved some, I reckon," Johnson said warily.

"You remember, too, then that I argued about it in English with him while old black Pompey interpreted?"

"Yep."

"Then I'd like you to tell everybody what I was saying, and what Pompey said the chief's answer was."

With every word begrudged, Johnson answered slowly. "You reminded him of the promise he made to you when you was first tooken by 'em, 'fore you led 'em back to camp."

"Which was?"

"That you had surrendered us to 'im only on Black Fish's word that he wouldn't let his party torture us er make us run the gauntlet, an' that now you was seein' that Black Fish's promises was empty an' not t'be trusted."

"And what was his answer?"

"He laughed fit t'bust an' said as t'how he was still livin' up t'his promise, which was that his war party wouldn't run us through the gauntlet, but that this here p'ticular gauntlet wasn't bein' set up by his war party, but by the villagers an' he hadn't said nothin' 'bout them. He sure was tickled over the look you give 'im!"

Boone laughed with what seemed to be genuine delight. "He tricked me all right, but he hadn't really broken his promise like I thought he had at first. Matter of fact, it wasn't really much of a gauntlet, was it? Mostly squaws and children and old men, and too cold to be standing out there in the wind and snow trying to whip a running man. Was anyone hurt?"

With his characteristic hunching movement, Johnson shrugged again. "Not to speak of. Few of the boys tooken a couple hard licks, but nothin' that caused no damage."

Boone nodded. "But that wasn't the first time I argued with Black Fish about the gauntlet, was it? What happened in our own salt camp the first afternoon of our capture?"

Johnson gave a little groan as he replied. "Black Fish set up gauntlet lines of his men."

"How did I act about that?"

"You was damn' mad, that's how," Johnson replied, "'cause you thought 'twas fer us an' that Black Fish had lied 'bout promisin' not t'make us run the gauntlet of his war party."

"And what was the chief's answer that time?"

For the first time since Boone had begun questioning him, Johnson grinned faintly. "Said he wa'nt breakin' no promise— that he had tol' you your men wouldn't haft' a run through a gauntlet by his men, but that he hadn't said nothin' 'bout you runnin' one."

"Then that gauntlet was for me?"

"Yep."

"And did I run it?"

"Yep."

"How many warriors formed the lines?"

"Oh, I reckon fifty-four, fifty-five each side. Four or five had t'keep guard over the rest of us."

"Was it a more dangerous gauntlet than the one that was later set up at Chalahgawtha?"

"Warriors is usually stronger an' faster'n squaws an' kids an' ol' men," Johnson grunted.

"How did I go through the lines?"

"Like a bat out'a hell, that's how, jiggin' an' jaggin' from side t'side t'keep from gettin' hit so much, but you took some purty good clubbin's, Boone."

Remembering, Boone nodded with a grimace. "Did anything unusual occur as I ran through?"

Again Johnson grinned, this time more broadly as he, too, remembered. "I reckon it did! That buck, Red Fox, he jest don't learn too good."

"What did he do?"

"Why, he stepped out squar' in the middle an' tried t'block you. By damn," he chortled, "you jest lowered yore head an' butted him in the gut so hard he was out for half an' hour. That son of a bitch was still rubbin' his sore belly when we got t'Chalahgawtha!"

Amidst the laughter this brought on, Colonel Trabue rapped his gavel and again rebuked the witness over his language, admonishing him to refrain from using such profanity.

"Yes, sir," Johnson said, nodding apologetically, "I sure as hell will."

Again the laughter swelled and Trabue looked at him sharply for a long moment but said nothing more. As the crowd noises died away, Boone continued.

"How did the other warriors in the line act when this happened?"

"Hell, Dan'l, you know how. They was laughin' so hard they couldn't hardly swing at you no more as you passed 'em. An' when you finished they all crowded 'round laughin' an' jokin' and shakin' your han'. Ol' Black Fish, he really thunk you was somethin'!"

The levity was suddenly gone from Boone and he eyed the little man coldly. "I've nothing more to say to you," he said. He turned his back and returned to the defense table where he sat down to the right of Harrod and Henderson, who immediately leaned forward to whisper to him. Both were smiling and Henderson thumped Boone's forearm on the table approvingly with his fist.

"Does prosecution have anything for this witness on redirect?" Colonel Trabue inquired.

"Yes, Mr. President," John Bowman replied. He moved toward the witness and said, "Only a few points, Mr. Johnson, if you please. Captain Boone has, in his very homey way, made it seem to the members of this court that he has refuted all your earlier testimony given during direct examination. We need to make clear that he has not done so. Is it not true that Daniel Boone failed to take such elementary defensive steps at the saltmaking camp as posting a regular guard to warn of approaching danger?"

"That's right."

"And did not Captain Boone voluntarily lead the Indians to the camp of the saltmakers and force his own men to surrender to them without making any attempt whatsoever to defend themselves?"

"Yep."

"And was he not on familiar grounds with the Shawnees and receive favorable treatment from them at virtually all times?"

"He was and he did."

"And did he not volunteer to aid Chief Black Fish and his warriors in the plan for a subsequent attack against Boonesborough?"

"Yep."

"And were not all his actions in those circumstances, in your full understanding of what constitutes such a crime, nothing less than acts of treason?"

"Yes, sir!"

"Thank you very much, Mr. Johnson. Prosecution has no further questions of this witness on redirect."

To the spectators, who had been closely following every word and were now whispering excitedly among themselves, it seemed that in one fell swoop the extremely able Colonel John Bowman had just demolished the entire morning's effort by Daniel Boone.

II

Immediately after John Bowman had finished his brief but devastating redirect examination of Andrew Hezekiah Johnson, the witness was excused and Daniel Boone requested the return of William Hancock to the witness chair. Again there was a sense of disappointment among the spectators who had expected Captain Callaway to be called. The judge advocate made the call and Hancock took his place, reminded that he was yet under oath.

For some time Boone studied Hancock from his own seat at the defense table. A big, broad-shouldered man, Hancock was far more the stylized picture of what a frontiersman should look like than was Boone. Hancock's features, well-formed though craggy, were quite manly, and framed beneath dense black hair that had seen neither comb nor scissors in many months, yet had fallen into its own pattern of growth in a rather attractive way. His small ears were nearly hidden by it and the heavy beard like a dense black matting merged without break with the hair of his head in front of his ears and at the rear of his jaws. He looked strong and tough until one saw his eyes, and there the whole aspect changed. They were a little too small, a fraction too close-set, wholly lacking in depth, entirely incapable of penetration. They were a mottled greenish-brown, darker than olive and yet not really brown. They were, in essence, muddy-colored. They also moved constantly, rarely touching the eyes of the individual to whom he spoke, or who might be speaking to him. More than anywhere else, he kept them directed toward the ground a few feet in front of him, imparting a perpetual hangdog attitude. In times of emotional stress, the fleshy node on his right temple tended to turn from a sickly ivory color to pink, and at this moment it was so suffused with that color that he seemed at first glance to have a wild rose pinned to the side of his head.

Boone approached him thoughtfully, unsmiling. Even when he stopped a few feet in front of him, the defendant said nothing for several seconds and the bearded man's nervousness increased.

"Well, Willie," Boone began casually, "I never figured you'd be able to get away."

"I don't doubt that, Boone, elsewise you'd not've told me all them things you said."

"If I'd known you'd get away, Willie," Daniel Boone corrected enigmatically and without warmth, "I'd probably have told you a lot more. You came here to Boonesborough from Savannah, right?"

"That's right."

"And before Savannah, New York?"

"Right."

"And before that, from Boston?"

"Yeah."

"Why did you leave Boston?"

The question seemed to startle Hancock and he was silent for a moment or two before mumbling, "'Cause I got tired of the place."

"You couldn't go back there, could you?"

"Huh?"

"Didn't you leave Massachusetts because there was a warrant outstanding for your arrest on charges of horse theft?"

"Objection!" Bowman was on his feet and angry. "Mr. President," he said, "not only is the question irrelevant and immaterial, it calls for a self-incriminatory response from the witness. May I remind the court that it is Captain Boone who is on trial here, not Mr. Hancock."

"What is the purpose of your present line of questioning, Captain Boone?" Trabue asked.

"Reckon it's sort of important to me, Colonel, to point out the kind of feller Hancock is before getting to the matter of what he claimed about me when Colonel Bowman was talking to him."

"Will knowledge of the character of the witness have direct bearing on the evidence you intend to elicit from him through your cross-examination?"

"Yes, sir," Boone replied. "Reckon it's going to amount to the whole making or breaking of what he said earlier."

Colonel Trabue considered this in silence for almost half a minute and then cleared his throat. "While it is true," he commented, "as Colonel Bowman has pointed out, that the witness is not on trial here, the defendant does have the right to establish certain facts dealing with the character and credibility of the witness. If there is, in fact, a warrant of arrest in effect for Mr. Hancock in Massachusetts, his admission of that is not necessarily an admission of guilt to the crime for which the warrant was issued, and so his reply to the question is therefore not self-incriminatory. However, if his departure from Massachusetts was predicated upon the fact that such a warrant was outstanding against him, his admission of such flight could be deemed, in effect, an admission of guilt. Would Captain Boone care to rephrase his question?"

Boone nodded, but waited until John Bowman had reseated himself before continuing. "Is there, to your knowledge," he asked Hancock, "a warrant for your arrest outstanding in Massachusetts?"

Hancock's temple growth had become a very deep pink now and he nodded. "Yes," he said, "but I ain't guilty of what it charges."

"Is there a warrant out against you at this time in New·York?" Boone asked.

"Well, yes," Hancock admitted, "but I ain't guilty of that, neither."

"Maybe," Boone said, "but what about Georgia? Ain't it true that when you came here to Boonesborough, you openly bragged about killing a couple of blacks in Savannah, which is why you had to leave there so fast?"

"Do I have to answer that, your Honor?" Hancock appealed to Trabue.

"If such admission was publicly made by you prior to this time, then the defendant's question must be answered."

Hancock's eyes returned to the floor in front of him. "It's what I said," he admitted, "but it ain't true. I was just talkin' so's people would look up to me. I ain't never kilt nobody— not even niggers."

Trabue was now frowning at Boone. "It seems to me," he said, "that the defendant has strayed quite far afield with this witness. I see no relevance to the issue at hand and must now direct that you leave this line of questioning and either apply yourself more to the matter of cross-examination or else excuse the witness."

"What I've been getting at, Colonel," Boone said, "is that some things I've known about Hancock's background for a long time don't sit too well with me. Now these things," he added hastily, as Bowman seemed about to interpose a comment, "may or may not be true. I don't much care one way or another. Most of them I heard from Willie himself, and some from others who say he told them. The point is, they ain't the sort of things that, once hearing them, would incline me to confide in him *anything* that I'd want to be kept a secret. Now I ain't denying that I told him what he claims I told him up in Detroit. I did. But I did it for a purpose. I told him because I knew he had a tongue that couldn't keep from flapping and that as sure as I told him something he figured was a secret, it wouldn't be long before everyone around knew it, too."

"Is this court to understand then," Trabue began, but suddenly broke off and began anew. "You are not presently sworn, Captain Boone, and you are not required to answer this question if you do not care to, but the court is curious. Are we to understand that you deliberately told Mr. Hancock the things he testified to under direct examination because you knew that he would broadcast those same statements to others, including this court?"

Boone hesitated. "Well, sir," he admitted, "I have to say that I didn't think Hancock had the know-how to get away up there and make it back here to Boonesborough, so I never really figured he'd be telling anybody *here*. It was up at Detroit that I expected he'd be wagging his tongue, and that was what I wanted."

"I see," Trabue said slowly. "Do you wish to explain now why you should have made such an extraordinary move at the time?"

"Reckon I'd rather wait a little while before I get to that, Colonel."

"That is your choice, Captain. Proceed."

"I have only one other thing to cover with him, Colonel." Boone looked again at Hancock, who was glaring at him angrily. "Willie, you told Colonel Bowman when he was questioning you that I received gifts in Detroit from General Hamilton and some of the other British officers there, right?"

"That's right. And, by God, you can't weasel out of that, Boone, 'cause I saw them things with my own eyes!"

"What did you see, Willie?"

"I seen plenty, that's what! I seen that nice horse they give you, 'long with the fancy saddle an' bridle an' so on. I seen blankets you got, an' clothes, too—good warm wools straight from London, shirts an' pants an' such. I seen 'em, all right, an' you can't deny it."

"I don't intend to deny it, Willie. But there was more than that, wasn't there? What else did I get from them?"

"Food for one thing. My God, they give you foods like you was visitin' royalty, 'stead of a pris'ner. Whilst the rest of us was locked in a room an' had to eat stale bread an' old meat an' drink water, you was gettin' cakes an' fancy breads an' wine. An' good brandy an' meats an' all sorts of foods cooked like I never tasted afore. They give you all kinds of—"

"Hold it!" Boone's words abruptly chopped off what Hancock was saying. "Back up a little, Willie. Foods like what?"

Hancock wrinkled his brow. "Well, like I said, foods like meats an'—"

"No," Boone interjected, "you said all sorts of foods cooked like you never tasted before?"

"That's right. We don't get fancy things like that down here in Boonesborough. Bettern' anything I ever..." His words suddenly trailed off as he finally realized what he was saying and he clamped his lips together in a tight line.

"You ate some of those foods, then?" Boone asked.

"Some," Hancock admitted. "You give me some."

"What about the clothing? Did I give you some of that, too?"

"Uh-huh." Hancock was suddenly reluctant to elaborate.

"And the blankets?"

"Yeah." Hancock's voice was hardly a whisper.

"Witness will speak up," directed the president of the court.

"He give me one," Hancock said loudly.

"What about the other ten men who were taken to Detroit with us, Willie?"

"What about 'em?" Hancock pretended not to understand.

"Did they also get some of the food and clothing and blankets that were given to me?"

"I think so."

"You *think* so! Willie, you danged well *know* so! Ain't it true that everything that was given to me but the horse, bridle and saddle I gave to you and the other ten to divide among yourselves?"

"Yeah."

"Did I keep any of the food and drink?"

"Not that I saw."

"Did I keep any of the blankets or clothes?"

"Nope."

"What did I do with them?"

"You give 'em to us."

"That's right, Willie. What about the horse and bridle and saddle? What about the silver trinkets you said were given to me? What did I do with them?"

"Give 'em back," Hancock mumbled, the words almost lost in his beard.

"Say it again, louder," Boone demanded.

"You give 'em back," Hancock brayed. "Damn dumbest

thing ever I seen. You give 'em back. Hell, that horse alone was worth fifty pounds!"

Boone stepped back and looked toward the bar. "I've got nothing more to ask from him, Colonel," he said. He strode back to the defense table.

"Does prosecution have anything on redirect?" Trabue asked Bowman.

The judge advocate brought his hand down from his moustache which he'd been preening and nodded. He spoke to the witness without rising from his seat.

"Mr. Hancock," he said, "how long have you known Daniel Boone?"

"Oh, couple years, I reckon, more'r less."

"Do you feel you know him pretty well—that is, his character and habits and manner of expressing himself?"

"I reckon."

"Mr. Hancock, Captain Boone would have this court believe that he used you as a dupe. Do you agree?"

"As a what?"

"Do you feel it is true that Captain Boone didn't trust you; that the only real reason he sought you out specifically and told you the things he admits he told you was because he thought you would betray his confidence?"

Hancock still did not fully comprehend Bowman's meaning and he shook his head. "No, sir! If ever I seen a man serious an' meanin' what he said, it was Boone. He picked me out'a all the others to tell what was goin' on 'cause he said he knew he could trust me. He even said he didn't have to ask me to give my word not to tell nobody else what he was tellin' me—that's how much he trusted me. No, sir, he sure didn't figger that word'd *ever* get out 'bout what he was tellin' Hamilton."

Bowman sighed audibly and addressed the bar. "No further questions, Mr. President."

"The witness is excused," Trabue said. "Defense may continue with its next witness under cross-examination."

There was a general shuffling and whispering among the spectators as Walter Bruther, the next witness for cross-examination, was called for by Boone, reminded of his oath by Bowman, and reseated. At a tap from Trabue's gavel, the noise ceased.

Although Walter Bruther effected a sense of composure, he was decidedly nervous. Daniel Boone had turned out to be considerably more formidable in cross-examination than anyone had expected and since, aside from Callaway's testimony, Bruther's had been longest and probably even more damaging, he was apprehensive about what manner of counterattack the defendant would launch. He was therefore shocked by Boone's opening remark to him.

"Mr. Bruther," Boone said pleasantly, "I have to say right at the start here that I believe you are a very good and honest man, and I don't know of one thing you said up here under questioning that wasn't true."

Bruther's eyes widened and he stared open-mouthed at Boone.

"I don't aim to keep you sitting here for too long," the frontiersman continued, "but there are a couple of small points you mentioned that I'd sort of like to develop a little more."

"Yes, sir?" Bruther said.

Boone scratched his jaw and jerked his head sharply to swing his trailing topknot of hair back behind his ear. He smiled at Bruther and spoke apologetically. "Still can't quite get used to this danged scalplock hanging down," he said. "I'll be glad when the rest grows out again all the way so I can feel more natural. Now, what I want to ask you about is something you mentioned that happened after I left Chalahgawtha. You said there were a couple of white men— French, but in British service—who you overheard talking about artillery which they'd brought along from Detroit to use against Boonesborough?"

"Yes, sir."

"And that they were complaining that Chief Black Fish told them they should leave the swivels there at the village?"

"Yes, sir. Evidently the chief had argued that the big guns would slow their progress on the march, especially when it came to rafting across the Ohio River."

"When they first showed up at the village with the two pieces, Mr. Bruther, did they say anything about them in particular . . . like maybe what they could do to a fortification or anything like that?"

Bruther pursed his lips as he concentrated. "Well," he said, "there was a good bit of excitement in Chalahgawtha when they showed up with them. As you know, the Shawnees are very much in awe of cannon. Most of them had never before seen one at close range and they were very interested in them. There was a lot of clamoring for a demonstration."

"Did the whites shoot one for them?"

"As a matter of fact they did, Captain. Their leader, Captain De Quindre, had one of them set up and primed and then aimed at an outcropping of rock overhanging the Little Miami River. The rock was already cracked and the captain evidently thought that a good solid hit would knock it all apart and impress the Shawnees."

"Did it?"

Bruther grinned. "As it turned out, the shot missed the rock entirely. Instead it hit a large oak tree growing up next to the cliff, exactly where the first big limb was growing out of the trunk. It shattered the limb in quite a dramatic manner, causing it to drop into the river with a big splash. I guess the Indians thought the cannon had actually been aimed at the branch and so they were extremely impressed. They did quite a bit of shrieking and jumping around. I heard De Quindre at that time tell Chief Black Fish that the same effect could be expected when the cannonball would strike the uprights of the fort. He meant Boonesborough, of course."

"Did they say that General Hamilton had ordered the artillery brought along?"

"Not right then, sir, but later on I did hear one of the other men—Lieutenant Drouilliard, I believe—saying he was glad they had finally persuaded the general to let them bring along the two 'convincers.'"

"Hamilton hadn't wanted them to take artillery at first?"

"Evidently not, sir." He hesitated, as if embarrassed, then went on. "From what I gather, General Hamilton had contended that such pieces would be absolutely unnecessary, since according to the agreement he had made with you, Boonesborough would be surrendered without resistance as soon as the general's letters were presented to you, either there at Chalahgawtha or at Boonesborough."

A broad smile was creasing the features of John Bowman as he leaned back in his chair at the prosecution table. That Boone had been able to do some damage to the testimony of both Johnson and Hancock had not been too great a surprise to him. With a man of the intelligence of Walter Bruther, however, he was obviously only digging his own grave a little deeper, and the judge advocate was pleased.

"But they brought the big guns anyway?" Boone was asking.

"Yes, sir. I take it that they convinced the general that it wouldn't hurt to have them along just in case. It seems, though, that they had been given instructions that whether or not they would take the cannon beyond Chalahgawtha would depend on how Chief Black Fish felt about it. The governor-general apparently wanted to make sure that no slightest hint of insult be made where the Indians were concerned. His instructions were that if Black Fish were convinced the artillery would be unnecessary, then his word was to be final."

"Was there any other reason given by Chief Black Fish to the whites for not taking the artillery, other than just that they'd slow them down?"

"I personally did not hear any other reason, sir, but later on, after they were gone, I heard bits and pieces of conversations among the Indians still there at Chalahgawtha and got the impression that the chief was so positive of your promises to him about surrendering Boonesborough that he ordered them left in the village. For one thing, he was sure you would be justifiably insulted when you came out of the fort to negotiate with them and saw that cannon had been brought."

James Harrod and Samuel Henderson, at the defense table, looked at one another in stunned disbelief. It was Henderson who puffed out his cheeks and exhaled a gust of wind. "Our Daniel," he muttered heavily, "is one hell of an attorney . . . for the prosecution!" Harrod grunted and made a faint motion with his head toward the bar. Henderson swiveled his head and saw what Harrod had—that a good number of the members of the court were whispering to one another and several others were jotting down notes on the papers in front of them. There seemed to be no doubt that in the cross-examination of Bruther, Boone was accruing testimony at least as damaging to himself as that which Bowman had elicited from the same witness.

Boone had paused and stepped a little distance away from the witness chair. He was lost in thought, with a distant expression in his eyes as he weighed something. Still the silence stretched out and a shifting of the onlookers became audible, along with whisperings from them.

"Is Captain Boone finished with his cross-examination of this witness?" Colonel Trabue finally asked.

Boone shook himself free from his thoughts and smiled crookedly. "No, sir," he said, "just trying to figure something. Sorry to keep you waiting. I'm ready now." He faced the witness again. "Mr. Bruther, I'd appreciate it if you'd tell the court some more about the way you said I was fixing up the guns for the Indians."

Bruther was puzzled. "The repairs you were making? I've already testified to that, Captain Boone."

"Reckon there ain't no doubt about that," Boone said ironically, grinning with the short wave of laughter the comment brought. "But what I think you ought to tell them is more about what I was actually doing."

Not sure yet that he was comprehending Boone's meaning, Bruther frowned. "Do you mean, sir, that you wish me to tell them more specifically about the various *types* of repairs you were making?"

"Yep."

Henderson groaned and slumped in his seat. "Double damn me for an idiot," he hissed to Harrod, "but I'm beginning to think this son of a bitchin' friend of ours is actually *trying* to get himself hanged. For God's sake, he doesn't seem to understand even the most fundamental precepts of cross-examination . . . or defense!"

Harrod was still looking at the defendant and witness and his reply was so soft that Henderson could barely hear it. "Could be," he said. "Then again, Sam, maybe it's just that he knows what he's doing and we don't. Let's hope so."

"Many of the stocks of the rifles you were repairing were cracked, Captain Boone," Bruther was saying, "and a number were completely broken at the narrow part—the grip, I guess you'd call it. I remember you telling me that they'd gotten that way because the Indians tended to use their guns for clubbing about as much as for shooting. Anyway, those that were cracked in the stock you were wrapping with wet stretched rawhide strippings so when they dried and tightened, they'd hold the stock together firmly. Those completely broken, you bored holes in each side of, and inserted wooden pegs, fitted the pieces together, and then firmly wrapped them with rawhide as you did the others."

"You're a good observer, Walter," Boone said. "What else?"

"Well, in quite a few cases the sights were bent or broken off. Those that were bent you heated and bent back into their proper position. Those that had broken off you replaced with makeshift sights you whittled from wood. On each of the weapons you made very sure that the pan was clean and straight, that the flash port was open all the way and not caked with grime, so that the charge inside would be sure to ignite when the flash in the pan occurred. You also made sure that the flints were in good shape and replaced all that were not. Where the trigger mechanism was concerned, you disassembled each one and made sure all parts, from hammer cock to trigger, were clean and that all rust or corrosion had been filed away. You must've cleaned three hundred like this, counting those brought in by the war party that was with you when you returned from the Scioto. When they were all good and clean, you lubricated each mechanism carefully with clear bear oil and reassembled them. Twice, as I recall, you discarded guns because the barrels had been bent or squeezed together too badly for any kind of repairs—from their having been used as levers, you said. Also, on each gun you checked, you bored small holes on the bottom of the forepiece and stock for attaching rawhide straps as carrying slings, which Black Fish thought was a good idea, but then which you finally decided you couldn't do because the wooden plugs you planned to use for anchoring the straps just wouldn't stay in place like metal buckles that could be screwed in. I must say again, sir, that you worked extremely hard on these guns and repaired them very well under the conditions. When you were finished, you fired two test shots out of each one."

"What was done with these guns when I was finished fixing them?" Boone asked.

"The majority were stored under heavy guard until it was time for them to be put into use against Boonesborough."

"Thank you, Mr. Bruther. I think that's all."

"Prosecution?" asked Trabue as Boone returned to his seat.

Bowman was content to leave well enough alone. "No redirect, Mr. President," he said.

"Then defense may call its next witness on cross-examination."

There was a decided stir in the gallery, a quickening of interest, a sudden intake of breaths in anticipation. Now, surely, it was Captain Richard Callaway's turn to be questioned by the man he had accused. At that moment Boone was listening quietly to urgently whispered comments from both Harrod and Henderson, calm in the face of their agitation. Both of them glanced at intervals at Boone's principal accuser.

Callaway himself, still seated at the prosecution table between Colonel Logan and Colonel Bowman, straightened in his chair, bracing himself for the calling of his name. This was the moment he had dreaded most. His features were grimly set and he had steeled himself for a most unpleasant session. John Bowman had warned him far in advance that Boone would almost certainly do everything in his power to make Callaway out to be a liar, motivated by personal hatred, vengeance, jealousy, vindictiveness or anything else he could think of, and that even though these things were not true, it was bound to be an angering and demoralizing period. Bowman had firmly cautioned Callaway against being baited into losing his temper, regardless of what Daniel Boone said or what fantastic charges the defendant might fling at him. The man would be fighting for his life, utilizing every trick he could devise, and so Callaway would be well advised to take the questioning in stride, as unperturbedly as possible and, in all cases, answering to questions with the greatest possible degree of brevity. The principal thought Callaway had to bear in mind, Bowman assured him, was that Daniel Boone was the guilty individual here and that it was only a matter of time until he would be sentenced and hanged. Nevertheless, despite all the instructions, encouragements and assurances, the portly Richard Callaway was very nervous. At the moment he was looking unseeingly at the witness chair, but a motion at the defense table made him shift and sharpen his gaze.

It was not Daniel Boone but rather James Harrod who had stood and faced the bar. "Mr. President," he said quietly, "defense has no further cross-examination."

Trabue's answer was instantaneous and sharp, cutting through the gasp from the spectators. "You've discussed this with the defendant?"

"It is the defendant's own wish, Mr. President. It is, I might add, against the advice of both Mr. Henderson and myself. However, we have been given no choice."

Trabue's slow head-shaking expressed his own silent disapproval. "I would hope, " he said, "that Captain Boone at least intends to question some witnesses for the defense."

"He does, Mr. President."

Trabue glanced quickly at his watch. "There is still time. Let him begin." He shook his head again faintly as Harrod turned away. In his entire career as an officer, he'd never encountered any situation even remotely like this.

III

As Daniel Boone prepared to call his first witness for the defense, the air of disappointment that overhung the gallery was pervasive. The testimony that had been given by Captain Richard Callaway against Boone to open this court-martial had been extremely detrimental to the frontiersman. Those who had clung to some badly undernourished belief or hope that Boone was not guilty and had looked forward with a peculiar desperation to the moment when Boone would lock horns with him and perhaps nullify at least some of the charges Callaway had made were deeply disheartened. Those who were convinced of Boone's guilt had also looked forward to an interchange between the men, sure that Boone would not be able to do anything to change Callaway's testimony and that when it was over, Boone would have become even more inextricably knotted in the web of his own guilt. Boone certainly hadn't been able to change or even soften any of the damning points that W. B. Bruther had testified to against him, so they were sure he wouldn't be able to do so with Dick Callaway, but they had nevertheless looked forward to seeing him try. Now the very fact that he was not going to call Callaway at all reinforced the belief of those who considered him guilty and caused those few who had still hoped he would somehow be able to extricate himself from this impossible mess to practically give up.

Given leave by the court, Boone talked briefly with James Harrod and Samuel Henderson as the gallery hummed with whispered conversation and the court waited patiently. John Bowman was talking softly with Callaway, who still wore an expression of shocked disbelief. The nauseating dread that had been in the principal witness earlier over having to be cross-examined by Boone was slowly being replaced by a savage satisfaction, a sense of jubilation and triumph. Indeed, Boone seemed to be where they wanted him and Callaway assured Bowman that there was no one the defendant could call as defense witness who could possibly get him out of the box he was in. Bowman did not appear so sure. To large measure, he realized, he had grossly underestimated Boone's ability in handling himself before the bar. The frontiersman had done much damage to Andrew Johnson's testimony and Bowman had been only barely able to salvage that session. With William Hancock, there had been no chance for such salvaging. Boone had shown the man to be stupid, and his testimony far less than credible. And so, Bowman was girding himself, prepared to watch Boone with greater care and wariness and not particularly reassured by Callaway's burgeoning optimism. More than anything else, at the moment, John Bowman was curious over whom Boone planned to call as defense witnesses. He was not long in learning the identity of the first.

Daniel Boone had approached the bar and spoke to Colonel Trabue, though Bowman had not been able to catch what was said. The president of the court nodded and turned to face Bowman as Boone stepped back several paces.

"Will the judge advocate please call and swear in the first witness for the defense, Mr. Benjamin Cutbirth."

Standing, Bowman faced the gallery and spoke loudly. "The defense calls Mr. Benjamin Cutbirth."

A neat but relatively nondescript man of about thirty-two who had been seated on an upright-log section in the first row of the gallery's left side, stood and walked to the witness chair. Unbidden, he stopped beside the chair and raised his right hand shoulder high. Bowman moved to a stop directly in front of him,, raising his own hand in similar manner.

"Do you solemnly swear," he said clearly, "that in the testimony you are about to give in the matter presently before this court, you will speak the truth, the whole truth, and nothing but the truth, so help you God?"

"I do."

"Please be seated."

Bowman looked thoughtful as he returned to the prosecution table and resumed sitting there. Callaway was frowning, but when Bowman looked at him he merely gave a shrug and said nothing. Boone in the meanwhile had taken a stance before the witness, a few feet distant.

"Hello, Ben," he said warmly. "Reckon you're supposed to start off by telling the court who you are and where you live."

"Cutbirth is my name," the man said. "Benjamin Robert Aylesworth Cutbirth. I live right here in Boonesborough."

Clad in faded gray linsey-woolsey shirt and trousers, Cutbirth was a medium man in most physical respects. Of medium height and weight, his features were regular and undistinctive, his hair a pale brown, haphazardly combed, his eyes deep brown and his complexion tanned. He smiled easily, showing even white teeth that were perhaps just a trifle too small. He was neither tense nor too nonchalant, but simply calmly alert.

"Ben," Boone continued, "how long have you known me?"

"We first met ten years ago, in 'sixty-eight, when we both had places on the Yadkin," Cutbirth replied, "but I didn't get to know you well until you returned from your first trip into this Kentucky country in 'seventy."

"You were with me as one of the party who set out to establish Boonesborough for Judge Henderson?"

"I was."

"Would you say that the relationship between Dick Callaway and me was strained at that time, or later on when we started building this place?"

"There was pronounced antagonism," Cutbirth said, "but it was mostly one-sided. Captain Callaway was very jealous of your being our leader and—"

"*Objection!*" This time Bowman had catapulted to his feet and was pointing angrily at the witness. "Mr. President, this cannot be permitted! The witness cannot attest to what the inner feelings of Captain Callaway were at any given time, and his interpretation of what he *thinks* he may have detected can only be the most wild of conjecturings!"

"Sustained," Colonel Trabue said. "Witness will confine himself to relation of factual occurrences, testifying to same and allowing this board of court-martial to draw its own conclusions based on the sum total of evidence presented."

"Yes, sir," Cutbirth answered meekly. "I'm sorry."

Boone was not to be diverted, however, and he framed his next question carefully. "What kind of disagreements did you personally witness, Ben, that came up between me and Dick Callaway?"

Cutbirth was as careful in his reply. "Captain Boone, from the time we set out from the treaty at Watauga until we got to this place here, where we decided to build the fort, Captain Callaway objected to practically every decision or suggestion you made, no matter how minor. Some of us were pretty disgusted with it all and wondered aloud to each other how you could continue to be so friendly with him and not take offense. Captain Callaway, as all of us knew, didn't really know a whole lot about traveling in the woods, especially in country where there were hostile Indians, and yet every time you gave us any kind of directions for seeing to our own safety, Captain Callaway had other ideas and kept wanting to call for a vote among the members of our party, in order to support his own views. I guess it would have been sort of funny if it hadn't been so damned dangerous as well."

"Colonel Trabue," John Bowman said, shaking his head disgustedly and standing with his weight on one leg, "must it really be requisite upon me to constantly remind this court that it is Captain Boone who is on trial here? Most assuredly it is not Captain Callaway. Thus far the full burden of Mr. Cutbirth's testimony has been to undermine the character and ability of a man who has long been known as one of the Kentucky country's most upright and solid citizens. Is such character assassination to be permitted to continue?"

At the defense table, Samuel Henderson also rose and, leaning over the table with both palms flat on its surface, he addressed the court even before being recognized. "Mr. President, the present testimony of Mr. Cutbirth is being elicited by Captain Boone on the strongest possible advice from Captain Harrod and myself. On direct examination, Captain Callaway testified in a manner which depicted Captain Boone as an ineffectual leader, with the inescapable insinuation that he was actually an enemy of his own people. Prosecution was not concerned in the least at that time with the matter of character assassination, as he puts it. What defense is here attempting to establish is that Captain Callaway had indeed become jealous of Captain Boone's leadership and did everything in his power to thwart Captain Boone, and that his testimony concerning Captain Boone was thereby distorted. Prosecution itself has opened this avenue of questioning and cannot now legally close it to the defense."

"It seems to the court," Trabue commented mildly, "that Captain Boone is undertaking his questioning of the witness in a reasonably suitable manner. If personal dislike and overt antagonism between defendant and plaintiff was and is a motivating factor in the testimony previously given by Captain Callaway under direct examination, then Captain Boone has been well-advised by his associates to establish this fact through the testimony of his own witnesses. Within, of course," he added, "the bounds of legality. The court rules in favor of Mr. Henderson and the defense. Captain Boone may continue."

Boone sent a hasty wink toward Henderson and then addressed the witness. "Did the situation you spoke of between Captain Callaway and me improve any when we finally reached this place and started to build the fort?"

"No, sir, it did not. In fact, it deteriorated. Relations between you became extremely strained, but primarily at Captain Callaway's instigation. The problem came to a head at about the time we were completing the initial construction here."

"How so?"

"You, sir," Cutbirth said, "were having a difficult time keeping the men at work. Captain Callaway consistently refused to do his share of the work in construction and spent at least a part of each day laying out his own land claims in the area. Other men seeing him do so were afraid he would get all the choice land and so they, too , neglected their work in order to stake out claims. It finally came to the point where you threatened to lock up anyone who should try to leave the fort to make such claims until construction was completed. Captain Callaway was furious about this and did considerable derogatory talking about you, openly suggesting to the entire party that they name a new leader."

"Who was it he wished to have named as leader in place of me?" Boone asked.

"Himself."

"But that didn't happen?"

"No, sir. The men knew you were right, that the Indians might well attack again, and that if the fort was not completed by then they could be wiped out. They didn't mind not being able to lay out land claims as long as the ruling applied to everyone, including Captain Callaway."

"Anything else happen that made Dick mad about that time?"

"One thing in particular right then, Captain Boone. When the fortifications were just about finished in their first stage, someone suggested that we had to have a name for the place. We'd been vaguely calling it Otter Creek Station up till then, but now we wanted something as a more permanent name. There were a lot of possibilities suggested, but when we finally voted on it the choice had been narrowed down to three. Hendersonville was one of the suggestions, which you yourself made, because this was to be the capital of Judge Henderson's Colony of Transylvania. Captain Callaway, however, contended that it should be named after one of us who was working so hard to build the place."

"Did he suggest a name?"

"Yes, sir. He thought we should call it Fort Callaway."

A roar of laughter erupted from the spectators and Richard Callaway glared angrily from the prosecution table, a deep flush coloring his features. Despite himself, even John Bowman's eyes were twinkling with amusement.

"Almost everyone, though," Cutbirth continued as the laughter died, "thought it should be named after you, since you were the leader and all. Some suggested Fort Boone or Boonesburg or Boone's Station, but we finally settled on Boonesborough, and that's the name we subsequently voted. Captain Callaway was very incensed about this and made no secret of how he felt."

"Was there any other specific thing between then and the first of this year where Dick Callaway and me argued?"

"Yes, sir. It was when your daughter, Jemima, and Captain Callaway's two daughters, Betsy and Fanny, were kidnapped by the Indians."

"When did that occur?"

"A couple of years ago—about June or July, I think, of 'seventy-six."

"Will you please tell the court what happened?"

At the prosecution table Richard Callaway was suddenly whispering in an agitated manner to Colonel Bowman, who was nodding his head at intervals. Bowman finally reached out and squeezed Callaway's forearm, spoke quietly to him for a moment, and then the two lapsed into silence.

Cutbirth had turned to face the court again, to address the officers directly. "Jemima, Betsy and Fanny," he explained, "had decided to take a ride in the canoe. That was Boonesborough's only boat at the time. It was a beautiful Sunday afternoon and they—"

"How old were the girls when this occurred, Mr. Cutbirth?" Trabue asked.

"Betsy was sixteen. Jemima and Fanny were both fourteen."

"Where were Captain Boone and Captain Callaway at this time?"

"Well, sir, Sundays were quiet days and after services most everybody just rested. Captain Boone saw the girls off, telling them to be sure to stay in sight. We hadn't been bothered by Indians for a considerable while, so it seemed all right. Then Captain Boone went back to his own cabin for a nap. It is my understanding that Captain Callaway was also asleep in his own quarters."

"Thank you," Trabue said, "please continue."

"Yes, sir. Well, the girls started off but somehow they got farther from the fort than they should have. They not only got out of sight, but out of hearing, too. When they came close to the opposite shore they were suddenly surprised by a party of Indians who had seen them coming and who had lain in wait. One of the warriors jumped into the water and grabbed the boat and pulled it to shore, despite the fact that Jemima was beating him over the head with her paddle. They quickly took the girls out of the beached canoe and headed away with them. No one at the fort knew anything about it and it was close to milking time before one of the boys who was out rounding up the cows saw the empty canoe on the opposite shore some distance downstream. He gave the alarm and there was plenty of excitement. Never before or since have I seen Captain Boone so alarmed. John Gass swam across the river and retrieved the canoe, since there was no other way for a rescue party to follow without otherwise getting their gunpowder all wet. By the time the party was ready, Captain Boone was back and—"

"Back from where, sir?" Trabue cut in.

"Oh. Well, Colonel, he'd swum across the river to look for whatever sign he could find of what happened. He was the one who told us for sure that Indians had got the girls. Up till then we had suspected it but we weren't positive. Captain Callaway was blaming Captain Boone for everything, because he'd let the girls go out alone in the first place. Captain Boone was blaming himself for the same thing, but Captain Callaway kept at it so hard that Captain Boone had to make him shut up."

"In what way did he do so, sir?" Trabue asked quickly. "Did he strike Captain Callaway?"

"No, sir. He didn't have to. He just looked hard at Captain Callaway and said, 'Dick, if you say one more word I'm going to knock you flat on your ass!' Well, Captain Callaway sort of sputtered but he kept pretty quiet for a while after that. Anyway, by then it was too dark to make any attempt to follow the trail, so we had to wait for morning, and that's when the search party led by Captain Boone set off. I was one of those ordered to stay behind and help protect the fort in case it was all a ruse to draw us away—those were Boone's orders. In the morning, by first light, the rescue party set off."

"How many men did it include, Mr. Cutbirth?"

"Uh, let's see... There was Captain Boone leading, and with him there was John Gass and John Holder, along with Sam Henderson and Nathan Reid. Then there was Captain Callaway and his nephew, Flanders, along with five of Captain Callaway's men. Then John Floyd and Levi Todd were along, and they had about seven of their men. I don't remember who-all, exactly, but there were about twenty-five men in all. Anyway, they hardly got across the river before there was another big argument between Captain Callaway and Captain Boone."

John Bowman had been waiting for this. He sprang to his feet with an objection. "The witness," he said, "cannot testify to any such matter, Mr. President, since he was still in the fort and not present during any portion of the rescue operation."

"Prosecution is correct. Objection is sustained. Witness may relate only matters in which he was personally involved."

For a moment Cutbirth did not know what to say and then he finally concluded lamely, "Well, they eventually got back to the fort safe with the girls, but after that Captain Boone and Captain Callaway hardly ever even spoke to each other."

Cutbirth looked to Boone for the next question, but the defendant was standing silently looking toward the bar but seeing no one, as he was lost in his own thoughts.

"Does Captain Boone wish to continue now?" prompted Colonel Trabue.

Boone started and then grinned sheepishly and shook his head. "No, sir," he said. "I'm all done with Ben for now."

"Does prosecution wish to cross-examine?"

"Yes, sir," Bowman said, rising.

"That being the case," Trabue put in quickly, "perhaps it would be best to put it off until tomorrow morning, since it is now close to time of adjournment."

"Sir," Bowman appealed, "we still have a little time left—about fifteen minutes, I believe—and I only have a brief point or two that I'd like to take up with the witness. I'm quite sure I can finish with him before three o'clock."

"All right, Colonel," Trabue said a trifle grumpily. "Proceed."

"Mr. Cutbirth," Bowman said as he approached the witness, ". . . you consider yourself a man of honor, do you not?"

"Yes, sir, I do."

"I have learned," Bowman continued, "that you are considered to be a man who will always extend himself to aid a friend. Is that correct?"

"Yes, sir, I've always been ready to help a friend, but that doesn't mean I'd testify here that—"

Bowman shot up an interrupting hand and shook his head. "Please, Mr. Cutbirth, do not elaborate; merely answer the questions."

The judge advocate ignored the flush of anger coloring Cutbirth's cheeks and went on. "All right, you've described yourself as a man of honor and a man always ready to help a friend. Are you also the type of man who unfailingly repays a debt, however small?"

"I am," Cutbirth replied tightly.

"And would you also consider yourself to be a man who is family conscious—that is, a man who would go to great lengths to aid a member of his family, or even a distant relative who might need assistance?"

Cutbirth hesitated and Henderson interjected an objection without rising from his seat. "Mr. President," he said, "this line of questioning by prosecution is neither relevant nor material. Colonel Bowman is obviously fishing for something, but doesn't seem to know exactly what."

"Colonel Trabue," Bowman spoke up before the president of the court could reply, "prosecution's questions at this time are neither irrelevant nor immaterial and if the court will have patience for a short while longer, this will be made quite clear."

"I'll hold a ruling on the objection in abeyance for a while longer, Mr. Henderson," Trabue said, "and allow prosecution the opportunity to develop his point."

Bowman faced the witness and spoke again as the disgruntled Henderson clamped his lips in a tight line. "You are married, Mr. Cutbirth?"

"Yes, sir."

"And prior to your marriage your wife's name was Elizabeth Wilcoxen?"

"Yes, that's correct."

"Is it not also true that Daniel Boone is her uncle and that she feels very deeply toward him?"

Benjamin Cutbirth looked disgusted and his reply was hardly audible. "Yes, my wife is Captain Boone's niece. She admires her uncle a great deal."

Bowman glanced toward the defense table and saw Sam Henderson poised to rise and swiftly went on in a different vein. "Mr. Cutbirth, is it not also true that you personally owe Captain Boone a great debt?"

Cutbirth swallowed. "Sir?" he said weakly.

"Isn't it true," Bowman bored in, "that you were a member of Daniel Boone's party when he opened the trail through Cumberland Gap to Boonesborough, and that during that time he saved your life when you were about to be slain by an Indian?"

Cutbirth was silent and Bowman was suddenly harsh. "Answer the question, sir, yes or no. Did Captain Boone save your life?"

"Yes, sir," Cutbirth nodded, "he did."

"Then I contend, Mr. Cutbirth, that because of a distinct family relationship to Captain Boone and because of the great debt you owe him for saving your life, your testimony is highly colored in his behalf and it would be pointless for me to question you further." Bowman began walking away.

"But," Cutbirth protested, "that's not—"

The prosecutor spun about and said sharply, "That's all, sir! No further questions."

Once again with his rapid-fire technique of examination, the prosecution had neatly undone much of what Daniel Boone had built in his own defense. A heavy murmuring was already rising from the crowd as Colonel Trabue slammed his gavel to the table and adjourned the fifth session of this court-martial.

James Harrod banged his fist against the defense table in exasperation as the members of the court began filing out and the gallery started milling.

"Damn that Bowman!" he said angrily. He started to say something else, glanced at the guards that had moved to within a respectful distance of the table and stood waiting, and abruptly lowered his voice to a whisper. "Damn him! He *knows* that's improper!"

"Of course he does, Jim," Henderson agreed. "But this gives you a good look at the way his mind operates. Take good note of it, too. He knew he could have waited until tomorrow morning to tackle Cutbirth, but he also knew if he could get some good licks in now, even though we could show him to be wrong later, the court members would be leaving with a last thought in Bowman's favor to dwell on for the night. Hell yes, we'll show it's improper in the morning, and you watch—Bowman won't say a word. He won't want to linger on it at all. He'll know the members have had a whole night to consider what he said, which sounds convincing so far. When we get around to disputing him, of necessity it'll be brief and not make nearly the impression that he has. Consciously the court members will know we're right. Subconsciously they'll be remembering Bowman's show. I've seen cases falter on less."

"Tricky sort of feller, ain't he?" Boone remarked.

"Tricky, yes, and dangerous as a rattler, too, Dan. More dangerous—he doesn't give any warning. Don't forget that."

6

It was exactly as Henderson had predicted it would be when court reconvened at eight in the morning on another gloomy, drizzly day. On advice from Sam, Daniel Boone had immediately recalled Benjamin Cutbirth. He established the fact that Cutbirth was noted for his veracity and would never have colored his testimony in favor of Boone, even though a relationship through marriage did exist and despite the fact that Boone had saved his life. Benjamin Cutbirth was shown to be a man of high moral character, a very honorable man. The court members took note of what was said but seemed unimpressed by the refutation and—again as Henderson had predicted—Bowman declined any further questioning of the witness.

Daniel Boone's next witness was a distinct surprise to everyone, including the man he called. "If there ain't any rules against it," he told the president of the court, "I'd like to question Sam Henderson."

Bowman came to his feet at once but remained mute at a swiftly upraised hand by Colonel Trabue. "It is not customary," the president remarked, "for any defense counsel to testify in behalf of his client. However, it is not prohibited. As was mentioned earlier in this court-martial, any person can be called by either side to testify. Bear in mind, however, Captain Boone, that in cross-examination the prosecution will have every right to question Mr. Henderson as a hostile witness. If you have no objection to this, you may go ahead."

Distinctly unhappy about it, Bowman called Sam Henderson and swore him in, then returned to his own place in a disgruntled manner. Boone got right to the point with Henderson after establishing his name and place of residence in Harrodsburg.

"Sam, you were with my party when we went out to rescue the girls, weren't you?"

"Yes, I was."

"Did you have any special interest aside from the fact that like everyone else you wanted to get them back?"

Henderson grinned. "No doubt about that," he said, then chuckled aloud. "I was engaged to Betsy Callaway at the time. Matter of fact, Betsy and I got married a month after we brought them safely back to Boonesborough. She's my wife and Captain Callaway is my father-in-law."

"Do you get along with Dick Callaway very well?"

"We've always gotten along together reasonably well," Sam said, then added with another short laugh, "but that'll probably end now."

A low laughter rippled across the onlookers as Boone continued. "Do you believe your relationship to Captain Callaway by marriage or your helping me in this here court-martial will keep you from giving testimony that ain't favorable to one side or the other?"

"As a member of the defense, it is my duty to help you, Dan, however I can. By the same token I owe some degree of consideration to my wife's father. But to my own way of thinking, both of these connections are set aside when I sit here in the witness chair. I consider it my duty to give testimony in as unbiased a manner as I can."

"All right, fair enough," Boone said. "Now, the question we couldn't get around to with Ben Cutbirth because he didn't actually witness it himself is what happened between Dick Callaway and me on this here rescue mission. Supposing you just talk to the court as if I wasn't here and tell them what happened."

Sam Henderson faced the court and spoke clearly, concisely, unhurriedly, yet effectively encapsulating what must have been a complex set of circumstances.

"Ben Cutbirth had everything fairly straight up to the point where we all crossed the river to try to trace the girls and their captors. In the dimming light the evening before, Daniel Boone had been unable to determine which way they had gone. After we got across the river in the morning, though, John Floyd there," he dipped his head toward the officer on the board of court-martial farthest to Trabue's left, "was the one to pick up the trail. The Indians had headed directly to an extensive stand of cane and immediately upon entering it had split up into several different parties. Captain Callaway was for splitting our own group similarly and plunging right in after them, but Dan argued against it and said he reckoned they had probably milled around in there for a long time to throw off pursuit and then slipped off, covering their tracks behind them as they left the canebrake until they got far enough away not to worry about that, and then set off at top speed. Well, Captain Callaway took considerable issue with that, not wanting to leave the trail, but since Boone knew Indian ways better'n any of us, we let Dan lead the way. He set out straight north, traveling fast for maybe three or four miles and then cut sharply northeast. Pretty soon we came to a little creek. Sure enough, we right away found footprints of not only the Indians, but the girls, too. By relying on Boone, we had saved untold hours of trying to unravel a trail that the Indians had done everything they could to hide."

Henderson paused briefly and then added, "I have to admit that instead of being pleased that we were this much nearer to saving Jemima Boone and his own two daughters, Captain Callaway was unusually put out that Captain Boone had been right and had outfoxed the Indians. He said some pretty unkind things about Daniel for a while, to which Captain Boone paid almost no attention, and this tended to make Captain Callaway madder than ever. Anyway, we got down to discussing how to proceed and Captain Callaway insisted that since we had 'lucked into the trail again,' as he put it, that we should now follow it with all haste. Boone disagreed. He said the Indians always kept a lone warrior traveling far in the rear to watch for pursuit. If he saw it coming, he would quickly overtake the others and warn them. At this the chances were, Boone told us, that the girls would be tomahawked so they would not slow down the Indians in their escape."

Henderson gave a mirthless little smile as he continued: "Captain Callaway didn't believe what Captain Boone was saying and just kept insisting that they all follow the trail, which at this point was heading almost straight west. Dan had had just about all he could take of the arguments and that, combined with the intense worry he was experiencing over the girls, made him lose his temper a bit. He grabbed Captain Callaway's shirtfront and shook him so hard I thought his teeth would fly out. Boone told Captain Callaway that he was in charge and he didn't want to hear any more talk from Dick about how they should proceed, since Callaway had never in his life been known to be right about anything. I really thought they would come to blows for a while. Finally, Dan ordered Captain Callaway and his nephew, Flanders, and their five men to head directly for a ford on the Licking which was about thirty miles or so ahead of us and which was where he anticipated the Indians who had the girls would cross. They were to set up an ambush there and wait. In the meanwhile, Boone said he would lead the rest of us across country directly to the northwest, in an attempt to once again cut the trail of the Indians and lop off more time in overtaking them. Captain Callaway, still extremely upset, set off with his party as Boone had directed and then Boone and the rest of us moved out. We traveled as fast as we could the rest of that day, camped without fire for the night and started again in the morning. It was late afternoon of that day when we came to a buffalo wallow around thirty-five or forty miles from Boonesborough, and here we found much fresher signs of the party again. The Indians had been following buffalo traces instead of the main Warrior's Path, but they were paralleling that principal route."

Sam Henderson paused to clear his throat and then grinned. "Captain Boone was really outthinking the Indians. By that time no one in our party had any doubt but that Dan could take us right to them. Boone said he was still sure they meant to cross the Licking ford at the place where he'd sent Callaway to establish the ambush, but that if we moved fast it was possible that we could overtake them before they got there. That far away from Boonesborough the Indians weren't being too careful anymore about their trail. We were now following cautiously on their actual trail and in less than a mile came to a freshly killed buffalo. They had only taken the hump from it and there was still some blood oozing from where it had been cut. Dan told us right then that we were going to find the Indians camped at a little no-name creek he knew about which was a couple of miles ahead. We continued moving along and pretty soon found a snake the Indians had paused to chop in half with a tomahawk. Both sections were still squirming pretty actively, so we knew we were mighty close."

The witness stopped and licked his lips. He exhaled loudly and said, "Have to admit I was pretty scared, and I guess most of the rest of us were, too. Captain Boone now made us keep absolutely silent and extremely watchful. In another couple of miles we came to the creek he had mentioned earlier. The tracks we were following went in on the south side but didn't come out on the north. Boone whispered to us that they'd gone downstream just a short distance to camp. In this way, he said, they could watch the creek and if they saw muddy water suddenly coming by, they'd know a party had crossed above them, which they could then follow and attack by surprise from behind. We slipped downstream about forty yards away from the south bank and in a couple hundred yards came to their camp. They didn't know we were there yet and our big concern was that we'd be detected and the girls would be killed before we could get to them. We backed out of sight and made our plans. Coming in from above and below them—Boone leading one group and I the other—we crept up. I could see Betsy leaning with her back against a tree and Fanny and Jemima lying on the ground with their heads in her lap. Only one Indian guard with a rifle was close to them. The others were busy cooking the buffalo hump, getting water from the creek in a kettle, and getting settled down. We'd been lucky to get that close unseen, but just then one of the Indians let out a yell and pointed toward Captain Boone's line of approach. We couldn't wait any longer. We fired and so did some of the men in Boone's group. The guard with the girls was hit and knocked into the fire, but he and three others that were knocked down all got up again and ran. Plain as day I heard Jemima scream out, 'That's my daddy!' Things got pretty confused along about then. The Indians all scattered with us chasing them, but they finally got into a big canebrake, where Captain Boone said it would be useless and possibly even suicidal for us to follow them farther, so we gave up. The important thing was that we'd got the girls back unharmed. Right away we sent word to Callaway's party at the ford to come in and, when they did, we went back to Boonesborough. Captain Callaway was relieved to see his two daughters safe, and Jemima too, but he was still furious with Captain Boone, and more so now, all of us thought, because Captain Boone had been right every step of the way. If we had listened to Captain Callaway earlier we—"

"Objection, objection, objection!" said Bowman, rising tiredly. "Mr. President, the witness has kept us all nicely entertained with his little happy-ending story—which, I might add, has precious little to do with the charges of treason against Captain Boone—but prosecution simply cannot sit here and listen to Mr. Henderson, who certainly knows better, blandly forming all sorts of conjectures and conclusions about 'Captain Callaway felt this,' or 'If Captain Callaway had done that,' and so on. Mr. President, prosecution has been extremely patient in this matter, in accord with the directions of the court, but isn't it about time that we more directly put our attention to the charges which this board of court-martial has been assembled to consider?"

"Colonel Bowman," said Daniel Trabue, "is well within his rights with such a request. This board of court-martial appreciates the lucidity but not the loquacity with which Mr. Henderson has presented his story. It has grown entirely too long for its purpose. It is clear that Captain Boone, in his examination of witnesses, has embarked upon an-initial attack of discredit to Captain Callaway, attempting to prove that Captain Callaway has perhaps not testified as fully as he could have, and equally to show that the plaintiff has exhibited marked antagonism toward him because of personal matters long before the issues of this trial came into being. The court feels that such points have been adequately made for some time and are now only being belabored, and that no possible benefit can accrue with further testimony along these lines. The defendant is therefore ordered to take his witness into areas of testimony directly dealing with the charges or else end his questioning and allow Colonel Bowman his opportunity for rebuttal through cross-examination if he wishes."

"Yes, sir," Boone said. "I don't have any further questions to ask of Sam."

"Colonel Bowman?"

The judge advocate hesitated. For a moment he was on the verge of rising, but after a long, direct look at Henderson who was openly smiling at him, he shook his head and settled back. "No cross-examination here, Mr. President."

"Mr. Henderson," Trabue said, "you are excused and may resume your duties. Captain Boone, you may call your next witness, with the repeated admonition for the court that questioning hereafter deal with matters which are directly related to the issue."

"I'd like to take a couple of minutes, sir," Boone said, "to

talk over at the table there with them." He pointed to where
Henderson was just then sitting down beside Jim Harrod.

"You may do so, sir," Trabue said. "If more than a few
minutes are needed, this court-martial can be recessed for
ten minutes."

"Thank you, sir. I would appreciate that."

The gavel banged loudly once as Trabue called the
recess.

II

Because of the inclement weather—a faint misting of chilly
rain was still falling—hardly any of the spectators left their seats
in the shelter of the roofed-over area during the short recess.
Members of the court whispered together, but not one left
his place.

Immediately upon the recess being called, Daniel Boone
had returned to the defense table where he sat to Henderson's
right. He began talking to both men in a low tone at once,
speaking steadily for two or three minutes. Henderson replied, followed by Harrod, and then a brisk *sotto voce*
interchange took place. At last, just as Colonel Trabue gaveled
the court back to order, Harrod nodded reluctantly and
Henderson shrugged. Boone straightened and stood up.

"The defense," he said in a more formal manner than
previously, as if parroting what he had been advised to say,
"respectfully requests that the court allow one of its members
to testify—Major Smith."

The burly and rather untidy officer seated next to the end
of the table to the court president's right, between Lieutenant David Gass and Captain Hugh McGary, sat suddenly
more erect and tugged briefly at the waistcoat rumpled over
his broad chest. Colonel Trabue sighed soundlessly, not
overjoyed at the request, but merely nodded to the judge
advocate.

John Bowman was no happier. He moved toward the
witness chair, calling as he did so, "Will Major William Bailey
Smith please come forward and be sworn in."

The officer moved around the end of the long table to
the witness chair, limping rather badly but using no cane or
other support. He raised his hand dutifully to be sworn and

then seated himself. He was not in the least ill at ease, nodding in a pleasant manner to the defendant as Boone came to a stop before him, and answering in a resonant bass voice when Boone asked him to state his name and residence.

"And how long have you lived in Boonesborough?" Boone asked.

"Two years," Smith replied, "almost exactly."

"Captain Callaway has testified that when I went out to meet with the Indians a second time after they surrounded Boonesborough, you accompanied me, all dressed up in fancy uniform, is that right?"

"I did."

"And at this time you pretended to be the new commanding officer of Boonesborough?"

"That's right."

"It was after that meeting that I am said to have advised the people inside the fort to seriously consider surrender?"

"Yes, sir, that is correct."

"Isn't it true, Major Smith, that I told you as we walked back to the fort together after the meeting that I was completely against surrendering?"

"You did, but you put the surrender proposal to them at my recommendation. And I also advised them to seriously consider the proposal."

There was a stir in the court at this. Bowman glanced sharply at Callaway beside him, who looked surprised and shrugged, then turned back to hear what else was being said.

"Will you please tell the members of this court why you made such a recommendation?"

William Bailey Smith swiveled in his seat so he was more directly facing the central table and directed his remarks to the court members in general.

"Under the circumstance," he explained, "it seemed to me the only reasonable thing to do. What Captain Boone and I had heard and seen in that short meeting with the Indians had convinced me that there was positively no way Boonesborough could defend itself against what was to be brought against us. Under that strong conviction, it seemed to me that the choice of surrender or fight to the death had to be something the Boonesborough people themselves decided, rather than something Boone and I decided for them."

Major Robert Anderson, seated to Colonel Trabue's left, spoke up. "That's a rather enigmatic statement, Major Smith.

Will you kindly be a little more specific in regard to what you saw and heard which made you feel the enemy was too powerful for Boonesborough to stand against?"

"I will, sir. Captain Boone and I had been told during that meeting that if the fort surrendered peaceably, as Chief Black Fish fully anticipated it would be, there would be no problem. He promised us that no indignities of any kind would be committed by his warriors against us, that we would all be transported first to Chalahgawtha and those who cared to do so would be allowed to remain there for subsequent adoption into the tribe. Those who did not wish this and who preferred instead to be turned over to the British would be safely escorted to Detroit and there turned over to Governor-General Henry Hamilton, who had promised kind and courteous treatment of all. However, Black Fish warned that if we refused to accept the offer, no consideration whatever would be shown to the Boonesborough people. He told us that when the fort was taken, after such a refusal, that only the healthiest survivors who remained among us would be taken back to the Ohio country alive. Those who had been wounded in the fight, those who were ill or weak, all the old people and all the little children who could not travel well, all these would be executed on the spot and their scalps taken. The surviving healthy prisoners would be taken to Chalahgawtha and there dispersed among the various other villages of the tribe to serve as virtual slaves. The healthy women would be made to do the most menial labor, as well as bear children for the tribe. The men would all have to run gauntlets of the most severe kind and those who survived that ordeal would eventually be sold to the British, either alive for ten pounds sterling each, or their scalps only for five pounds each. The implication was there very strongly that it would be much less trouble to merely sell the scalps."

"Major Smith," Colonel Trabue said, as the witness paused, "I'd like to ask a couple of questions of my own here, if I may. Captain Boone?"

"Go right ahead, Colonel," Boone said.

"Thank you. Major Smith, I find it difficult to believe that you, a military officer, would have been swayed by mere threats against the people of Boonesborough. In line with the question you were answering that was posed by Major Anderson, was there anything other than such threats that you've not yet told us that would have led to your extraordinary recommendation to Captain Boone?"

"Yes, sir, there was. Despite all the repairs that had been done to the fort under Captain Boone's direction after his return here, Boonesborough was still in pretty bad shape for any kind of defense. We were at that moment outnumbered in fighting manpower at a ratio of about eight to one. That alone would not have made us even consider surrender, but there were two things in particular which we felt the fort could not possibly stand against if they were brought into use—fire and artillery. Chief Black Fish promised us that he planned to use both against us if surrender was not agreed to."

Trabue scowled. "Mr. Walter Bruther," he reminded, "has testified that the artillery was left behind in the village of Chalahgawtha."

"Yes, sir, that's true. It was. But Mr. Bruther did not get back here until long after the siege against us was over and we did not have his intelligence then. As far as we knew, the opposing force did indeed have artillery on hand. In fact, in the letters addressed to Captain Boone from Governor-General Hamilton, it was expressly outlined that two three-pounders were being brought along by the English officers accompanying the Indians and that this artillery was not to be used unless Boonesborough refused to surrender; but that if such refusal was made, then it was indeed to be used."

"And you believed that?"

"Not at first, sir. But then Chief Black Fish not only told us that the cannon in question were on hand here, but he described them very closely—in such a manner that we knew he had to have seen them himself. As a final proof, he had one of his men show us the three-pound balls that they meant to throw against us. With such weapons brought to bear against our gates and walls, there would have been no way to keep from being destroyed."

"You were both convinced that the cannon were actually on hand?"

Major Smith shook his head. "No, sir. Captain Boone whispered to me that he doubted that they had such artillery with them. He said he thought that the Indian pride was such that if they did have them, they would have shown them rather than just talking about them."

"This wasn't your belief, Major?" Trabue asked.

"No, sir, it was not. I had no doubt that Chief Black Fish had actually seen such artillery. His descriptions were too exact not to have seen them. By no stretch of the imagination could I believe that having seen them, he would not also have brought them along to be used against us. Thus, I told Captain Boone as we returned to the fort that in fairness to our people, they should be told what they were facing and that they be given a choice in the matter. When we did get back to the fort, it was I, not Captain Boone, who most vigorously expressed the alternatives to our people. I was quite willing to try to defend this place, but did not feel that we had the right to place so many women and children in jeopardy without giving everyone a chance to speak. In fact, I still felt this way until we were able to determine that the enemy did not have the cannon they said they had."

"When was this determined?"

"Well, Captain Boone first assured me of it the next morning, though he didn't say how he knew and I suspected he was merely trying to bolster my courage. But then I became convinced he knew what he was talking about on the first night of the actual siege."

"You mean by the fact," Trabue persisted, "that cannon were not immediately brought into use against Boonesborough's defenses?"

Richard Callaway had been whispering to the judge advocate and now Colonel Bowman, grim-faced, came to his feet saying, "Colonel Trabue!" and effectively cutting off Major Smith's reply.

"Sir," Bowman continued as the president of the court turned toward him with an irked expression, "the prosecution must strongly object to the president of this board of court-martial suddenly assuming the duties of defense counsel. If there is information to be brought out here, it should, by rules of procedure, be brought out in direct testimony by defense counsel—in this case by the defendant himself—and not by the court."

"I'm sure," Trabue responded stiffly, "that I do not need to remind the judge advocate that any member of this board of court-martial may interpose questions to any witness, defense or prosecution, at any time he cares to during the course of the trial. In most cases, I admit, boards of courts-martial are content to sit quietly and assimilate the testimony elicited from witnesses by both defense and prosecution. But it is incumbent upon any member of this panel to interject himself as questioner at any time he feels greater clarity—and perhaps a truer degree of justice—can be the result by the response to his questions. Whether or not the information I am presently asking of this witness would have been revealed in direct examination by Captain Boone or in your own cross-examination, is not a matter of great issue. What is important is that it seems we are in a crucial area of discussion here and must closely establish certain facts which it is entirely possible that Captain Boone, through inexperience, might allow to pass. You are out of order in this respect, sir, and the court requests that you be seated."

With poor grace, Bowman dropped back into his chair and sat scowling, his arms tightly folded across his chest. He made no reply when Callaway leaned over to whisper something to him.

"Captain Boone," Trabue went on, "I do not intend to act the part of direct examiner on your behalf, but I am considerably curious as to this matter of artillery. I will ask only a few more questions on this topic and then turn the witness back over to you."

Even as Boone began to nod, Trabue addressed the officer in the witness chair, picking up where the testimony had broken off at Bowman's interruption.

"Major Smith, was it because cannon were not used against Boonesborough that first night of the siege that you were convinced that the enemy did in fact have no artillery with them?"

"No, sir, it was not. Firing—rifle fire, that is—was very heavy against us at first. After darkness had fallen and Captain Boone had gone out to rescue Mr. Buchanan, I didn't see him—"

"Excuse the interruption, Major. You say Captain Boone went out to rescue Mr. Buchanan? Explain that, please."

"Well, at that last meeting when we eight went out to supposedly sign the peace treaty with them and the Indians turned on us, we all managed to break away and run toward the fort. I am convinced that the only reason we were as successful in this as we were, was because of Captain Boone. Having broken away form the two Indians who were gripping him, he charged at Black Fish and struck him a tremendous blow which knocked him unconscious. Shots were being fired at the time from the fort and seeing their chief fall and lie unmoving so disconcerted the Indians that for a few moments they hesitated, not knowing what to do. This gave us the opportunity to put some space between them and us. Captain Boone was by far the swiftest among us and he reached the east gate first, snatched up the rifle he'd left leaning against the wood outside and came running back toward us."

"The Indians were firing at you eight men by this time, Major?"

"Yes, sir, they were. By the time Captain Boone came running back toward us, two of our men had fallen. One was Squire Boone, who had been shot. The other was Mr. Buchanan, who had stumbled in a hole or over a root or something and severely sprained his ankle. Squire had fallen about halfway from the meeting place to the fort, but Mr. Buchanan was closer to the gate. Boone ran past Mr. Buchanan and yelled at him to crawl and take refuge behind a stump there and then lie still. He—Boone, that is—continued running away from the fort and stopped only once to fire at a warrior who had run up to Squire Boone and was just then raising his tomahawk to hit him. Captain Boone shot the Indian, then ran up and picked up Squire Boone in his arms and ran back to the fort with him."

"Weren't the Indians firing at him?" Trabue asked.

"Oh, yes, sir, indeed they were. There must have been a hundred shots or more fired at him as he ran, but except for one ball that made a hole in his shirt, he wasn't hit. Squire was trying to reload his brother's rifle while being carried, but not doing very well. As Captain Boone ran past Mr. Buchanan a second time, he again yelled at him to lie still and not move a muscle or he'd be killed. I had picked up Squire Boone's gun at the east gate as I ran past it and brought it inside. We had the gate all but closed and as soon as Boone ran inside, we closed and locked it. Captain Boone had carried his brother at a dead run for about forty or fifty yards and was breathing very hard, but he still wanted to go back outside to get Mr. Buchanan. We wouldn't let him because by then the fire against us had grown much hotter and we didn't want to lose him. Anyway, Mr. Buchanan stayed out there all the rest of the day, lying still as Captain Boone had directed. Right after dark, in spite of our objections, Boone made us open the gate just enough for him to get through and then he crawled on his stomach all the way to where Buchanan was. Firing had tapered off at dark and there were only occasional shots then. Mr. Buchanan's ankle was so badly swollen that it looked broken. He couldn't even attempt walking, much less running, so Captain Boone got him to his feet and then scooped him up in his arms the same way he'd carried his brother and ran for the gate. The Indians saw him then and started firing pretty heavily at them, but Boone made it to the gate and got inside again without being hit. We immediately closed and locked the gate again. Well, anyway, shortly after that I didn't see Captain Boone anymore until about one or two o'clock in the morning. He came to where I was then, in the southeast blockhouse, and told me that he had been right, that the Indians didn't have any artillery."

"How did he know that, Major?"

"He didn't explain, sir, even when I asked him. He just said I needn't worry any longer because he knew for certain that they didn't have cannon."

"Thank you, Major Smith. Captain Boone, you may continue with the witness."

"Major," Boone said, moving up to stand near him again, "what was the condition of Boonesborough at the time of the attack? I mean, how good was it defensively?"

"Only fair," Smith said. He snorted, adding, "But a whole lot better than when you got away from the Indians in June and came back here."

"Do you want to explain that? To them," he said, pointing at the central table, "not to me."

"Well," Smith said, "when Captain Callaway had insisted on staying at Boonesborough in January when most of the men went to make salt, Captain Boone placed him in temporary charge of the place with explicit instructions to continue the construction of defenses. Captain Callaway didn't do much of a job of it and—"

"Objection!" It was Bowman. "Colonel Trabue, sir, must it be constantly necessary for me to keep reminding the court that Captain Callaway is not on trial here? The entire case by defense so far, it seems to me, has been to undermine the character of Captain Richard Callaway in any manner conceivable. The court has already reminded Captain Boone that it wished to hear no more along those lines. Prosecution requests that the president reinforce this admonition."

Trabue shook his head. "The present testimony is dealing most pertinently with Boonesborough's defenses or lack of them, upon which it is evident that certain of Captain Boone's actions or statements were predicated. The matter is entirely relevant and the court will allow it without being unduly concerned over whether or not it tends to depict Captain Callaway unfavorably. Continue, Major Smith."

"As I was saying," Smith went on, his deep voice far-carrying, "not too much was done and by late June, when Boone got back here, the defenses of the fort just weren't much better than when he left. Captain Boone was pretty upset about that and he told Captain Callaway about it in no uncertain terms. Right away Boone set up work details and had everyone laboring day and night to improve the defenses wherever possible. In less than six weeks he got much more done in that respect than Captain Callaway had accomplished in the six months Boone was absent. If we had had to undergo the siege with the fort in the condition it was in when Boone first got back, the Indians would have taken us even if they'd only had war clubs!"

"Objection!" Bowman was striding toward the bar. "Witness is stating conclusions as fact and—"

"By God, Bowman," Smith suddenly thundered, "what I'm saying is what I *know*! You think I have no knowledge about defenses? I—"

The crack of Colonel Trabue's gavel stopped the interchange and the president of the court glared at the witness. "Major Smith," he barked, "you are out of order! You are well enough versed in military procedures to know that it is not in your province to reply, either as a witness or as a member of this court, to objection. You will refrain from doing so and comport yourself in the manner of an officer and a gentleman. Prosecution's objection is valid. Equally, the witness's point concerning defenses here has been made. Captain Boone will now continue with questioning."

Though Smith mumbled a subdued "Yes, sir," Bowman was still very angry. He had paused midway between witness and bar, his brow pinched and moustache trembling. He seemed on the point of saying more, but then merely stalked back to the prosecution table, a picture of indignation.

"Bill," Boone said, "you were one of those who accompanied me on the mission to the Scioto Valley, weren't you?"

"I was."

"Captain Callaway has testified that this was on the eve of expected attack against Boonesborough. Is this true?"

"Only partially. Four days prior to the date when we expected attack, basing the expectation on what Willie Hancock told us about his escape from the Indians, you and I and Captain Holder made a reconnaissance on horseback. We moved as fast as we could and scouted almost all the way to the Ohio River and back."

"What did we find?"

"Nothing! There was no fresh Indian sign anywhere. If the Indians were really coming against Boonesborough on July twenty-nine, as we'd been led to believe, they'd already have crossed ground that we covered and would probably have made a war camp in the vicinity of the Blue Licks. There was absolutely no sign of that and so we knew that attack was not as imminent as we believed."

"This was explained to the men at the fort when we returned?"

"Yes, sir, but Captain Callaway and a few others did not believe it. They were scared."

"Objection! Witness cannot testify to the mental state of another."

"Sustained. Final remark will be stricken by the clerk."

"Did I," Boone continued, "confide to you what my reasons were for undertaking the trip into the Ohio country at that time?"

"You did. You informed me that when you had been in the Scioto Valley with the Indians on the saltmaking trip just prior to your escape, you had visited with them the village called Kispoko Town, which is on the Scioto about ten miles above where Paint Creek empties into it. This, you had learned, was the village of the present Shawnee war chief, She-me-ne-to, better known to us as Black Snake. You said if we scouted it out and found it pretty well deserted of warriors, then they had probably moved out to assemble at Chalahgawtha and attack from there was probably soon to be on its way against Boonesborough. But if there were lots of warriors there at Kispoko Town, then it would be a sure sign that the Shawnees were not planning any more major campaigns against us this year."

"Why was that important to know?"

"Because we had numerous small plots of crops in the fields around Boonesborough—corn, pumpkins, squash, beans and so on. It'd soon be time to harvest them and you said if the Indians attacked while we were trying to bring those crops in, they might be able to kill a lot of us in the fields before we could reach the safety of the fort again. We had no idea whether it would be safe to harvest or not."

"What about the matter of getting horses and beaver skins?"

"Those were only secondary possible benefits so far as you were concerned, although for most of those who went along, they were the most important consideration."

"What did we determine on that expedition?"

"We found the villages practically deserted—only women, girls, little boys and old men there. The warriors and almost all the horses were gone."

"And it was then that we came straight back here?"

"That's right, but you had to argue pretty damned hard to get us to give up. With the village virtually empty, a lot of the men were for going in and raiding them for the furs and the horses that were left. There wouldn't have been much risk involved for us. I have to admit," he added, shaking his head ruefully, "that I was one of those who insisted on hitting the village. None of us were any too happy when you ordered us to head back toward Boonesborough as fast as we could."

"Why did I do that?"

"Well, you scouted around and found sign where the warriors had ridden out westward toward Chalahgawtha on the trail you said led there. You read that trail to be seven-eight days old. The way you figured it, you said we'd have to ride fast to reach the fort before the Shawnees, but that you figured we'd find them war-camped at the Blue Licks preparing to come against us."

"And?"

Smith grinned and rubbed his chin vigorously. "Just like you said. We rode hard and came up on them camped at Blue Licks. Monstrous war camp! We sneaked in close enough to see them painting their faces. Then we backed off and made a wide circle around them without being discovered and got back to Boonesborough ourselves the day before they arrived."

Boone looked at his witness for a long moment and then said quietly, "I guess that's all the questions I have for you, Bill."

Prosecutor John Bowman wasted no time launching into his cross-examination, firing his first question at William Bailey Smith even while he was rising from his seat at the prosecution table.

"Major Smith, how long have you known Captain Daniel Boone?"

"Just over three years. I met him first after coming to settle at Harrodsburg."

"How long did you remain at Harrodsburg?"

"About a year, then moved here to Boonesborough."

"Why did you move?"

"Oh, I liked the river valley here and planned on claiming some of the land. Then, too, Boonesborough was weaker than Harrodsburg and I was needed here, although it's part of my job to move from fort to fort on a circuit to check on problems, needs, Indian activity and so forth."

"Isn't it true, Major, that a large part of your reason for moving here was because you had become good friends with Daniel Boone and wanted to be closer to him?"

"That was part of the reason, but I wouldn't really say it was a large part of it."

"Is it not also true that at least twice over the past two years Captain Boone has saved your life?"

Smith was getting wary. "Yes," he said shortly.

"Do you not, then feel some sort of obligation to him—an obligation which might well cause you to color your testimony in his behalf?"

"No, sir!" Smith was indignant. "Daniel Boone is my friend, I'll grant, but I would not lie on his behalf in a trial such as this. I have, sir, given my oath to speak the truth, and that is what I have done!"

Bowman's attitude was gallingly skeptical, but he went on. "Major, about a third of that party of men with which you left Boonesborough for this extraordinary mission became so apprehensive about it, did they not, that they tried to get Captain Boone to give it up, and when he did not, they broke away and returned to Boonesborough?"

"Yes, sir."

"Why did this happen?"

Smith was suddenly uncomfortable. "What happened as we left the fort was bothering them."

"You mean the scene which developed, as testified to by Captain Callaway, where Captain Boone was being cursed and called a traitor?"

"Yes, sir."

"And where many of the residents of Boonesborough were crying with the expressed fear they felt that Captain Boone was going to turn this party of men over to the Indians, too?"

"Yes, sir."

"Did Captain Boone deny being a traitor?"

"Hell, no, he didn't. He didn't answer them at all. He just ignored them as we rode out."

"But some of the men who were with him didn't?"

"Some did. Others didn't."

"Which ones didn't?"

"Well, some of the wives were calling and crying and begging their husbands not to go."

"Because?"

"Because they said Boone was going to betray them to the Shawnees."

"But those men went along anyway?"

"As far as Blue Licks, yes."

"What happened there?"

"Everything seemed to come to a head when we got to where the saltmakers had been taken the previous February. Captain Boone saw that some of the men were ready to abandon him, so he didn't give them a chance."

Bowman jerked his head up at that. "What do you mean? They did leave him and come back to Boonesborough, didn't they?"

"Yes, sir, they did. But Captain Boone knew they were on the point of going and he didn't want them to be guilty of desertion, so he ordered them—the eleven who were getting ready to desert—to go back and help with the continuing work on the fort's defenses."

"They did so?"

"They did."

"And nineteen of you continued to the Scioto Valley?"

"Yes, sir."

"Did you have any trouble with the Indians?"

"A brief skirmish is all. We killed a couple of Indians."

"Who did?"

"Simon Kenton. He'd been scouting ahead and saw two coming toward him riding the same horse. He shot once and got them both. Then he discovered that they were just a boy of about fifteen and an older man with a deformed leg. He felt very badly about it then."

"Did Simon Kenton come back with you from that mission?"

"No sir, he—"

"Alexander Montgomery was also on that mission, wasn't he?"

"Yes."

"Did he come back with you from it?"

"No, but—"

"Is Montgomery now dead, killed by the Indians?"

"Yes, but—"

"And is Kenton also presumed dead, killed by the Indians?"

"Well, that's right, but—"

"Major Smith! Do you honestly feel—yes or no!—that this Scioto Valley expedition of Boone's was worth the lives of two of our staunchest defenders?"

"Of course not! But they were killed—"

"Exactly, Major Smith! They were killed, and the reason they were killed is because of accompanying Captain Daniel Boone on a mission undertaken from Boonesborough when no one should even have considered leaving the place. They were killed because Daniel Boone fully intended leaving Boonesborough as weak as possible in the face of an approaching enemy! They were killed because Daniel Boone betrayed them, just as—"

"Objection! *Objection!* Sir! Colonel Trabue, this is improper!" Sam Henderson's voice was unsteady because of his anger. "The prosecution is leading the witness, badgering him, browbeating him, not giving him a chance to answer the questions being asked and drawing his own conclusions which he is stating as fact. Defense objects most strongly!"

"Objection is sustained," Trabue ruled, not much surprised by the remarks of either Bowman or Henderson, "and prosecution is reminded to adhere to proper cross-examination procedure."

Bowman gave Trabue only a brief, cold nod and continued. "Major Smith, you have testified that you saw the letters sent to Captain Boone by Governor-General Henry Hamilton of Detroit."

"I did."

"What did the letters say?"

"Objection!" This time it was James Harrod who raised his hand. "It has already been established what the contents of the letters were."

Trabue was mildly puzzled. "That, Captain Harrod, does not preclude Colonel Bowman from discussing them again. No one heretofore has testified to actually seeing the contents of the letter. Prosecution may continue. The witness is directed to answer the question."

Smith slouched a bit in his seat and tipped his head to one side in an offhand manner. "I didn't memorize them," he said, "but they were essentially what they've already been testified to as being. Hamilton reminded Captain Boone in them of the promises that Boone had made to surrender Boonesborough and turn the Boonesborough people over to the Indians who would in turn deliver them to him in Detroit."

"Where are those letters now, Major Smith?"

William Bailey Smith was suddenly occupied with scratching an itchy forearm, then with crossing his legs and then with clearing his throat noisily, but he did not reply.

"Major Smith?" Bowman asked more sharply. "The letters. Where are they now?"

"Destroyed."

"Destroyed! Who destroyed them?"

"Captain Boone."

"How?"

"He burned them."

"Why did he burn them?"

"He told me that he thought it wouldn't be a very good idea to have them around."

"Those were his exact words—that it wouldn't be a very good idea to have them around?"

"Well, no, not exactly his words, but—"

"What *were* his exact words, Major?"

Smith shifted uneasily. "Near as I can remember, he said he'd never be able to deny anything, if it came to that, if those letters were still around."

Bowman homed in on that like an attacking wasp. "He then *anticipated* being charged with treason?"

"Hell, yes," Smith shot back. "Callaway had already threatened that he would bring charges against him."

"And this was his reason for destroying the damning evidence?"

"I guess it was."

"You guess! Did you not, as a responsible officer, make some effort to stop him from destroying this evidence?"

"I did."

"How?"

"I grabbed for them."

"What did Daniel Boone do at that point?"

"He jerked them out of my reach and told me that he had

no intention of letting them stay around so that a rope could be put around his neck." Smith sent a look of misery toward Boone, who was watching him and who smiled faintly as he saw the major glance at him.

"But you still tried to preserve them?" Bowman dug on.

"Yes, sir. I told Captain Boone that he had no right to dispose of them and that it was possible that they could be of help to him rather than harm him. I was trying to reason with him."

"Come, come, Major! Did you really believe they would *help* him?"

"No, sir." Smith's booming voice had become quite subdued.

"No, you didn't! I contend, sir—and is it not actually true—that you yourself, close friend of Daniel Boone, believe him to be guilty of treason and were torn between loyalty to a friend and duty to your country?"

Smith did not reply and Bowman leaned down toward him, his eyes blazing. "Is that not true, Major?"

"Yes," Smith said, "I guess it is."

"But you did endeavor to get the letters?"

"Yes! I've told you I did!"

"But you were not successful?"

"I was not."

"Did Daniel Boone threaten you, sir?"

"No. Well, not directly."

"Indirectly?"

"I suppose there might have been an implied threat there, but nothing overt."

"Explain that, please."

"He held the letters and he just looked at me in that way he has that can make you feel cold. Then he laughed and said, 'All right, Bill, you've done you're duty. Don't press it.'"

"What did you do?"

"I just ignored it and advised him again not to destroy them."

"But he did so anyway?"

"Yes, sir. He threw them in the fire right after . . ." He broke off abruptly with a grimace of self-exasperation.

"Right after what, Major?"

Smith shrugged. "Nothing, really."

"Major Smith," Bowman's words were pointed and evenly paced, "what took place immediately before he burned those letters? Did he say something?"

"Yes."

"What, Major? What did he say?"

Smith took a deep breath. "He said he was going to get rid of them right now before Dick Callaway saw them or . . ." He stopped.

"Or? Or *what*, Major Smith?"

". . . or he—Captain Callaway—would *really* be able to nail him for treason."

Bowman let a stifling silence fill the air after Smith's final words. The seconds ticked by until more than twenty had passed before the judge advocate spoke again, and when he did his voice was icy, deadly.

"He was so right, Major, but with or without those letters, I assure you, Captain Daniel Boone will be nailed for treason! No more questions."

III

Immediately after Colonel John Bowman's final remark to Major William Bailey Smith, Colonel Daniel Trabue had excused the witness and then rapped the table with his sitting-bear gavel and announced a recess of fifteen minutes. More of the spectators than had left during the first recess went out this time, but the majority still remained seated. Three of the members of the court—Captains James Galloway and John Todd and Colonel Trabue himself—left the roofed-over area, ducking their heads against the chill drizzle as they moved rapidly out through the fort's west gate and along the mucky relief path.

Judge Advocate John Bowman spoke in guarded whispers for half the recess with Colonel Benjamin Logan and Captain Richard Callaway, then busied himself leafing through a stack of papers and making some notes. A similar conference took place at the defense table between Harrod, Boone and Henderson, but this one lasted until the three officers of the court returned and the session was once more brought to order.

"Captain Boone," Colonel Trabue directed, "you may call your next witness for the defense."

Boone approached to within a few feet of the bar. "Sir," he told the president of the court, "there's another member of the court present here that I'd like to call—John Holder."

John Charles Holder, captain and acting major of the Boonesborough Militia was a slender officer of about twenty-six, good-looking despite his high, hawkish nose. His thin black moustache was a complement to the aquiline features. Sworn and seated, he listened attentively to Boone's first question.

"Cap'n Holder, you were one of the party of men I took to the Blue Licks last January first to make salt, weren't you?"

"I was."

"But you were not captured?"

"No, I wasn't."

"Will you explain, please, why not?"

"I was not there when the capture took place, Captain Boone. I was one of the three men who had regular guard duty at the camp, but at that particular time I was in Boonesborough."

"It has been testified on several occasions here, John, that there were no guards at the saltmaking camp."

"Well, that's not quite true, Captain Boone. It's true that there didn't happen to be any at the time the Indians captured everyone, but that was an unusual circumstance. Normally you insisted on there being four regular guards on patrol. I was one of them, Flanders Callaway was another, and Mike Stoner a third. Depending on which way you went out from camp in the morning to hunt, the other three of us would go out in the other three directions and make a regular patrol, being especially watchful for Indian sign. You yourself would make the same sort of guard patrol in the fourth direction while you were hunting."

"But you were not running such a patrol when the capture took place?"

"No, sir. The three of us—Flanders, Mike and I—were sent back to Boonesborough with the first lot of salt. That way, none of the men working in salt production would have to be pulled off their jobs, and since there had not been that first trace of Indians for over a month and it was the time of year when Indian danger was always least, we all felt that it was reasonably safe to break the pattern and let the guards take the salt in and inform everyone at Boonesborough that everything was fine."

"What happened when you came back to the Blue Licks salt camp from Boonesborough?"

"Well, we got there I guess only a few hours after you were

taken away, since there was still a little warmth in the fire ashes. We could see all the tracks and the dumped salt and figured out what happened, and so we immediately hustled back to Boonesborough with the news. After a week passed and there was no attack on the fort, we realized that there wouldn't be any, and so we went out and gathered up the salt that had been dumped, salvaging about ninety percent of it. We brought that back to Boonesborough, along with the big salt kettles."

"Where were you, Captain Holder, when the actual fighting broke out at Boonesborough?"

"I was in the fort. I'd been put in charge, by you, of the riflemen on the walls. All of us there, according to your instructions, took beads on the Indians you were signing the peace treaty with. As soon as we saw the Indians grab you, I gave the order to open fire. I personally fired at one of the Indians holding Major Smith and killed that Indian. Lots of other Indians dropped then, too, and we figured they were killed. Then you eight men broke free of the Indians and we laid down a covering fire for you."

"Was the firing very heavy at first?"

"On our side it was as heavy as we could make it, but the firing from the Indians was not especially heavy, at least not at the very beginning. Quite soon, though, the firing from them became much hotter than our own and at times the balls hitting our palisades sounded almost like hail."

"How long did the heavy firing continue?" Boone asked. "From the Indians, that is?"

"It continued very hot during the day but then eased off at nightfall. It picked up again briefly when you went out after Mr. Buchanan, but then for the rest of the night firing was largely sporadic."

"What about on the following days of the siege?"

"Mr. President," Bowman complained in a bored tone of voice, "the details of the siege are known well by virtually everyone here. Can we not move on to matters of more relevance to the charges against the defendant?"

"Captain Boone?" Trabue raised his eyebrows questioningly.

"Sir," Boone replied, "what I'm asking John Holder here, and what I'm going to be asking him yet may deal with the siege, all right, but as for it being irrelevant, that ain't the case at all."

"The court," Trabue declared, "will rule for the defense on

this point, with the understanding that the defendant will soon show the relevance of the testimony."

"Thank you, Colonel," Boone said. "Now, then, John, how heavy was the shooting on the following days?"

Holder considered that carefully. "I would say without hesitation that there was more shooting on that first day of the siege, at least on the part of the Indians, than on all the rest of the days put together. The second day the firing from them was about half as heavy as the first day and after that it dropped way down. Toward the end of the siege there was hardly any gunfire, but a whole lot more arrows were coming in. What we were worried about most at first was the artillery they claimed to have. We were still pretty worried about that the next day, too, even though word had gone around that you had claimed that the enemy had no cannon. Most of us didn't really believe that, because Major Smith was so sure that they *did* have it and, of course, had seen the cannonballs when he was out with you to talk with the Indians before the fighting began. But since we never did get shot at with cannon, Captain Boone, it turned out you were right."

"How many of our people were killed during those nine days of the siege?"

"Just three. The first one was a Negro named London. He was Judge Henderson's servant, who had stayed here on Henderson's orders to await his return. Anyway, London stood up to shoot at an Indian who'd crept in pretty close, and when he pulled the trigger, the hammer just snapped. The Indian killed him with a shot through the head. The second one was William Torrence, who got killed when he ran outside with me to pour some water on a fire the Indians had started along the north wall. We got the fire out all right, but he got killed while we were running back to the gate. Then the last one was Mrs. Bryce, Edgar Bryce's wife. Somehow a rifle ball came through a crack in the palisades about sunset the third day and caught her in the throat. She lived until just before dawn, but then she died."

"How many Indians were killed?"

"We don't know for sure, but figuring on the basis of everyone who was very sure he made kills, there were probably at least thirty or forty, plus lots more that were wounded."

"There weren't any bodies outside the fort after the siege ended?"

"Not Indians. I guess they took their dead away, like they usually do. But the black man, Pompey, was lying dead out there. They'd left him."

"How did Pompey get killed?"

"You killed him, Captain Boone. He kept climbing up a big tall beech tree way out there, around three or four hundred yards from the fort and kept screaming at us to surrender or die. It was sort of funny at first, but after the fifth day of it the whole business was getting on everybody's nerves. You finally loaded up Tick-Licker with an extra-heavy powder charge and a one-ounce ball, took a bead on him and knocked him out of the tree. When he was found by us later on under that tree, he had a bullet hole as big as my thumb square in the middle of his chest and a hole big as my fist in his back where the bullet came out. Best shot I ever saw!" He looked admiringly at Boone.

"You say, John," Boone went on, ignoring the praise, "that after the first two days, gunfire from the Indians fell way off but that arrow shooting increased. How else did they try to take the fort?"

"Well, there were a couple of direct charges tried at the walls, but each time we repulsed them with rifle fire. We killed a lot of them that way, but the bodies would always be gone by the time the next morning came around. They did a lot of firing into the fort from the hill behind us, and from the hill across the river—with guns and arrows both. Your daughter, Jemima, for example, was carrying gunpowder and loading guns and so on like the rest of the women when a rifle ball from the hill across the river hit her in the . . ." he paused and then added, blushing ". . . in the fleshy part of her lower back." There was laughter from the gallery at this, but he rushed on. "It wasn't too bad, though, and just pulling on the cloth of her dress, which had been forced into the wound, pulled the ball out with it. The ball was just about spent before it hit her. Squire Boone's dog, Old Spot, got hit the same way and was nearly killed. One of the cows was killed when hit by an arrow that was lofted in. Several people got slightly wounded by arrows the same way, but nothing really serious. What was bad was when they started lofting fire arrows at us and throwing torches at the walls. We had a bad time dousing all the fires on the cabin roofs. Those they tried to start with torches thrown against the walls we got out, too, but there were a couple times when it looked pretty bad for us. One fire just about got out of control when it started to rain and put it out."

"How did you put out most of the wall fires?"

"Either by dumping water over the walls or, if that didn't work, running outside with buckets of water to dump on them, which is what was happening when Bill Torrence was with me and got killed."

"You weren't hurt?"

"No."

Bowman was standing, but the president of the court, knowing what he was going to say, ignored him and addressed Boone.

"Captain Boone, it still seems to the court that this sort of questioning is getting us nowhere in particular. I will have to insist, as I'm sure the prosecutor wishes me to do, that you address yourself now more directly to the issue."

Boone scratched his head. "Is it addressing myself to the issue, Colonel, if I show what I did to help Boonesborough withstand the siege?"

"To a certain extent, perhaps, Captain Boone, and you are given rein to do so, as this could possibly mitigate in your favor. But it must be to the point, sir."

"Yes, sir, Colonel. I'll stick more to what we're after from here on out. John, how else did they try to get at us?"

"At one point, early in the morning, they pretended to raise the siege and leave. we could hear them loading horses and making lots of noise. The lookouts saw them file away until they disappeared in the woods about a mile away, and everyone was elated and all set to open the gates and run outside. We were sure it was all over, but you ordered everyone to be quiet and stay inside."

Holder looked from Boone to the bar and addressed his next remarks to the court directly. "There were some," he said, "Captain Callaway for one, who were extremely angry at Captain Boone for this. You've got to understand," he added hastily, "that we'd been under fire for quite a while and we were crowded, uncomfortable, didn't have good food or water, and our nerves were pretty ragged. Captain Callaway actually went so far as to open up the gate, but Captain Boone ran up, jerked him away from it and locked it again, and then hit Callaway on the side of his face with his fist. It knocked Callaway flat. Boone then said if anyone else tried to go out until he personally gave the order, he would shoot that person.

We all knew he meant it, too. Things remained pretty tense for an hour or so and then one of our lookouts gave a yell. Indians were suddenly jumping up from where they'd been hiding behind every stump and log and they were hightailing it for the woods. I guess they'd taken cover there during the night and had stayed hidden all day while the others had pretended to leave. If we'd been more ready, we could probably have killed a dozen of them. As it was, only one was dropped by one of the lookouts. After that everyone was pretty subdued and within an hour all the Indians were back shooting and lofting arrows at us again."

Daniel Boone was unmoved by the relation of his actions and only moved on to his next question. "Was any other kind of attempt made to take the fort, John?"

"The way that worried us most," the young captain said, nodding, "was when they started to dig a tunnel from the riverbank to the fort. They dug for five or six days, I guess."

"How did you learn about it?"

"You were the one, Captain, who saw that the river water was suddenly getting muddy from there they were digging out of sight of us and dumping the excavated dirt into the river and you figured out what they were doing. You said you thought they meant to dig as far as the wall and when they ran into it you were pretty sure they intended to put a big explosive charge against the underground part of the palisades and blow a big hole in the wall. If that happened, we'd be done for sure."

"What did we do to counteract it?"

"Well, first you ordered us to start digging ourselves and to throw the dirt over the wall on that side to make them think we were digging a cross-trench to intercept them. But when that didn't stop them, you fired the artillery at them."

"The *what!*" Colonel Trabue had leaped to his feet in his astonishment, as had Bowman at the prosecution table. "Captain Holder, do I understand you to say that Boonesborough had *artillery*, which it fired at the enemy?"

"We did and we didn't, Mr. President," Holder told him. He looked at the defendant with an attitude of great respect and pride. "Actually, it was all Captain Boone's idea. He had decided to make some artillery."

"*Make some!*" Trabue was completely bewildered. "How could he possibly make some artillery?" As always whenever artillery was mentioned, the president of the court was showing strong interest. He glanced at Bowman who was on his feet again and shot a hand out at the judge advocate in an impatient gesture. "Sit down, Colonel!" he ordered. Then he dipped his head at Holder to continue as he sat down again himself.

Holder cleared his throat. "Starting about the second day of the siege, sir, Captain Boone had all the younger boys of the fort begin hollowing out a long elm log that was on the ground in the fort. It was about twelve feet long and maybe a foot or a little more in diameter. The log already had a small hole running down the middle—a natural cavity, I guess. He had them saw it into two six-foot sections, then put them to working on it hard and fast in shifts that spelled each other about every fifteen minutes or so. Even then it wasn't until the eighth day that they were finished with a nice smooth hole about three inches, maybe even four, straight down the middle. Anyway, once they were bored and drilled for a fuse, a big heavy wooden plug was hammered into the back end and then held in place with bent pieces of iron wagon-tire, nailed across in an X-shape. At one-foot intervals down the length he also had bindings of the same iron stripping wrapped around them as snug as we could get them. He had them blacken the whole thing—both of them—with charcoal, but he kept saying that he wished we had had enough of the elm log to make a third one, because he needed three shots."

"Three shots?" questioned Trabue. "Why three?"

"He just said we *had* to have three shots, but since we only had two of the wooden guns, we'd have to make it work out. He said that after the third shot was fired the Indians would call off the siege. Nobody could figure out what he was talking about and nobody really believed him, but since no one else had any ideas, we did what he said."

"All right, go ahead. What happened?"

"None of us were any too anxious about trying to shoot them like real cannon because we were pretty sure they'd just blow up and kill anybody standing near them. Captain Boone said he would fire them. He had us use ropes to haul them up to the platform about five feet below the inside top of the wall on the east side. We fixed up a couple of wooden tripods to set the breech end on and rested the muzzle end between two of the sharpened ends of the palisade uprights. First, though, we loaded one with a heavy charge of black powder from the magazine and about twenty or thirty ounce-sized rifle balls. All of that was put in the one wooden cannon that

Captain Boone thought was the weakest. In the other one he put about half as much powder but no charge. The women had made three thirty-foot powder fuses like Captain Boone had ordered and one of these was in the port of the first cannon and stretched to the ground below. Captain Boone put a few men in the northeast and southeast blockhouses to watch out of the rifle ports. Everyone else he ordered to get under cover. Then he climbed back up to where he could see over the wall and yelled out to Chief Black Fish."

"Yelled out to him? Why? What did he say?"

"Sir, he said that he had warned Black Fish the night before that if he kept on, this was going to happen. He said that he had tried to convince the new commander of the fort not to use his artillery, but that Major Smith was now very angry about this seige and intended to teach Black Fish a lesson."

"You're sure he said he had *warned* Black Fish?"

"Yes, sir, Colonel Trabue. That's what he called out. We all heard him."

"And you also heard him shout to Chief Black Fish that it was the previous night that he had given him this alleged warning?"

"Yes, sir."

Trabue's confusion increased. "Go on," he said at last.

"Well, he came back down, made sure everyone was in the cabins or blockhouses or under cover somewhere and then scrunched himself up against the base of the east wall and lighted the fuse. It was an extremely fast fuse and the fire got to the gun in about three or four seconds. It exploded with a tremendous boom. The lookouts in the blockhouses said they could see small branches clipped off trees and spurts of dirt tossed up from the ground way across the clearing, and they heard some Indians start yelling."

"And the gun?"

"It had blown to bits, sir. Pieces of it shot every whichway and there was a big cloud of smoke. There just wasn't much left of that first cannon at all, but nobody inside the fort got hurt."

"What then?" Trabue was leaning forward, fascinated, as were several others of the court officers.

"Immediately after that Captain Boone rigged the second log cannon with a fuse like the first, but he firmly roped the barrel of this gun to the platform. By then a whole bunch of

Indians had come into sight at the far edge of the clearing, jumping up and down and laughing. We heard someone—I guess it might have been one of the white men with them— yell out that Captain Boone had now blown up his wooden cannon, so what was he going to do?"

"Did Captain Boone answer them?"

"Yes, sir, he sure did. He called back, addressing Chief Black Fish again, and saying that there was no wooden gun in Boonesborough—only a fine strong cannon that he had hoped they would not have to use. He said he would fire one more warning shot, as he had promised the chief he would, and that if they didn't end their siege with that one, then he would have to fire at them in earnest. They were still laughing at him when he came down and lighted the second fuse."

"This was the one with the powder charge only?" the court president asked.

"Yes, sir. It ran up fast like the first one did and made a big bang, much louder than a rifle, but nowhere near as loud as the first blast. The recoil had caused the log to spin backwards and hang from the platform by the rope, but it really wasn't damaged and Captain Boone and I and some others got up there and pulled it back up. The captain checked the gun and found it hadn't even cracked from the light charge. He ran some damp wadding down the barrel to snuff out any live sparks and when there was no more smoke coming out, Captain Boone fitted the third fuse and loaded the gun again."

"The same way?"

"Not exactly, sir. This time he put in a much larger powder charge—larger even than the first one. He rammed it down with a pole and wadding and then shoved in a cylinder of wood not quite the diameter of the hole in the log. In a couple of places it was a pretty tight fit, but he finally got it rammed down all the way. When he was satisfied, he poured in what must have been three or four pounds of assorted sizes of rifle balls, including quite a lot that were out of shape that we had picked up inside the fort, shot at us by the enemy. By now there were more Indians than ever in view—maybe as many as a hundred. One of them, who claimed to be Black Fish—although Captain Boone said it didn't sound like him— yelled out, 'Sheltowee lie. No thunder gun. Black Fish not afraid Sheltowee warning.' Well, Captain Boone positioned the gun so it was aimed just over the heads of the men we could see, locked it into place as firmly as possible with some timbers propped against the platform, and then yelled that if that was how they wanted it, then we would now really begin making war, though he regretted hurting his father's people. He came down and lighted the fuse and this time, sir, when the gun blew it sounded like the crack of doom, believe me! Even with the blast, the lookouts said they could hear the rifle balls screaming through the air like grapeshot and some of the Indians fell—maybe eight or nine of them. All the Indians dropped flat then, but in a moment they jumped up again and ran off, but at least seven of them had to be carried away by the others."

"Was there any damage inside the fort?"

"The platform was knocked down and the gun itself had simply disintegrated and scattered all over, but not a soul inside Boonesborough was hurt. It was late in the afternoon then and still raining—it had been raining on and off all day—after that it got pretty quiet except for some scattered shooting from the Indians and us. It continued raining all night and in the morning everything was quiet. It stayed quiet until noon without the lookouts sighting one of the enemy, but no one wanted to be the one to go out and check to make sure they were gone. Finally, though, Captain Boone himself went out and ran from cover to cover toward the river. He got out of sight of us and was gone for about half an hour. When next we saw him he was walking straight across the clearing toward us and waving. We knew then that the Indians had lifted the siege and were gone."

"Thank you, Captain Holder," Colonel Trabue said, "for your excellent presentation." The president of the court turned an appraising eye on Daniel Boone and looked at him steadily for several seconds. "Captain Boone," he said at last, "you may continue."

Boone nodded. "Captain Holder, when the siege was definitely over and we were able to leave the fort, what did you do?"

"I went on a tour of the whole area, sir, along with you and Major Smith and Captain Callaway."

"For what purpose?"

"We wanted to see the diggings that the Indians had been doing, as well as to check out their campsite, look for weapons, dead men, and so on."

"What did you find?"

"Well, for one thing, we found that tunnel they'd been digging had reached a point only a dozen feet from the north wall, but the all-day and all-night rain had weakened it and it had caved in. We also collected about a dozen tomahawks and twenty-six—I think it was twenty-six—anyway, twenty-six or twenty-seven flintlock rifles that had been broken in half."

"How had they been broken?"

"It looked like they had been deliberately smashed across tree trunks or rocks. The stocks on all of them were broken, most of the barrels were bent, and the triggers were missing. It was obvious they had been broken so we would not be able to fix them for our own use when we found them."

"Anything else?"

"We also found their main camp, which was in the valley behind the hills across the river from us, but there was nothing of value there. We also found the body of Pompey, too, and buried it."

"There were no Indian bodies?"

"No, sir."

"All right, Captain Holder, thank you. No more questions."

Daniel Boone turned and moved back to the defense table and sat down. Immediately he was the target of a barrage of whisperings from Harrod and Henderson, but he merely held up a hand to cut them off, indicating that he wanted to pay close attention to Bowman's cross-examination of John Holder.

For his own part, Colonel Bowman looked a little dazed. Twice Colonel Trabue asked him if he wished to cross-examine before he finally nodded slowly and stood. He walked with deliberate thoughtfulness to a point three or four feet in front of the witness and stopped there. Still it was a long while before he spoke.

"Captain Holder," he said at length, "it is highly distressing to prosecution to learn that one of the members of the court is so strongly biased in favor of the defendant. Do you not feel you should disqualify yourself at this point from returning to the board of court-martial?"

"Colonel Bowman," rapped out Trabue, "that question is entirely improper. You are the individual who, as judge advocate, administered the oath of this office to Captain Holder and who heard him swear to impartiality. Equally, as a witness he is bound to the oath of truth and there is no indication that he has testified otherwise during these proceedings. I think it is quite clear that he has acted well, both as court member and as witness. I am equally sure that he will continue to serve as a member of this court in as unbiased a manner as is required of him."

"Sir, may I speak?" It was Captain John Holder. At Trabue's nod, he went on. "Sir, I feel that others here may wonder at my impartiality considering my testimony as a witness. I can say in all honesty that I believe I am still impartial, and state that I have testified only to my own knowledge of events which actually occurred here. I have made no judgment yet in my own mind as to either the guilt or innocence of the defendant. But if it will serve this court and the administration of justice, I will step down as a member of this board of court-martial and some other officer could be called in my stead."

"That is not necessary, Captain," the president of the court said. "You may continue to give testimony if Colonel Bowman intends cross-examination, but when it is completed you will then return to your place on this board of court-martial and fulfill the remainder of your duties there. I have no doubt— and feel certain that no other member of this court feels any doubt whatever—that you will be able to continue your duties as prescribed by the Articles of War, the Mutiny Act, and the Code of Military Law. Colonel Bowman, you may now cross-examine."

Glowering, Bowman had thrust his lower jaw out in a pugnacious manner and his bulging eyes were flint-hard as he stared at the witness. Hooking one thumb in his waistcoat pocket he said acrimoniously, "Captain Holder, you have told an interesting story of Captain Boone's ingenuity in the defense of Boonesborough, but I noticed in his examination Captain Boone steered well clear of anything pertaining directly to the charges lodged against him. A man who robs his neighbor and then, later, dives into the river to save the life of a drowning child may well be admired for his act of rescue, but it in no way diminishes his original crime. In the same way, the heroic acts you attribute to Captain Boone in the defense of Boonesborough might be admirable and praiseworthy, but sir, *in no way* do they mitigate the crimes of which he is charged here. Captain Boone has, by his own admission, collaborated with the enemy and plotted the overthrow of his own fort and the people therein. That, sir, is treason, and that is only part of the case that has developed against Captain Boone. Is it not true that if Boonesborough had not been attacked in the first place, two men and a woman—residents of Boonesborough—would still be alive?"

"Yes, sir, that's true."

"Is it not also true that if Boonesborough had not been attacked, great hardship would not have been wrought upon his people here, and that the many who were wounded would never have been injured?"

"Yes, sir."

"Is it not also true that Daniel Boone, in leading his seven fellows to the final meeting with the Indians before the siege began, exposed them to extreme danger?"

"Well, in a way, sir, it's true, but—"

"Merely answer the question, please, Captain. Is it not also true that as a result of that meeting Major William Bailey Smith was struck a tomahawk blow which injured him and might well have ended his life had the Indian's aim been better?"

"He was struck, sir, yes; but if the Indian's aim had been better he'd have hit Captain Boone rather than Major Smith, since it was Captain Boone he was aiming to strike."

"But Major Smith did indeed receive a dangerous wound?"

"Yes, sir."

"And is it not also true that Daniel Boone thought so little of his own brother's life that he exposed him to this danger and that as a result, Squire Boone was shot by the Indians and at this moment still lies gravely wounded in his cabin?"

"No, sir."

Bowman's mouth dropped open, then snapped shut. "What do you mean, 'No, sir'? Daniel Boone exposed his brother Squire to danger by asking him to be one of the eight who attended that meeting, did he not?"

"Yes, sir."

"And Squire Boone was subsequently shot while fleeing from the Indians, wasn't he?"

"Yes, sir."

"And still lies very seriously wounded?"

"Yes, sir."

"Then I don't follow you. Please explain yourself."

"Squire Boone," said Holder quietly, "was not shot by the Indians."

Bowman was thunderstruck. "How can you possibly say that," he demanded, "when a score or more of people watched him get shot down as he ran with his brother and the other men to escape the Indians."

"Sir," Holder said, "when Captain Boone rescued his brother and brought him into the fort, it was not until later in the evening that he was able to see him again. Squire was in great pain and Captain Boone, after examining the wound carefully, said the bullet would have to come out right away or his brother would die. He asked me to help him, which I did, along with Jemima. It was Captain Boone who opened the wound and removed the bullet."

Bowman was undoubtedly quite confused at this seeming *non sequitur*. Holder paused for a moment and then went on. "The point is, sir," he said levelly, "that when we finally got around to treating him, we saw that the bullet which struck Squire Boone had entered from the front, not from the back where the Indians were. It seems," he added remorsefully, "that I or one of my men on the wall in Boonesborough, in our desire to lay down a protecting fire for the escaping men, inadvertently shot Squire Boone."

Bowman grimaced and clenched his fists at his sides, mentally chiding himself for walking into a pointless situation which placed him in a bad light and which abraded the points he had been establishing against Boone. He coughed briefly and attempted to recover.

"Be that as it may, Captain," he said, "the facts of the matter remain clear. Captain Boone has drawn from you not one trace of testimony that refutes any of the evidence against him, that in the events prior to the siege of Boonesborough he was guilty of treasonable acts. I have no further questions."

Even as he excused the witness, Colonel Trabue brought his gavel down sharply on the tabletop and announced adjournment of the court-martial until eight o'clock in the morning.

7

Although it was a bright and cheerful morning on this seventh day of the court-martial of Daniel Boone, there was a subdued sense to the assemblage which had gathered under the expansive roofed-over area in Boonesborough. The crisp chill of the morning air turned exhaled breaths into tiny, momentary plumes of vapor, as if a page in the seasons had abruptly been turned. It was no longer summer weather. Overnight the subtle presence of autumn had come with its promise of bitterly cold days ahead, and eyes automatically went to the trees, expecting that somehow, miraculously, the leaves had burst into glorious fall colors, but they hadn't. The oaks and maples, hickories and elms and walnuts remained as green as they had been yesterday and the only splash of color was one side of a tall sweet gum tree which, in the way of such trees, had turned scarlet a week or so ago.

The six men seated at the two smaller tables to right and left of the long, presently empty central table spoke little among themselves. Several times Captain Richard Callaway had attempted to engage Colonel John Bowman in conversation, but the judge advocate's replies had been terse and without warmth, and so Callaway had given up and sat idly fingering a button on his frock coat. On the other side of Bowman, Colonel Benjamin Logan sat with his hands quietly folded on the table before him, his thoughts turned inward, his features devoid of any expression.

Across from them at their own table, Daniel Boone, Samuel Henderson and James Harrod were also quiet. Boone sat with his arms folded across his chest and his eyes all but closed. Henderson was in the middle, the scratching of his pen abnormally loud as it raced across the sheet of foolscap before him, the dancing, feathered length of the quill pausing at regular intervals to be raised and moved as the pared tip

241

was plunged precisely into the inkpot to Henderson's right. James Harrod sat much as Logan was, his hands folded before him, paying little attention to either Henderson or Boone. Unlike Logan, however, he was not lost in introspection. His eyes moved in turn from Logan to Callaway to Bowman, studying each of them, as if by look alone he might find some clue to weakness. Harrod sighed, wishing this whole business was behind them. He looked over his shoulder for a moment and then settled back into his previous position.

The members of the board of court-martial had not yet left their nearby cabin and a stir of unrest was growing in the gallery. A sibilance of whisperings rose in a scattered manner from among them, punctuated now and again by muted coughings and throat clearings, by occasional louder words, but at no time by laughter. There was no apparent levity among the spectators gathered here today, nor even much of a sense of unity among them. Though they all sat together, they were mostly islands of themselves, listening with half an ear to the murmurings of their neighbors and replying, if at all, in short, low-pitched phrases. Mostly they sat and waited with diminishing patience, sometimes looking toward the officers' quarters, sometimes toward the prosecution table, but mostly, as if drawn by magnetism, to the stoical Daniel Boone.

In their attitudes as they gazed upon him there was a sense of disappointment, of unfulfillment, as if they had expected this man over the past week to shuck off his veneer of impassivity and bare his innermost feelings to all, and he had failed them. Only the one time—when John Bowman had driven home the vicious little barb about Rebecca Boone— had the defendant momentarily reacted with anger. Before that and since then he had remained unreachable, a silent and unreadable man even when questioning witnesses.

There had been the sense throughout this trial thus far that Daniel Boone was scornful of any efforts to help him; that he was stubborn and uncooperative; that without moving from his place, he was striding alone through a wilderness of sorts, memorizing the boulderlike placement of words here and there, wading swiftly through a grassy sea of testimony, noting little occasional clearings, almost hidden, where something may not have been which should have been; noting the presence of each tall tree of fact behind which might be crouched a deadly foe named accusation; moving steadily, alert without seeming alertness, reading as much from a word, an inflection, a glance, as he might in the forest wilderness from the flitting of a bird, the twitch of a deer's ear, the bent or broken blade of grass. There was a feeling of subdued incensement, of subtle antagonism toward him because of this—as if they resented the idea that any man could remain isolated from all others, depending upon his own resources only in the face of staggering obstacles. It made them feel less capable of themselves, less confident in their own strengths and abilities, and because of this reaction it made many of them feel that Daniel Boone deserved whatever happened to him now, whether just or not.

Throughout the evening yesterday and much of the preceding night before this morning's gathering, Boone had been discussed and rediscussed, his guilt or innocence reassessed, the small mountain of testimony thus far given against him climbed and then reclimbed from all possible approaches. The evidence against him had mounted inexorably, like the massive, heavy blade of a great guillotine pulled ever higher by the strongly braided rope of testimony as witnesses in turn told of what he had said and what he had done; climbing ever higher until locked into place by the deft hand of John Bowman, but ready in an instant to flash downward in one swift and fatal passage.

Daniel Boone's defense to this point had been interesting, but less than spectacular. He had shown a skill in questioning that had been unsuspected, and under this questioning, both in cross-examination and direct, small points of damning testimony against him had been altered or expanded to present a new aspect, perhaps, but the undeniable fact remained that the principal charges had not been refuted or hardly even touched in dispute. Courage and heroism and ingenuity might well have been apparent on his part during Boonesborough's great crisis, but would such a crisis have developed at all had not Boone said and done what the witnesses had testified to?

There could be no doubt of it—the attitude of the onlookers had subtly changed over the past two or three days. The belief in Daniel Boone's guilt had not diminished; had, in fact, been strengthened, even cemented in many cases. Few any longer vacillated in their conviction of his guilt. Yet now, oddly enough, there had been an abatement of the anger, a banking of the fires of hatred which at times had approached the point of conflagration. Now there was something akin to sympathy in them, yet it was a paradoxically merciless form of sympathy. Though it was not articulated, it was as if they were saying to one another that, yes, Daniel Boone was guilty, and wasn't it a pity that a man such as he would have to die?

Among the onlookers, Jemima Boone Callaway sat in a tight shell of misery, gleaning little comfort from the protective arm of her young husband as he held her close to his side. Her eyes were haunted, mirroring the unspeakable specters that prowled behind them, and occasionally she gave way to a small shiver. She had been relatively relaxed as she sat there, but now her body abruptly stiffened and Flanders noticed it at once. His gaze followed hers and locked on the little cabin to their left, closest to the northwest blockhouse. The door had opened and in single file, in the order of their seating, the thirteen members of the board of court-martial filed out and wordlessly took their seats at the long central table.

For a minute or two they settled themselves, arranging their papers on the table before them and checking the neatly sharpened nibs of the quill pens. They did not speak to one another, except for the president of the court, who briefly murmured to the officer at his left and nodded once at Major Robert Anderson's equally brief reply. Immediately, then, the gavel banged loudly one time on the table.

"This court-martial is hereby reconvened," Colonel Trabue said. "The defense may continue with its examination of witnesses."

Daniel Boone took several steps from the defense table and stopped, dipping his head respectfully toward the court. "Colonel," he said, "I'd like to have John Bowman take the witness chair."

There was a considerable stir in the court, a strong murmuring of wonder and surprise. Bowman himself was taken aback and was suddenly more alert and very suspicious. He looked at Boone steadily for a moment and then at the president of the court, who nodded.

"Colonel Bowman will rise and be sworn by the court," Trabue said.

A distinct scowl on his face, Bowman walked to the witness chair and stood there facing the court, his right hand upraised, palm forward. At the central table Colonel Trabue had also risen.

"Do you," he asked Bowman, "solemnly swear that in the testimony you are about to give in the matter presently before this court, you will speak the truth, the whole truth, and nothing but the truth, so help you God?"

"I do."

Both colonels seated themselves simultaneously and Boone casually approached the one in the witness chair.

"Reckon you know you're supposed to tell the court your full name and residence now," he said.

"Bowman," the witness said crisply. "John Wilcox Bowman. Colonel. Temporary residence, Harrodsburg."

"Colonel Bowman, do you consider me guilty of treason?"

At the defense table James Harrod groaned audibly and Samuel Henderson shook his head. Bowman was momentarily startled but then half-smiled at the unexpected opening.

"I do," he said evenly, "beyond any shadow of doubt."

"And as prosecutor in this case against me, you would do anything to see that I am convicted of treason?"

Bowman almost smiled at what he considered Boone's clumsy effort to entrap him with a damaging admission. "It is my duty," he replied carefully, "to prosecute you to the fullest extent of my ability, within the realm of legality."

"Would you deliberately lie to get me convicted?"

"I would not!" Bowman was assertive but not incensed.

"Would you deliberately withhold evidence in order to get me convicted?"

"I would not, sir!"

"Would you knowingly prevent a witness from testifying to matters which might damage your own case against me?"

Bowman hesitated for just an instant before answering. "As prosecutor in this case," he said guardedly, "I am obliged to draw on all my resources to bring a conviction against the accused. I am not obliged to voluntarily elicit from witnesses testimony which might be favorable to the accused."

"In other words," Boone continued, "if you knew that a witness for the prosecution had information which might be of assistance to me, you would carefully maneuver the witness away from expressing such information?"

Bowman was becoming more wary by the instant. The usual homey, nonchalant, backwoodsy nature of Daniel Boone was hardly noticeable. He was sharp, direct, in positive control of how he expressed himself and boring in with a sharpness and penetration that was both annoying and unnerving. Bowman no longer smiled and a veil had been raised, masking the protuberant blue eyes. He became even more circumspect in his reply.

"It is possible," he admitted, "that I would do so, but only within the bounds of my right to do so. It is not and never has been the responsibility of prosecution to prompt testimony from his witnesses which might be damaging to his own case."

Neither the court nor the gallery could understand where this line of questioning by Boone was leading, but there was an electric increase of interest on everyone's part and John Bowman's own wariness mounted proportionately. The bulging eyes regarded Boone steadily, frigidly. Boone returned the gaze, measuring the man before him. Abruptly he turned and walked a few paces away before turning back to face the witness again.

"Colonel Bowman," he said, "here and there throughout this whole trial you've mentioned the two men who were part of my expedition to the Scioto Valley in the Ohio country— men you made sure to point out who never returned to Boonesborough. Do you recall which men I mean?"

"I do. Simon Kenton and Alexander Montgomery."

"Do you know that Simon Kenton was my closest friend?"

"I knew you were companions and had roamed the woods together a great deal."

"Do you know that Alexander Montgomery was also a very good friend of mine?"

"I had heard he was."

"And Alexander Montgomery is now dead?"

"He is. Killed by the Shawnees and scalped."

"And Simon Kenton?"

"He was captured by them, tortured and is now also believed to be dead."

"*How,* Colonel Bowman," Boone shot at him, "do you know these facts?"

Bowman moistened his lips with the tip of his tongue and the faintest glimmer of alarm showed briefly in his eyes. "From the statement of a man who was with them when they were caught, but who managed to escape."

"Who was this man?"

"His name is George Clarke."

"George Rogers Clark?"

"No. Clarke with an 'e.' No relation to George Rogers Clark."

"Not many white people here in the Kentucky country I don't know," Boone mused. "Strange that I don't know this George Clarke. Where's he from?"

"He lived in Harrodsburg. He was a newcomer to Kentucky who settled in Harrodsburg in July."

"You knew him before he came here?"

"Yes. I had met him, but I didn't know him well."

"Where did you meet him and under what circumstances?"

"In Williamsburg. He knew my younger sister, Olive."

"He came here because you were here?"

"I cannot say for sure. Evidently the letters I wrote to my sister about this country were read by her to him. He is only twenty and very impressionable. Apparently he admired me through my sister and had certain romantic notions about becoming a frontiersman."

"He made his way here and came to you because he thought you would help him become one?"

"I believe this to be true." Bowman was becoming a bit agitated despite his efforts to remain unperturbed, but he relaxed a little at Boone's next question.

"Where is this George Clarke now?"

"He has returned to Williamsburg, having decided that frontier life was not quite as pleasant as he expected it to be."

"But it was from him that you learned of what happened to Simon Kenton and Alexander Montgomery?"

"Mr. President," Bowman said, suddenly turning to face Colonel Trabue, "although I am now being questioned as a witness, I am still the prosecutor and I must, under the cape of that office, object most strongly to the line of questioning the defendant has embarked on. It is certainly irrelevant and immaterial. Captain Boone is quite obviously blindly fishing in unknown waters and desperately hoping for some kind of a nibble. I submit that his questioning should be more directly related to what he is supposed to be dong here—that is, refuting if he can the six counts of treason with which he is charged. His straw-grasping efforts at probing into the actions of a twenty-year-old would-be frontiersman who is no longer even in this country can hardly be considered as being germane to our purposes here. I request that the court direct him to leave this line of questioning and concentrate more directly on the issue."

Trabue considered this for a moment and seemed favorably inclined toward Bowman's argument. He raised his eyebrows toward the defendant. "Captain Boone?"

Boone also faced Trabue and shook his head in a measured way. "Well, sir," he said, "I grant that I don't know a whole lot about what I'm allowed or not allowed to do up here, but it seems to me I recollect from what Sam Henderson told me that I'm within my rights with this questioning. If he," Boone dipped his head at Bowman, "was allowed to talk to his witnesses about Kenton and Montgomery and make out like I was responsible for them being killed by the Indians, then according to what Sam said, I should be allowed to dig into the same subject and maybe show that I ain't."

Trabue turned his attention back to the witness. "Colonel Bowman," he said, "the defendant is quite correct. Prosecution having opened the matter of the two men in question and indirectly implying that Captain Boone was responsible for their deaths, the defendant has every right to pursue the matter further in his own defense. Prosecution's objection is overruled and, as a witness, you are directed to answer the questions put to you by Captain Boone along these lines."

Boone turned back to John Bowman and his tone of voice suddenly sharper. "Well, Colonel, was it from Clarke that you learned about what happened to Alex Montgomery and Kenton?"

"Yes." The set of Bowman's lips gave the impression that he now intended to answer as shortly as possible with nothing extraneous volunteered.

"Huh," Boone muttered, scratching his jaw and squinting at the witness, "seems to me something don't fit here. According to what the different witnesses have said up to now, Colonel, how many men, including me, were in the party that left Boonesborough?"

"Thirty."

"That's right. And how many of 'em turned around at Blue Licks and came back to Boonesborough?"

"Eleven."

"Right again. Reckon that means there were nineteen of us that went on into the Ohio country, right?"

"Yes."

"And how many of us came back to Boonesborough the day before the Shawnees showed up there?"

"Seventeen."

"All but two, eh? Which means that the missing two were Kenton and Montgomery, right?"

"Yes."

"Now that's mighty peculiar to me. I know those two elected to stay behind and try to grab a few of the horses of ours that the Shawnees still had there, but it was just those two. So what bothers me now is, how'd this Clarke feller get involved?"

Bowman didn't answer and Boone evidently didn't really expect him to, since he went on after only the briefest pause. "This George Clarke, Colonel, he wasn't a member of the party that left Boonesborough, was he?"

"No."

"Fact is, he'd never been to Boonesborough, had he?"

"No."

"Ain't it a fact that he never in his life saw either Kenton or Montgomery before the party left Boonesborough?"

"I don't know."

"No," Boone admitted, "I reckon it's possible you don't know. A man can't be expected to know who-all any other man knows or may have met somewhere."

Boone swung away and walked slowly toward the defense table, but before reaching it he turned and came back to stop a couple of paces from the witness chair. In the distance a bobwhite whistled crisply and a small black-and-white woodpecker drummed briefly on one of the palisade uprights before bobbing out of sight in its distinctive flight. They were the only sounds that broke the stillness until Daniel Boone suddenly thrust out an arm and pointed at the witness.

"Colonel Bowman," he demanded harshly, "ain't it true that *you* saw both Kenton and Montgomery after my party left 'em?"

Bowman's voice betrayed no emotion but his face was set in hard lines as he replied. "Yes."

A swell of surprised murmurings erupted from the assemblage, and even as he was tapping his gavel for order Colonel Trabue was frowning, and his attention was locked on John Bowman. Boone went on without pause.

"Where?" he asked. "*Where* did you see Kenton and Montgomery?"

"At St. Asaph."

"In other words, after we left 'em over in the Ohio country, they did come back across the Ohio River and into Kentucky?"

"Yes."

"But instead of coming back here to Boonesborough, they went directly to Logan's Station?"

"Yes." Bowman had lost some of his color.

"Why?"

"They had recovered some horses from that village of Kispoko Town. Four of them. All had originally been taken by the Indians from St. Asaph. Kenton recognized Colonel Logan's black mare among them, and one or two others."

"And so they brought them directly back to Ben Logan?"

"Yes."

"And you happened to be there at Logan's Station—St. Asaph?"

"Yes."

"Colonel, I can't see any point in my having to squeeze all these answers out of you. How about you telling the court yourself right now what happened after that?"

John Bowman was boxed in and he knew it. His shoulders slumped a little and a deep breath escaped him, but he said nothing. It was Colonel Trabue who spoke up in an icy voice.

"Colonel Bowman, you have been directed to explain to this court what transpired after Simon Kenton and Alexander Montgomery came to St. Asaph. You *will* do so!"

"Yes, sir." Recognizing that there was now nothing to do but go ahead with it, Bowman steeled himself and gave his accounting swiftly, briefly, emotionlessly. "When Kenton and Montgomery returned with the horses and gave them to Benjamin Logan, I saw this as a good opportunity to call upon their resourcefulness for a mission I had been considering. William Hancock's escape from the principal Shawnee village of Chalahgawtha had given us our first concrete evidence as to its location. I felt that we should know more about it—its strengths and weaknesses—for a possible expedition against it in time to come. Kenton had been a scout and spy for George Rogers Clark and was experienced in moving about in enemy territory and observing accurately. Montgomery was also highly experienced. I ordered them to infiltrate the enemy country, scout out the village of Chalahgawtha and report back to me at Harrodsburg with information on it. I also ordered them to take along George Clarke, who was at the time with me at St. Asaph. They set out and scouted the area as ordered, but again they decided to take some of the horses the Indians had there which had originally been stolen from us. This was a mistake. The Indians discovered their loss quickly, followed them and caught up with the three men and the seven horses they had taken, overtaking them on the north bank of the Ohio River. Kenton was captured first and tied to a tree. Montgomery made the mistake of showing himself to take a shot at Kenton's captors. He missed and they chased him, caught and killed him and then scalped him. George Clarke had avoided detection by taking refuge in a hollow tree and he witnessed all this. He saw the Indians torture Kenton to some extent and then take him away to the north with the recovered horses. When they were gone, Clarke kicked his way across the Ohio River while hanging onto a log. He made his way back to Harrodsburg and reported to me. Immediately thereafter he decided he had had enough of the frontier and returned to the East."

Colonel Daniel Trabue regarded John Bowman sternly for a long, silent period after the witness had ceased speaking. At last he spoke and his words were implacably cold and harsh.

"Colonel Bowman, by what the defendant has drawn from you in questioning and your own statement just given, you have shown yourself to be guilty of at least a gross dereliction of duty, if not actual perjury. Your offense is grave in the extreme. You have, through careful avoidance of facts known to you, through careful avoidance of any mention of acts instigated by you, and equally through the emphasis of misleading facts, cast false implications of guilt upon the defendant in an obvious effort to bias the court against him in the charges under which he is accused. Your behavior is inexcusable and totally reprehensible and this court officially reprimands you and condemns your actions. Zeal on the part of prosecution is expected and desirable, but not deceit and false witness. You have disgraced your office and your rank and you have brought dishonor to yourself and the court. Because of your actions, in which you have been found out, this court has no other choice than to lodge an official action against you with highest authority in Williamsburg, with the strong recommendation that you be at least demoted in rank and stripped of your powers of judge advocacy, and that you not again be allowed to serve courts-martial in any capacity whatsoever!"

Trabue was breathing rather heavily and the fury he was keeping contained was immense. He continued. "As for the remainder of this present court-martial, Colonel Bowman, the court will allow you to continue in your office, but your conduct henceforward as witness, prosecutor or judge advocate will be under the closest possible scrutiny by the court. Any further suggestion, however faint, sir, that you are abdicating or corrupting your responsibilities and you will be removed from these proceedings and placed under actual arrest and confinement!"

Trabue paused in his diatribe, still glaring at Bowman, but then he shifted his attention to the defendant. "Captain Boone," he continued in a somewhat less agitated tone, "because of what has occurred here, your rights have been subducted and you are given leave to move for mistrial."

Daniel Boone shook his head. "No, sir, I don't want to do that. I want this whole business settled right here and now. But one thing," he added grimly, looking at Bowman, "I sure don't have any more questions for him!"

"The witness," said Trabue curtly as Boone returned to the defense table and sat down, "is excused."

Bowman acted like a man lost in some incredible kind of nightmare. Moving in a trancelike manner, he moved to the prosecution table and sat down, still staring stonily ahead of him. Neither Logan nor Callaway looked at him.

"Defense may call its next witness," Colonel Trabue declared from the bar.

Samuel Henderson was deeply involved in something of a heated discussion with Boone and neither man appeared to have heard. James Harrod stood and addressed the president of the court.

"If the court please, sir, may we have another few moments?"

"Granted," Trabue said. He busied himself with writing swiftly on the paper in front of him while defense discussion continued in muted voices, with Harrod also interjecting comments here and there. For fully two minutes more they talked and then Sam Henderson rolled his eyes upward, slammed one palm down on the table's surface and reluctantly came to his feet. Immediately the soft conversations among the spectators ended and all eyes were anchored on him.

"Mr. President," he said, "Captain Boone has requested that I undertake examination of the next witness."

Trabue nodded.

"The defense," Henderson announced quietly, "calls as its final witness Captain Daniel Boone."

II

As if it had been an electrical charge surging through them, the spectators virtually jumped at Samuel Henderson's declaration. Everyone seemed to be talking at once. Because of Daniel Boone's own handling of cross-examination and his direct examination of defense witnesses thus far, it had generally been taken for granted that he would not himself be taking the stand. The interest in the proceedings, which had never waned throughout the trial, took on an even greater intensity now.

Probably no one was more surprised than Colonel John Bowman. He had been holding himself under rigid control since being reprimanded, allowing no sign of what he was thinking or feeling to become evident, but this seemed to shake him from his trance. He visibly relaxed and even permitted the ghost of a smile to touch his lips. One hand went up and automatically preened his moustache, and then from the papers before him he withdrew a clean sheet, dipped his quill pen and swiftly wrote a few words before getting up. Daniel Boone was already on his feet, moving with his peculiar grace toward the witness chair, and Colonel Trabue was rapping his gavel in metronomic cadence on the table. Only gradually was silence restored in the gallery and by that time Bowman had sworn Boone in and returned to his table.

"State your name and place of residence," Henderson said, approaching the seated witness.

"Daniel Boone. Boonesborough."

"You are a captain in the Virginia Militia?"

"I am."

"Captain Boone, let us move to the incidents beginning last January. It has been testified that you were in charge of the party of thirty saltmakers who left Boonesborough on January one for the Blue Licks and that all went well until the seventh day of February, is that correct?"

"It is."

"Will you please tell the court what occurred on February seven after you left the salt camp for your usual hunt?"

Daniel Boone nodded and hitched his chair around slightly to better face the court directly. "Snow was pretty deep that day," he said. "Six, maybe seven inches. Buff'ler don't much like it, especially where it drifts up in the open places, like around the licks. At times like that they tend to bed down in and around the more protected canebreaks. I headed downstream along the Licking for five or six miles, then started a wide swing southwest toward some canebrakes I knew about. Sure enough, the buff'ler were there. I kilt three of 'em and then spent the rest of the day cutting them up and loading the best cuts of the meat on my horse. It started snowing hard again about the middle of the afternoon and by the time I got to leading my horse back—first back to the river and then upstream—toward Blue Licks it was blizzarding so bad I could hardly see. First I knew there was any trouble about was when my horse snorted. Looked back and saw four Shawnees running up on me about thirty paces away. Whipped out my knife and tried to cut the tugs and drop the meat so I could ride the horse, but the handle was still slick from buff'ler fat and I lost it. I let go of the horse then and took out running. They chased and I'd maybe have outrun 'em, but one buck cut the packs off the horse and started riding me down."

"Were they shooting at you?"

"Yep, but most Shawnees can't hit a standing deer, much less a running man. One shot come too close, though. It hit the tug on my powder horn and cut it loose. That left me with just the one shot in Tick-Licker, and I knew if I shot one of them I was done. So I just stopped, leaned the rifle against a tree and stepped behind it, so that when they came up they'd know I wasn't going to shoot—and so they wouldn't shoot me."

"They captured you then?"

"Yep."

"Did they harm you?"

"No, they just tied my hands and walked me to their camp which wasn't far off, close to the Licking on Hinkson's Creek. Turns out the ones that had got me were a scouting party sent out from the main war camp toward Blue Licks to see if there was anyone there."

"A war party, Captain Boone? At that time of year?"

Boone shrugged. "Wasn't usual, but then Shawnees ain't always usual. Mostly they don't come against us in winter, but I reckon this time they just figured they would."

"How many were there?"

"Hundred and twenty, near as I could make out. They had a fire forty feet long next to a rock ledge alongside the creek and they were all sitting hunched in their blankets, some of 'em in the process of getting their faces painted up for war. Found out they were planning to move against Boonesborough in the morning."

"There were some white men with them, Captain?"

Boone nodded grimly. "Three of them. Two of the same four that came for the siege—Charles Beaubien and Peter Drouilliard. The other was a Frenchman who ran a trading post way up in the Ohio country, Peter Loramie."

"Did the Indians recognize you, Captain Boone? If so, what was their reaction?"

"Oh, they recognized me all right! They carried on like you wouldn't believe, figuring I was quite a catch. They'd been trying to catch me for a long time. Lot of them came over when I was untied and shook my hand and patted my back and all, as if I was a long-lost friend instead of an enemy. It was their way of showing respect for me. A whole lot more of them than I would've guessed had had run-ins with me and somehow I'd always managed to come out best. They all started telling stories about these run-ins, going back as far as seventeen sixty-nine, to the time when John Stuart and me stole some horses back from them that they'd taken from us. That's the kind of thing that really appeals to them. They admire bravery a whole lot, but even more than that they get tickled when someone pulls off something unusually audacious against them. Guess they'd been keeping score where I was concerned, ever since that horse incident, and by the time we managed to outguess them and get Jemima and the Callaway girls back after they were taken from Boonesborough, they figured I was some kind of great warrior. I didn't mind. Getting treated the way they were treating me was, the way I figured it, a whole speck better than being tied up and tortured, which was what I expected, so I just figured I'd play along with them and pretend to admire them as much as they admired me. Of course it come out right away that they were on the move against Boonesborough, with one of the prime objects being trying to catch me. The fact that I'd just about walked into their camp made them figure that the Great Spirit was sure enough smiling on them."

"It was Chief Black Fish who was leading this war party?" Henderson inquired.

"Yep, and he had me sit close to him and we ate and talked way into the night. At that time I knew some Shawnee words, but I couldn't speak or understand it very well, so the whites who were with them and the black man, Pompey, interpreted whenever we got bogged down."

"What did you talk about?"

"Well, they were mighty curious as to what I was doing out there all by myself and I just let on at first that I was out doing some hunting and that's all there was to it. Pretty soon, though, another little scouting party of five came in and told Black Fish they'd spied the fires of my party at the Licks."

"You told them then that these were your men?"

"No, not right away. I sort of talked around the subject for a while and all the time I was thinking pretty hard. I knew Boonesborough's defenses were so poor at that time that they'd never be able to hold off even around twenty warriors, much less six times that many. Remember, we'd left Boonesborough with only ten men and twenty boys to guard around fifty women and girls, and there wasn't even a stockade up all the way around it yet. But since the Indians were already aware of the party at the Blue Licks and they weren't sure at all what to expect at Boonesborough, I told them a tale about the fort having four strong companies of soldiers on hand and that they couldn't possibly take it without a whole lot of their number being killed, and probably not even then. I got them to thinking maybe it was too risky."

"Did the white men with them believe what you said?"

"No, and that was the biggest threat I had to put down. They kept insisting that the Indians should surround the salt camp at Blue Licks during the night and then by first light in the morning attack unexpectedly and kill everybody there, which they could have done easily enough, and then move on against Boonesborough according to the original plan. I knew enough about Indian ways to know that if there was any way for them to make a big coup without exposing themselves to danger, they'd elect to do that. So that was when I convinced them that Boonesborough was mighty strong right then and they couldn't possibly take it, but that later in the spring when the soldiers I'd told them were there had gone away on a mission that was planned, they could take the place easily. I added some sugar to it then by saying I'd even help them to do it by going in with them then and talking those in the fort into surrendering. It began to sound pretty reasonable to them, despite what Beaubien and Drouilliard and Loramie were saying. Still, there were a lot of bucks there who were suspicious of me. I knew by then that my men at the salt camp had no chance at all, no matter what the Indians decided. If they fought they might manage to kill a few Indians if they got warning enough, but all of them were going to be wiped out if I didn't do something fast. It seemed to me they'd be better off alive and in captivity with a chance of possibly escaping than dead and the Indians still on the move against Boonesborough. Besides, they were a whole lot more likely to survive a winter march into Indian territory than the women and children. Not one in ten among those still at Boonesborough would've survived such a march."

"Objection! Mr. President," Bowman said, "that's entirely conjecture on the defendant's part."

"No, I think not," Trabue said. "As aware as Captain Boone was of the rigors of a forced winter march, he is undoubtedly correct in his evaluation. The defendant may continue."

"Well," Boone went on, "that was when I made my decision and told them that I would not only surrender Boonesborough to them later on in the spring after the soldiers were gone, but that the next day I would show them a way to take all the saltmakers without anybody being hurt on either side."

"This idea appealed to them?" Henderson asked.

"Of course it did. They knew they were going to take those men no matter what, but if there was a way of doing it without exposing themselves to any risk, then they were all for it. Besides which, a scalp only brings them five pounds from the British at Detroit, but live captives are worth ten pounds apiece. Black Fish wanted to know what my plan was, so I told him that if he'd give me his word not to kill my men after they were taken, or torture them, or make them run a gauntlet of his warriors there, I'd go in alone in the morning and convince the saltmakers that they had to surrender without fighting. Black Fish thought about it and then gave his promise, so that was that."

"Your promises, then," Henderson said, "to turn over your own men to them then and Boonesborough to them later were *not* the acts of treason they have been interpreted as being, but rather a desperate move on your part to save all the saltmakers and probably most of the Boonesborough women and children from certain death?"

"That's right. The actual surrender of the saltmakers was just about like Johnson and Hancock and Mr. Bruther told it.

I went in the next day and convinced them they had no choice but to surrender or be killed—which was true."

"And Chief Black Fish honored his promise when you honored yours?"

"Yes, except he caught me by surprise on a couple of counts—like making me run the gauntlet at the salt camp, even though the men were spared this, but then making them run the gauntlet at Chalahgawtha because he'd only promised me they wouldn't have to run a gauntlet of his warriors at the Licks. You've got to be careful when making deals with the Shawnees," he explained with a smile, "because they're nearly as tricky as us whites."

"But despite Black Fish's promises to you," Henderson pressed on, ignoring the light laughter in the gallery following Boone's remark, "there was still a vote called for regarding going against Boonesborough, once your men were taken?"

Boone nodded. "The whites with them didn't give up easy. They kept trying to convince them—especially the young bucks who were hot for war—that with all these saltmakers from Boonesborough captured, that there was probably hardly anyone left at the fort guarding it, because I was probably lying about the soldiers being there. They were pretty convincing. Now Black Fish is chief, but in matters like that, where part of the Indians want to do one thing and another part wants to do another, it always goes to a vote and the majority rules. When a vote was called for, Black Fish had no choice but to let it be taken, but he insisted that *I* be given the right to vote, too, because he knew it was going to be very close. He also told all the warriors to very closely consider the alternatives, that on the one hand they had me and the twenty-seven other captives without a single warrior being hurt. Bringing us back to the village would be a great victory, a reason for tremendous jubilation, a fantastic coup. On the other hand, attack against Boonesborough might result in many of them being killed or wounded. He was very persuasive about taking what they had and leaving, but so were Beaubien and Drouilliard and Loramie about killing all the prisoners and going on against Boonesborough. The vote was taken, like Andy Johnson said, and it was close, but it came out all right."

"Why, Captain Boone, was all that valuable salt dumped and not taken by the Indians? They use salt, don't they?"

"They do, but Boonesborough and the other settlements

needed that salt and we'd worked hard to make it, so I convinced Black Fish that because it had been rendered in white men's kettles over fires built by white men, that now there were white spirits in it and it would be very bad luck for them to take it. I told them they could destroy it by dumping it in the snow, where it would be ruined, but they'd have terrible misfortune if they took it. They believed me and dumped it out, figuring the snows and rain would make it worthless before anyone found it, which would have been the case if it had laid there for too long. But I also knew that the three men I'd sent to Boonesborough with the first salt would be back soon and they'd see the salt and salvage it—which, as it turned out, is just what happened."

"Captain Boone," Henderson said, "didn't it occur to you that in deceiving the Indians, as you were doing in making them believe that you were helping them and that you would turn Boonesborough over to them, you might also be deceiving your own men, who would think you guilty of treason?"

"Reckon the thought occurred to me," Boone said drily.

"Then why didn't you explain to your men what you were doing?"

Boone shook his head. "The very fact that my own men were considering me a traitor made Black Fish and all his men all that much more certain that I was not deceiving them. All it would have taken was one man among us knowing that I was pulling the wool over their eyes and then letting that slip out and everything would've been ruined. Figured I could worry later on about what my own men thought about me."

"And so you kept up the act?"

"Yep. That's why I laughed and joked with the Indians and acted like I was one of them. And that's why, too, I knocked that warrior named Red Fox flat when he tried to make me carry a brass kettle. It's just what any of the other warriors would've done to him if he had tried to make one of them carry a kettle. It was a little risky for me to do it, but it worked out all right and made them even more sure I was with them."

Colonel John Bowman at the prosecution table was no longer taking notes. His expression was drawn, his entire attitude dulled. He was listening but a vital spark seemed to be going out of him. Few noticed it, though. The attention of the whole gathering was riveted to Daniel Boone's testimony.

"All right, Captain Boone," said Henderson slowly, "let's

move on to the next matter. It has been testified that in Detroit you colluded with the British, discussed the taking of Boonesborough with Henry Hamilton, and made him certain promises about switching your own allegiance to him and then turning Boonesborough over to him later in the summer. Will you please explain your actions to the court?"

"I figured that Boonesborough was in pretty near as much danger from the British," Boone said, facing the bar, "as from the Indians. There just wasn't any doubt that pretty soon there was going to be a big army of Indians or British or both moving against Boonesborough. I wanted to do anything and everything possible to keep it from happening, but if that didn't work and a force did come against Boonesborough, which is what I expected, then I meant to act in a way that delayed it as long as possible to give Boonesborough a chance to strengthen defenses, and I also meant to say things that might possibly make the enemy give up some of its advantages. The thing that worried me most about the British was artillery, which I knew Boonesborough couldn't stand up against even if it was in excellent shape, which it wasn't. So I decided I had to get Hamilton's confidence and convince him that he wouldn't need any cannon when it came to taking Boonesborough."

"How did you do that?"

"First by passing on information to him that was true, which he didn't know about yet but soon would, which would tend to make him believe other things I said which were lies."

Colonel Trabue wore a slight frown. "What kind of information do you mean, Captain Boone?"

"Well, sir, one of the last reports we'd had in Boonesborough of the war in the East was that our own General Gates had just managed to make British General Burgoyne's whole army surrender to him. Black Fish and his men hadn't known anything about that, so I assumed the Detroit garrison hadn't gotten the word yet. When I got to Detroit, the first thing I told Hamilton when he questioned me was that he had to get word as fast as he possibly could to General Burgoyne, because the Americans were laying a trap to take him and his whole army at Saratoga. I told him I'd heard about this from one of the colonels who had just come to Boonesborough. He didn't really believe it, of course, but then three days after we arrived word got to him of that surrender and from that point on he believed almost anything I told him."

"What else did you tell him?" Trabue asked.

"I also told him that the people in Kentucky just weren't getting much help from the East and were getting very disgusted. I told him that there was no reason for him to think that the Kentucky forts were solidly allegiant to the United States and that it wouldn't take much to convince them to support the British. I gave some pretty broad hints that with the Kentucky forts in British hands, a flank attack against the United States from the west could possibly turn the tide of the whole war. Hamilton took the bait a lot easier than I thought he would. He even began talking about what a hero he'd be back in England when King George realized that the Americans had been defeated because of Hamilton's strategic moves in the West."

It was Colonel Isaac Shelby, seated to Trabue's right, who spoke up now. "Captain Boone," he said, "I must admit that I find it difficult to believe that Governor-General Hamilton, who certainly cannot be considered a stupid man, could have been gullible enough to be taken in by your stories to him."

"Colonel Shelby," Boone replied at once, "meaning no disrespect to you, sir, you're wrong. If Hamilton was really a smart general, he'd've been leading an army in the East where the war action is, not holding down an isolated outpost on the frontier and buying American scalps from the Indians. He's not only not very smart, Colonel, he's also an ambitious man who likes a lot of praise and thinks highly of himself and his own abilities. I figured him as being an officer who was mighty anxious to make a big mark for himself and held out some hints on how he could do it. Like I said, he took the bait and pretty soon he was going over all kinds of plans with me about how he'd march out of the Kentucky forts and straight into Williamsburg before the Americans realized what was happening. Matter of fact, he took to the idea so fast and got so enthusiastic about it that in a day or two he was believing the whole thing was his plan."

"What, exactly, did you promise Hamilton, Captain Boone?" It was Colonel Trabue speaking again.

"The first thing I told him was that I had made a deal with Black Fish to surrender Boonesborough to him in the spring, as soon as the big army that was presently in Kentucky—four companies of it at Boonesborough—had moved out. I told him that if he preferred, I'd hold off doing that until his own soldiers showed up down there. By then, I told him, I hoped to be back at Boonesborough and would have gotten everyone there to agree to back the British. As soon as they showed up with letters from Hamilton himself, we'd all swear allegiance to the Crown and turn over the fort to them. He'd been planning to send a couple of hundred troops he was hoping to get from Montreal, with artillery and supported by Indians, against the Kentucky forts, but I told him that it really wouldn't be necessary now. All he'd have to do was send a few officers as his representatives to take command in the name of King George. I also promised him that the first thing we'd do here would be to rename Boonesborough and call it Fort Henry Hamilton. He all but licked his chops when I told him that."

"Did General Hamilton say when he had intended sending his hoped-for troops, supported by artillery and Indians, against the Kentucky forts, Captain Boone?" asked Samuel Henderson.

"His plan had been to do so late in the spring if he got the manpower, but I told him that there was a good chance the American companies would still be in the forts at that time, but that I knew they'd be gone by midsummer and that the fort would be at its weakest about in August."

"And he changed his plans in accordance with your supposed inside intelligence?"

"He told me he would, but I wasn't too sure of it. In fact, I wasn't positive he believed *any* of what I'd been saying. I only knew it was worth a try. I could tell pretty soon, though, that he wasn't bothered too much any more about the possibility of not having a lot of soldiers to send against us. Turned out that he did believe me, all the way, after all. I reckon he really wanted to believe there was a big chance for military glory for him. There's just nothing I know of that's more important to him."

"It was testified by Mr. William Hancock," Henderson continued, "during your cross-examination of him that you had given him and the other prisoners the gifts that were given to you by Hamilton and some other officers. Why did you accept these gifts in the first place?"

"I couldn't very well refuse them without arousing suspicion, and besides, I knew that the men needed those things badly. The only thing I couldn't give them was the horse, and this I gave back to Hamilton telling him I couldn't accept so fine a gift from him then, but that when he came to Boonesborough himself to take command and begin his big strike at Williamsburg from there, he could give it to me as a reward then."

"You are convinced that it is because of what you discussed with General Hamilton that British troops and artillery were not brought against the Kentucky forts?"

"I am now."

"All right, let's move on. You returned with Black Fish and his men to Chalahgawtha and there you voluntarily became adopted into the tribe as the son of Chief Black Fish himself, is that correct?"

"That's right."

"Will you explain to this court," Henderson went on, "why you so willingly agreed to this?"

Boone grinned. "Well, I got to admit that a small part of it was because I'd always had a hankering to really get a good closeup look at what life was like among the Indians, and there'd never been a better chance than that. Still, that was only a small part of the reason. The big part was that I stuck with the belief that the Shawnees were the most dangerous enemy we had to face down here, mainly because they were so close to us and because I knew that Black Fish was planning a major attack before too long."

"How did you know that?"

"Black Fish told me himself. So, by sticking around and becoming one of them, I figured I might be able to learn what their plans were and do whatever I could to ruin them. I decided I'd stick with them until they were about ready to move against us, and then I'd light out with a warning to the forts. First off, though, I had to build up their confidence in me a good bit more, because there were still plenty of the younger ones who were suspicious of me."

"That was why you joined in their activities as you did?"

"That's why. I was adopted and had my hair pulled out and fixed like this," he indicated his still Indian-appearing scalp, "and I dressed like them and acted like them. I hunted with them, competed in sports and shooting matches and all till most didn't have any doubts left that I was solidly with them. I worked hard for them in any number of ways, and though none of them could shoot anywhere near as straight as me, they get jealous and resentful pretty easy, so I always made sure to let them beat me at least half the time. Got to admit, though, that even when Black Fish was letting me sit in on councils, there were some who didn't trust me."

"How were you able to finally convince them of your supposed sincerity? " Henderson asked.

"They'd given me pretty much freedom," Boone replied, "but I knew they were watching me close, sometimes from hiding, giving me a chance to run if I wanted to. One day I went out hunting with Black Fish and five of his men. Without them realizing it, I'd managed to get the balls out of their rifles before we left. When we got out in the woods I suddenly started walking away from them. Black Fish called out to me to stop and asked me where I was going. I was thirty-four yards away by then and I told him I reckoned I was going home to Kentucky. He warned me not to go any further or he'd have his men shoot me through the legs. I just laughed and told him I was much too fast for any bullets to hit me. Black Fish always did have a pretty short temper and this got his dander up and he actually did order his men to shoot. All five of them raised their guns and fired at me. I jumped around, pretending to be catching things in midair, then walked back up to them and handed Black Fish the five bullets, which I'd had in my hand all along. Told him then that I wasn't really going anywhere after all, that I was just having some fun with him and that I *never* wanted to leave 'em. Reckon it made quite a sensation."

"And that's when they really began to trust you? How could you be sure of that?"

"Well, for one thing, they gave Tick-Licker back to me, which they'd taken from me back in February down at Hinkson's Creek. For another, they started bringing me their busted guns to fix for them."

"You fixed them?"

"Sam, I fixed them guns so they were in better working condition than they'd ever been since the Indians first got them."

"You must have known that those guns and others like them were going to be used against the settlements, Captain Boone. How could you have brought yourself to fix them so well?"

"Sure I knew they'd eventually be used against us down here," Boone said. "That's why when I fixed the first few batches of 'em, I fixed 'em just as good as I possibly could—because I wanted them to wind up bringing me every gun that was going to be used against Boonesborough. That's just what they did, eventually, exactly like William Bruther testified. Fixed 'em up the best I knew how—but I done something else to 'em, too."

Henderson noted that the officers at the central table were listening raptly to every word. "What was that, Dan?" he asked.

"The guns that they used for hunting," Boone explained, "I had to fix good, since they were using them regular. But the stock of guns they'd set aside for the next war party against Boonesborough was a different matter. When they saw how well I fixed the hunting guns, that's when they brought me all the others. Like Mr. Bruther said, I cleaned them and oiled them, repaired broken stocks and sights and all. Also took the workings apart on each one of them, cleaned them out good, filed away rust and corrosion and so on. But I did a little more than just that."

Boone paused, let his eyes move across the officers of the court and then return to stop on the president. For the first time he addressed them on a more direct level than previously, and with greater intensity.

"Colonel Trabue, officers of the court, up till now what I've told you I done could have been things I just made up to get me out of this trouble. They all fit together pretty well and there'd have to have been a whole lot of coincidences to have it work out, but I reckon there could still be some doubt about me; that maybe I was just sort of making what happened *seem* when I explained about it that I hadn't really been committing treason, right?"

Trabue nodded cautiously. "That possibility is there, Captain Boone, and I'm sure all the gentlemen on this board are aware of it. You have, of course, had sufficient time since first being charged to develop a plausible story to fit the acts. But, as you are evidently inferring, there has been no evidence of a tangible nature to lend proof to what you are saying. You are coming to such evidence now?"

"Yes, sir, I am." He looked across the officers again and spoke clearly. "Maybe you don't know about the way Indians shoot, so I'll tell you something: somehow they just won't learn that you have to squeeze the trigger instead of jerking it. They always jerk it hard when they shoot, which is why most of them can't shoot any too straight. Sometimes they get lucky and hit what they're shooting at, but most often not, unless they're pretty close to whatever they're shooting at. Well, while I was filing away the rust and such off the mechanisms, I was also doing some pretty hard filing on the backsides of the triggers, way up at the top where they attach. Filed every one of 'em pretty near through. When I put the workings back together, you couldn't see the filing at all. Even if they were shot once or twice there wasn't any way to tell anything was wrong. But with continued jerking on the trigger like they do, the trigger'd gradually bend backwards. In maybe four-five shots it'd be so far back and up that it'd have to be bent straight again to shoot it anymore. And when they attempted to do this, the trigger'd break off, way up inside, and then the gun was just no good at all."

The third officer to the president's left, Captain James Galloway, spoke up during the brief pause. There was just the faintest trace of Scottish accent in his speech and his gaze was very penetrating. "Captain Boone, one of the officers of this board—Captain Holder—has testified that gunfire from the Indians was fairly heavy for the first day or two but then slackened sharply and soon there was more bow-and-arrow shooting than rifle fire. He also testified that after the siege close to thirty enemy rifles, deliberately broken by the Indians, were recovered and that the triggers were missing from all of them. It is your contention that this is the result of your undertaking at Chalahgawtha when you were supposedly repairing the guns?"

Daniel Boone grinned. "That's right. Nobody's taken the workings of those recovered guns apart yet, but when they do they'll see that the base of the trigger on each was nearly filed through. That's why it broke and made the gun useless, and why some of the Indians got mad and busted 'em up when they wouldn't work. And I don't reckon they left behind more'n just a few that the triggers broke off of. Probably took the rest back to try and fix 'em. Another thing that'll show them to be the guns I worked on is the little holes I bored in the wood of the forepiece and stock, which was supposed to be for slings. Never had any intention of putting slings on them, but I wanted to mark 'em some way and figured that way was best."

Colonel John Bowman, now leaning with one elbow on the prosecution table and his chin cupped in his hand, was staring at Boone with an unbelieving expression, his jaw muscles working and causing the dense brown moustache to move rhythmically. Callaway wore a look of scorn and Benjamin Logan an expression of genuine interest. Logan's attitude was definitely reflected in each of the members of the court.

Sam Henderson spoke up after a moment. "Moving on now, Captain Boone," he said, "it has been testified that you proposed a plan to the Shawnees whereby Boonesborough could be taken without the Indians themselves being exposed to danger. Kindly explain to the court about this."

Boone nodded, sitting back a little more comfortably in the witness chair and crossing his legs. "Mr. Bruther was right when he testified that I didn't realize he could understand the Shawnee language," he said, "but it wouldn't have made any difference if I had known. During the councils I told Chief Black Fish just about what I told Hamilton. First I said they had to hold off their attack for a while longer than spring, because Hamilton was going to send them some support for the attack, but not until a little later in the summer, when he was positive that all the soldiers at Boonesborough were gone. Of course there was always the possibility that Black Fish wouldn't want to wait and would come against Boonesborough without British support. I told him that if he did that, which would be all right too, that all they had to do was surround Boonesborough and then send in Pompey with the message that they were there. At that point I would come out to supposedly negotiate a peace with them. I was trying to set it up so that they'd let me leave Chalahgawtha early enough to get back to the fort by the time they showed up. Mr. Bruther testified to that, as you remember, but then he had to leave the council and didn't hear what followed."

Boone smiled crookedly and shook his head. "Got to admit," he said wryly, "that that idea didn't sit too well with them—not even with Black Fish. Even though they trusted me by then, none of them liked the idea of turning me loose. Black Fish decided they'd just take me along on the war party with them and then send me in to negotiate the surrender when we got there. I didn't want that at all. The whole point in the idea of getting back first and having them call me out to negotiate the matter of surrender was to buy some extra time for Boonesborough to prepare its defenses and to give me a chance to figure out the enemy strength. I knew that no matter what was done, we wouldn't be prepared enough. I

did expect the fort would be in reasonably good shape when I
got back, like I'd ordered Captain Callaway to get it fixed
when my party left for the Blue Licks, but even so, I knew
that every extra minute we had to prepare for them after they
showed up here was going to be to our advantage. I also
knew that come what may, I was going to have to get away
from the Shawnees as soon as I knew they were in the final
stages of preparing to leave Chalahgawtha against us. Even
then I tried to prime Black Fish for my leaving. I told him
one night that I never wanted to permanently leave my new
Indian life, but that sometimes my heart got to aching for my
woman and children and there might be a time when I'd just
up and leave to go see them without saying anything to
anyone. Black Fish didn't much like that and warned me not
to do so, but I pretended to take it just as his concern for my
safety. I assured him that if I ever did go, he had my promise
as a true Shawnee that I'd be faithful to him and live up to
every promise I'd ever made to him—including the one
about turning Boonesborough over to him, even though I
didn't say so just then in so many words."

"Could you be so sure, Captain Boone," Trabue asked,
"that the negotiations you hoped to enter into with them
would provide the time needed for Boonesborough to secure
its defenses?"

"No, sir," Boone admitted, "not positive at all, but reasonably sure of it. If you know Indians at all, you know that it
takes a whole lot of talking for anything to be decided, even
when they're just deciding things in council among themselves. I figured if I could keep them from instantly attacking
when they first got there and get them to ask for negotiations
because they really believed the fort would be surrendered to
them, it'd give us at least a couple extra days to prepare,
maybe even longer. And I was pretty sure they'd want to
negotiate if at all possible. The Shawnee tribe, sir, will never
under any circumstances consider the lives of its own people
expendable in the taking of an enemy except as a last resort. If
there is the slightest hint that warfare will not be necessary
and they can get through bloodless negotiation what they
want, pretty much on their own terms, then that's the course
they'll take. I was depending on that. I figured I could get at
least two days, because the first thing I could tell them was
that I was no longer in charge, because of my absence, and
that they'd have to negotiate with the new commander. I also

knew that when I called on Major Smith to act the part of the commander, he'd be pretty quick to catch on to what I was doing and fall in with it, which he did when it actually happened." He dipped his head toward William Bailey Smith and smiled.

"Captain Boone," Henderson said, "there are a couple more important points which need to be brought out for the officers here. When the Shawnees did arrive here at length under Chief Black Fish, with the several British representatives of General Hamilton who accompanied them, you went out alone at first to meet them. What did you discuss?"

"Not much, actually," Boone said. "They right away asked me to surrender the fort like I'd promised I would and I told them I was willing, but that I wasn't in charge anymore, that Major Smith was, and so we would have to convince him of the wisdom of surrendering. But I told them that I was pretty sure the major was really a Tory—begging your pardon for the lie, Bill," he said quickly, looking apologetically at Smith, who seemed a bit shocked at first, but who then smiled faintly and dipped his head to signify his understanding. "Anyway," Boone went on, "I told them I thought he was a Tory and wouldn't really need much convincing, and that I'd help them convince him. But before I went back in after Major Smith, Black Fish must have become a little suspicious of me."

"How so, Captain?" Trabue asked.

"He suddenly told me that although he believed me and was sure that I was going to live up to my promises, because I was his son Sheltowee, that just in case he had been wrong in his judgment of me, the British officers with him had brought along two cannon. He said that it grieved him to possibly offend me that way, but that he hoped I would understand. He said that he would positively not let the cannon be used, because he knew it wouldn't be necessary. But just in case I hadn't been telling the truth about surrendering, then he would have to very reluctantly agree to their use."

"You believed him?"

"Sir, I didn't know whether to believe him or not. I certainly didn't *want* to, but I just couldn't be sure. I countered by telling him that *we* had a cannon, too, and would not like to have to come to the point of using it, but that we would if it came to that. I said it was a cannon that had been left here for us by the soldiers that had been here the previous winter and spring."

"Did he believe you?"

"No, sir, I know he didn't believe it at all, because he said, 'My son Sheltowee is catching more bullets in his hand.' I just told him I hoped it would never become necessary to prove it. As for his artillery, as I say, I wasn't sure myself whether to believe him or not. I wasn't inclined to, but I also knew that if he actually did have such artillery, then Boonesborough was finished. There was no way we could hold the place against that. When Major Smith came outside with me then and Black Fish showed us the actual cannon-balls, I was even more concerned. I told Major Smith that I didn't think they had the artillery or they'd have flaunted it, but I wasn't all that sure inside. Which is the reason I agreed with Major Smith to put the matter of whether we really surrendered or not to serious discussion among the men when we returned to the fort. I have to say," he added, "that I felt right proud of 'em when they decided to stand and fight, even if the enemy had their big guns." .

Colonel Trabue was leaning forward keenly interested in what the defendant was saying. At Boone's pause, he spoke up. "When were you able to determine for certain, Captain Boone, that the enemy did not in fact have the artillery with them?"

"Well, the first time was that first night after we talked with them. I fixed myself up like an Indian, which wasn't hard the way my hair still looked, painted my face and chest and slipped out in the middle of the night. Scouted around the perimeters for a couple of hours, staying to the shadows, but sometimes having to answer in Shawnee when someone saw me, but keeping from being found out. I didn't see anything of artillery anywhere around the fort, so I was all but positive then that they didn't have any. I told Major Smith in the morning that I was sure Black Fish was bluffing."

"You say that was the first time? Does this imply there was a second time?"

Boone nodded. "By the time the siege actually began, I got a bad feeling that maybe the guns just hadn't been brought up yet when I checked before and had still been in the main encampment. If that was the case, it was possible they were being brought to bear on us right then. So after getting Buchanan safe into the fort and tending to Squire's wound, I dressed up Indian-style again and slipped out. Figured if the artillery was there, our only chance was going to be for me to spike it. I checked all the perimeters again and didn't see them, so I crossed the river and checked out the main encampment. No cannon there, either, so I knew positively then that we were safe from that threat."

"You weren't detected by any of the enemy when you went out like that?" Trabue asked.

"I was stopped by two different warriors."

"What happened?"

"I cut their throats."

A woman's voice in the gallery rose clearly in a revolted "*Oooooh!*" and this was followed by a nervous little laugh from some of the men. Boone was expressionless and after a moment's pause, it was Henderson who began questioning Boone again.

"One final point, Captain Boone. In his testimony, Captain Holder said that when you rigged up the wooden artillery here in the fort out of the elm log, you shouted over the wall to Chief Black Fish that you had warned him the night before that the fort's artillery would be used if he persisted in his attack. How could you have warned him the night before?"

Boone looked at Henderson and then back at the court. "I left the fort again," he explained, "like I had the two times before, dressed like an Indian. Slipped out and moved around cautiouslike till I found a warrior lying in wait pretty much by himself, watching the fort. Got around behind him and pinned him face down on the ground with my knife against his throat and told him who I was. I told him I had cut the throats of two of his brothers before and his was next unless he carried my message to Black Fish. He knew about the two throat-cut warriors, of course, and he also knew I meant business. He said he would take my message to Black Fish."

"What was this message, Captain Boone?" Henderson asked.

"I told him to tell Chief Black Fish that I had warned him during our first meeting outside the fort that we had a cannon inside that had been left by the soldiers. Told him to say that until now I had prevailed on Major Smith not to use it, as I did not want to see so many of my Indian father's people hurt. But I said that now Major Smith had become too angry and I could no longer keep him from using the terrible thundergun. I told him to tell Black Fish that we would fire it once in a general direction toward them tomorrow, to prove to them that we had it. If Black Fish persisted after that, we would fire one final warning shot. If *then* Black Fish did not immediately pull his people away and end the siege, the artillery would be turned on him and his warriors in earnest and we would destroy them all."

"Was there any doubt in your mind," Henderson queried, "that despite his promise, the warrior you were telling this to wouldn't give the message to Black Fish?"

"Not much," Boone said, "but I had to make sure that he *couldn't* keep from delivering it."

"How?"

"I twisted his arm behind him and held him that way while I used my knife tip to carve the sign of Sheltowee—the Big Turtle—on his back, so Black Fish would have no doubt I was the one who sent the message. I then shoved the warrior down a steep embankment and ran back to the fort. So that was the reason for my calling out to Black Fish as I did about the warnings."

There was a prolonged silence after that. The entire assemblage—gallery, members of the court, plaintiffs and prosecution—were stunned by the revelation. Major John Bowman appeared positively deflated. Only Samuel Henderson, James Harrod and Daniel Boone himself were not virtually speechless with surprise. It was Samuel Henderson, clearing his throat, who broke the spell.

"No further questions, Mr. President," he said. "The defense rests."

For the first time in many minutes, the president of the court shifted his gaze to the judge advocate. "Does prosecution wish to cross-examine?" he asked.

John Bowman was still staring open-mouthed at Boone and it was a moment before he slowly looked toward the bar. Twice his lips moved soundlessly before his words finally came out in hardly more than a whisper.

"No questions."

Daniel Boone began getting up from the witness chair but the suddenly outthrust hand of Colonel Trabue stayed him.

"Captain Boone, there is one point the court would like to clarify."

"Yes, sir?" He settled back in his seat.

"You have stated that on three different occasions—once prior to the siege and twice during it—you left the fort under cover of darkness dressed as an Indian. In no testimony given here has the court been informed that you had done so. Why is this?"

"Because, sir, with the exception of Captain Harrod and Sam Henderson here, who both learned of it from me just since the trial began, no one knew about it."

Trabue shook his head, nonplussed. "There is no way, sir," he said, "that you could have left and reentered the fort without someone manning the gate for you."

"Colonel Trabue," Boone said simply, 'I didn't use a gate."

Trabue digested this for a moment in silence and then said, "Explain that please."

"In my quarters, sir," Boone said, "there is a hidden trapdoor under one of the beds. It leads to a crawl passage eight feet below ground level, which I and my brother Squire constructed, unknown to anyone else, over a period of several months last year. Knowing Indian ways as we do, and the hazards of being helplessly pinned inside a fort, we felt that it might one day become useful. It did. The passage goes for about eighty yards underground and then comes out inside a large hollow stump. We rigged a false cover of dirt, old wood chips and brush over it that has to be opened from the inside. It was this passage that I used on those three nights."

"Then that also means," Colonel Daniel Trabue said slowly, "that your confinement to quarters under guard since these charges were brought against you was not confinement after all, and that at any time you chose to do so, you could have gone away." He stopped, then repeated himself. "Any time you chose."

"Yes, sir, Mr. President," Boone said softly, "that's just what it means."

Epilogue

Daniel Boone stood beside his horse twenty yards outside the widely opened east gate of Boonesborough, a small, crooked smile on his lips as he listened to the words of one of the four who had walked outside the fort with him. Behind them, inside the fort, people moved about in casual activity, pausing occasionally to glance their way. The heads of a couple of guards could just barely be seen above the log palisade spikes, moving slowly, pausing to scan the surrounding countryside now and then, and moving on again. The scraping and faint clanging of a shovel could be heard from inside as work continued on the fort's still unproductive water well.

It was difficult to believe that less than two months ago this fort was under siege; that less than a week ago these bullet-pocked stockade walls had borne witness to the unclimactic conclusion of the court-martial of Daniel Boone; that they had witnessed a prosecutor for the first time in his years of judge advocacy decline to make a concluding statement in support of his case to the board of court-martial; that they had witnessed a quietly unanimous vote of not guilty for the defendant; that they had witnessed an acquittal not only with honor, but with promotion.

"You *will* be back, Dan, won't you?" Sam Henderson was saying. He tilted his head toward the fort. "They need you, and they know it now more than they ever have. *We* need you, Dan."

Boone clasped the extended hand and squeezed Henderson's forearm with the other hand. He nodded. "I'll be back, Sam. Count on it."

He turned to James Harrod and accepted the proffered hand warmly, wordlessly. Flanders Callaway grinned as Boone gripped him with one arm around the shoulders and further tousled the already windblown hair on the young man's head.

"Take care of my little girl now, hear?" the frontiersman said, and Flanders nodded.

The instant Boone turned away from his son-in-law, Jemima flung herself at him, hugging him fiercely and burying her face in the broad, buckskin-covered chest. He stroked her hair and gently kissed the top of her head, then kissed her again. She turned her face up toward him, smiling, her eyes glinting with tears not quite of happiness, nor of sadness.

"Give mamma my love," she said. "Tell her we're waiting. Tell her we've missed her."

Boone nodded, kissed her forehead and turned away. In the wonderfully flowing, graceful movement so characteristic of him, he was suddenly in the saddle and looking down at them.

"Better not forget Tick-Licker, Dan," Harrod said, handing the long rifle up to him. "You may need it."

"Hope not, Jim," he said, balancing it crosswise on the pommel, "but you never can tell."

He dipped his head at them all and kneed the horse into a brisk canter toward the distant trees. They watched him go, standing silently until he had almost reached the clearing's edge, and then Jemima stepped apart and cupped her mouth.

"Good-by Daddy!" she called, and then after an instant, "Good-by, Major Boone!"

ABOUT THE AUTHOR

ALLAN W. ECKERT, recently awarded an Honorary Doctorate in Humane Letters, Bowling Green State University, Ohio, is a historian, naturalist and playwright who has written twenty-nine books, including the highly acclaimed *Winning of America* series and his new children's fantasy series, *The Mesmerian Annals*. A five-time Pulitzer Prize nominee, he has also written over two hundred *Wild Kingdom* television scripts. He has received many awards for his writing, including a Newbery Honor Book award for *Incident at Hawk's Hill*, the Friends of American Writers award for *Wild Season*, and the Ohioana Book Award for *The Frontiersmen*. He has also received an Emmy Award for television writing.

ALLAN ECKERT'S NARRATIVES OF AMERICA

Allan Eckert's Narratives of America are true sagas of the brave men and courageous women who won our land. Every character and event in this sweeping series is drawn from actual history and woven into the vast and powerful epic that was America's westward expansion.

The true story of what may have been the most destructive serial murderer in the annals of American crime. Herman Mudgett, alias H. H. Holmes, built a mansion in the early 1890's on Chicago's South Side: a hundred-room carnival house of horror, complete with trap doors, hidden passageways, a crematorium and a dungeon.

Prices and availability subject to change without notice.

TERRY C. JOHNSTON

Winner of the prestigious Western Writer's award for best first novel, Terry C. Johnston brings you two volumes of his award-winning saga of mountain men Josiah Paddock and Titus Bass who strive together to meet the challenges of the western wilderness in the 1830's.

☐ 25572-X **CARRY THE WIND** $4.95

Having killed a wealthy young Frenchman in a duel, Josiah Paddock flees St. Louis in 1831. He heads west to the fierce and beautiful Rocky Mountains, to become a free trapper far from the entanglements of civilization. Hot-headed and impetuous, young Josiah finds his romantic image of life in the mountains giving way to a harsh struggle for survival—against wild animals, fierce Indians, and nature's own cruelty. Half-dead of cold and starvation, he encounters Titus Bass, a solitary old trapper who takes the youth under his wing and teaches him the ways of the mountains. So begins a magnificent historical novel, remarkable for its wealth of authentic mountain lore and wisdom.   Coming in October 1986.

☐ 26224-6 **BORDERLORDS** $4.50

Here is a swirling, powerful drama of the early American wilderness, filled with fascinating scenes of tribal Indian life depicted with passion and detail unequaled in American literature, and all of it leading up to a terrifying climax at the fabled 1833 Green River Rendezvous.

Look for these books wherever Bantam books are sold, or use this handy coupon for ordering:

Roe Richmond is one of that rare breed of Western writers whose novels continue to be read by generation after generation. In the tradition of Luke Short and Ernest Haycox, he is a storyteller of power and passion who brings back to life the authentic Old West.

Roe Richmond has these great westerns to offer you: